For Nicholas

Critical Acclaim for
THE POISON TREE

'A debut to die for ... *The Poison Tree* is several
notches more intelligent than most of its genre ... So
assured is the writing that I found it hard at times to
believe that *The Poison Tree* is the author's first novel.
Debuts don't come much better'
The Times

'Witty, assured and clever ... Well-drawn characters, a
horribly ingenious plot and a heart-stopping climax
make for an accomplished literary thriller'
Cosmopolitan

'Assured and clever'
Manchester Evening News

'A sexy, disturbing, Gothic thriller ... [*The Poison Tree*]
is a breath of fresh spring air and Tony Strong is a
novelist whose talent is clearly in full bloom. Just read it'
Oxford Mail

'There are indeed few first novels which are as assured
as *The Poison Tree* ... A dark and creepy mixture of
male rape, wife-swapping, bitching academics, poetry –
and murder ... A tale well told of colossal vanity,
rampaging egos, and a mind twisted by the need for
revenge ... A stylish and gripping triumph'
Oxford Times

'A remarkably assured piece of writing ... Incredibly
powerful and disturbing ... An exciting debut'
Publishing News

The Poison Tree

Tony Strong

BANTAM BOOKS

London • New York • Toronto • Sydney • Auckland

THE POISON TREE
A BANTAM BOOK : 0 553 50542 4

Originally published in Great Britain by Doubleday
a division of Transworld Publishers Ltd

PRINTING HISTORY
Doubleday edition published 1997
Bantam edition published 1998
Copyright © 1997 by Tony Strong

The right of Tony Strong to be identified as the
author of this work has been asserted in accordance
with sections 77 and 78 of the Copyright Designs
and Patents Act 1988.

Extracts taken from:
p.94 'The Destruction of Sennacherib', George Gordon, Lord Byron.
p.122 'The Epipsychidion', P. B. Shelley, 1821.
pp.150 and 407 'Little Gidding', V, *Four Quartets*, T. S. Eliot,
Faber and Faber Ltd. Reproduced with permission.
p.180–1 'Adonais', P. B. Shelley, 1821.
p.182 'A Defence of Poetry', P. B. Shelley, 1821.
p.184 'Love's Philosophy', P. B. Shelley 1819.
p.186 'Dolores', A. G. Swinburne, 1866.
p.281 'The Sick Rose' from 'Songs of Experience' William Blake,
1789–94.
p.282 'Proverbs of Hell' from 'The Marriage of Heaven and
Hell', William Blake, c 1790–93.
p.321 'The Guilty Vicarage', *The Dyer's Hand and other essays*,
W. H. Auden, Faber and Faber Ltd. Reproduced with permission.
p.323 *Writing Crime Fiction*, H. R. F. Keating, A & C Black, 1986.

Set in 11/13pt Sabon by Falcon Oast Graphic Art

Bantam Books are published by Transworld Publishers Ltd,
61–63 Uxbridge Road, London W5 5SA,
in Australia by Transworld Publishers (Australia) Pty Ltd,
15–25 Helles Avenue, Moorebank, NSW 2170,
and in New Zealand by Transworld Publishers (NZ) Ltd,
3 William Pickering Drive, Albany, Auckland.

Reproduced, printed and bound in Great Britain by
Cox & Wyman Ltd, Reading, Berks.

Acknowledgements

Acknowledgements are due to Francis Warner, playwright and Lord White Fellow of St Peter's College, Oxford, from whom I have borrowed a soldering iron, a room and a harpsichord; to author Nancy Friday, on material from whose books several of the letters in *The Poison Tree* are based; to Steve from Australia, whose letter to *Fiesta Magazine*, reprinted in *The Fiesta Letters* (Star Books, 1986, ed. Chris Lloyd), I have also adapted; to Keith D. Wilson, M.D., author of *Cause of Death: a writer's guide to death, murder and forensic medicine* (Writer's Digest Books, 1992), and Michael Dibdin, whose account of a visit to a post-mortem, *The Pathology Lesson*, in Granta 39, I have used as source material; to my friends Dr Ian Wylie, Dr Siân Griffiths, Katie Reader and Charles Stewart-Smith, who read the book in manuscript and made many useful suggestions; to Judy Turner and Ursula Mackenzie of Transworld; to Jane Wylie, owner of 57 West Street at the time of the fictional events described in this book; to my sons Tom and Harry, for allowing me to waste valuable computer time when they could have been playing *Warcraft*, and to my wife Sara, without whose unceasing scepticism and gentle mockery this book would never have been written.

I was angry with my friend:
I told my wrath, my wrath did end.
I was angry with my foe:
I told it not, my wrath did grow.

And I water'd it in fears,
Night & morning with my tears;
And I sunned it with smiles,
And with soft deceitful wiles.

And it grew both day and night,
Till it bore an apple bright;
And my foe beheld it shine,
And he knew that it was mine,

And into my garden stole
When the night had veil'd the pole:
In the morning glad I see
My foe outstretch'd beneath the tree.

William Blake
'A Poison Tree' from *Songs of Experience*

Prologue

At last the dog stops barking. I wait another minute, just to be sure.

Another minute for him to live.

Stepping back into the darkness of a doorway, I watch the street. No one around. A light rain makes the street-lights hazy and soft as dandelion clocks.

I am aware that my awareness is heightened, that all my senses are loaded and brimming like a paintbrush loaded with paint. Drizzle prickles in my scalp like a cloud of gnats. It feels good. More than good: godlike.

I pull the balaclava and the swimming goggles out of my pocket and put them on, goggles first, so that the eye-pieces fit through the holes in the balaclava. I cross the street. The goggles make my vision prismatic. Thumb-smears of pink and green leap off the wet tarmac.

The door's unlocked and the stink hits me. Earlier, there was a party, though the house is silent now. The bulb above the stairs has been swapped for a red one, to create an atmosphere.

I swim through the atmosphere, through the bloody-mary light. A bottle of wine on the bottom stair catches my eye and I pick it up thinking, Dutch courage, but even in that light and through the goggles I see two or

11

three cigarette butts floating in it, bloated and bursting open.

Hugh's room is right there, at the bottom of the stairs. The only bedsit on the ground floor. I go in. A stink in here, too, but different – party smells overlaid with sex smells. Him, or other partygoers? Not that it matters now. He is lying on the bed face down, naked, the duvet wrapped round his legs. Pissed out of his tiny brain, of course. The subject was inebriated. Red light from the hall fills the room but he doesn't stir.

He really is breathtakingly beautiful – broad shoulders, biceps sleek and salmon-fat. But I'll not scar that whiter skin than snow. Othello.

I withdraw to the kitchen, looking for an electric socket. When I find one I take the soldering iron from my coat pocket and plug it in, lying it across a beer glass so that the tip isn't touching anything as it heats up.

Time passes.

Suddenly a noise. I swing round, alerted. False alarm. That ridiculous cat is oozing through an open window. It startled me. Not startled me. I am beyond fear. Angered me then.

It comes to me, purring, trying to lean against me, asking for food or love or whatever it is animals want. I grab it, rolling it over onto its back, right hand round its throat where the claws can't reach me, pinning it down. I touch the tip of the soldering iron once, twice, three times to the black belly. Smell of fur and a glimpse of burning pink. The noise, yowling or whatever, is indescribable. For a moment I think: error. Too much noise. Run. But then it's gone, back the way it came, off wailing into the garden and beyond.

Again I wait. Silence. All pissed.

I put a finger near the iron's tip and I can feel the heat. Time to kill him.

I open the door to his room and everything goes white, like an explosion or a scream. I struggle through it, trying to see him, but I can't. And I'm there but I'm

12

simultaneously back here again, back in the present day, sitting on this hard bed, the cigarette falling from my fingers. Forcing myself to breathe.

Pushing against the threshold of memory, finding it gives a little more with each feeble shove.

Laid out on the bed beside me are the things I will need again tonight: dark clothing, the balaclava, the goggles, a Stanley knife.

But for a while I just sit here, breathing.

My head rolling slowly into the basket of my hands.

One

The two men had been watching the street for some time now and the car was fuggy with their breath and the damp, steaming burgers they were eating. The older of the two was getting impatient – where was she? why the hell hadn't she showed? – but the younger man was relaxed, enjoying himself, watching the occasional pretty student walk past. It was the first sunny day of spring, and there was more bare flesh on display than there had been for months. He wished he had brought his sunglasses. It would have been exactly like a Hollywood cop stakeout then.

'There she is.' The older man pointed. 'That one just coming round the corner.'

'What makes you so sure?'

'Instinct. Watch.'

The woman he had pointed out was in her late twenties. Her hair, which was long, dark, and exuberantly ringleted, hinted at Mediterranean blood; though even at this distance her eyes were clearly some lighter colour, light blue or possibly grey. Good-looking rather than beautiful, her clothes too looked as if they had been chosen for comfort rather than allure. She was wearing a light blue tea dress without a coat, evidently being one of those who believed that the morning sunshine was not some transitory fluke, though the effect was somewhat offset by the pair of heavy Timberlands on her feet.

The older man had been right: it was her. She had stopped in front of the house and unslung a small knapsack from her back. From it she took a copy of the documents.

Peter whistled. 'Worth the wait.'

'Come on then.' The senior man wiped his fingers on his handkerchief, then swivelled the rear view mirror so that he could check his appearance. 'This is probably our last chance, so let's do it properly.'

As they got out of the car they both did up their suit jackets simultaneously, then walked purposefully to where the woman was peering up at the For Sale sign.

'Mrs Williams?' Nick, as the senior partner, held out his hand to her. 'Nick Woolway. We spoke on the phone. May I introduce my colleague, Peter Soames?'

Her handshake was firm and her smile amused. '*Two* estate agents? I am honoured. Sorry I'm late, by the way. The train from London was held up.'

Nick didn't hesitate. 'We always come out in force for a cash buyer.'

'Well. I haven't exactly brought along wads of fivers.'

'But I am right in thinking you want to buy straight away?' He spoke with just a trace of anxiety, Peter thought, but probably not enough for Mrs Williams to notice.

'Oh, definitely. I need to find somewhere before the university term starts.' There was a pause. 'I like the outside. Shall we go in?' she asked.

'Of course, of course.' Nick was fumbling in his pocket for the key. Peter suppressed a smile. His boss had a tendency to become flustered around attractive women. 'Here, Nick, allow me,' he said smoothly, taking the key from him and smiling at Mrs Williams with practised charm.

'I see you've had an intruder,' she said conversationally as he worked the key into the lock.

Both men froze. Peter was quicker. 'Pardon?' he said casually.

'Up there.' She took a step back on the pavement and pointed to where the For Sale sign had been mounted on the wall. In the triangle of the board's two sides there was a round dark shape the size of a tennis ball. As they looked, a small bird flickered out of it and was gone over the rooftops.

'It's a house-martin's nest, I rather think,' she said.

'I can't think how that got there. The house has only been on the market for a very short time,' Nick lied.

'You'll have to promise me something. If I do buy, I want you to leave the sign up.' She smiled at him. 'I wouldn't want to throw them out of their new home just as I'm moving into mine.'

'Of course, of course,' Nick said cheerfully, though he was groaning inwardly. A woman who worried about little birdies in their nesties was hardly going to want to set up her family home in a house like No. 57.

'As you can see, the house has been used for student accommodation and would benefit from some minor refurbishment.' Peter was well into his spiel now, moving smoothly from room to room, throwing open doors and then standing in the doorway so that Mrs Williams' delightful breasts or her surprisingly muscular buttocks were forced against him as she squeezed by. 'But overall the condition is good—'

'Is there a damp course?' she interrupted.

'I'm, ah, not certain about that,' he confessed.

'It's a bit moist under this wallpaper,' she muttered to herself, pulling at a loose join. 'It doesn't really matter. I'd be putting in an injection damp course anyway.'

'Er, right. And this is the master bedroom.'

'Not that we're meant to call it that these days,' Nick interjected. 'Bedroom One is considered more politically correct.'

She glanced at him thoughtfully but said nothing, allowing herself to be led passively on their well-planned tour. After a while she simply tuned them out – what was the point in any case of listening to someone who could open the door to a bathroom and announce 'This is a bathroom'? She found herself more interested in the strange resonance their words made in the empty rooms than in the words themselves.

She had, she realized, never been in a house that felt so utterly bare, so devoid of its past. No room was furnished: here and there a series of round indentations in the carpet, mysterious as crop circles, indicated where beds and cupboards had once stood. Other rooms had been stripped even of their floor coverings, revealing their pale boards to the sunlight like the first white sunbathers of spring. Differently coloured squares and oblongs on the walls, their corners dotted with Blu-Tack, were all that remained of pictures and posters, and on the back of a bedroom door the faint shadow of a triangle, airbrushed in dirt, showed where a coathanger had hung for years undisturbed. It was as if the whole house had been unexpectedly blasted, Hiroshima-like, and its inhabitants smeared sideways into angles of light.

The telephone was mounted on the wall in the kitchen, and with flagrant disrespect for college property the wall around it had been used as a notepad, a two-foot aurora of scribbles, numbers and whimsical caricatures. Someone had tried to scrub the wall clean, with only partial success, so that even here the doodles seemed to have paled under the flash of some enormous force.

Nick sneezed suddenly. She said 'Bless you', and he sneezed again.

'I'm terribly sorry,' he explained, 'I'm just a little allergic to dust.'

'You're in the right business, then,' she retorted with a wry smile. 'Looking round old houses.' The smile vanished, replaced by a look of frowning concentration as she touched her finger to the window sill and examined the result. 'There's an awful *lot* of dust, though,' she said, half to herself. 'Not house dust, exactly. It's too white. Like flour. Or it could be chalk.' She blew gently at her hand, watching the grey, smoky residue lift and cloud the sunbeam. 'What could it be? Not rot spores, but . . .'

With a sinking heart Nick realized that he was going to have to grasp the nettle. 'Mrs Williams,' he said formally. 'It's fingerprint powder. We have had the house cleaned, but it takes an age to settle.'

'Fingerprint powder?' she repeated, puzzled.

'Part of the reason the house is for sale is that there was a . . . criminal incident on the premises.'

'An incident?' She laughed sardonically. 'Believe me, I'm used to those. In the last five years I've lived in Clapham, Tooting, Brixton and Stockwell. I've had more Victim Support letters than gas bills. Never had the fingerprint people round, though.'

'As a matter of fact, this wasn't a burglary. Tragically one of the students who lived here was,' Nick tried to think of a euphemism and couldn't. 'Was killed.'

'Really? How?'

'By an intruder.' He cleared his throat. 'Frankly, Mrs Williams – er, Theresa, isn't it? – we've had some very interested purchasers who didn't want to go ahead once they found out – women on their own, couples with young children, and so on. Well, you can understand it in a way.'

'Ah.'

'Would the Williams family be bothered by a thing like that?' he prompted delicately.

She turned away from him and looked out of the window before replying. 'I suppose most houses, old houses that is, have had someone die in them, when you think about it. It's where people used to want to die, before we decided that birth and death are illnesses that should be pushed into hospitals.'

'That's a very sensible attitude,' he said, unsure where this was leading.

'There isn't a Williams family, by the way. I'm separated, almost divorced. A woman on her own, as you put it.'

'Oh dear. I do apologize—'

'So there's no-one else I need to consult,' she interrupted him. 'If you'll knock ten grand off, I'm interested.'

'There are four other buyers coming to look round this evening, Mrs Williams, er, Theresa,' he said, lying to cover his surprise.

'Well, if they give you the asking price you'll be able to throw out my offer, won't you?' She smiled at him sweetly. 'And please, I'm called Terry.'

As they were about to leave she stopped him. 'Would it be all right if I stayed for a bit? I just want to try and visualize things, where I'm going to put stuff. I'll pull the door shut when I go.'

'Of course.' He offered her his hand. With some

21

young women you could employ a little old-fashioned gallantry and kiss them goodbye but not, he suspected, with this one. 'I'll be in touch.'

She waited until they were gone, then went out into the garden and scrabbled about in the rubble until she found what she was looking for: a length of rusty metal, about a foot long and solid as a crowbar. Kneeling down behind the kitchen window, she started hacking methodically at the bricks, about a foot above the ground. Ah. As she'd thought, there was a damp course already, quite a good one too by the looks of it. The house was scruffy as hell, but structurally it had been well looked after. Terry wiped her fingers on the grass and stood up.

A flash of blue caught her eye, a piece of plastic a couple of inches long fluttering on a bush. She reached out her hand to it. One end was coagulated from having been in a fire – there was a burnt patch on the lawn, which looked quite recent. Looking at the plastic in her hand, she realized that it was part of a police scene-of-crime tape.

Suddenly she was aware that she was being watched. A woman was standing at one of the windows of the house next door, a redhead of about her own age, wearing a white bathrobe and drinking from a bright green coffee mug. The mug and her eyes were the same striking colour. Terry nodded politely: the woman continued to watch her, her face expressionless, then abruptly turned away as if in response to something that had been said to her.

She went and ran one of the kitchen taps to make

sure the water hadn't been turned off, then used the loo. On the back of the door some student wag had written in felt tip FARTING IS THE FREEDOM CRY OF THE REPRESSED SHIT. She looked at it thoughtfully, then decided that it might stay. Of course, no-one else would realize that the repressed shit she'd be thinking of was her ex-husband David. She opened the estate agent's particulars again and began to leaf through them.

Number fifty-seven West Street, Osney, is a terraced property approximately one hundred years old. It currently comprises four bedrooms, having recently been utilized as accommodation for students: one of these bedrooms is on the ground floor and could easily be reconverted to a dining or sitting room.

Whilst in good overall condition the house would undoubtedly benefit from some cosmetic refurbishment. There is a garden of approximately one-eighth of an acre at the rear, mainly laid to lawn, although it has been neglected in recent years.

Osney itself is one of Oxford's most sought-after locations. Though benefiting from a secluded village-like atmosphere, it is well within walking distance of the amenities of Oxford city centre. Known by residents as Osney Island, it is bounded on one side by the Oxford Canal and on the remaining three sides by tributaries of the nearby River Thames. There are two Public Houses on the Island, one overlooking the river, a shop, and a thriving Residents' Association. Although there is some multi-occupancy student accommodation on the Island, it is less than in most comparable areas.

Properties in this area very rarely come on to the market, and early viewing is urgently recommended.

Please do not hesitate to contact me or one of my colleagues if you have any queries or wish to arrange an appointment.

Yours sincerely
(illegible)
For Woolway, Webb & Co.

When she had finished she unceremoniously tore a strip out of the particulars to wipe herself with and pulled the handle. I've marked my territory now, she thought, wriggling back into her knickers, I'll have to buy it. She walked slowly back down the hallway, its sides scarred by the handlebars of generations of students' bicycles, and closed the front door behind her.

While Terry sat on the train back to London, members of the university staff were attending evensong in the tiny cathedral of Christ Church College.

If the choirboys resented having to give up part of their holidays in order to be present, if they fidgeted and winked at each other from behind the safety of their high pews in the choir, it didn't show in their singing. As ever, it was perfect, the high quivering notes swooping and diving through the stony spaces above the congregation like a blur of swallows.

There was a special ritual attached to this part of

the Easter service. Whatever other litanies or psalms might be sung, it always concluded with Allegri's arrangement of Psalm 51, the psalm of contrition. The lead was taken by a solo treble voice, the child's purity making the words of abjection and repentance even more poignant:

Behold, I was shapen in wickedness,
and in sin hath my mother conceived me.

As the choir sang, the candles at the end of each pew – the sole illumination in the great space – were extinguished row by row until those on the altar itself were the only points of light remaining. Then these too were abruptly snuffed, until through the darkness came the first words of the second half:

Thou shalt wash me with hyssop, and I shall be
    clean:
thou shalt wash me, and I shall be whiter than
    snow.

As the other, older voices in the choir took up the chant again, weaving their deeper melodies through the clear unbroken treble, the candles were relit, row by row, so that by the last lines of the psalm the cathedral was once again filled with light, only the stench of burnt wicks and a faint tracing-paper haze in the air showing that they had once been snuffed. The last lines of the psalm were also the last lines of the service:

Thou shalt be pleased with the sacrifice of
  righteousness,
with the burnt-offerings and oblations:
then shall they offer young bullocks upon thine
  altar.

The congregation remained on their knees while the choir filed silently out, then one by one got to their feet and stretched. Here and there they rubbed knees that had spent too long pressed against the hard oak of the pew in front. As they moved slowly towards the exit hands were shaken, smiles exchanged.

In the middle of a pew towards the front one man knelt on, apparently oblivious to the fact that the service had ended, and oblivious to his neighbours, who eventually filed out either side of him. With his head bowed it was impossible to tell if he was deep in prayer, lost in thought, or simply asleep.

Only when the congregation had gone did he finally raise his head and gaze at the altar. Reaching into his breast pocket for an immaculately folded cloth handkerchief, he silently wiped away the tears that glistened like snail-tracks on his smoothly shaven cheeks.

As he made his way to the door he felt someone touch his arm.

'Brian?' a voice murmured.

They had clearly been waiting for him. Two of them. Like him, they were wearing formal academic gowns over their dark suits.

'Might we have a word?'

'Of course, Master.' He nodded at the second man, acknowledging him. 'Dean.'

'I thought we had better discuss *damage limitation*,' the Master murmured as they emerged into the dark night air. His voice sank even lower as the three men strolled slowly after the departing congregation.

Two

It was one of Terry's rituals, whenever she moved somewhere new, to start by unpacking her books. Everything else – the disconnected cooker, the curtainless windows, the boxes of glasses wrapped up in tissue paper like tangerines at a grocer's – were ignored until she had arranged her precious texts, by subject and then alphabetically within each subject, on the bookshelves.

It had driven David mad, which was why she'd started doing it. Now that there was no David fuming silently behind her, it felt even better.

The shelves in front of her were like a particularly colourful rock strata, a slice through the ages of her life. At the bottom were the greys and blacks of the Penguin Classics and Arden Shakespeares she'd had since school. On top of these was a bright green seam of Virago, which she'd discovered at seventeen; then a layer of thin, shale-like volumes of poetry topped in turn by an orderly block of white

King Penguins. Above them came her first under-graduate hardbacks, proper scholarly editions of Joyce and Yeats and Eliot, and pressing down on these the books about books, works of criticism and academic essays. Towards the top there was a row of detective paperbacks and thrillers, their spines a jumble of lurid colours, while the books from her most recent existence, her life in London, were the biggest but fewest in number, sitting on the very top shelf: books on DIY and home furnishing, *The Joy of Sex*, the *Reader's Digest Book of the Home*, a couple of old Habitat catalogues, back issues of *Interiors* and *Tatler*.

By way of contrast, the first thing Mo had done was to set up the stereo. Tracy Chapman was now preaching revolution to the peaceful burghers of suburban Oxford through the open front door, while Mo finished carting in from the van the bin liners in which Terry, having run out of boxes, was transporting her worldly goods from Mo's flat to Oxford.

'Funny, isn't it?' Terry said as the other girl passed. 'We'd never have left the door open like this or the van unlocked in London.'

Mo shot her an amused glance. 'There's crime everywhere, Terry. Or have you forgotten what happened in your new home?'

'Sorry. I was just—'

'You were just trying to sell me on the move. You don't have to, honestly. If you want to come and vegetate in an ivory tower, that's up to you.'

She spoke lightly, though Terry knew she was

more hurt than she admitted. They'd been sharing Mo's flat for six months now: no-one at the agency had ever realized just how close they'd become. Leaving Mo, Terry thought, felt a bit like the first time she'd come here, as a gawky first-year undergraduate, leaving the familiar safety of her parents' suburban home.

'You don't think I'm running away?'

'From me? No way. I'll be down here every chance I get. You don't get rid of me that easy.'

The books finished, Terry knelt down and started pulling crockery out of boxes. 'From real life, then,' she suggested.

'Come off it, darling. You weren't exactly a street-radical activist, were you? And if you start to get really provincial I'll post you little emergency parcels. A copy of *Time Out* and an Afro-Jewish takeaway. Or you can come and join me on the odd demo. Me in my Doc Martens, you in your gown and mortar board.'

Terry gave her a hug, just as the doorbell rang.

'Visitors already?' Mo said. 'Perhaps it's the vicar come to say see you on Sunday? Or could it be the Women's Institute come to ask you to tea? Ow!' Terry had pinched her to make her let go. A woman of about forty was peering through the open door.

'Mrs Williams?' she asked.

'I'm Terry Williams. This is my friend Mo Dawson.' Terry held out her hand.

'Sheila Gibson. From next door.' The woman approached and waved vaguely in the direction of her own house. 'I just popped in to say welcome to

Osney.' She looked at the piles of bin liners doubt-fully. 'Gosh. Your husband's making you do all the heavy work, is he?'

'There's no husband, actually. I'm divorced.' Every time she said it, it got a little easier. 'But Mo here's giving me a hand.'

'Lucky you.' As if realizing Terry might have thought she was referring to the divorce rather than the help, she coloured. 'Well, it's lovely to have you here. I must say, I think you're very brave.'

'Why's that?' Mo asked.

'Oh God. Have I put my foot in it?' Sheila put her hand over her mouth, but her eyes had lit up.

'I already know about the history of the house,' Terry said firmly. 'It doesn't bother me.'

'Oh. Good,' Sheila said, though she looked dis-appointed. 'Anyway, I'd better leave you to it. I just wanted to say, if you need anything, anything at all, just knock. We might even persuade the old man to give us a drink if you've got time.' She paused, then said in a rush, 'It'll be so nice to have a proper resident in here again. Those dreadful students with their parties and their bicycles cluttering up the pavement. But of course they didn't care, they were only staying a year at the most, and as soon as you got to know their names they were off again. I did remind one of them to clean the windows, they were absolutely filthy, but she just laughed at me. We've got a Residents' Association; I know you've only just arrived but I do hope you'll think about joining us as soon as you possibly can.'

Terry muttered something non-committal.

'The net curtains are twitching,' teased Mo when Sheila had departed.

'Don't. Come on, we need to find a Paki shop. I'm getting hungry.'

'Oh, we don't have Pakis in Oxford,' Mo said, imitating Sheila's middle-class tones. 'Such dreadful people, not the sort who become members of the Residents' Association at all.'

Their second uninvited visit came later.

It came in the middle of the night, long after they were asleep. It started with a scream; a high-pitched, anguished howl that sliced as effortlessly as a razor through the thick muffle of Terry's dreams.

She was accustomed to sleeping through the white noise of the London night. But this unfamiliar screech had her suddenly wide awake, her heart racing.

She was still a bit drunk. They had found, not just a corner shop, but the largest and most expensive delicatessen she had ever seen. Once she'd managed to stop Mo making caustic and entirely unfair remarks about student grants and honest taxpayers' hard-earned money, they'd had a field day: two bottles of chilled Perrier-Jouët champagne, a hunk of crumbling Stilton, some chicken-liver pâté and a large shareable slice of cheesecake. To her delight, Mo had also found a student's guide to Oxford. Since there were no chairs they ate upstairs, sprawled across Terry's double mattress like a couple of schoolgirls having a midnight feast, guzzling champagne while Mo read out gems from the guide.

'"Hertford Drama Society. Last year we produced an acclaimed production of *Midsummer Night's Dream* set entirely in winter, bringing out the bleak side of Shakespeare's comedy. Serious thespians always welcome." Sounds cheery. "The Heffalump Society. Activities include a termly Pooh Sticks championship, searching for the North Pole and saying our prayers." Jesus wept! Whatever happened to sit-ins and changing the world? Listen, here's another. "The Hyacinth Society. Dedicated to drinking, decadence, and Sandlers' proposition that poetry is the synthesis of hyacinths and biscuits."' Mo snorted derisively and tossed the book onto the floor. 'I'd heard that students today were boring and self-centred, but if I'd known that this was what you were coming back to I'd have tied you to my kitchen table.'

'I'm not eligible to join those societies,' Terry pointed out mildly. 'I'm not an undergraduate. And I didn't join them when I was.'

She knew and understood why Mo was being grumpy. They'd never be this close again: on Monday Mo would be back in London, photographing sanitary towel ads, while Terry would start catching up with the latest critical thinking on her doctorate subject. Despite Mo's promise to come down at weekends, their worlds were diverging. Getting drunk tonight had been a kind of ritual goodbye.

Sitting up in bed she listened, waiting. The

screeching that had woken her was repeated, so close that for a moment Terry thought it was actually in the room with her. She held her breath, trying to make no sound.

At the uncurtained window two blazing eyes in an elfin head stared angrily at her through the glass. Instinctively Terry flinched, then breathed a slow sigh of relief. It was just a cat. There was a lean-to just below the window: the animal must have simply walked up the sloping roof.

She got out of bed and went towards it, trying not to frighten it away. Behind her Mo mumbled something, still half asleep. She reached the window, but the cat seemed to panic. It turned and half-fell, half-slithered down the slates. Just for a moment she had a brief impression of something pink and gaping on its behind, like a wound; it was already gone before she realized that it had been the animal's vulva, glistening and distended. Looking down at the unkempt garden, snowy with moonlight, she thought she caught a glimpse of it again, picking its way through the shadows.

Behind her Mo turned on the light. Instantly the garden vanished, replaced by the blacksilver reflection of Terry herself, naked except for a T-shirt, her hair wild with sleep.

'What's up?'

'It was just a cat,' Terry said, getting back in beside her. She shivered. 'It was odd,' she said. 'It's bum was all open.'

'Perhaps it was on heat.'

'For a moment when I heard it trying to get in . . .

Christ knows I'm not superstitious, but . . .'

'Don't let people wind you up about that kid who died,' Mo said softly. 'They'll try, you know. They won't like the fact that you're a girlie and you aren't frightened, so they'll try to spook you.' She reached out and touched Terry's hair. 'Come here,' she whispered.

Mo's mouth was sticky with sleep, a faint ghost-taste of toothpaste and champagne. Terry kissed her deeply, exploring the familiar tininess of her teeth as their bodies fitted into each other, breasts resting between breasts, her right thigh pushing into the hollow between Mo's legs. She caught her breath, amazed as always by the simplicity of their arousal. With David, sex had been energetic; foreplay a matter of kneading and squeezing and movement. With Mo, all they had to do was lie together: within moments she felt as if she was part of some purring, gyroscopic machine, lifting them effortlessly towards orgasm. Licking her fingers, she reached between the other girl's legs.

Afterwards, Mo was asleep instantly. Terry held her, listening to the unfamiliar sounds of a new building. Even the distant traffic sounded different from London, subtly changed by the reverberations of the empty house.

David and she had been a college couple, though it wasn't until afterwards, when he had already taken a job in the City and she had started the first year of her postgraduate studies, that their relationship became serious. It was the era of financial

35

deregulation – nicknamed the Big Bang – and the merchant banks were offering ludicrous salaries: he earned more in a year, even as a trainee, than she would get as a grant for the whole of her doctorate. When David started putting pressure on her to get a job in London, she hadn't taken much persuading. A friend who worked as an account executive in one of the top advertising agencies got her an interview as an account planner, helping to create the strategies for new campaigns and then researching the creative work in consumer focus groups. Rather to her surprise, she found that she was good at it. Experience of decoding texts and analysing literary symbolism helped her to interpret the consumers' responses as well as simply report on them, and she soon had a reputation as a planner who fought hard for quality work. The creative department loved her, even if she had to fend off the attentions of drunken Geordie art directors on a regular basis.

One of David's perks was a low-interest mortgage, and the two of them had thrown themselves into the Eighties property boom. Everyone had been doing it – everyone like them, that is, middle-class professionals with two incomes, no children, and no ties to any area or community. Sometimes when she looked back on it, it seemed to Terry that it had all been like that building society commercial of the time in which an endless blur of potters from Potters Bar, cooks from Cookham and bankers from Balham whizzed through the society's branches, borrowing and depositing, selling up and buying up and doing up, but always above all moving up, up that invisible structure known to everyone as the property ladder. It was, she thought to herself later, an interesting metaphor: a ladder, after all, is something solid and useful, as real as bricks and mortar itself. At the time no-one had ever considered that the ladder might turn out to be a bubble.

Over the next two years the boom created a diaspora effect, scattering professionals like themselves out from the traditional heartlands of Fulham and Clapham into the newly gentrified areas of Balham, Stockwell, Brixton and Lambeth. David and she had been pioneers in Tooting, doing up and selling at a handsome profit. Six months later, they were selling up in Battersea and planting the first yellow skip of spring in a run-down street in Kennington. A year after that, they bought a house in more upmarket Wandsworth, which they intended to reconvert from flats into a six-bedroomed house. When David lost his job in the crash of '87, it seemed the easiest thing for him simply to continue to work on the house, only without employing so much help from builders. He bought a Labrador puppy, replaced his company BMW with a second-hand Range Rover and drank more, but otherwise their lives seemed unchanged. Terry still rushed home from work and donned a pair of overalls to start painting or stripping or hacking rotten wood out of newly exposed beams. It was six months before she found a pair of women's knickers in the glove compartment of the

Range Rover. Her first thought, ludicrously, was that David had developed some kind of secret fetish: her second, once she had realized what it meant – she still blushed with shame and anger when she thought about it – was to examine the elastic to see if David's mistress took a smaller size than she did.

David had been having an affair with a neighbour for over a year. She had initiated it, he said, as if that was somehow an excuse. And to him, she realized, it probably was. Like so many men he simply went with the path of least resistance, with whatever flow – the City, the housing boom, infidelity – happened to have caught him up in its currents. At her request, he moved out while she considered her options.

Cunningly, he played a trump card by going to her mother, confessing all and asking for her help in obtaining Terry's forgiveness. Her mother's appeals took the form of oblique pep talks, which Terry was soon able to anticipate and break down into their component themes within moments: Stand By Your Man. ('I did, Mother. The problem was he didn't stand by me.') David's Learnt His Lesson. ('He may well have done. But it was a marriage, not a tutorial.') You're Not Getting Any Younger. ('I'm twenty-seven, Mother. These days you can have a baby when you're forty-five.') And, most unforgivably of all, Well I'm Not Getting Any Younger And I Do So Want To Enjoy My Grandchildren Before I Die. ('What about my brother Mark? He and Rachel will give you grandchildren – if you pay them enough.') Finally, there was David's A Man And Men Have Different Sexual Needs. This last talk was abruptly terminated when the Labrador, which David had left at the house, took it upon itself to thrust its nose up her mother's sensible skirt, promptly developed an erection like a furry gun turret, and began energetically humping her mother's leather-booted leg, dribbling quantities of thin doggy come over it as he did so. Rushing into the kitchen for a cloth, Terry had had to stuff it into her mouth and bend double over the cooker to prevent herself from laughing out loud. There were no more pep talks after that.

In the five years they had been married most of the wedding presents hadn't even been unpacked. There hadn't seemed much point when they'd always known they'd be moving on in a few months or so. Now, for the first time, Terry went through them all, methodically separating ice-cream makers, crockery, pasta jars and so on into boxes. Her friend Mo, a photographer she'd met on an advertising shoot, came round to help one night with a bottle of vodka and they got carried away. When David was eventually allowed back into the house he found the sofa, the bed and the dining room table neatly sawn in half with one of his own power tools. The Labrador had a dotted line drawn in black felt tip round its midriff: 'His' had been written on the front half, 'Hers' on the back. It had been Mo's idea, but the writing was Terry's.

*   *   *

She'd known, from rumours at work, that Mo was supposed to be gay, but put it down to sexual envy. In the predominantly male and laddish environment of the agency's creative department, any drop-dead crop-haired blonde who could take her portfolio round with a stud in her nose and her arse hanging out of a rip in her jeans was going to take a lot of flak. But when Mo had eventually asked her if she'd like to be her lodger for a while, she'd added casually that Terry might have to be broadminded about some of the people who stayed the night.

'By people, I take it that you don't mean men,' Terry had said.

'Correct,' Mo said, holding her gaze defiantly.

'No problem,' Terry had replied, and it hadn't been. She certainly hadn't been jealous of Mo's girlfriends, just mildly curious as to what they actually did together. She couldn't imagine it being one half as satisfying as what she still thought of as real sex; though one day, looking in Mo's bedroom for a sanitary towel, she came across a drawer full of sex toys and accessories of such extravagant and unexpected diversity that her imagination boggled.

She was basically celibate during this period, though she did miss sex. When someone at work organized an Ann Summers party, Terry ended up ordering herself a vibrator. She'd used it once, then accidentally dropped it in the bath: within a few days the batteries had started oozing radioactive-looking yellow gunk. The problem with vibrators, she told Mo later, was that they were basically frigid. Great at providing orgasms, they weren't that fussed themselves. It was what had always bothered her about sex with men, that impression she'd always had that they were constantly looking for the buttons to press, that they were either great or lousy lovers depending on how many hits they could notch up on their partner's orgasmeter. Compared with her mother's generation, she knew hers had it easy. But it seemed to her that while the goalposts might have moved in the right direction the game was still too much about scoring goals.

Mo started giving her massages. She was careful to keep clear of the erogenous zones, but they both knew that Terry got aroused, even if they chose to ignore it. Then one time Terry simply asked her not to stop. It wasn't fireworks or earthmoving or any amazing self-realization: it was simply something nice, something she wanted, and which she felt a little bit guilty about afterwards. They became lovers, but Terry still didn't think of herself as gay. Then she realized that Mo had stopped bringing girls home. When she asked her why, Mo said she was in love with Terry.

Terry reacted badly, going off and sleeping with one of the drunkest and most egotistical of the Geordie art directors. Then she came back to Mo's flat and threw up. Mo cleared up the sick without reproach: Terry ended the night in Mo's bed.

The two of them were together for six months. They made no formal or spoken commitment to each other, but like schoolgirls or nuns in convents their monthly cycles slowly synchronized, a kind of marriage of bodies that seemed to Terry all the deeper for being unwilled.

She knew, however, that it was a relationship without a future, and that it would be her, not Mo, who brought it to an end. In any case, she wanted to make a decision – any decision – anything to prove to herself that she wasn't simply bobbing along, like David and so many of her contemporaries, on whatever tide happened to be rising at the moment. She wrote to her old tutor, asking if she could come back to Oxford. To her surprise, he replied warmly. He had already heard of the break-up with David, and would love to have her back to finish her doctorate. He couldn't do much to help her get a grant, of course, but he would do his best to give her some teaching work with the undergraduates. By this time the house in Wandsworth had been sold: David and she were both coming out of their marriage richer by around eighty thousand pounds. David immediately reinvested his share in a smaller house in Streatham, a rung or two down the ladder. Terry started looking in Oxford. She wanted to renovate something, if only because that was the skill she had acquired in the years of her marriage, but she was also determined to find a house that she would live in, not just invest in.

She waited until she had already exchanged contracts before she broke the news to Mo.

She was almost asleep when she heard the cat again. Perhaps an hour had passed, but the sound jerked her instantly awake. It was different this time. Whereas before it had been a howl of anger, this was more piteous, a staccato high-pitched mewing. The sound of an animal in pain.

It was coming from downstairs, from somewhere inside the house.

'Mo?' she said softly. There was no reply.

For the second time that night she slid quietly out of bed and prepared to confront her fear. The naked bulb on the landing was hideously bright to her sleep-accustomed eyes. She tiptoed down the creaking stairs. The noise seemed to be coming from directly under her naked feet, from the space where they had been chucking all the empty cardboard boxes and bin liners. She paused for a moment and the sound redoubled, a sudden wail of such purity and agony that the hairs on the back of her neck rose in a single movement.

Even with the light on, the recess was hard to see into. Terry went as close as she dared – if the cat was in pain she didn't want to be on the receiving end of its claws or teeth. Then she saw it. It was in one of the boxes, the blazing eyes staring balefully at her from a nest of something white. The whiteness wriggled, and she realized she was looking at a pile of newborn kittens.

The cat howled again, and another glistening package slid out and began to struggle free from its bag of slime.

It made sense now – the screams, the desperate attempt to get inside through the bedroom window, the distended pelvis she'd glimpsed as the cat had

turned away. She'd just been trying to find somewhere quiet to give birth. Terry swallowed and
made some soft inarticulate sounds of reassurance.
The mother started to lick the latest arrival clean,
while the two that had already been born scrambled
for teats. There was a long strand of placenta
attached to the sac: as Terry watched, the cat began
to suck it up like a gourmet with a piece of spaghetti.

Knowing Mo would want to see them, she went
and shook her awake. 'We've got some visitors,' she
said, enjoying Mo's look of sleepy incomprehension. 'Come and see.' She led her downstairs
and pointed to the box. Puzzled, Mo went and
peered in it; then, seeing the kittens, she gave a little
cry of surprise and delight.

'Where did she come from?' she whispered after a
moment's cooing.

'I don't know. She must belong to one of the
neighbours. I can't even see how she got in. Do you
think she needs anything?'

Mo shook her head. 'Some milk maybe, when
she's finished. Other than that, she's best left alone.'

'We don't need to call a vet?'

'I shouldn't think so. My parents' cats were
always having kittens. After a while we just let them
get on with it. Nature knows what she's doing.'

They checked her occasionally, able to tell from
the cries when another kitten was on its way.
Eventually the afterbirth appeared, and the cat
seemed to be done, lying back on her side exhausted
but purring contentedly while the kittens wriggled
and rolled round her belly.

44

While Mo warmed up some milk Terry wandered into the front room and leant her elbows on the window. It was almost dawn now. The view wasn't anything much, the terraced houses identical to the ones she'd looked out onto in London. The only difference was that several had bicycles leaning against them, four or five in some cases, completely blocking the pavement. Those would be the student houses the neighbour had complained about.

Two figures came jogging out of the pre-dawn darkness. They were running seriously, dressed in identical Boat Club tracksuits, with handweights strapped to their wrists and Walkmans clipped to their waists. They passed within inches of her, but she might as well have been invisible behind her window.

Simultaneously, a red sports car turned into the street, an old MG. It parked outside the house opposite, and a young couple got out. The man was wearing full black tie and the woman a taffeta ball-gown. Terry was glad Mo hadn't been there to see it: her stereotypes, an uneasy combination of *Brideshead Revisited* and *Inspector Morse*, were ingrained enough already.

Mo brought her coffee, and the two of them stood watching the street for a few moments.

'Well,' Mo said at last, 'they seem to be doing fine. We may as well go back to bed.'

'I was just thinking . . . She could be a stray. What if we can't find the owner?'

Mo grunted. 'We? What's this we?'

'What if *I* can't find the owner, then?'

45

'Then you'll have a cat of your very own. Not to mention four kittens.'

'Five, you mean. I counted them. But—'

'No, four. I counted them too.'

Terry dashed to the box and frantically counted the kittens. Four. 'There must be one underneath her. We'll have to move her, she might be squashing it,' she called to Mo, who came and helped her lift the unprotesting cat. But there was nothing underneath.

'I know there were five, Mo, I counted five. One must have escaped,' she said, desperately pulling boxes out of the space.

'Calm down, Terry. Look, it couldn't have escaped, there's no way one of these little things could climb out of that box. The sides are far too high. Besides— Oh, Christ, look, it's . . .'

Terry somehow knew, even before she turned, what had made Mo gasp, what it was she was about to see. As if in some terrible dream she watched the cat lower its head delicately back down to what it was eating. She caught a glimpse of tiny, mouse-sized entrails, a hairless body bitten right across in cross-section. A tiny high-pitched squeaking, so quiet Terry had barely been aware of it, stopped abruptly. The cat threw its head up to swallow better, gulping the remains of its baby down greedily, like a pelican swallowing a fish. Terry turned away.

'Jesus,' Mo said quietly.

Three

From his bathroom at the back of number fifty-nine, Harry Gibson could just see the punky-looking blonde in the garden of fifty-seven. She was walking round looking at the plants, eating a bowl of cereal at the same time. Her hair was short, and he admired the long curve of her neck. It was sunny rather than warm, but she was wearing a thin dressing gown that didn't leave much to the imagination. Not that it mattered much, since Harry's imagination was well-practised at filling in details. She went inside, but he closed his eyes and pictured her letting the dressing gown fall, the tennis-racquet tautness of her stomach, the nipples on her gently swaying breasts teased to erection by the chilly wind. Gulping, he reached through the gap in his pyjamas.

The doorbell went, and he froze. Sheila would answer it, but if it was something that required his attention he might have to go downstairs. As he listened to the murmur of voices his erection was letting itself down in a series of little jerks. He heard Sheila's footsteps on the stairs.

'Harry? There's a girl from next door who wants to know if we know anything about a cat they've found.'

'I'm just coming,' he called. There. Just about decent. Twisting his pyjamas sideways so that nothing could be glimpsed through the fly, he pulled back the lock on the door.

Dorling Van Glught was not a happy man. His wife had started buying free-range, wholemeal, virtually vegetarian eggs from the shop with the jokey name on the Botley road – Eggs Eggcetera, that was it – and as a result his breakfast egg was fertile. A brown speck the size of a tadpole lay on his teaspoon as he waved it accusingly at his wife.

'Oh come on, darling,' Julia said crossly. 'It's nothing to make a fuss about. It's perfectly natural.'

'I just happen not to like them like this, that's all,' Dorling retorted, putting down his spoon. 'Do we have marmalade?'

'In the cupboard.'

The doorbell rang. Julia ignored it, so after a few moments Dorling went. She stopped eating and listened. 'No,' she heard him say, 'I can safely say that we have never possessed a cat, though my wife can be a bit feline sometimes. I suggest you put a notice in the shop window. That's what we generally do round here when we mislay something, and it seems to work. Not at all.'

'Who was that?' she said when Dorling came back.

'Our new neighbour is sharing her house with an unwanted moggy. I told her we didn't know anything about it. The papers are here, by the way.'

Dorling took the book section first, while she flicked through the *Style* magazine.

'Brian's done another full-page review,' Dorling said. 'Some American book on Wordsworth. He massacres it, of course.'

'Of course,' Julia murmured. For a while there was silence, broken only by the occasional chuckle from her husband.

'What's she like?' she asked.

He pretended not to understand. 'Who?'

'That girl.'

'Seems all right.'

'Sheila said there were two of them. Very affectionate with each other, she said, which is Sheila-ese for queer. The one who's bought it used to live in London, apparently. Though why anyone should want to leave London', she said thoughtfully, picking up the magazine again, 'to come back to this dump is completely beyond me.'

Giles Chawker heaved himself out of the bath and towelled himself briskly, admiring the lean athleticism of his body as he did so. Then he turned to the girl who'd been sharing the bath with him. Her eyes were closed, though he knew she'd have been watching him as well. A nipple protruded through the water. Rolling it in his fingers, pinching just enough to hurt, he chuckled as her eyes opened and she squealed at him.

'Got to go, my lovely. Have you seen my kit?'

'It's in my bag. I washed it for you. I was doing a load of my stuff anyway,' she added, though in fact she hadn't been. Emma was eighteen, a student at one of Oxford's hundreds of secretarial colleges, and totally besotted with Giles.

'Going to do anything while I'm out?'

'Sleep,' she murmured happily, closing her eyes again.

'Shouldn't sleep when you've been up all night. It's best to go right through.' He yawned. 'Thank God today's only training.'

'Didn't you train when you were at home?'

'Don't need to. Bonking keeps me in shape.'

'Bonking who?' she asked fearfully.

'Everyone in sight, my precious.' He was pulling on the trousers of his tracksuit as he spoke. The tracksuit was a plain blue one, bearing the crossed oars of the Oxford University Boat Club. 'Going to seem a bit odd, training without Hugh.'

'Was it really terrible, talking to the police?'

Giles shot her the look that terrified her, the look that said she was pestering him. But he spoke gently. 'I don't actually want to discuss it.'

'Sorry.' She started soaping her firm little breasts, hoping he'd be distracted enough to give her a quick one before he went.

He sighed. 'I'll take the car. You won't need it if you're just going to sleep.'

'All right,' she said meekly. 'The' car was actually

hers, a little MG her doting father had given her for her eighteenth birthday.

'We'll probably go to the Bear for some lunch.'

'Can I come?'

'No, actually. I'll want to talk to the chaps. Haven't seen most of them since last half.'

'With Hughie dead,' Emma said thoughtfully, 'does that mean you're more likely to get a place in the boat?'

His face darkened. 'God, women are pathetic sometimes,' he snapped. 'What a thing to say.'

'I'm sorry,' she said desperately. 'I was only thinking out loud.'

'And you've been wearing my Blues sweater, haven't you? It reeks of that French pong.'

'I wore it when you weren't here,' she said. 'It reminded me of you.'

'Well, don't. You'll stretch it. Christ, I look as if I'm growing a pair of tits,' he said, regarding himself in the mirror. He went through to the bedroom, and she heard him whistle under his breath. 'Talking of tits,' he said.

'What is it?'

'Red-hot totty alert. Must have moved into Hugh and Rollo's house.'

Emma came and stood beside him in a towel, shivering and wet. Terry was crossing the street just below them. 'She can't have. The For Sale sign's still up. Perhaps she's only looking.'

'Likewise,' Giles murmured. He kissed her perfunctorily on her wet shoulder. 'See you later.'

When he had gone Emma got back in the bath

51

and lay with her eyes closed, thinking about Giles. The doorbell rang, but by then she was half asleep and she couldn't be bothered to answer it.

Terry had tried most of the houses in the immediate area now, and not one of them produced someone who had lost a pregnant cat. In a couple of cases, where there was no reply, she pushed a note through the letter box. She decided that she would try one more, and if that didn't work she'd take Dorling's advice and stick a notice in the window of the local shop.

Number fifty-five, the house on the left of her own, turned out not to have a doorbell but a grandiose mock-Gothic knocker. It was so heavy that when she rapped it the door, which was unlocked, swung open. The layout was an exact mirror image of her own house next door, but there any resemblance ended: while her house was bare and dilapidated, this had been furnished by some-one who knew what they were about.

She rapped the knocker again, and heard move-ment upstairs. While she waited she admired the sculpture of a face which had been hung on the wall by the door so that, white on white, it seemed to be emerging from the wall itself. She touched it, wondering what kind of marble it was made of, and was surprised to find that it was dry and porous to the touch. Not marble at all, but plaster of Paris.

'I see you've met Percy.' The voice belonged to a man of about forty who was standing at the top of the stairs in a dressing gown, watching her.

She jumped. 'I'm so sorry. The door was open, and I was curious.'

'Please, don't apologize.' He indicated the sculpture. 'Do you recognize him?'

'Should I?'

'I was told you were a student of literature.'

'News does travel fast,' she said dryly.

He came downstairs slowly. His feet and legs were bare and, she couldn't help noticing, inordinately hairy, as was the v of chest revealed by the dressing gown. 'Your clue', he said, 'is that he really was called Percy.'

'When was it sculpted?'

He laughed. 'It isn't a sculpture. It's an eighteenth-century Italian death mask, one of only three made from the original mould.'

She looked at the mask more closely. The features were fine and almost girlish below the high forehead. 'Is it Shelley?' she hazarded.

'Very well done.' He was standing next to her now, and she realized that he was in fact quite a small man, at least an inch or two shorter than herself. Although his body looked as if he kept it in shape, there was grey in his hair. He was also intensely, radiantly physical: so much so that she felt her body space invaded even though he was not particularly close. 'It's beautiful,' she said truthfully. 'Where did you get it?'

'Percy and I are old friends. I wrote a book about him, and in return he allowed me to track this down in a private collection.'

'It must be worth a fortune. Isn't it risky leaving

it right next to the door? Particularly if you don't lock it.'

He smiled. 'All risk is relative. Besides, he's my household god. That's why he's next to the threshold. By having him here I actually reduce the risk of being burgled.'

'Really?' Terry said politely, not sure if he was being serious or not.

'Anyway, congratulations. You've passed the first test, which is identifying him. Now you can enter, and I will offer you hospitality. A cup of coffee, perhaps.' He spoke in a strange, slightly lilting way, as if he couldn't decide whether or not to give his sentences an ironic twist, though his eyes suggested intense amusement. Whether he was amused by her or himself Terry couldn't have said.

'I came round to ask if you'd lost a cat,' she said.

He raised an eyebrow. 'You've found one?'

'Well, several really.'

She explained about the events of the night. When she had finished he said, 'I'm afraid I can't help you. I don't notice animals,' managing to make it sound as if it would be somehow extraordinary if he did.

'Wait,' he said, and thought for a moment. 'I tend to have a small party on the first night of term. Will you come? Tomorrow at about eight? A lot of the Islanders will be here.'

'Islanders?'

He waved his hand to indicate the area around

54

them. 'Osney Islanders. We like to think we're a race apart. Anyway, it would be a chance to meet some of your neighbours and ask them about your feline friend.'

'Thank you, I'd like that. I'm Terry Williams, by the way.'

'I know. I'm Brian Eden. Stay there, I want to give you something.'

After a few moments he returned with a book, a hardback the thickness of a brick. It was entitled simply *Shelley*, its cover design a richly coloured portrait of the poet when he was barely more than a boy. Terry blushed: she'd seen the book in the shops the previous year, when it had been in the best-seller lists. Brian Eden. She recognized the name now: as well as being a biographer, he was one of the most readable of the Sunday book critics, destroying reputations as much with his languid, well-turned witticisms as with his formidable scholarship.

He wrote something on the flyleaf, breathed on it to dry the ink from his fountain pen, and handed it to her. She glanced at what he had written:

To Terry Williams, who admired my mask.

Mo, she thought as she returned to her own house, is going to kill me for this.

Brian watched the door close behind her and stretched lazily. He heard her own door thump closed, then the muffled clumping of Terry's footsteps through the wall. Turning towards the death mask, he bent and slowly kissed it on the lips.

His wife was still in bed when he took her up some coffee. 'Who was that?' she asked.

'The girl next door. The actual girl next door, I mean, not the dramatic stereotype. Definitely not the stereotype.' He glanced down at Carla, reaching out a hand to run his fingers through her red hair. 'I've asked her to come tomorrow. We'll get everyone else to have a look at her.'

'She's pretty, is she?'

Brian laughed. 'Ravishing, in an amazonian sort of way. I wonder what her circumstances are.'

'You will be careful, won't you?'

'Whatever do you mean by that?'

Carla drank her coffee and said nothing.

In their house in Scotland, Edward Pearce was about to confront his father.

He had chosen the day and the time carefully. His father was at his least irascible in the mornings; but if things did go wrong, at least there was only a day left until term started.

He waited patiently through breakfast, drinking cup after cup of coffee to try to lubricate the dryness in his throat. The old man, immersed in the sports section of the *Sunday Telegraph*, didn't notice.

Eventually Edward took the plunge.

'Dad, can I talk to you?'

'What about?'

'About Oxford.'

His father drank some more tea, though he glanced up automatically at the painted oar that hung on the wall above Edward's head. It was painted with the names of the rowers who had been victorious in Eights week, more than thirty years earlier. One of them was his own. Then he turned back to his paper. Edward knew he wouldn't be reading now, though. He'd be calculating. God, how he hated having to ask him for anything. But it had to be faced.

'Is something wrong?'

'Not exactly. It's about my degree course.' The old man was wearing a silk dressing gown with a Chinese dragon on it. He'd picked it up on his travels, the memento of a shore leave in some foreign port or other. For a moment Edward had the fantasy that he was talking directly to the baleful eye of the dragon itself, but he forced himself to continue. 'I've decided to change it. To English Literature, in fact.'

Still no response. 'What makes you think they'll let you?' his father said at last.

'I've asked them, and they seem to think it's OK.' No need to go into Hugh Scott's death now. 'Basically, they've got a vacancy, and the tutor's said he'll have me.'

'I'm sure he did,' the old man murmured. 'Keen to get anyone they could, I expect. For English Literature.'

Don't rise. Don't rise to anything he says. Behave like an adult and he'll have to treat you like one. 'It's something I've been thinking about for a bit. Basically I'm not finding Engineering as challenging as I'd hoped.' That was something he'd planned to

57

say, to head off any implication that he was taking a softer option.

'And what will you do with your English Literature degree? Become a teacher?'

'Not – not necessarily. There are plenty of jobs for arts graduates at the moment. Probably more than there are for engineers. I could go into management.'

'Management,' his father repeated. Not attacking yet, just circling: looking for an opening. 'And what about your scholarship? Is this tutor who's so keen to have you keen enough to go on paying your scholarship?'

Here it came. 'Well, I can do without that. It's only five hundred.' His father snorted. 'The real problem is that I'll probably have to go without a grant for a year.'

'And you want me to pay for you.' His father put down the paper at last and stared at him.

Edward reckoned he'd got this far pretty well. At least he'd been able to make his case. 'Yes. It's going to be nearly two thousand. I'll pay you back, of course.'

'From the money you make in management.' His father smirked. 'What exactly do you intend to manage again?'

Suddenly Edward could feel the helplessness and the anger rising in him like vomit. The temptation to lose control was almost overwhelming. He wanted to shout and scream and break things. He drank some more coffee and said nothing.

'Something artistic. A ballet company, perhaps.'

His father flipped his wrist over in a grotesque parody of a queer. 'Oh, do come and read some poetry to us, Edward.'

Edward couldn't think of anything to say.

'Gays don't do that, actually,' he said at last, indicating his father's mincing wrist.

'Don't they? I bow to your superior knowledge. I don't know many homosexuals.' He pronounced it hommasexuals.

'I'm not gay just because I want to read English, for Christ's sake. You're mad.' Edward realized he was going to start crying, and the shame of the realization precipitated the actual tears. Blubbing, his father called it. 'I'm going to do it anyway,' he said through the choking snot. 'I'm going to start next week. I'll manage on my own if you really won't help me.'

'Well,' said his father, picking up his paper, 'I see you've already started to behave artistically.'

Five hundred miles away in Northumberland Andrew Harris was lying in bed, trying to discuss his daughter Emily with his wife. Ben, their three year old, had wriggled between them and was now seeing which of his parents he could kick the hardest.

'All right,' he agreed, 'so I don't understand. Why doesn't she want to go back to Oxford?'

'She gets homesick,' Maggie said. 'I think she's lonely down there.'

'She's got loads of friends,' he argued. 'She's spent all holiday going on about how boring it is at home.' He couldn't understand the change in his daughter. She'd been the top achiever of her year at her school, the local comprehensive. She'd got an Exhibition to Oxford, and had come home after her first two terms full of self-confidence and chatter about life in college. Then, this last vacation, she'd been moody and aggressive. He had a sudden thought. 'Is it boy trouble?' Maggie sighed, which meant yes.

'Come on, she's my daughter too. What's the story? She's never mentioned a boyfriend.'

'I don't think he was a boyfriend exactly,' Maggie said carefully. Ben started to hit his father over the head with a toy submarine that was somehow lying in the bed with them. She offered him an alarm clock instead to divert his attention. 'It was a bit more off and on than that.'

'What on earth do you mean?'

'I think she was keener on him than he was on her.'

'Well, there's always next term.'

'Not in his case.'

'Why not?'

'You remember she told you about the boy who was killed?' Andrew nodded. 'That was the one she was keen on.'

Andrew stared at the ceiling. 'Christ. No wonder she's feeling a bit odd.'

Giles parked the car on Donnington Bridge and trotted down the towpath to the boathouse. The others were already hard at it, working on the ergonometers or doing press-ups under the watchful eye of Roddy, the coach.

'Sorry I'm late,' Giles said pleasantly, slowing to a walk.

'You're certainly late, but I doubt if you're sorry.' Roddy pulled on a cigarette and regarded the young man shrewdly. 'You'll have to catch up. Fifty sit-ups should sweat some of the alcohol out. And next time you turn up to one of my training sessions, make sure you've been to bed the night before.'

Cursing under his breath, Giles wedged his feet under a bench and started the sit-ups. Roddy was right, damn him: within moments he was sweating like a pig.

Nominally Roddy was the college Fellow of Modern History. In fact, his only passion was rowing. Forty years ago he had rowed stroke for the Dark Blues in the Boat Race, in a contest that was still talked about by his generation. He had coached the St Mary's Eight for over fifteen years; in that time only Oriel had been Head of the River more often. Yet it was said that in all the time he had been coaching he had never himself set foot in a rowing boat. The antithesis of everything a modern coach should be, Roddy smoked and drank and swore and indulged himself at every High Table in Oxford. There was a time when he had jogged alongside the training crews, shouting instructions from the towpath; later, as he became less fit, the shouting was done through a megaphone and his ever-increasing bulk wobbled precariously on a bicycle. When even that became too much he appeared on the river one day with a CB radio and a Suzuki moped, on which he proceeded to roar up and down the muddy towpath, flagrantly disregarding both local by-laws and common sense. Many were the dog-owners who had had to leap out of the way as Roddy, his attention fixed on the water, charged down on them, steering one-handed and operating the radio mike with the other. Somehow, though, their complaints were never acted upon. The police reckoned they had enough town-versus-gown conflicts to resolve without taking on fanatics like Roddy.

'How's that feeling, laddie?' Roddy enquired genially as Giles staggered to his feet. He puffed cigarette smoke into the boy's face. 'Not feeling sick, I hope?'

'Not in the least,' Giles lied.

'Have a go on the erg, then.' The college only had one proper ergonometer, but Roddy had had half a dozen more built by John, the boatman. A bench with a sliding rowing seat had mounted at one end of it an exercise bike wheel and a handle. When you pulled the handle, the wheel went round. A Nobel Prize-winning Professor of Physics had designed the meter which indicated the stroke rate: Roddy liked to say it was the most useful work he'd done in his life.

As Giles grunted and heaved at Roddy's torture machine, the other man crouched down and spoke to him.

'Word to the wise, Giles. I need rowers, not passengers. Considering the way you treat your body, I will admit your performance is nothing short of miraculous. But I have to consider what putting you in the boat would do to the others. Whether they'd see you swanning around and think they could start doing the same.'

'Come off it, Roddy,' he gasped. 'I've been rowing in Eights since I was fourteen.'

'Hmm. Do you know Edward Pearce?'

'Never heard of him. Where'd he go to school?'

'Nowhere you'd think of as a school. The point is, it was on the other side of a loch. Rowing there was the only way to avoid a three-hour bus ride. His father taught him to scull: he was a Worcester man himself, as it happens. Rowed stroke for their Eight.'

'You're winding me up, Rodders.'

The older man nodded, lighting another cigarette from the stub of his old one. 'Of course. The question is, how are you going to respond? Are you going to get serious, or are you not?' He squinted at the young man across his cigarette smoke. 'That dining society of yours, for example.'

'What about it?'

'Let's just say that if you're really serious about *this*,' he slapped the ergonometer, 'you might demonstrate it by spending a little less time with your socialite friends.'

'It never bothered you with Hugh.'

'Young Hughie's dead. And he didn't die in very nice circumstances, did he?'

'What's that got to do with anything, Rodders?'

Roddy sighed. 'Those of us in college with long memories think that certain individuals would be well advised to keep a low profile for a while. And you in particular, if you want to get into my boat, are going to have to do just that. It's up to you, laddie.'

When Roddy had stomped off to harass some other unfortunate, Adrian Mills came over and climbed on the next ergonometer.

'Giles. How are you? Good vac? I see Roddy was giving you one of his pep talks.'

'Good to see you, Ade. Yeah, the usual stuff. What's this Edward bloke like? Roddy seems to think he might give him Hughie's seat.'

'You've heard that loch-and-bull story too, then? Two miles there and two miles back?' Adrian picked up some weights and began swinging them casually. 'He had a chat with me as well, earlier. I got the impression he'd been asked to lean on Hugh's friends. They seem to be terrified of any publicity.'

'Why, for God's sake? There are plenty of other dining societies to worry about.'

'Yes, but there's only one that Hugh was involved in. I think this must all have something to do with his death.' He looked thoughtful. 'You went to the inquest, didn't you?'

'Yeah,' Giles paused. 'It was a bit of a non-event, actually.'

'It was very cleverly managed. Think about it. Did anyone speak to you about what you should say, by the way?'

'My tutor phoned me,' Giles admitted. 'But he

64

didn't try to coach me or anything. Just said he understood how I felt about gossip, and that I shouldn't repeat any unless I knew it to be true.'

'Gossip? What gossip?'

'Didn't you know? Hugh told me a couple of stories . . . but nothing to do with his death. And nothing to get Roddy in a tizz.'

'Anyway, it's all very peculiar,' Adrian murmured. Roddy blew a whistle, and the two of them jogged towards the next part of the circuit.

Four

Terry rested the flat of her hand against the end of the champagne bottle and launched it into space. There was a moment of silence, and then a satisfying explosion of breaking glass echoed from within the metal container. She had always liked bottlebanks. There were basically, she reckoned, only two sorts of people who used them: those who were simply too anal to throw anything away, who released their bottles of Sainsbury's Cabernet Sauvignon gingerly, holding on to the neck until the last possible moment, and those like her for whom the pleasure was entirely that of legitimized delinquency and who relished every muffled clang and smash.

She had given up on finding the cat's owner, at least for the time being. Mo was getting bored, and since they had the van for the rest of the day it seemed sensible to make use of it. She needed white paint, gallons of it, so they combined a run to one of the DIY superstores with a trip to the bottle bank she'd seen in its car park. The boxes of empties she'd found cluttering up the lean-to were soggy and foul with dregs, and had a tendency to split when she carried them to and from the van. After ten solid minutes of feeding them bottle by bottle through the metal porthole she lost patience and began simply chucking them over the top. A young man of student age, definitely in the anal category, who was standing next to her carefully separating his carrier bagful into clear, brown and green glass, looked at her disapprovingly.

'White with a hint of Lavender,' Mo said cheerfully, returning from the store with a trolley full of paint. 'Just the thing for a vanilla lesbian with a hint of dominatrix like yourself.' There was a sudden crash as one of the student's bottles slipped from his fingers and shattered on the tarmac. Getting down on his knees, he shot them a wounded look and began picking up the pieces, shard by shard.

'Where now?' said Mo, when Terry had got her safely back in the van. Mo insisted on doing the driving: Terry suspected she was actually fantasizing about being a builder, and that given half a chance she'd wind down the window and wolf-whistle at some unsuspecting housewife.

'Your friend's place?' Terry suggested. Mo had a gay friend in Oxford who ran a café in a Women's Centre, and who had bought some of the photos at her last exhibition: she'd said that if Mo was ever in Oxford she should come and see where they were hung.

'Why not?'

They drove in silence for a while. 'You know, I've been thinking about the cat,' Mo said at last.

'What about her?'

'You know the vet said it could be caused by stress or trauma?' No vet's surgeries had been open, it being a Sunday, but they'd eventually got through to one on the phone. He hadn't been able to help much. Cannibalism was just one of those things that sometimes happened: it would probably stop after a few days, once the kittens started to grow. In the meantime they should just let the cat rest and be careful not to startle her. 'I was wondering – did you feel those lumps under her fur?'

'What lumps?'

'When I was stroking her I felt some scabs. On her stomach, just above her nipples. I thought she'd just been in the wars, but it suddenly occurred to me – well, it's a horrible thought.'

'What is?' Terry said, puzzled.

'They could be burns from a cigarette. You know, like someone's been torturing her.'

The Women's Centre was located in an old Victorian fire station in the centre of town, and consisted of a bookshop linked to the café run by Mo's patron, Lizzie. It was reasonably full, dotted with small groups of women having brunch and reading the Sunday papers.

The photographs were mounted all along one wall. Terry looked at them and felt her neck turn crimson.

'You didn't tell me it was these particular shots,' she hissed at Mo. She felt as if everyone was looking at her.

'You never asked. Relax, will you? It's not as if you'll be recognized.'

That at least was true. In her private work, as opposed to her advertising commissions, Mo aspired to be a sort of female Mapplethorpe. The nudes in Lizzie's café were beautiful, in richly toned black and white, delicately lit and printed on the finest paper, but they were also extremely explicit. They were from what Mo called her non-sexist nude series. The model's head had been cropped off, and the photographs had been printed in such strong sepia tones that it was impossible to tell even if she was black or white. In fact, it was Terry.

She couldn't help thinking that of all the cities these photographs might have ended up in, anywhere would be preferable to here. It wasn't rational – Mo sold few enough photographs anyway, so she ought to have been delighted for her, and it wasn't as if her body was in any way identifiable. But somehow she didn't think she'd be spending a lot of time in the Women's Centre.

Mo stopped a waitress and asked if Lizzie was around. The girl flashed them a smile. 'Sure. She's in the kitchen. But she won't see you if you're reporters.'

'Tell her it's Mo Dawson. The photographer.'

A few minutes later Lizzie appeared, a surprisingly young and frail-looking American. Terry caught herself thinking that she didn't look like a

dyke, and instantly reproached herself for the crass-
ness of the thought. For that matter, what signals
did she herself give off? Mo introduced them, and
they ordered coffees. Mo complimented Lizzie on
the way the pictures had been displayed. To Terry's
relief she didn't mention her own part in them.

'They're so beautiful. Everyone's been asking
where I got them,' Lizzie said.

'Really? I'll send you some cards, if you like. All
commissions gratefully received.'

Lizzie suddenly looked tired. 'That's if we're still
open, I guess.'

'Why? It seems like business is booming.'

'Oh, this business is fine. It's that other business
that's the problem.' When they looked blank she
said, 'Sorry, you don't live here, do you? You
wouldn't have heard. We're the suspects in a
murder case right now.'

Mo glanced at Terry. 'Not a murder in Osney, by
any chance?'

'That's the one. You have heard about it, then?'

'Terry bought the house where it happened.'

'No – you bought the famous house of slaughter?
That's pretty cool of you. Cool in the English sense
of the word, I hasten to add, not cool as in where I
come from.'

'It was just a nice house,' Terry said, 'I wasn't trying to make a point or anything.' But she had been,
she realized, if only to that pompous estate agent.
If she'd known the murder was such a *cause célèbre*
she might have acted differently.

'So why are you involved?' Mo asked.

Lizzie sighed. 'It's so stupid, really. They've had a letter claiming responsibility for the murder, written on the notepaper we sell. Like, our customers are so stupid they'd kill someone and then not spot they were giving the police a clue.'

'Is the paper very distinctive?' Terry asked.

'Well, it's recycled and bleach-free, so it's not totally common or garden. But more to the point, each page has got a line of type at the bottom saying that it's sold in aid of our women's rights Legal Fund.'

'That hardly implicates the Centre directly, though. Anyone could have got hold of a piece of writing paper.'

Lizzie shrugged. 'I guess they haven't anything else to go on.'

'Was there an inquest?' Terry asked. 'They'd have to say what they knew then.'

'There was one, but the police adjourned it.' She looked at Terry sharply. 'You seem to know the procedure pretty well.'

'I know they're not allowed to harass you, if that's what they're doing, without a reason,' Terry said.

'Again, it's only guesswork, but we've heard they've got a psychologist advising them, some bigshot professor from the university. I suppose he thinks that if the police keep leaning on us they'll eventually flush something out.' She looked around at the busy café. 'What you see here is solidarity, not custom. It's sweet of them, but sooner or later they're going to get tired of being intimidated and they'll just drift away. Meanwhile, word has mysteriously got round the townies that we're involved, so we've had the attacks.'

'Attacks on you personally?'

Lizzie shook her head. 'Not so far. A couple of windows smashed. And a little bit of spraycan stuff. You saw the sign outside that says Lizzie's Café? The first i got changed to an e.'

'That seems a bit subtle for townies,' Terry said thoughtfully. 'That's more like university humour.'

Lizzie looked at her in surprise. 'You're right. I hadn't thought of that.'

The room suddenly went quiet, then resumed its former noise level. The women were all studiously ignoring the three people who had just walked in. A policeman and WPC in uniform, and a second man wearing a waxed jacket, walked ostentatiously up to the counter, then over to the toilets. A brief look inside each, and then they walked equally slowly back through the tables towards the door. As they passed the table where Terry was sitting, she heard a voice from the all-female crowd remark, 'Nice uniform, love. Want to come and try out your handcuffs sometime?' There was a roar of laughter. The back of the WPC's neck went red, but she kept walking without breaking her stride.

'That was probably unwise,' Lizzie murmured.

'So that's what happens?' Mo asked when the police had gone, leaving behind them a buzz of indignation.

'Pretty much. Sometimes they stop customers on the way out, question them or frisk them for drugs.

72

My lawyer's made an official complaint – she's great, she's one of the customers here and she's not charging for her time. But apparently they're not doing anything they're not entitled to. So we just have to wait till they turn something else up, I guess. Or until someone else gets killed.' She spoke lightly, but the strain showed in her drooping shoulders. 'My own theory, given the way the guy got killed, is that it was a man. A pretty mixed-up man, too. I can't imagine a woman doing anything like that.'

'Why? How did the student die?' Terry asked.

'You mean you don't know?' Lizzie looked surprised. 'He was stabbed with a soldering iron.'

Terry and Mo exchanged glances.

'Are you thinking what I'm thinking?' Mo asked.

Terry nodded. 'The cat. Burns. Wait, Mo—'

'Where exactly was he stabbed?' Mo asked Lizzie.

'You mean where in the house or where in the body?'

'Where in the body?'

Lizzie grimaced. 'If you're a psycho, there's only one place you insert a red-hot soldering iron, isn't there?' She nodded. 'Right up the ass.'

The cat lay back on her side, kneading her paws and purring as the remaining kittens, tiny as little white field mice, peered myopically through their milky-blind eyes and burrowed into her stomach. There were only two now. Another one had been eaten while they were out.

'Here, feel the scabs,' Mo said.

With a finger she gently parted the cat's fur, revealing a brown circle of matted blood about half a centimetre in diameter. 'Can you feel those lumps under the fur when you stroke her? They're mostly healed now, but they must have been quite bad.'

'Are you sure they're burns?'

'Not a hundred per cent. They could be scars from leeches. But I can't see where a cat would get that many. Sheep ticks cause the same sort of thing, but I've only ever heard of dogs getting those.'

'How do you know all this stuff?' Terry asked.

'I grew up on a farm. Don't look so surprised. Why d'you think I'm such a rampant townie? When you've spent your childhood watching grass grow, and the highlight of your week is a trip to W. H. Smith, Camden Market looks like dyke paradise.'

Terry shivered. She was wondering where in her quiet little house a body had lain with a soldering iron sticking out of it. Oh, of course. The downstairs room. The one with no carpet. Taken outside and burnt once the police had finished with it.

'A soldering iron,' Terry murmured. It seemed inconceivable.

'Yup. Just like Edward the Third.'

'Second. Edward the Second,' Terry corrected automatically.

'Whatever. But the symbolism hardly lends itself to a crazed feminist psychopath, would you say?'

'I don't know,' Terry said. 'In the play – Marlowe's play – Edward's killed on the orders of the Queen, who's been abandoned for Gaveston.'

74

She sighed. 'People assume that the red-hot poker was because of his homosexuality, but actually it was a fairly common way of murdering people when you didn't want it to be obvious how they'd died. The wound was nearly invisible, you see.'

'Terry,' Mo said carefully, 'have you thought about going to the police?'

'Why? They might just be burns from a cigarette, like you first thought. We don't know for sure that they've got anything to do with this soldering-iron maniac. Besides, how's it going to help the police to know about the cat? She can't give a statement. They might even want to take her away, have you thought of that?'

Mo said nothing.

Suddenly angry, Terry slammed her hand against the wall. 'It's fucking nothing to do with me. This is my home. I don't know anything about any murder. I don't want to know anything. I just want to be left alone.'

'Sounds fine to me,' Mo said calmly. 'Shall we do some painting?'

That evening was Mo's last in Oxford. She would be driving the van back to London the next morning. Gradually the sense of impending parting affected them both, and they became awkward and reserved. Terry suggested that they stop work on the house and go out, but Mo said she'd rather continue to paint. Terry guessed that in some obscure way she was laying claim to the territory. She didn't mind. Together they got the stairwell and half a bedroom done, then Terry went out to get a take-away.

When she came back Mo shyly handed her a large, thin parcel wrapped in newspaper. 'A present, girlie. Sort of a housewarming gift.'

'Oh, Mo.' Terry felt guilty: she hadn't even thought of getting anything for Mo. Opening it, she found one of Mo's photographs of her, a delicate close up of one of her shoulder blades, printed on rich, silver-black paper and in a simple black frame. Terry surprised herself by starting to cry, though whether from gratitude, guilt at deserting her friend, or homesickness for a home that no longer existed, she couldn't have said.

That night they tried to make love, but it didn't work out. One or other of them wasn't reading the signals properly, and after a while it became clear there simply wasn't any point. That was one of the things about two women, Terry reflected afterwards: you couldn't fake it and there was consequently nowhere to hide.

She woke up sometime in the night. Mo wasn't there, but there was light coming through the open door. Getting out of bed, she crept out to investigate.

Mo was painting. She was in the bedroom they'd half finished earlier, still naked, furiously swinging the brush to and fro. Lumps of paint were flying in all directions, and Mo herself was liberally splattered by White with a hint of Lavender.

Hearing Terry, she looked round. Her eyes were

red and swollen. She turned back to the wall without a word and went on painting.

Terry went and stood behind her. There was an unused brush lying at her feet, its bristles still protected by a sleeve of cellophane. She picked it up and pulled the sleeve off. Then she ran the brush softly down Mo's back.

Mo stopped. Her back twitched like a horse shuddering off a fly, and her eyes closed. Terry ran the brush down her back a few more times, finding the spot between the other girl's shoulders that made her back arch involuntarily, teasing her, then moved the brush round to paint the ribs on first one side, then the other, letting the outermost bristles just touch the side of her breasts. Mo put her hands on the wall and rested her weight on them, like someone being frisked. Terry kept her own hand moving, keeping the rhythm of her brushstrokes slow and steady. When she had touched every part of Mo's torso she squatted down and started on her buttocks and the backs of her thighs. She could smell Mo's arousal, and the pungent familiar smell of her began to turn Terry on too. Putting the brush down, she entered the other girl with her fingers, spreading wetness over her labia and clitoris. Mo groaned and threw her head back.

Terry stood and clasped her from behind, humping Mo's buttocks viciously with her pelvis, reaching up for her breasts and gripping them, using the thrusting of her pubic bone to grind Mo's hips into the fresh, slippery paint. She put her hand on Mo's clitoris and simply left it there, letting the pounding motion do the rest. They'd never made love this way before. It was violent and masculine and completely unexpected. Mo started to come, gritting her teeth and grunting in time with Terry's thrusts. The noise of it startled Terry into coming too and they collapsed against the wall, laughing and roaring, their bodies slick with paint and sweat.

Five

Terry paused on the landing outside her tutor's rooms, partly because they were on the top floor and she needed to get her breath back, and partly because she wanted to listen to the Bach coming from the other side of the door. As an undergraduate she'd once teased Reg that to have a harpsichord in your rooms verged on the pretentious; he'd looked mildly surprised and said, as if it were perfectly obvious, 'But I couldn't have got a piano up the stairs.' He'd proceeded to play her a rousing pub version of 'Knees up Mother Brown', though quite frankly on the delicate, tinkling strings of the harpsichord it sounded like Bach anyway. That was Reg: proud of his working-class roots, he was apparently unaware that a lifetime spent in the rarefied climes of academia had left him rather less working class than the average pope. Terry could still remember his mortification at discovering that his students had nicknamed him Regina.

She knocked. The playing stopped, and she heard him call 'Come!', just as he had done every week for three years when she'd climbed these stairs for her tutorial.

'My dear Terry.'

'Reg.'

They embraced. The room even smelt the same, Terry realized, a rich odour redolent of sun-dried leather chairs and sherry. Reg hadn't changed either: a short, hyperactive man now in his early fifties, the only difference she could see was that instead of wearing ironed jeans under his formal tutor's gown Reg was now sporting a pair of track-suit trousers, the better to accommodate a small beer belly.

'Please,' he said, indicating one of the leather arm-chairs. Before he sat in the other he paused and flicked the wings of his gown up in a gesture that, even more than the smell or the harpsichord, brought her student days flooding back. 'Tell me everything.'

She did. Reg was an excellent listener, the result of a life spent listening to undergraduates read out their essays – it was typical of him that, whilst quite happy to encourage students like Terry to pursue the wildest and most radical feminist critical theories, abandoning the age-old tradition of read-ing a weekly essay out loud to your tutor would have been unthinkable. He was also deeply charm-ing. Every year he bedded two or three of his most intelligent and beautiful female students: Terry suspected that one of the reasons he had been so keen to have her back was that she had never

80

succumbed to his oblique but unmistakable advances. He had taken no offence at her refusals, so she had taken none at his propositions. It seemed to her to be an eminently civilized way of going about things, although she knew that many students, and some of his colleagues, considered it to be an unforgivable abuse of his position.

She quickly filled him in on the events leading up to her separation from David. Reg said little. She suspected that he had never thought it would work anyway. Skipping the bit about Mo – not for fear of shocking him; Reg would have loved it, but unfortunately he was a notorious gossip and she wanted this part of her life kept private – she concluded with the purchase of the house on Osney Island, and the visitation of the cat.

He raised his eyebrows. 'So it was you who bought the college house? I should have guessed from some of the wilder descriptions that were going round.'

'It was cheap. And it's a very nice little house.'

'Yes, it was always very popular with the students. Some of them were rather cross it was sold, in fact, given how little housing stock the college can offer. Doubtless it was explained to them that the sale was purely motivated by fears for their safety, and not in the least by the fact that house prices are going to fall over the next few years.' He beamed cynically.

'Did you know the dead student then, Reg?'

'Hugh Scott? Certainly. One of my own second years.'

'What was he like?' she asked curiously.

Reg put on a sombre face. 'A golden boy, absolutely golden. A talented young mind with all his life ahead of him.'

'Reg!'

Reg giggled. 'Aren't we wicked? Actually, he was one of those rather dreary Hooray Henries who only get in because they've been so well taught. Absolutely beautiful, no soul whatsoever, though I don't think he realized it himself. He wrote appallingly bad poetry from time to time, but it was clear that he was destined for an upper second and a job in a merchant bank. He reminded me of your tedious ex-husband, in fact.' Terry tried to look disapproving at this levity, but actually it was a great relief not to have to be serious about it for once. He giggled again.

She said, 'The thing is, I ought to go to the police.'

'Why on earth do you want to do that?'

She explained about the cannibalistic cat and the burns that might or might not be from a soldering iron.

'Let me give you some advice,' he said, serious now. 'The university is very intent on keeping a low profile over this one.'

'It wasn't the university's fault, though, surely?'

'No, but . . .' Reg looked at her for a moment – almost, she thought, as if he were trying to judge how much to tell her. 'We are *in loco parentis*, after all,' he said. 'And there could be some silly publicity. He was a member of the Catamites, you know.'

'The Catamites?' Terry vaguely remembered a college dining society of that name. Its sole function, so far as she had been aware, was to throw parties, each more lavish and outrageous than the one before. She had a fuzzy memory of attending one herself: the theme had been Fur Coat And No Knickers. A certain amount of cautious debauchery and recreational drug-taking had taken place, to be sure, but nothing particularly excessive by the standards of the time. 'What have the Catamites got to do with it?'

'You know what journalists are like. They love a good dining society story. Privileged youth with more money than sense, that sort of thing. And given the nature of young Scott's demise . . .'

'Just because they're called the Catamites, you think someone might assume there's a connection? Come on, Reg. No one ever thought the Catamites were really raving queers – quite the reverse if I remember rightly. It's just a way for public schoolboys to *épater le bourgeois*.'

'Of course, you must do what you think best,' Reg said mildly.

She sighed. 'No, I'm going to have to get it over with. I'll go down to the police station this afternoon.'

'You must admit,' he said thoughtfully, 'it's somewhat ironic, your talking to the police about a murder.'

'You never really approved of my thesis subject, did you?'

Reg tutted energetically. 'You mustn't think that.

As it happens, having an expert in your field in the college will be very handy for us, when the new Chair's announced.'

'A Chair of detective fiction? At Oxford? You're pulling my leg!' The detective novel was a fashionable literary subject just then, undergraduates tending to feel that enough had already been written on The Role of Nature in Wordsworth, but amongst the older academics it was still considered a genre too frivolous to be worthy of serious critical analysis. Postgraduates who, like Terry, wanted to make detective fiction the subject of their doctorate generally found that their supervisors looked askance.

Reg tutted gently at her. 'Where have you been, Terry? I thought out there in the real world people at least read the papers. Oxford's all about market forces these days; hence the proposed Pensung Chair of Detective Fiction, sponsored by Kim Chong. You have heard of Dr Chong, presumably?'

'Chong – isn't he a Korean?'

Reg nodded. 'Electronics millionaire. In fact, to judge by today's three point stock market rise, probably a billionaire. He's also a fanatical reader of crime books.'

'I had heard of him, actually. But I didn't know he was a doctor.'

'By a happy coincidence, Terry, an honorary doctorate was bestowed on Kim Chong just over two years ago by this very college.' He beamed. 'We grabbed him before the others. Well, Edinburgh had a go but we saw them off easily enough. These events were not unconnected with the fact that Kim

Chong, MA, is a St Mary's alumnus. You would have overlapped, in fact. He matriculated seven years ago.'

Terry searched her memory. There had been one or two Asians around, she seemed to recall, but they hadn't spoken much English and with the arrogance of youth she had simply tuned them out. 'And will the new professorship be attached to St Mary's?' she asked.

'Not necessarily, though of course we'd like it. He's already paid off his debt to us with a rather fine music room. And McGilchrist is trying to get the Chair for Magdalen.'

'McGilchrist? I went to his seminars. Is he still a Marxist?'

Reg nodded. 'Rabidly so. I hear he offers his undergraduates fizzy lager instead of sherry.'

Terry looked hard at him, but it was impossible to be sure whether or not he was joking. 'Won't his, um, extremism be a problem with Dr Chong?'

Reg sighed ostentatiously. 'Really, Terry. Don't you know anything about the politics of Korea and their economic relationship with the emerging market economy in communist China?' Terry shook her head, afraid she might laugh. 'Well, I won't go into it now. The point is, St Mary's needs to be seen to be doing something on detective writers, which is why I'd like you to do some teaching on them. Only the dead ones, of course: we haven't completely abandoned our standards.' This was a reference to the fact that at Oxford literature had to have been written before 1960 in order to qualify for inclusion on the syllabus. As far as the university was concerned, death was a necessary accompaniment to genius. 'It's just a few seminars I'm after, though if you can publish something as well, so much the better. I've taken the liberty of asking McGilchrist to prepare a reading list.' He handed Terry a sealed envelope. The whole thing was strangely redolent of a spymaster briefing one of his operatives; which, she realized, was probably why Reg was enjoying it so much.

'This is from McGilchrist?' she asked as she took it. 'Isn't that rather magnanimous of him?'

'Of course. You're not in Commerce any more, Terry. Here we're all on the same side: the pursuit of knowledge, beauty and goodness.'

What Reg was pursuing was rather more bankable than beauty, Terry reflected, but she kept the thought to herself.

'Speaking of other academics,' she said as she stood up to go, 'do you know Brian Eden at all?'

'Certainly. There's an example of what I mean when I say the university is changing. An absolutely brilliant mind, still young – there was a time when he'd have had to wait his turn for all the academic honours, but these days someone like that has recognition heaped upon him. He's very telegenic, too. The American universities are desperate to have him, but for the moment he seems quite loyal to us.'

'I'm going to a party at his house tonight. He lives next door to me, you know.'

'It should certainly be entertaining. Though from

what I gather,' Reg said thoughtfully, 'he'll be keeping a rather low profile for a while, too.'

'Why?' she enquired. But Reg didn't elaborate.

When he showed her out onto the landing there was an undergraduate waiting to see him, a nervous-looking young man with dark hair and very pale skin. 'Have you met Edward, Terry?' Reg asked.

'No, I don't think so.' The boy shook her hand shyly and looked at his feet.

'Edward will be joining the second years. You'll be teaching him, so in a sense you'll both be the new boys.' For some reason this made the young man blush even more. Terry gave him what she hoped was an encouraging smile and left him with Reg.

She strolled out of the college, noting the new music room Reg had mentioned. By anyone's standards, St Mary's wasn't one of Oxford's more photogenic colleges. Admittedly, there was a fine chapel, once a parish church, around which building styles of various centuries radiated outwards, like rings in an oak tree. First came the quadrangle of Victorian staircases in intricately patterned brick where Reg had his rooms. Beyond this, almost fluorescent by comparison, were the red-brick halls of residence which housed the first-year undergraduates, which in turn were surrounded by the glass-and-metal constructions of the last fifteen years. A series of archways and apparently random gaps led from one period to the next, adding to the ramshackle effect. Here and there benefactors had attempted to brighten the place up or commemorate their achievements with brick-built fountains, but the uses found for them by unruly undergraduates had prompted the college authorities to fill them in with earth. Institutional lobelias and scraggy conifers now stood where their designers had imagined flowing cascades and waterspouts. In Terry's day it had been a common sight to see gaggles of American tourists, accustomed to the idea that all Oxford colleges were places of dreaming spires and tranquil gardens, wandering in through the porter's lodge ('Plodge' in the college jargon) with their cameras at the ready, only to lower them in disbelief and beat a hasty retreat.

Terry paused in the lodge to see whether she had been given a pigeonhole yet for her mail. She had, though it was empty. What next? she wondered. There was so much to do: the house, the work for her doctorate, a note in the shop window about the cat, Reg's blasted reading list. Since she was in the vicinity, it seemed sensible to go and renew her membership of the Bodleian library. There was a quaint oath you had to swear, not to kindle flame in the library's precincts: medievalese for No Smoking. But first she'd better get the police thing out of the way. She started walking briskly in the direction of the St Aldates Police Station.

Detective Inspector Richard Girdler was not best pleased. He had a murder investigation that was going nowhere, he'd cricked his neck playing rugby in the police side the day before, and the desk sergeant had just phoned up to say that there was a woman downstairs who'd walked in off the street and announced that her cat had witnessed the killing. Just what he needed right now: half an hour with some old loony who thought her pet was Sherlock Holmes. He put the phone down wearily and scanned the desks outside his office for a couple of faces to do the interview for him, but unfortunately everyone was out apart from a young female detective constable, working through the pile of fingerprint reports.

'DC Hughes, with me,' he said curtly, pulling on his jacket.

'Sir?' Jane Hughes came over eagerly, grateful for anything that might break the monotony.

'Don't get excited, it's just an interview. Room seven. A lady whose cat may have solved the murder. Let's hope she hasn't been abducted by aliens before we get there,' he added under his breath.

Five minutes later, Girdler's attitude was rather different. It wasn't just that the woman had turned out to be young and attractive, Jane Hughes admitted to herself: the DI was better than most of her male colleagues at ignoring the skirt factor when he had to. He'd started to fill in the Interview Sheet, and had asked for her name and address.

'Terry Williams, fifty-seven West Street, Osney,' she had replied.

Girdler's eyes narrowed. 'Did you say fifty-seven?'

'Correct,' Terry replied, holding his gaze.

'Been there long?'

'I moved in this last weekend.'

'You know we're investigating a suspicious death that took place there?'

'Yes, I do.'

He looked at her thoughtfully for a moment. 'If it's any help,' he said, 'our experience shows that violent crime rarely happens in the same place twice.'

'Thank you,' Terry said. 'I have been getting a bit jumpy, what with one thing and another.' She explained about the cat, and the burns which might have come from the same soldering iron that killed the student.

'There's a connection here with one of the neighbour's statements, sir,' Jane interjected, digging through the file. 'Sheila Gibson. The only thing she heard once the party was finished was a cat fight, just before three. If that wasn't actually a fight, but the sound of this cat getting burnt, and we assume it happened immediately before the murder, it gives us a more specific fix on the time of death.'

'Mrs Williams, your information has been extremely useful,' Girdler said, putting his pen away.

Terry looked doubtful. 'Yes, that's good about the time. But the reason I came in was because of the Women's Centre, you see. I met the woman who owns it, and I heard about that letter you got sent.' She paused.

'Yes? Do you have any more information for us, Mrs Williams?'

'Not more information, no. It's just— Forgive me, but I'm not sure you've grasped the implications of what I've told you.'

The two police officers looked at her quizzically. 'You remember I said that the cat's been eating its babies,' she went on. 'Well, I'm no expert, but even I know that means we're dealing with a female of the species here, right? And if your theory is that this student was killed simply because he was a man, then it doesn't make any sense. Why torture a female cat if your object is to terrorize males?'

There was a long silence while Girdler digested what she was saying. 'It's certainly something to speculate about,' he said at last.

'May I see the letter?'

'See it? Certainly not. It's evidence in a murder investigation. We're grateful to you for coming forward, but—'

'I'm not asking out of prurience, Inspector. I'm an academic. Literature – writing – is what I study. Presumably even the police have noticed that the killer's *modus operandi* has strong similarities with Marlowe's play about the death of Edward the Second. The letter might contain a reference to the play, for example, in which case passing up the opportunity to show it to an expert would be a little stupid, wouldn't it?'

Girdler pursed his lips, then nodded at Jane, who opened her file and took out a photocopy. The original had been a piece of notepaper, on which two or three lines had been typed. Terry took it and read it aloud.

' "*Hugh Scott was killed because he was a man. Save fuel, burn men. All men are rapists. The sisters of unmercy shall prevail.*" ' At the bottom of the page, just as Lizzie had described, it said that the notepaper was sold in aid of the Oxford Women's Legal Fund.

'Well?' he asked.

She shook her head. 'Sorry.' Having set herself up as an expert, she now felt a complete fool.

'What were you expecting?' The DI asked curiously.

She shrugged. 'I don't know. I just had a notion you were barking up the wrong tree with the Women's Centre.' She read it again. 'Who are the sisters of unmercy?'

'If we knew that, we'd have a much stronger idea of what we're looking for. We thought it might be an undergraduate group – there are thousands of clubs and societies, but none with that name. And it's not a national organization, or it would have an entry on the police computer. Our guess is that it's something the writer made up on the spur of the moment. Cranks like to pretend they belong to groups. It gives them a sense of power.'

'Hugh Scott was a member of a dining society called the Catamites,' Terry said. She felt a pang of disloyalty – Reg had specifically warned her not to make a big thing about that – but to her surprise Girdler shrugged and said, 'We know. So far as we can tell, it's just a drinking club.' She stared at the words on the page again, willing them to mean something.

'Wait. There might be something after all. Can I borrow a pen and a piece of paper?'

Jane Hughes obliged, and Terry started to write the words out again. 'Look,' she said when she'd finished. 'If you change the line breaks, you get this.' She showed them what she'd written:

Hugh Scott was killed because he was a man.
Save fuel, burn men. All men are rapists.
The sisters of unmercy shall prevail.

'Yes?' said Girdler, uncomprehending.

'It's just that it's very close – uncannily close – to being blank verse. You know, ten-syllable lines of iambic pentameters.'

'You've lost me,' the DI confessed.

'Blank verse is a form of poetry, sir,' Jane Hughes explained. 'It doesn't rhyme, but it's got a regular rhythm.'

'What did you read at university?' Terry asked her.

She grimaced. 'Police training manuals, mostly. And it was Hendon, not university. I did some Shakespeare at school for A levels. You'll have to remind me about iambic pentameters though.'

Terry picked up the pen. 'Rhythm in poetry is measured in what are called feet. There are different sorts of feet, to describe different rhythms – an iamb is short-long, so an iambic rhythm sounds like de-dum de-dum de-dum de-dum. A trochee is the opposite: dum-de dum-de dum-de. An anapest is de-de-dum. That's an easy one to remember because it sounds like horses' hooves. "*The Assyrian came down like the wolf on the fold, And his cohorts were gleaming in purple and gold.*" A spondee is two long syllables: dum-dum.'

'I'm with you so far,' Girdler said.

'So if a rhythm is iambic, it simply means the feet are short-long. Pentameter refers to how many feet there are in the line, i.e. five. Look.' She used the pen to annotate the lines she'd copied. 'The curve means it's short, and the line means it's long.' She passed the paper across the desk.

Hŭgh Scōtt wăs kill̄ed bĕcaūse hĕ wăs ă mān.

'That's classic blank verse. The other lines aren't quite so regular, but they're still a lot more like iambic blank verse than you'd expect normal speech to be.'

'Did Marlowe write in iambic pentameters?' Girdler asked, passing the paper back.

'Yes. Yes, I suppose he did. Though to be fair, so did virtually every other poet who ever lived, until this century at any rate.'

'So our murderer, or at any rate our informant, is a dead poet. That's narrowed the field a little,' Girdler said mildly. Terry shot him a surprised look: she didn't expect irony from a policeman.

'Or someone who studies dead poets, Inspector. Like an academic who's got these rhythms going round and round in his head, and who unconsciously uses them when he writes.'

Now it was Girdler's turn to look surprised. 'I

take your point,' he said quietly. Terry suddenly found herself rather attracted to him: she liked men who were confident enough to admit when they were wrong.

Jane Hughes broke the silence. 'So what we've got is a letter written on Women's Centre notepaper, perhaps by an academic. Therefore, we might be looking at a female academic.'

'No, not at all,' Terry said. 'My whole point is that this could easily be written by someone who's trying to make you think that the Women's Centre has something to do with it. Someone with a grudge against feminists – there must be plenty of men around who feel threatened by them, for God's sake, particularly in an age-old bastion of male supremacy like a university. My guess is this has absolutely nothing to do with the murder what-soever. Someone just saw a chance to make things difficult for them. I'd say you were closer with the Marlowe thing: some kind of homosexual con-nection.'

'Possibly,' Girdler conceded. 'Except for one thing.'

'What?'

'When we found Scott's body, the word *rapist* had been written on the wall with lipstick. Which could be another reason for the manner of his death, wouldn't you say? A violent penetration for a violent penetration?'

Terry said nothing.

'The letter writer couldn't have known about that, unless it was written by a member of my investigation team – we didn't reveal it until the inquest, which was after this letter had arrived. As for homosexuality, of course we've checked it out, but Hugh Scott seems to have been exclusively and enthusiastically heterosexual.' He studied her face for a few moments. 'Thank you for coming, Mrs Williams, but I think you'd better leave the detective work to us.'

Six

The party started as a murmur of voices through the wall, punctuated by slamming car doors and an occasional descant of laughter. By half-past eight it was a piercing hum, and getting louder by the minute. Terry waited as long as she decently could, then went next door.

She hadn't been able to decide whether a university party required one to dress up or down. In the end she'd settled for her one designer outfit – a Rifat Ozbek little black dress with red-indian-inspired silver chasing down either side of the cleavage – but very little make-up, just a smudge of kohl in the corners of her eyes to make them look bigger. She'd washed her hair and teased it out with the hairdryer so that it fell in unruly black waves over her shoulders. She half wanted to take a coat, just for psychological protection, but that did seem crazy when you were only going two yards.

The door was opened by a young girl in a maid's

uniform. Another maid stood a little further down the hall with a tray of champagne, next to the priceless death mask, which was wearing a party hat and a pair of dark glasses. She took a glass of champagne and saw Brian Eden himself at the door to what must be the drawing room, the epicentre of the noise. He was wearing a tailcoat and a white bow tie, but somehow, on his neat frame, the effect wasn't quite as comical as it might have been. Smiling, he took her elbow and led her into the room.

'What a beautiful dress,' he murmured. 'I hope you have good hunting.' Terry smiled but, having heard a variation on this joke from her friends every time she wore this particular dress, it was a thin smile. It didn't seem to deter Brian in the least. He was looking at her body with undisguised interest. 'And you're so muscular. However did you get all those muscles?'

'Doing up houses, I suppose.'

'You like doing men's work?'

Taken aback, she managed to shrug and say, 'I've never really thought about what is and isn't men's work.'

He cocked his head. 'Listen. Do you like this music?'

She could barely hear it above the noise. Then she caught the soaring treble solo and recognized it. 'Allegri, isn't it? The "Miserere"?'

'Absolutely. But – this is my point – it's a real boy's voice. You can get these imitations now, with women taking the treble parts. But it doesn't have the same purity. Women pretending to be men, men pretending to be women – it doesn't work. History shows us that.'

Terry had stopped dead, her mouth open. She had expected to encounter sexism when she went to work in advertising, though she'd actually found very little. She certainly hadn't expected to find such blatant sexual hostility from a best-selling academic biographer. She took a deep breath to still her rising temper. 'Actually,' she said carefully, 'Allegri would have written this for a castrato. So even your boy treble is a sort of imitation. Your example defeats your argument instead of supporting it.'

To her surprise she saw that he was laughing at her. 'Of course. I wasn't being serious. Now, come and meet some people. Carla!'

A woman of about her own age turned from a group. 'This is my wife, Carla. Carla, this is Terry, who's moved in next door.' Terry recognized her face as the one that had watched her from the window when she'd been looking round. Brian had left them. 'Hello,' she said. 'You've got a lovely house.' It was a pretty trite pleasantry, but you had to start somewhere, and she was still seething with anger at the way Carla's husband had tried to wind her up.

'Thank you,' Carla said frostily. 'I'm sorry, I must dash to the kitchen.' Then she was gone, leaving Terry on her own and wondering what on earth was going on. 'What curious people,' she said aloud.

She suddenly realized that this was the first party

she'd been to without David. At least if you were with someone you could pretend to talk to them. Oh well: if she was going to be a wallflower, she might as well not be embarrassed about it. She grabbed another drink from a passing maid and looked around her.

She needn't have worried about being over-dressed, that was for sure. All of the women were glamorous and most were pretty. A smattering of men were wearing black tie. She thought she spotted a couple of familiar faces from the telly.

Another face she vaguely knew stopped in front of her. 'Mrs Williams?' It was one of the neighbours she'd met yesterday, though he was now wearing a dinner jacket and, rather alarmingly, a monocle on a black braid. 'Remember me? Dorling Van Glught. And this is my wife Julia. Did you find your cat owner?'

'No, I – well, I ended up going to the police about it.'

'The police? Don't they have better things to do these days than trace missing pets?'

'I decided it might have something to do with the murder.' Terry explained about the burns and the theory that the cat's cannibalism was caused by trauma.

'Wasn't there a Hollywood movie in which a dog revealed the identity of the killer?' Dorling mused. 'I think he started barking whenever the villain hove into view. Do you think your cat might do the same?'

Dorling, it turned out, was an illustrator and

writer of children's books. She asked him if he'd started writing for his own children, but he and Julia didn't have any.

'I just wanted to stay on in Oxford,' he explained. 'There was a whole group of us who never left. The clever ones like Brian did doctorates and then got academic posts, and the thick ones like me had to find another way of earning a crust. But I've always been able to draw, and Brian fixed me up with a commission from a friend of his in publishing. I've got a character called Dickie the Little Dragon who basically keeps me in the black. All I have to do is write another three stories a year and the bank manager's happy.'

'It's all deeply Freudian,' Julia interjected.

'Sorry?' Terry said.

'His dragon stories. I mean, he called the damn thing Dickie for a start. Don't have to be a genius to work out what that's meant to symbolize.'

Dorling grinned amiably, presumably having heard this interpretation of his *œuvre* many times before.

'I'll have to show you the stories,' Julia went on, 'and you'll see what I mean. Basically, they're all about this dragon who everyone expects to be big and strong and fierce, but who actually is the size of a very small poodle. Oh, and his fire keeps going out. He's always having to eat curries to get himself going again.'

'They sound sweet,' Terry said politely.

'They sound exactly like Dorling's anxieties about the size of his cock, but so long as they keep

101

me in dresses what do I care?' Julia shrugged and turned away to scan the crowd.

Not wanting to get involved in their marital sparring, Terry said, 'I feel terrible – I don't know anyone here.'

'Really?' Dorling murmured. 'I feel terrible for precisely the opposite reason.'

To Terry's extreme relief, someone stopped, looked at her and said, 'I don't believe it. Terry?'

'Allison!'

She hadn't seen Allison since she'd left Oxford, but she was certainly pleased to see her now. Smiling a goodbye to the Van Glughts, she made her escape into the crowd.

'Have I just rescued you?' Allison asked.

'I think so. Is it just me or is this a very weird party?'

'Oh, Brian likes weird. You get the feeling these are acolytes, not friends. Maybe that's what happens when you get on TV.'

'You're not an acolyte, are you?'

Allison laughed. 'Christ, no. My date brought me, but he's buggered off somewhere.'

'Your date? You're not still with your American, then?'

'It's a long story, but no, I'm not. What about you? Is David here?'

'No. That's a very short story. We've split up.'

To Allison's credit she didn't say she was sorry. Terry was getting rather fed up with people treating her divorce as some sort of bereavement.

Carla Eden passed them in the mêlée, saw Terry, and turned away again.

'What do you know about Mrs Eden?' Terry asked.

'She was one of Brian's undergraduates, I think. Sweet, but not nearly as clever as he is. I suppose there's only room for one giant ego in the marriage.'

'She's not being very sweet to me. I think she thinks her husband's going to make a pass at me.'

'And is he?'

'Who knows? That's just the problem. When he does, I shall tell him to get lost, but I can't do that until he actually asks, can I? In the meantime, he's just playing these strange mind games.'

'Try talking about his wife the whole time. That usually works. Look, speak of the devil.'

Terry turned. Brian was approaching with a bottle of champagne – real champagne, she noticed, not blanc de blancs. Somehow he managed to make even filling her glass a sexually suggestive act. She told herself not to be so paranoid.

'Your hunting's gone well, then?' he said in a low voice, indicating Allison. He knows about me and Mo, thought Terry. Suddenly paranoia seemed a reasonable state of mind. She smiled weakly and lit a cigarette.

'I do like to see beautiful women smoking,' he continued. 'It makes them look dangerous. You know, I've always thought the tobacco companies have got it all wrong, marketing cigarettes that are lower and lower in tar. It's the little three-minute brush with death that makes cigarettes so

103

attractive, isn't it? What they should do, it seems to me, is make them more and more lethal. Then you'd really be making a statement by lighting up. May I?' He indicated the packet. She gave him one, though she was damned if she'd flick the lighter for him too.

'My first cigarette in five years,' he said thoughtfully, letting the first snake's-tongue of smoke flicker through his fleshy lips before sucking it back, inhaling with gusto. 'What a strange effect you must have on me, my dear.' Terry said nothing. The man was impossible.

'We were just talking about adultery, Brian,' Allison said, shooting Terry a mischievous look.

'With reference to sexual liaisons, rather than to my champagne, I hope?' he enquired, unfazed. Terry watched him. She'd never seen anyone play with the smoke from their cigarette so much. At any given moment he was breathing it from his nose in great palaeontological tusks, blowing through his pursed lips like a trumpet, and barking it out between each spoken word. 'That is, of course, its original meaning. Latin *adulterare*, to corrupt or dilute, as in the practice of adulterating good wine with cheaper liquid. One can of course see why that was considered a deadly sin. The other meaning is a modern invention of much less significance. Excuse me, I must circulate.' And with a final lingering glance at Terry's breasts he was gone.

'Smartarse,' Allison muttered as he joined the next group.

'A total shit,' Terry agreed. Unfortunately, and

despite all her better judgements, she realized that she found Brian Eden rather attractive. He was a clever self-confident bastard, and that type, for some reason, opened whatever mysterious stopcocks and conduits controlled her body's signals of desire.

Angry with herself, she said, 'Do you feel like getting out of here? Come and have a drink. I've got a bottle of single malt next door.'

'Sure. I've had enough of these oddballs.'

Making sure that Brian saw them, Terry pushed her way through the throng. Their eyes met briefly, and he raised his eyebrows, whatever that was meant to convey.

'So we'd been together for three years, and Harvey's visa ran out. It was one of those tricky situations: if he married me he'd be able to stay. On the other hand, if he hadn't needed to stay, we'd probably never have thought about marriage.'

'What happened?'

'He wanted to, I wasn't ready. I think I might have been, in another few years, but we didn't have a few years.' She sighed. 'So I gave him the boot.'

'That's terrible,' Terry said, appalled. 'What an iniquitous system.'

'Worse things happen. Anyway, I'm keeping busy. I'm a Junior Fellow now, which sounds a bit like a trainee transsexual, but it means I'm working hard and', she shrugged, 'going to a lot of parties. Sleeping with a lot of men. It's a classic reaction. Maybe I should write myself up.' She took another swig of the Scotch. 'What about you?'

'I fell straight into another relationship. That's over now too, sort of.'

'On the rebound? Was he totally ghastly?'

'No, not at all. It was a friend who became a lover. That's been the tricky part, because I don't want to lose this person as a friend.' God, it was so cathartic to tell someone, even in these vague terms. 'I moved in for a few weeks, just for somewhere to stay, and suddenly found myself in the middle of this intense, wonderful relationship.'

'So why leave?'

She reached for the bottle. 'I don't know. I suppose it felt a bit frightening. This friend wanted to love me.'

'Terry? Can I ask something personal?'

She laughed. 'More personal than this?'

'You never say he. You always say this friend.'

'Yeah. Yeah, well spotted.' Terry took a deep swig. 'Her name's Mo. I forgot you were a psychologist.'

'It wasn't that. Rats are my field. I tend to cut them open, rather than have penetrating insights into their emotional lives. I just noticed, that's all.' She stood up. 'Let me get some more water, and then you can tell me all about it.'

Miles Lambert was cruising, so far without success.

He looked at his watch. Almost two, and he still hadn't made so much as an eye contact, let alone pulled. After nine weeks of the vacation, holed up at his parents' house in a sleepy market town with

106

no gay scene whatsoever, he was completely desperate.

He'd tried the Red Lion, which was packed with drunk students. The big craze at the moment was ordering lager in cans, biting right through the metal and sucking the lager out before it spilt. The place was awash with beer and blokiness. Pur-leese, Miles thought to himself, and slipped out to try the Scotch Pony.

The Scotch Pony was a gay pub, almost the only one in Oxford. He met up with a couple of acquaintances, but the talk was all about the murder at the end of last term. Miles didn't want to talk about the murder. He wanted to get laid.

'It's obvious what happened,' Grant kept saying. 'He pulled some trade, they went to bed, and in the dark he just grabbed the nearest object that came to hand. Ooh, you're a bit warm, he said.' He giggled. 'What a wonderful way to go.'

'Come on,' Miles objected, 'he's dead. Don't talk like that about it.'

'She's feeling sensitive tonight. Got your period, Miles?'

'Miles? Should be called inches from what I heard,' said Paul, Grant's friend. 'Who wants another drink?'

'Heard about the boy who got himself raped in the Parks last week?' Grant whispered theatrically.

Miles hadn't. 'What boy?'

'Someone Rupie Johnson knows very well was *accosted* by a big hairy knifeman.' He giggled. 'Some people have all the luck.'

107

'Did he go to the police?' Miles asked.

'Ooh yes. They sent him away with a spanked wrist.' He waggled his finger at Miles. 'Going to have to be a little bit *careful*, aren't we Miles?'

As soon as he could Miles made an excuse and slipped away. Grant and Paul were just a little too camp for his liking.

Miles ended up in the Coven, a nightclub down by the station that had a licence until three. The crowd was mixed, straight as well as gay, which made pulling more difficult. He chatted up a French boy for a while, a language student, who kept telling him in broken English that he wasn't gay and that he was off to find a woman on the dance floor. He'd disappear for a few minutes and then come back again, flirting sulkily. Eventually Miles lost patience and wandered off.

There was a cottaging area outside, round the back, where you could go for a few minutes of impersonal relief. It wasn't what he'd been after but it was better than nothing. He went outside and lit a cigarette. He heard a grunting sound from the bushes and made out the outline of two men, one standing and the other kneeling in front of him. The standing man looked in Miles' direction and laughed. Miles threw the cigarette down and walked off. He might be desperate, but not so desperate he was going to stand in line for it.

He was rounding the corner when he heard footsteps coming after him. He turned. For a moment he thought it was the French boy. Then something caught the light, something that wasn't either the other person's eyes or a pair of glasses, and he realized he was looking at a pair of swimming goggles. And a black balaclava. All he could see was these goggles sticking out of the holes in the balaclava and a little hole where the mouth was. He froze.

The man had a knife and he was holding it in front of him, pointing it straight at Miles' face.

'Turn round.'

He tried to do as he was told but he was actually too frightened to move, his limbs wouldn't respond, and the man took his inaction as a sign of resistance. He waved the knife in Miles' face and repeated the instruction. This time Miles did turn round. He wasn't sure if the man was a queer-basher or a mugger but either way he knew this was going to be awful. 'Drop your trousers,' the man said and for a moment as he complied Miles found himself thinking, that's good, he's only going to rape me. I'm not going to die. Then the man's arm with the knife was round his throat and with his other hand he was guiding himself in and it hurt, it hurt terribly. Miles screamed but the knife came round to his mouth and the scream died in his throat.

He fell down on all fours with the man's weight on him and they continued like that. He had one of his hands in Miles' groin now, trying to stimulate him. 'Fucking tart,' the man hissed. 'You're enjoying it, you tart.' He finished and pulled out. Then with his foot he pushed Miles over onto his side and stood over him, holding his cock. He's going to piss on me, Miles thought, but the man was still too erect and with a grunt he put his penis back in his trousers. Then he lunged at Miles' face. Miles felt something swipe across his cheek and screamed. But the man just laughed and showed him his hand. He was holding something else now, not the knife, something small and stubby that might have been a pen. 'You enjoyed that, bitch,' the man said again. Then he walked off.

Miles stood up, sobbing, and pulled up his trousers. He could still walk, though sometimes there was a sharp stabbing pain in his guts that brought him up short. He went back to his college and let himself in with his night key. Some people he knew passed him in the quad and called out, 'Hey, Miles. Come and have a nightcap.' 'No thanks,' he called back. Why am I behaving normally? he wondered. He got back to his rooms, ran the hottest bath he had ever run, and tried to clean himself up with a roll of toilet paper. He was bleeding, a bit. He got into the bath, the water stinging where the man had torn him, and watched the pink stain spreading up between his knees like an oil slick.

He lay there a long time. He could go to the police, he supposed. But everyone knew what the police were like. He'd have to explain what he'd been doing going round the back of the Coven – not that it would need much explaining, the police knew what went on there. They'd say he'd been asking for it. They'd ask him if he'd resisted and of course he hadn't, so they'd say he must have wanted it. Had he wanted it? When the man had stimulated him he'd got an erection. Miles looked down at his cock, which was starting to become erect. Oh no, he thought, I can't be. He closed his eyes and masturbated himself slowly. Touching himself was a relief, it stopped him thinking. When he came he felt sick. He lay in the bath for another hour, staring at the ceiling, hating himself.

It wasn't until he got out and looked in the mirror that he saw that what the man had swiped across his face was lipstick.

Seven

It was a beautiful morning. Her windows still curtainless, Terry was woken at six by the brilliant sunshine and the racket of the spring dawn chorus. She stretched and decided to get going. It was a day for a big project, like plastering the bathroom. Picking the Ozbek dress off the floor where she'd dropped it, she put it carefully onto a hanger, then pulled on a pair of overalls. What a fashion contrast, she thought to herself: from bitch to butch. But if the truth were known, she felt sexier in the overalls. She liked the feel of the rough fabric against her naked skin.

For an hour she hacked the existing plaster off, her mouth and nose protected from the dust by a ventilation mask. Where it had been penetrated by the damp and mould the plaster came off easily, peeling away from the bare bricks of the outer wall like wet dough, but elsewhere it needed to be chipped away inch by inch. She was soon damp with sweat.

112

This was the kind of work she liked best, as engrossing and physical as a dance, leaving her mind free to wander. In some strange way she felt it brought her closer to the house, stripping away its old, worn-out petticoats and tired make-up, hacking her way back to the bricks and mortar to start the life cycle all over again.

She'd been working for an hour and a half when Allison stuck her tousled head round the door, still slanty-eyed with sleep.

'Morning,' she grunted. She glanced at the bath, now full of lumps of plaster. 'Not much chance of a bath, then.'

'There's a shower behind the door. I'll make some breakfast.'

Allison waved her hand. 'No food,' she groaned. 'Coffee.'

Standing in her kitchen, Terry could see part of Brian and Carla's garden next door. To her amazement, the party was still going on. Half-a-dozen people were standing around bleary-eyed, smoking cigarettes or tearing chunks from a loaf of bread that was being passed round. She watched as two women came out of the house and said something to one of the men. Both girls were wearing dinner jackets but their legs were bare. The man picked up his own jacket and followed them into the house. It was an odd, rather painterly scene. *Petit déjeuner sur l'herbe.*

Allison had to get home to change before she gave her first tutorial, which suited Terry as it meant she could get on with the bathroom. Even so, it was ten before the old plaster was all removed and she was able to start working up a new mixture.

Plastering was a real skill she had, one she was proud of. David had paid someone to come and do their first house, but Terry had taken one look at the beautiful expanses of bluey-green plaster, smooth as skin, and decided she wanted to be taught how to do it herself. All day she quizzed the poor boy as he worked, getting him to hold her arm until she'd mastered the complex, circular movements, as endlessly repetitive as t'ai chi. Now, five houses later, she still wasn't quite up to professional standards, but only a professional would have known it.

Soon after she'd started, the doorbell rang. Cursing, Terry was tempted to ignore it, but then it occurred to her that it might be someone coming to claim the cat. 'Come in,' she yelled down the stairs. 'I'll be down in a minute.' No, that wasn't true. She really couldn't stop now. 'Can you come up?' she shouted. 'I'm in the bathroom.'

She heard footsteps on the stairs, then a girl of about twenty put her head round the door. Seeing Terry, her eyes widened behind wire-framed granny specs. 'I'm terribly sorry,' she said nervously.

'It's all right,' Terry said brusquely, not meaning it. 'Now you're here, what can I do for you?'

'I'm sorry, it's nothing. I'll go away.'

Few things brought out Terry's vicious side as much as women who dithered. 'Well, you must have wanted something,' she said sternly. She knew she'd feel guilty later, but honestly, some women just asked to be trampled on.

Like a terrified gazelle edging towards food, the girl slid a little further into the bathroom. She was holding, rather incongruously, a bunch of flowers, blue irises mixed with bright yellow daffodils. My God, thought Terry, the daft thing's come to welcome me with a bunch of flowers. She waited, turning the plaster on her hand-board over with the trowel to keep it fresh. The girl remained tongue-tied.

'Are those for me?' she prompted. This must be how the Queen feels, she thought, when she's confronted by a five-year-old with a bouquet.

But to her surprise the girl said, 'No. Not exactly. They're—' She stopped again.

'They're?'

The girl said in a rush, 'They're for Hugh. I just – I thought I'd better ask your permission. I was going to put them outside, on the pavement, next to where his room was, and then I realized someone had moved in and it seemed rude not to ask you.'

'While you're at it,' Terry said crisply, 'why not put up a headstone? A nice tasteful number with a skull and crossbones on it. Here died whatever-his-name-was.' She sighed. 'For the love of God, it's a house. Not a mausoleum, not a cemetery, not a shrine, and certainly not a fucking tourist centre. My house. Where I live.'

There was an awful silence, in which Terry

115

immediately wished the words unsaid, and the girl's eyes filled with tears.

'God, I'm sorry,' Terry muttered, putting down the trowel, 'I don't know why I said that. I'm a bit hung over and I'm foul when I'm working.'

'It's my fault,' she sobbed, 'I had no right to bother you. I've been thinking about him all vac, and I just wanted to do *something*.'

'Was he a friend of yours?' Terry asked gently, partly to make amends and partly because she knew from experience that it's hard to talk and cry at the same time.

'He was my lover,' the girl announced somewhat theatrically. She took her glasses off and wiped her eyes with her sleeve.

'Look, why don't you put the kettle on and make us both some tea? And of course you can leave the flowers outside. I'm sure he would have been very touched.'

'No he wouldn't,' the girl admitted. 'He'd have thought it was silly. It's for me, really, not him.' She looked around for something to blow her nose on and Terry offered her the loo roll.

'What's your name?'

'Emily Harris.'

It rang a bell. 'A first-year English student?'

The girl looked surprised. 'How did you know?'

'I saw your name on Reg's teaching list. I'm Terry Williams, one of his postgraduates. I expect I'll be teaching you at some point.'

'Oh, God. How embarrassing.'

'More embarrassing for me,' Terry said firmly.

116

'I'm the one who's been rude, remember? Now, how about that tea? You can talk to me while I plaster.'

'The thing that's bothering me', Terry said when Emily returned – two cups on a tray, and a bottle of milk, and a bowl of sugar, because, the girl explained anxiously, she wasn't sure how Terry wanted it – 'is that I'd sort of got the impression from the way he was killed that Hugh was homosexual.' She watched Emily carefully to see if she was going to start crying again, but she seemed to be OK now.

She shook her head vigorously. 'Oh no. Not Hughie. After all, I'd have known, wouldn't I?'

'Well, not necessarily. Some people can go both ways,' Terry said, unsure just how naïve Emily was.

'Oh, I know that. But Hugh wasn't. I mean, he went to a public school, so he was pretty relaxed about queers. But he definitely wasn't one himself. He didn't like boyish girls or anything. I mean, look at me. He was a tit man, he always said.' It was true: Emily was full-bodied and large-breasted. She blushed and added, 'I wasn't this fat when I met him, actually. I've been eating all vac because I've been so miserable.'

Oh well. So much for her Marlowe theory. What was it the Detective Inspector had said? Enthusiastically heterosexual. That probably meant he was promiscuous. 'Did you ever tell the police you were Hugh's girlfriend?' she asked.

Emily blushed. 'I couldn't. I mean, I wasn't exactly a girlfriend. Not formally.'

117

Ah, the complexities of adolescent relationships, thought Terry. 'How, er, informal was it, if you don't mind my asking?'

'Basically Hughie was very busy with his rowing and his work,' Emily explained. 'So although we went out sometimes, we weren't tied down to each other.' Terry had the eerie feeling that she was listening to an echo of the dead boy's own words, pronounced and inflected just as he himself had said them to Emily.

As if guessing what she was thinking, the girl said defiantly, 'The first few times we went to bed, we didn't even do anything. I mean, he wanted to of course, but I'm not that easy. I kept my knickers on.'

She made it sound, Terry reflected, like the latest form of contraception.

'But you did eventually? Take the knickers off, I mean?'

'He got the most terrible blue balls,' Emily explained. 'You know, it's really painful for men to be that aroused and not do anything to relieve it.' Terry raised an eyebrow but said nothing. 'So – well, we did other things at first, but it's not the same, is it? And it's not as if I was a virgin.' She sighed. 'I've never been in love with anyone before, though, the way I was with Hughie.'

It wasn't in Terry's nature to proffer advice to other women on their personal lives. She said hesitantly, 'There will be others, Emily. It's good that you've mourned him, but now you're alive and he isn't. Whatever you do, don't let him become a reason for not getting on with your life.' It came out like some fatuous agony-column cliché, but it seemed to have a powerful effect on the girl, who started crying again. It was, Terry guessed, as much at the thought of a boyfriend-less future as at Hugh's death. Following the train of her own thought she added, 'I haven't got a boyfriend at the moment, either. So we're in the same boat there.'

Emily looked aghast. 'Haven't you? Why not?'

Now was not the time to go into her complex private life. 'I'm separated from my husband. And I'm not looking for anyone at the moment.' But was that really true? she wondered.

'My trouble is,' Emily confided, 'I'm really drawn to the Heathcliff type.'

That's because you're still looking for someone to worship, Terry thought, but what she said was, 'So that's the sort Hugh was? A Heathcliff?'

Emily laughed. 'No, not really. But he was so tall and good-looking. He rowed for the college. And everybody liked him. He was really funny and confident. He was such good value, you know?'

It was, Terry reflected, an odd phrase to use of a human being, when you thought about it.

Emily eventually dragged herself away, her spirits restored by several cups of tea and a spirited discussion of which men in Shakespeare's plays they would most like to go to bed with. Terry had managed to finish one wall while they talked, but she was glad to be able to concentrate again. She found a local station on her radio and got back to work, laughing occasionally at the impossibly quaint, small-scale advertisements – after London, announcements that the local pick-your-own farm was now open for spring asparagus or that the second-hand car showroom on the Botley road had a new car to sell seemed almost idyllically provincial. Even the news was given a local slant: the currency crisis in Germany was followed, as if of equal importance, by the robbery of a post office in Wycombe.

Once again, just as she was hitting her stride, the doorbell went.

The one person she certainly hadn't expected to see on the doorstep was Carla Eden.

'I'm sorry, I'm disturbing you,' she said, seeing Terry's plaster-streaked overalls.

'No, come in,' Terry said, still taken aback. 'I can't stop, but come and have some coffee and we'll talk while I plaster.'

They went into the kitchen. Terry busied herself with the cups, wondering if this was going to be some sort of confrontation. But the coolness Carla had seemed to display at the party had vanished.

'I just wondered if you'd dropped an earring last night,' she explained. 'We found one on the carpet today, and it looks quite valuable. So I'm traipsing round the island like Prince Charming, offering it to everyone to see who it fits.' As she spoke she dangled the earring so that the diamond caught the light. With her short red hair and green eyes she looked more like Buttons than Prince Charming.

'Not mine, I'm afraid,' Terry said. 'I wasn't wearing earrings.'

'Could it have been – oh, I've forgotten her name. That girl you left with?' She put a deliberate inflection on *left*.

'Allison? I'm not sure.'

'Will you be seeing her any time? Perhaps you could check.'

'Um – I'm not sure. I could drop a note off at her college if you like,' Terry said evasively, wondering which the point of the visit was: the ear ring or the blatant probe into the nature of her relationship with Allison.

As if sensing her thoughts, Carla said, 'I'm sorry, I didn't mean to pry. You must think us very nosy round here. The truth is, no one's got any secrets on the island. We're like a little village, with Sheila Gibson as our village telephonist.'

Sheila Gibson. Of course: the neighbour who had caught her and Mo embracing. 'Ah. So I've got Sheila to thank for the fact that everyone seems to know about my private life, have I?'

''Fraid so. It doesn't bother me, by the way, I hope that goes without saying.'

'Actually,' Terry began, and then stopped. If they wanted to think she was an out-and-out lesbian, perhaps she'd better let them. She was damned if she'd give the Osney grapevine any more details of her sex life to exclaim over.

They went upstairs. Carla perched herself on the edge of the loo and watched Terry at it.

'To be perfectly honest, I can't help envying you

a bit,' she said after a mouthful of coffee. 'I went to an all-girls school – well, I'm sure you know what *they're* like. Then I met Brian when I came up to Oxford – he was one of my tutor's postgraduates – and bang, we got hitched. Not that marriage necessarily means you stop experimenting, of course,' she added thoughtfully.

'Um,' said Terry, who thought it did. She remembered how she'd felt when she'd found out about David's affair.

'Oh, it depends on the marriage, of course.'

The conversation seemed to Terry to be taking a very strange turn.

'Have you read Brian's book yet?' Carla asked.

'I'm afraid I haven't had time,' Terry confessed.

' "I never was attached to that great sect,

Carla quoted dreamily,

' "Whose doctrine is, that each one should select
Out of the crowd, a mistress or a friend,
And all the rest, though fair and wise, commend
To cold oblivion, though it is in the code
Of modern morals, and the beaten road
Which those poor slaves with weary footsteps tread,
Who travel to their home among the dead
By the broad highway of the world, and so
With one chained friend, perhaps a jealous foe,
The dreariest and the longest journey go." '

'Shelley,' Terry said, ' "The Epipsychidion". But if that's what you both feel, why do you envy people who aren't married?'

'Good question. Well, perhaps that isn't why I envy you exactly.' She drained her mug and stood up to examine Terry's plastering, stroking it with the back of one of her fingers. 'How do you get it so smooth?' she wondered.

'Practice,' Terry began. Then, to her astonishment, Carla lifted the hand up, turned Terry's face towards her, and kissed her on the lips. She felt a brief, slippery contact from the other woman's tongue before she pulled away. The amused green eyes looked at her for a moment.

'And you thought it was going to be my husband who made a pass at you,' she said softly. She smiled. 'Thanks for the coffee. I'd better go. But think about it, will you?'

She was halfway down the stairs before Terry had gathered her wits sufficiently to go after her.

'Mrs Eden?'

Carla turned. 'Carla, please.' She was still smiling.

'I just want you to be absolutely clear', Terry said firmly, 'that there's nothing to think about. I'm a person, not an experiment.'

She watched the smile die from the other woman's eyes and wondered if she'd been too harsh. 'I'm sorry,' she added.

Carla looked at her for a moment. 'Yes,' she said dumbly. 'Yes.' Then she was gone.

Shit, Terry thought to herself. That was all she needed: emotional complications with someone who lived next door. She wondered if she should have handled the situation more evasively.

*   *   *

Ten minutes later, visitor number three turned up. The bell rang, and she heard the door being opened.

'Hallo?' a male voice said.

'In here,' she called wearily. It was, she thought, like one of those stage plays in which one door opens to let a character in just as the previous one departs.

'Hallo, I'm Giles Chawker,' said the good-looking young man who stuck his head round the door.

'Come in, I'm almost finished,' Terry said. She was sponging the smooth plaster down with a cloth to take any bits of gunk off it.

'I saw your card in the shop,' he explained. Unlike Emily, who had loitered in the doorway, or Carla, who had sat on the loo seat, Giles hoisted one buttock onto the basin, folded his arms and watched her with undisguised admiration. She turned her back on him, though she could sense that his eyes were still on her. 'About the cat.'

'She's yours, is she?'

'Not exactly. I was a friend of Hugh's. He used to live here – I don't know if you heard?'

'I've heard,' she assured him.

'Well, um, it's a bit complicated.'

'Was the cat Hugh's?' she prompted.

'Not exactly. What happened was that there's this sort of dining society. It's a bit of a joke, really.'

'The Catamites?'

'Yes.' He seemed surprised that she'd heard of it. 'Well, as the, er, Grand Bamboozler of the, er . . .'

124

'Catamites?' she prompted.

'Yes . . . Well, Hughie had this idea for a mascot. The Bamboozler's Familiar. The thing was just a stray that he sort of adopted.'

'Tell me,' Terry said, turning round so that she could see his eyes, 'did you or your friends ever burn that cat with cigarettes? Or anything else for that matter?'

Giles looked genuinely shocked. 'Christ, no.'

'What about Hugh? Could he have done that?'

'No way. Hughie loved animals. I used to go shooting with him.'

'A real animal lover,' she said sardonically.

'What I mean is, he's always had dogs and things around. He was really upset that he couldn't bring his Labrador to Oxford.'

'Did this dining society give the cat a name?'

'Er – Pussy Galore, actually.'

Typical, thought Terry. 'And do you want Pussy Galore back?'

'Well . . . It's a bit difficult. I think we're going to get closed down.'

'You know she's had kittens, I suppose?'

He looked appalled. 'No. Mind you, we had some pretty wild parties. I'm not surprised Pussy Galore managed to join in the fun.'

'I hardly think that when a cat does it, it counts as fun.'

'Look . . . if you'd like to keep them. We'd be awfully grateful.'

'Why should I want to do that?' Terry said

sternly. 'They're expensive to feed and they'll destroy my house.'

He looked confused. 'I thought perhaps . . .'

'Oh, God,' Terry groaned. 'Just because I'm a woman, I must want to look after anything that's cute and helpless, is that it? And just because you're a man, you're absolved of all responsibility. Welcome to the twentieth century, lad. It doesn't work like that anymore.'

'So you won't have them,' he said anxiously.

She counted to three. 'Of course I'll bloody have them,' she said through clenched teeth. 'Anything's better than leaving them in your tender care.'

Giles grinned. 'Attagirl.'

Terry eyeballed him. 'Call me that again,' she enunciated clearly, 'and I will ram each one of those kittens down your thick public school neck.'

'Sorry. Tell you what. By way of thanks, we'll invite you to Hughie's wake.'

'Oh, great.'

'No, it'll be fun. A real orgy. If we're going to be closed down, we're going to go out with a bang.'

'Do you think that's altogether tasteful?'

Nodding made his hair fall into his eyes, and he brushed it back again with a big, sweeping gesture over his head, like someone pulling off a beret. 'Oh yeah. An orgy is definitely what Hugh would have wanted.'

'And you think I'd like to go to an orgy with you and your friends?'

Again the nod and the hair-sweeping gesture. 'I

quite fancy you, actually. Particularly now you're all sweaty. It's turning me on.'

She looked at him for a moment, considering her options. A swift knee to the groin? In the confined space of the bathroom he'd have no hope of getting out the way. But when all was said and done, he was only a kid. Attractive, charming, self-confident . . . boys like this had driven her mad when she'd been an insecure undergraduate herself, but only because she hadn't been able to see then what narcissists they were.

'Thank you for the invitation,' she said, 'both of them. But no.'

'Perhaps another time?' he said, and when she, simply to get his overpowering male presence out of her bathroom, said, 'Perhaps,' he pretended to swoon with rapture at her feet. 'Get out,' she said, kicking him and laughing; though on reflection later she didn't think it quite so funny that as soon as he had gone out of the front door he had opened it again, standing there holding out the bunch of flowers Emily had left on the pavement, fluttering his eyelashes like a pantomime Romeo.

This time she was given an hour before the doorbell rang again and Julia Van Glught's voice floated up the stairs, asking if anyone was in.

Ostensibly she'd come to tell Terry that a Mrs Phelps who lived in the next street was looking for a kitten as a present for her daughter. But it was soon clear that the real purpose of her visit was to moan about her husband. Terry pointedly went on with her plastering. Unbothered, Julia sat herself on the loo and launched into an involved recital of her spouse's failings, dodging flying gobs of plaster without breaking her flow. Terry suspected that being chosen as Julia's confidante would involve a lot of sympathetic nodding. It was something Terry was gradually discovering: just as doctors can't go anywhere without being told about other people's ailments, so some women assumed that a divorcee would understand their own marital problems. Which was a bit crazy when you thought about it, Terry decided, since advice from someone whose marriage had failed could hardly be construed as coming from an expert.

Julia went to make some coffee and returned with an envelope. 'There was a letter on the mat. Want me to open it for you? Your hands are mucky.'

'No thanks,' Terry said quickly. She opened it and glanced quickly at the contents.

It was a typewritten note, three lines long, on cheap A5 writing paper, the sort that came in pads with a topsheet of lined blotting paper. There was no salutation.

You will be glad to know that someone was
watching the two of you at it last night. Please
keep it up (and keep the curtains open). Believe
me when I say your little shows are much
appreciated.

Terry read it again, more slowly, looking for

iambic pentameters. *Believe me when I say your little shows* . . . de dum de dum de dum de dum de dum.

She suddenly realized she'd just been asked a direct question.

'I'm sorry?'

'I said, haven't you got any curtains?' Julia had been reading the note over her shoulder. Terry let her take it from her.

'No. I've ordered them, but they take an age to come through. Three weeks they said at John Lewis, and that was the fastest I could find.'

'I shouldn't worry. It'll just be one of the peepers then.'

'Peepers?'

'This area's notorious for them. All the courting couples come down by the river, you see, so the peeping Toms go down to the towpath with their binoculars. If they can't find any action there, they wander round the island. They'll tell you they're looking for wildfowl, but no one believes that. I can't say it's ever worried me, but then I'm a rampant exhibitionist.' She cackled merrily. 'Give them a real flash and they run a mile.' Before Terry could stop her she had folded the letter up and torn it into a dozen pieces. 'There. That's the only thing to do with those.'

'There's not much courting for them to see in my house, anyway.'

Julia looked quizzical.

'Darling, no one need go without in Oxford. It's crawling with fit young men. Or whatever else takes your fancy.'

129

So Julia was on the rumour circuit too. Terry made a non-committal noise and, to change the subject, asked, 'Speaking of young men, I had a visit from one of Hugh Scott's girlfriends this morning.'

'Ah. That explains the flowers on the pavement. We had quite a bit of that, immediately after he died.'

'What was he like?'

'Hugh? I don't know. He seemed OK. You'd have to ask Brian and Carla. They were the ones who got pally with him.' She sighed. 'There were four of them in here. Roland and Trish, they were a couple, and Hugh and Anne, they weren't. They were all a bit noisy and the bikes outside were a bit of a problem – people with pushchairs used to complain there wasn't enough room left on the pavement. Typical students, really.'

'Someone told me today that Hugh was good value.'

'Would that have been the flowergirl?'

Terry nodded.

'Snotty little student. What the hell would she know,' Julia said. She smiled slyly. 'If you want to know about *that*, you really should ask Carla. She used to call him Huge.'

'I don't think she meant . . . Are you saying that Carla and Hugh had a thing?' she said, astonished.

'Oh, God. Me and my mouth.' Julia thought for a moment. 'There was some gossip, that's all. You'll think us very wicked, particularly when someone's died, but there's bugger all else to do round here except speculate about other people's private lives.'

130

She looked round. 'Have you got another loo here? I'm dying for a pee.'

'I'm afraid not. Look, I'll get out of your way—'

'Oh, don't worry about it. I'm not shy if you're not.' Julia stood up and started to unbutton her jeans.

'No, really.' Faintly embarrassed, Terry edged out of the bathroom and waited until the other woman had finished.

'I've got cystitis,' Julia confided when she came back. 'Too much red wine last night, I expect.'

It was only much later, when Terry came to look for the pieces of the poison-pen letter, that she realized Julia must have flushed them down the loo.

Eight

She was plastering the final wall when her fifth visitor of the day rang the bell.

'Oh it's you,' she said tersely.

If Brian Eden had been up all night, it certainly didn't show. 'May I come in?' he asked brightly.

'I'm plastering. You can come up, if you promise not to crowd me. And I warn you, don't try anything clever. I've already nearly brained a member of your sex today.' Not to mention the fact that your wife made a pass at me, she thought.

'You'd better be careful, saying things like that.'

'Why?' She went upstairs and he followed, a little closer than she'd have liked.

'I believe crazed feminists are high on the police suspect list at the moment.'

'Ah. One other precondition. Don't try to say anything clever, either. You may succeed in provoking me, and believe me, you wouldn't like that.'

'As you wish,' he murmured. True to his word, he

stayed outside the bathroom and watched her work.

'Did you actually want something?' she enquired as the silence grew longer.

'Mmm – not exactly. I noticed you left early last night. I just wanted to make sure you hadn't been . . . made to feel unwelcome.'

She didn't like where this was going. 'Your wife did seem a little wary of me,' she said, putting a strong emphasis on the word *wife*.

He shrugged. 'She knows I find you attractive. It doesn't bother her, you understand. She just thinks it might be bad for my career if I started sleeping with you and there was any gossip.'

Amazed by his effrontery, she swung round, ready to attack. 'What!'

'We have a very open marriage,' he said, grinning at the effect he'd made.

'So I gather,' Terry murmured cryptically. 'You do realize I'm not interested in the least?'

'And now, of course, having spoken to Sheila, I understand why. No hard feelings?'

'None whatsoever,' Terry said, gritting her teeth.

'Oh, by the way. Could I possibly borrow back that book I gave you? I've got to look something up for my publisher, and I don't have any other copies at the moment. I'll return it as soon as I can.'

'It isn't here, I'm afraid. It's in my locker at the library. But I can get it for you tomorrow.'

He inclined his head gracefully. 'Thank you.'

*　　*　　*

Eventually she got rid of him. She'd finished the plastering and cleaned all the debris off the bathroom floor, but she wouldn't be able to have a bath until the plaster and sealant were completely set. While she waited she phoned Mrs Phelps, the woman who according to Julia might want a kitten. The phone was answered by a child, who said that they would both come round straight away to choose one if that was all right. A minute later they were at the door, a woman and a little girl of six or seven. It wasn't hard to guess why she was being given a pet. Her mother was pregnant, and the kitten was clearly compensation for the redirection of parental attention.

'There's not much to see yet, I'm afraid,' Terry explained, taking them to the box. The kittens' eyes were fully open now, and they were developing some fur, but they still weren't large enough to have much individuality.

'Can I pick them up?' the girl asked.

'I don't see why not. Just put it back if the mother gets agitated.'

The girl picked one up and held it against her cheek ecstatically. 'Oh, Mummy, I want this one,' she squealed predictably. Terry and the mother exchanged amused glances. 'Are you sure that's all right?' the mother asked.

'Of course. I'm just delighted someone wants one. It can't be weaned yet, of course, but I'll make sure no-one else has that one. You'd better start thinking of a name, young lady.'

'Dickie!' the girl breathed without hesitation.

'She's mad about Dorling's Little Dragon books,' her mother explained. 'Aren't you, darling?'

'He wasn't very big, and he wasn't very tall, Little Dickie Dragon was very, very small,' the girl chanted happily.

'Well, let's just check whether it's a boy cat first, shall we?' Terry said, scooping the little mite off the girl's lap and turning it upside down. 'I think a girl cat might object to being called Dickie . . . Ah. I'm afraid you'd better think again.'

The girl screwed her face up and thought hard. 'Rebecca!'

'Sounds good to me,' Terry said. 'Rebecca it is.'

'Why are you called Terry?' the girl asked curiously. 'That's not a girl's name.'

'Polly, don't be rude,' the mother scolded.

Terry laughed. 'That's OK. It's short for Theresa. My mother changed her mind after I was born.'

'Can I come back and see Rebecca sometimes?'

'Of course. Come whenever you like.'

'Can I really?' the girl said, her eyes wide. Terry suddenly realized she would be coming on a regular basis. But it was too late to withdraw the offer now. 'Anytime at all,' she said firmly.

She was shattered. She drained a glass of wine, lay down on her bed in her overalls, and was asleep within seconds. When she woke it was after nine, and the light was going.

Still groggy with sleep, she tottered downstairs and fixed herself a sandwich. She noticed that the door to the front room was open, but thought

135

nothing of it. Hugh's old room was doubling for the moment as her storeroom, piled high with bin liners of clothes and boxes of papers.

Pussy Galore saw the open door too. She was exploring a little further every day now, remarking on every change Terry had made to her old home with an outraged bleat. Terry saw her go in, and followed her without really thinking why.

In the fading light she barely saw it for a moment. It was a piece of white string hanging from a hook in the wall. Or it was a white boiler-suit suspended from the ceiling. But even as she thought these things, part of her brain was saying that she hadn't left either string or boilersuit in that position. She flicked on the light.

She didn't scream. Nearly, but not quite.

On the wall in front of her someone had drawn an outline in chalk on the dark wallpaper. It was a rough drawing of a figure, like a police outline marking the position of a body. But whoever had drawn this particular outline had added a large, spurting phallus, crude and diagrammatic as a fertility symbol cut into a hillside. On the floor in front of it lay a crumpled pair of Terry's knickers, an old pair from one of the bin liners. She swallowed vomit.

Girdler was at her house within ten minutes, another reminder of how small Oxford was compared to London, pressing his police ID against the wavy glass in the front door so she could read it before she let him in. He looked at the drawing quickly, almost casually, then drew her aside.

'I've called the station,' he said quietly. He was still holding her elbow, and she realized she was shivering uncontrollably. 'They'll want to take photographs, and probably fingerprints. That'll mean you'll need to be fingerprinted too. I've asked for a WPC—'

'No,' she said quickly. 'You. I want you to stay with me.'

'Of course,' he said. 'Look, there are a few things I'll need to ask. Did you see or hear anything? Anything at all?'

'No.' Her teeth chattered on the word. She clenched them tightly to control it.

'Has anyone been here in the last twenty-four hours? Any visitors? Phone calls even?'

She laughed uncontrollably. 'That's the funniest thing I've ever heard.'

He was watching her anxiously. 'Don't worry, I'm not hysterical,' she assured him. She managed to stop laughing. 'It's just that it's been busier than Piccadilly Circus round here. Since last night?'

'Yes.'

She ticked them off on her fingers. 'A friend I met at the party, a female friend, came and stayed over. Today, a girl called Emily Harris, a student at St Mary's, came. Carla Eden came. Julia Van Glught. Giles, what was his name, Giles Chawker. Brian Eden. Mrs Phelps and her daughter from the next street. You. I fell asleep earlier upstairs, someone could have got in then. And Brian Eden had a party last night, attended by about a hundred people, any

137

of whom could have seen me there and worked out that the house was empty.'

'And you didn't notice anything unusual?'

'No,' she said again.

He seemed to notice that he was still holding her arm and let go. 'Come into the kitchen. I'll make some tea.'

'I don't want any,' she said, but he ignored her. She watched him liberally spooning sugar into two mugs and thought, he thinks I'm in shock.

Two mugs, came the next thought. He needs one too. He's frightened for me. She felt her guts knot.

'Who else has a key?'

'No-one. No – I don't know. I mean, I haven't changed the lock since I moved in. Anyone could have one. I don't even always lock the door. Sorry.'

He was writing notes in his police notebook. When she told him this last part he sighed but said nothing.

'Could it – could it have been the killer?'

To his credit, he didn't attempt to fob her off with a platitude. 'It's possible, of course. Then again, I don't see why it should be. You're an attractive woman living on your own, and you don't take any security precautions. It was probably just some nutter getting off on the thought of giving you a shock.'

'Julia said the island is notorious for peeping Toms.'

'That's true, though there's a difference between peeping and this.'

'Oh, God, that reminds me.' She ran her fingers

through her hair. 'There was a letter today, a note rather. It said whoever wrote it had enjoyed watching me at it last night.'

'Where's the letter?'

'Gone. Julia – Mrs Van Glught – destroyed it. But the point is, it couldn't have come from a peeper. Whoever wrote it was lying – there was nothing to see. To put it bluntly, I didn't have sex last night.'

'Did you tell Mrs Van Glught this?'

'No.' Terry shrugged. 'She and everyone else assumed that I'd left the party with someone for – well, for that reason.'

Girdler consulted his notes. 'You said that the friend who stayed last night was female.'

'Yes. Allison Duckworth. She's at St Hugh's.'

Girdler wrote down the information without comment, though he looked thoughtful.

'Did you have any idea who might send you a note like that?'

'Not exactly.'

He looked up. 'What do you mean?'

She took a deep breath. 'It was very short . . . but I'm fairly sure that there was an iambic pentameter in it. Like the note you were sent.'

He made a note, then picked up one of the books stacked on her kitchen table. 'Why have you got this?' he asked curiously.

She took it from him. It was *The Feminine Sleuth*, by Anne Legame. 'It's one of the most important studies in its field. Why shouldn't I have it?'

'As I said last time we met, I think you'd be well advised to leave the detective work to the police.'

She laughed. 'No, you don't understand. It's not a handbook for amateur sleuths. It's a study of detective fiction from a feminist standpoint. That's my subject, Detective Inspector.'

'Oh, I see. I assumed – who else would have seen this?'

'Any of the people I've mentioned. They've all been in the kitchen, most of them on their own.'

'It's possible that one of your visitors might have thought you were thinking of investigating Hugh Scott's death yourself,' he explained. 'One other question. Do university teachers like yourself use chalk? On blackboards?'

She managed a weak smile. 'Not since the Middle Ages.'

'OK. Just a thought. Did you have any chalk in the house?' She shook her head.

Sirens came, and blue flashes of light filled the uncurtained rooms. Her little house was suddenly full of men, and a uniformed WPC at whom she saw Girdler surreptitiously shake his head, and who withdrew quietly to help her colleagues in the front room.

'Wait here.' He left her for a moment and returned with a little inkpad in a case, like a child's printing set. 'Fingerprints,' he explained. He lifted her fingers one by one onto the pad, rolling them for her from side to side to spread the ink, then carefully pressed them onto a sheet of paper. It felt strangely comforting to surrender control of her limbs to him.

A constable came in. 'We're done, sir.'

'Have you got rid of it?'

'Not yet.'

Girdler gestured with his head. 'Wet cloth in the sink.' He was not, she was beginning to realize, a man to waste words.

He looked at her carefully. 'I can have the WPC stay here tonight,' he offered. 'At least for a while.'

Terry shook her head. 'Can't you stay? Just you.'

'I'm not on duty,' he explained. 'And it's a uniformed job. They'd be able to stay awake; they go off shift in the morning.' But they both knew that wasn't what she'd meant.

'I don't need anyone. Really. Before you go, though, there's a couple of things I haven't told you.'

'Yes?'

'I'll do a deal. I want you to tell me how he died first.'

'We don't do deals,' he said, taking refuge in pomposity.

She snorted derisively. 'I'm not asking for a plea bargain. I'm asking you for the facts. Presumably I could get them from any newspaper archive.'

'Are you sure', he said carefully, 'that you really want to know?'

'Yes.'

He looked at her, then seemed to make a decision. He walked into her front room, waited for her to follow, and gestured under the window. 'He was found here,' he said, 'but not until the next morning, when one of his housemates, Roland Danreuter, realized he'd be late for his train and came in to wake him up. He'd noticed a burning smell but had assumed it was something to do with the party.'

'Go on,' Terry said. The constables were leaving. One of them called, 'Goodnight, sir.' Girdler raised his hand to them and continued:

'Hugh Scott was lying face down. He was naked, and basically he was stuck to the bed with his own blood. A soldering iron had been plugged into a wall socket and then inserted with some force into his rectum, puncturing his lower bowel and incinerating all the arteries and body organs within a two- or three-inch radius of the wound. He died from a combination of shock, loss of blood, and partial suffocation – the killer was probably sitting on his neck to prevent him from struggling. From tests on some spare corpses, the pathologist puts the time of death at between midnight and five in the morning. He had last been seen at about one-thirty, when the party started to draw to a close.'

Terry nodded.

'As I said, with the killer on his back he wouldn't have been able to struggle, but in any case the pathologist found so much alcohol in what little blood was left he wouldn't have been capable of doing much more than stagger around and sing rugby songs anyway. From tests on his penis we think he had intercourse some time that evening, though the traces of semen may have been caused by shock to the prostate as it fried. There were no signs of an intruder although subsequent interviews with the other occupants of the house revealed that in any case the door was usually left on the latch.' He glanced at her. 'As it still is.'

'I'll buy them tomorrow,' she said. 'A new door lock, window locks, a chain, the works.'

'Tests on the soldering iron revealed nothing in the way of fingerprints: the killer probably wore gloves. It was a standard twenty-five watt iron, of a type found in the university engineering faculty amongst many other places. A total of forty-eight different good prints were taken from different parts of the house, of which seventeen are still un-accounted for. We assume most of these are the partygoers', but we haven't been able to eliminate them because the hosts don't seem to have bothered with anything as formal as invitations or a guest list. Many of those who turned up were unknown to the three surviving occupants, and quite possibly to Hugh as well.'

'What about the writing on the wall?'

'Lipstick, as you know, though we kept that quiet until the inquest. Just the one word – "rapist" – though the lipstick had also been used to scribble on his shoulders and back. That was probably the last thing the killer did before he or she left.'

'What colour was it?'

'Flame red. Shocking red in my book. Not, as I understand it, a colour normally worn by ladies of a retiring disposition. But available in any High Street.'

She blinked, aware suddenly that he had finished. 'Is that it?'

'That's everything I can tell you, yes.'

'Thank you.'

'Not at all. What else was it you wanted to tell me?'

'Emily Harris. The girl who came to see me today. She said she slept with Hugh a couple of times.'

'Right.' Girdler made a note. He didn't seem surprised. 'We'll talk to her.'

'Something else. Gossip, this time, but I'll tell you anyway. Carla Eden and Hugh were supposed to be having an affair.' She watched him closely, but he didn't write it down. So he knew already. Or perhaps gossip didn't count? 'The cat belonged to Hugh. You can verify this by talking to Giles Chawker, Hugh's friend, who lives in the house opposite. And—' she paused.

'Yes?' he prompted.

'Those notes. I think they were written by Brian Eden.'

'Why do you think that?' he asked carefully.

She went and got Brian Eden's book on Shelley from her bedroom and showed him the inscription. '*To Terry Williams, who admired my mask,*' she read out loud.

'I'm not with you,' he confessed.

'Give me your pen.' She annotated it for him, just as she'd done with the letter. 'De-dum de-dum de-dum de-dum de-dum. If you make a very slight elision on my surname, it's a perfect iambic pentameter, just like the ones in the letters. Hardly surprising, when you consider that this is a man who spends his days grubbing amongst the work of the Romantic poets.'

144

'It isn't evidence,' Girdler said thoughtfully, tapping his teeth with his pen.

'And that letter? "The sisters of unmercy" is almost a direct translation of "*La Belle Dame Sans Merci*", a poem by Shelley's contemporary John Keats.'

'Hmm. It still isn't evidence.'

'Brian Eden and his wife are both serial flirts. Carla Eden is supposed to have been having an affair with Hugh Scott. So Brian had a motive for killing him. He could have written that word on the wall, and the letter, to distract your attention.' Only as she said it like this out loud did she realize how obvious it was, and how terrifying. 'He might have genuinely felt that Hugh's seduction of Carla was tantamount to a rape. He's egocentric enough.'

Girdler had closed his notebook and was watching her intently.

'And another thing. I went to see my tutor the other day. He virtually told me that the university in general, and Brian Eden in particular, is trying to hush up the circumstances of Hugh Scott's death. Why would that be happening unless they suspect he's involved?'

The Detective Inspector sighed. 'You're a sharp lady,' he admitted.

'So? What are you going to do about it?'

'Wait. You're sharp, but you're also arrogant as hell. Do you think we're so stupid we didn't think of all this? Not the poetry, of course. But the first things we look for in any suspicious death are the obvious things – sex, love, money, envy. Brian Eden

145

was our first suspect. He's been questioned, he's been investigated with a fine tooth comb, he's been questioned again. And as a result, he's one of the few people whose alibi for the night of the murder has been established without a single shred of doubt.'

'Where was he then?' she demanded.

He paused for an unnaturally long time before replying. 'He was at a big academic conference at the Hyatt Hotel in Birmingham,' he said at last. 'I tell you that simply to reassure you that you're not living next door to a murderer, you understand? Strictly speaking, it's privileged information.'

'And Carla? Was she there too?'

'We have a corroborated alibi for her too.'

'All night?'

'Sort of.'

'Oh, I get it,' she said, seeing the implication. 'That doesn't surprise me in the least.'

He shrugged. 'People's private lives aren't really my concern.'

'But even if he didn't do the murder, he might have written that letter.'

'That's true enough. And from what I know of Dr Eden, he's certainly silly enough to think that he could do something like that and get away with it. These university types live in a fantasy world, I'm afraid.'

She smiled faintly, and he said, 'Oh, I don't include you in that.'

'No offence taken,' she said.

'I'll have a word with him. Make sure this isn't

some stupid game he's playing.' He stood up to go. 'A squad car has instructions to drive past whenever it's in the area tonight. And remember, if you're worried about anything, you can always call me at home. Here's my number.' He wrote on a card and left it on the table.

'Your wife must be furious,' she said, glancing at the clock. It was already after one.

'Married to the job, I am,' he said lightly.

'In which case, can I interest you in a kitten, Inspector? They're a lot less demanding than a spouse.'

He laughed. 'Will you call me Richard?'

'I'll call you anything you like, if you'll take one of these bloody kittens off my hands.'

'Sorry, it's out of the question. I'm in rented accommodation at the moment. The wife got to keep the house.'

'Damn, I didn't realize . . .'

He waved her apology away. 'It's been a while now.'

'Me too.' She thought for a moment. 'Stay the night, Richard. Have some food and then we'll go to bed like the couple of grown-ups that we are.'

He blinked. 'Are you sure?'

'I never ask unless I'm sure.'

'I'll make a phone call.'

'Hang on,' she said suspiciously, 'I thought you said you were unattached.'

'I am.' He grinned. 'I'm just cancelling that squad car.'

'And I', she said fiercely, 'will go and rig up some curtains.'

Nine

'In many ways,' Terry said, 'the detective novel is not a novel at all.

'When the novel was invented in the eighteenth century, it was a completely new form of fiction: literally and genuinely novel. Up to then there'd been an assumption that the storyteller's job was to retell universal, accepted stories and truths. Originality as an artistic concept barely even existed – you certainly won't find an original plot in, say, Shakespeare or Chaucer. Even when the subject matter hadn't been used in literature before, like the story of Macbeth, the writer was expected to show that it could conform to certain universal plot requirements: the formal rules of tragedy, for example, laid down a thousand years earlier by Aristotle.

'The novelists rejected all of this. Their stories – *Moll Flanders*, *Robinson Crusoe*, *Clarissa* and so on – were the stories of realistic individuals, and the only truth they recognized was the truth of the individual's experiences. In other words, they were saying that character creates plot, instead of the other way round: *cogito, ergo sum*, as a contemporary philosopher was saying, instead of *sum, ergo cogito*.

'But detective fiction is different. It's structured, plot-based, and ultimately predictable. This isn't because detective novels are bad novels: rather, it's because they can trace their roots back to a literary tradition much older than the novel, the medieval Romance.

'Romances were poetic narratives, but they were also the Hollywood blockbusters of their day, spoken out loud by wandering troubadours who went from court to court, putting on their shows much as a studio publicity machine rolls a new film out round the world. Like the Romance hero, the detective is a Quester: someone seeking the answer to a question. And in the course of his quest he encounters various trials, deceptions and enemies. Getting past them – solving them if you like – requires not so much intelligence as insight; not just knowledge, but self-knowledge. The attainment of this self-knowledge by the hero is, of course, the true goal of the quest, though he may not realize this himself at first; the classic instance is the knight who discovers the Holy Grail only to find that after all his searching he is content to leave it where it is. I'm sure you're all familiar with Eliot's spin on this in *Four Quartets*:

' "And the end of all our exploring
Will be to arrive where we started
And know the place for the first time."

'Interestingly enough, Eliot was himself a passionate devotee of detective fiction. One of his dinner-party tricks was to amaze others with his detailed knowledge of Californian law, picked up from the novels of Raymond Chandler. And Chandler's first detective was called Malory, after *his* hero, the author of the Romance cycle *Morte D'Arthur*.'

Terry paused and drank some water, surveying the rows of seats in front of her. Like all the lecture rooms in the English Faculty, Room 6A had been built to house a hundred or so eager under-graduates. A dozen or so had turned up to hear her, scattered in desultory ones and twos round the vast emptiness of the auditorium. At least most of her own students had come – well, she thought of them as hers, though of course really they were Reg's. She hadn't expected more than this, knowing from her own experience that students studying Eng. Lit. at Oxford had far better things to do with their time than go to lectures.

As a planner working in advertising she'd regularly made presentations to the boards of multinational companies, men whose combined monthly salary would put this group of students through three years of university, but she'd been far more nervous today. In fact, she was grateful that there weren't more listeners. But she knew that Mo,

150

sitting patiently at the back, would assume the low attendance was an embarrassing failure.

'I say he when I refer to the knight-detective', she continued, 'because this holds good for most of the male detectives I have referred to. We should not forget, however, that since its beginning the detective genre has been dominated by women writers, and often women protagonists. Dorothy Sayers and Agatha Christie straddled the so-called "Golden Age" of the whodunit, while recently we have had women authors as diverse as P. D. James, Ruth Rendell, and Patricia Highsmith.' She stopped, conscious that she was violating Reg's injunction only to talk about the dead ones. 'What is less well known is that there were women detectives in fiction even before Conan Doyle published the first Sherlock Holmes story in 1887. Hayward's *The Revelations of a Lady Detective* and Forester's *The Female Detective* were published in 1861 and 1864 respectively; curiously, their female protagonists were working for Scotland Yard in fiction some twenty years before the police first took on any feminine recruits.

'So what is it about the female sex that makes male and female writers alike want to create female detectives? Partly, of course, it's because detective work is about sleuthing rather than slaying; in other words, it relies on such traditionally feminine virtues as nosiness, gossip, intuition and of course intelligence.' Cheered by the faint chuckle this raised from the girls in the audience, Terry continued, 'But I think there's something else as well, something which can best be explained by another comparison with the Quest narratives.

'Some of you in your work on *The Waste Land* will have come across the theory that Romances are themselves the folk-remnants of an even older literary tradition, the myths of death and rebirth that accompanied mankind's first religious rituals. This religion was a feminine-worshipping one: its purpose was to ensure the renewed fecundity of the land itself. And if you look carefully at some detective novels, I think you can still discern faint echoes of this same narrative structure. To take just one example, Christie's Miss Marple is portrayed as a kind of spirit of the English countryside, a modern-day witch, repeatedly compared by the author herself to the avenging spirit Nemesis.' Terry scanned the seats in front of her, and saw that her audience was flagging. One young man was openly asleep, his head cradled in the folder in front of him. 'In short,' she concluded, 'there is a strong argument for seeing the detective genre as an essentially feminine one, which is why it is so appealing to feminist critics today. That's the tack I'll be taking over the next few weeks, and I hope that as many as possible of you will join me. Does anyone have any questions?'

No-one did. Already they were busy snapping their notes into their ring binders and stowing books away in their backpacks.

'Congratulations,' Mo said when everyone had gone. 'You were terrific.'

'No I wasn't. I was nervous as hell and I pitched

it too high for the first-years. All they really want is for me to run through some of the storylines for them, to save them the bother of reading the books themselves. But I was OK. The real work gets done in the one-to-one tutorials.' They wandered out onto the concrete steps of the faculty building, blinking in the sudden glare of the sunlight. 'What do you fancy doing with the rest of the day?' Terry asked. 'I haven't really made any plans.'

Mo shrugged. 'I'm a tourist now. What do tourists do round here?'

'Well, we're right by the University Parks if you fancy a wander. There's the river over there, and it's a lovely day. We could head in that direction and sit in the sun while we decide what to do next.'

'Sounds good to me.'

As they meandered through the Parks Mo took Terry's arm in hers. Together, Terry knew, they made a striking sight, and she was conscious of the admiring glances from male undergraduates stretched out on the grass. For some reason it made her feel awkward, and she was glad when Mo took her arm away to put her sunglasses on.

There was a distance between them now that she felt was largely her fault. Although they'd spoken on the phone, it wasn't the same as sharing a house. Their telephone conversations were, she reflected, not unlike bad sex: one of them had to go first and talk about what she'd been doing, and only then would it be the other's turn. And looming over them now was the added complication, which neither of them had yet referred to, of tonight's sleeping arrangements.

Above the rise in front of them a dozen or so tall poles waggled in the air, for all the world like lances at a tournament. Mo looked puzzled, until she came over the bank and saw the river below them filled with punts. The water was high, and most of the punters looked decidedly inexpert.

'Of course,' Terry said. 'I'd forgotten. The first of May. It's the start of the punting season.'

'Can you do that?'

'Can Michelangelo do decorating? Want to have a go?'

'You bet.'

'You surprise me,' Terry told her. 'I thought you'd think it was decadent.'

'I told you, I'm a tourist now. Where do we get the boats?'

Terry took her the short way, through the playing fields of the Dragon school. There was a game of cricket in progress: thirty or so little boys, and one or two girls, no older than nine or ten, dressed in perfect whites like miniature adults. Looking at the idyllic scene in front of them, with the smell of freshly mown grass in their nostrils, it was hard to reconcile it with the terror she had felt when she had found the effigy in her house.

Mo read her mind. 'Cricket and murder,' she said. 'It's like something out of one of your detective novels.'

'Don't kid yourself. No-one's going to be unmasking the butler in the drawing room.' She sighed. 'Particularly not me. If someone drew that thing to scare me off, they succeeded.'

'You still think it was the slime next door, don't you?'

'If it wasn't him who wrote that letter it was another academic like him. But the police are adamant that he couldn't have been involved in the murder, so I have to take their word for it. They seem to know what they're doing, even if they haven't caught the killer yet.'

Mo snorted. 'A police force that knows what it's doing? I'll believe it when I see it.'

Terry said nothing. She'd told Mo most of what had been going on, but she hadn't got round to explaining about herself and Richard Girdler yet.

At the Cherwell Boathouse there was a queue for punts. Faced with the prospect of waiting an hour or so, Terry was about to give up when she saw a face she recognized on one of the incoming boats. It was Giles, the undergraduate who'd come to see her the other day, with a group of others. They were very drunk, and making a huge amount of noise. One of them was carrying a box of empty beer bottles, which he was lobbing into the water one by one, narrowly missing some of the other boats. One of the girls in the punt was wet through, having obviously fallen into the river at some point. She was shrieking with laughter.

'All the Bright Young Things,' Mo said disgustedly.

They finally got the punt tied up and, just as Terry had feared, Giles spotted her. He swayed over.

'Terry,' he declared loudly. 'Terry my own true love. Terrifying Terry. Tell me that you love me. Or tell me that this gorgeous creature with you loves me,' he said, running his eyes over Mo.

'Can I hurt him?' Mo said, judging the distance between them. Her Doc Martens twitched.

'Please, Mo,' Terry said under her breath. 'There are about a million people here, and I'm staff. Tact and diplomacy.'

Mo smiled sweetly at Giles.

'Please, beautiful ladies, take our punt,' Giles offered. 'The seats are a little wet, but it's a very nice punt.'

'Isn't there a queue?' Terry said.

'Not for this punt. This punt is a college punt. So long as you are holding this little blue ticket this is your punt.'

'Well, thank you,' Terry said, taking the ticket. 'Mo, jump in.'

'You may return the favour at any time,' Giles declared, leering drunkenly. Terry smiled at him, placed the end of the punt pole squarely in his stomach, and pushed off. He sat down suddenly, and they glided away from the pier.

'Upstream or downstream?' Mo asked.

'We go past Parson's Pleasure if we go upstream,' Terry warned her.

'What's Parson's Pleasure?'

Terry giggled. 'I'll show you. You'll like it, actually.'

'What do I do with this?' Mo asked, waving the

little wooden paddle. 'Do I have to steer?'

'No, it's only for emergencies. Just sit back and relax.'

She punted well, letting the aluminium pole drop through her hand, waiting for the faint clang as it hit the stony river bed before leaning on it with a practised, rhythmic motion. Soon they were over-taking the struggling beginners going round and round in circles near the boathouse. Large men, getting wet and sweaty as they tried to overcome the inertia of the water with brute strength, glared at her with equal amounts of lust and envy as she slid effortlessly past them.

'The secret', Terry explained, 'is to get it straight before you push.'

'I don't know why you're bothering to tell me,' Mo said. 'As long as you're in the boat, I'm not lifting a bloody finger.'

They punted in silence for a while. Mo took off her socks and dangled one foot over the side into the water. They passed a boat full of young lads, one of whom wolf-whistled. Mo gave him the finger, which for her was a fairly laid-back response.

'That one at the boathouse seemed like a nice boy,' she said after a while.

'You sound like my mother.'

'I suppose this place is full of young men who fancy you. Not just pillocks like that.'

Terry grunted non-committally.

'What I'm trying to say is,' Mo paused, 'don't feel you have to ask me or anything. When the time comes.'

'Thanks,' Terry said, meaning it. 'You neither.'

Mo laughed. 'I didn't. I went down to Dyke-U-Like last week and picked me up a femme.'

'Good for you,' Terry said. Dyke-U-Like was the most rampantly outrageous lesbian club in London, full of leathergirls and supermodels getting off together. Mo had taken her there just once, and she'd left after half an hour.

'What about you?'

'Yeah, me too. Prepare to be shocked, Mo.'

'Nothing shocks me, girlie. You know that.'

Terry took a deep breath. 'His name's Richard and he's a policeman.'

'Fuck. A policeman.' Mo laughed. 'OK, you've shocked me.'

They rounded the bend to Parson's Pleasure. Terry watched Mo doing a double-take, and with an effort kept a straight face. Today wasn't too bad, in fact. Although it was sunny the water was still cold, and there were only half a dozen or so scraggy naked bodies parading themselves round the small, fenced enclosure which constituted the University Fellows' nude bathing area. Ancient, sagging scrota proudly on display, the old men stared greedily at the two girls as the punt glided past. It was more like a scene from some East European lunatic asylum than something you might expect to find in the touristic environs of Oxford. One old crone, his pubis as grey as his wispy sideburns, started towelling his half-erect penis energetically as he held Terry's gaze.

'Terry,' Mo said carefully, 'is it my imagination,

or is that wrinkly wanking?' Her voice carried across the water, and the don grinned toothlessly.

'Don't ask me,' Terry said neutrally.

'Well, let's give him something to bloody well wank about then.' Leaping to her feet with an alacrity which caused the punt, and Terry standing at the back, to rock alarmingly, she turned her back to him, unbuckled her jeans and mooned.

'Take a good look, you saggy old git, and I hope it gives you a heart attack,' she yelled over her shoulder. 'Right, Terry,' she said as she did her jeans up, 'now get us out of here.' Terry obliged with an extra turn of speed, and they were soon round the next bend of the river.

'What a bunch of weirdos,' Mo said, shaking her head. 'Still, I don't think they'll forget us in a hurry.'

'Well, they'll soon have a reminder,' Terry pointed out.

'What do you mean?'

Terry laughed. 'There's only one way back to the boathouse, Mo, and that's the way we've just come. And you're going to be punting on the way back, not me, so you'll have plenty of time to engage them in constructive dialogue.'

'I think I preferred you as a dyke,' Mo muttered, closing her eyes. 'They're so much less bitchy than you straight girls.'

In the event, they tied up for an hour under a tree and dozed on the riverbank: by the time Terry punted them back up the river – after one brief go with the pole, during which the punt started to drift backwards with the current instead of in the direction she wanted, Mo flatly refused to do any more, maintaining that holding the pole felt too much like a penis for any true lesbian – the light was going, the wind cool, and Parson's Pleasure was deserted.

'Pity,' Mo said. 'We could have fixed you up with a date.'

Instead, since Mo seemed to be in the mood to do the whole Oxford tourist experience, Terry took her to Brown's. This time there was no way to jump the queue, and they got smashed on banana daiquiris while they waited for their table.

'I've got a confession to make,' Mo said after the second one. 'I really fancy that waitress.'

'I'll tell you what,' she said after the third one. 'That waitress keeps looking at me.'

After the fourth, as the pretty waitress left them at their table with a smile, Mo leant over and hissed dramatically in Terry's ear, 'She's begging for it!'

'You'd run a mile,' Terry said. They both knew it was true, but it was one of the rules of the dialogue that Mo deny this indignantly. Being laddish was part of Mo's front; Terry knew her well enough to know that she would drop it before it got to the stage when it would become boring.

'Ask her back, then,' Terry suggested jokingly.

Mo pretended to be shocked. 'For both of us? I'm not having your seconds.'

'You can take her to the spare room.'

'Ah. The spare room.'

Terry thought it best to say nothing.

'The visitor's room. The guest room. The people-who-come-down-at-weekends room.'

'I've put a bed in there. It's up to you, Mo, honestly. If you want us to share a bed tonight, that's fine too. I don't want to lose my best friend,' she said urgently.

'But no nookie?' Again Terry didn't reply. 'Did you paint over the wall, by the way? Is our piece of action art obliterated?'

Terry reached out for Mo's hand and kissed it, not caring what anyone might think. 'No, I left it. It's there for as long as I am.'

'Thank you for that,' Mo said. She brightened. 'Hey! Do you think we should sign it?'

In the end they went to separate beds, but in the small hours Terry was half-woken by a warm body slipping in beside her, Mo mumbling something about a bad dream. For the rest of the night they held each other gratefully. Whatever recidivist moments like this one or other of them might need, an important bridge had been crossed without casualties.

It was after midnight when Edward Pearce let himself into the training gym at the boat house. He had been working on his essay all evening, and he was too hyped up to sleep.

Quickly he stripped off his tracksuit top and picked up some handweights. When he was warmed up he switched to the ergonometer, gradually letting the stroke rate build up, losing himself in the hiss of the spinning bicycle wheel in front of him and the movement of the seat as it slid backwards and forwards with each pull. Soon his bare chest was glistening with sweat.

At last he rested. It was then that he lifted his head, wondering if he'd heard a noise. The training room was partitioned off with simple glass screens from the rest of the boat house, a dark warehouse where the boats were kept upside down on racks. He hadn't turned the lights on in the main building, only in here. Straining his eyes beyond the brightness, he thought he saw a figure, watching him. But he couldn't be sure.

'Is there anyone there?' he called. His own voice sounded querulous and thin as it echoed round the hangar.

For a while there was no reply. Then, just as he was about to turn back to the rowing machine, a large figure stepped out of the darkness.

'Oh, it's you.'

'Good evening, laddie,' Roddy said. 'You're here awful late.'

'I like to train last thing,' Edward said. 'It's all right, isn't it?'

'Of course, laddie. I was about to lock up, that's all. But I'll wait for you. Please, carry on.'

Edward bent back to the handle of the machine, uneasy now that Roddy was watching him.

'You're starting to pull too early. Here, I'll show you when.' Roddy put his hand on Edward's bare back, pushing when Edward should begin his slide forward on the moveable seat. 'Good,' he commented after a while. 'Can you feel the difference?'

162

'Yes,' Edward gasped.

'Fine. That's enough for now. You'd best take a breather.' Roddy lit a cigarette while Edward panted and gasped. 'I've not seen you here for a while. You've been coming late, is that it?'

Edward nodded, still catching his breath. 'I've got a lot of work to do,' he said between gasps. 'Catching up. I've changed courses.'

'I know, laddie. You've taken Hugh Scott's place, haven't you?'

Edward nodded again.

Roddy put his hand on his shoulder. 'It's not easy trying to balance work and rowing,' he said sympathetically. 'But I would say this to you. If you do keep up with your rowing, you've got a strong chance of being in the first boat.'

'Really? That's great,' Edward said. He thought of what he could say to the Old Man. Look. I can change courses *and* get in the boat.

As if reading his mind, Roddy said, 'Your father rowed, didn't he? I remember Pearce. What was it, 'fifty-five? You'll be at least as good as him.' With his free hand he ruffled Edward's damp hair. Then, almost reluctantly, he said, 'But you'd better be off now. I'll need to lock up.' He watched as Edward pulled on the tracksuit top, pulling a bunch of keys out of his pocket and nodding goodnight as the student made his way to the door.

Ten

By eleven o'clock on Monday morning Girdler had Brian Eden and his solicitor in the police station for an interview. He pushed the letter across the desk and waited.

Eden read it through and calmly handed it to the lawyer. 'What's the question, Detective Inspector?'

'I want to know if you wrote this.'

'Mmm. Not technically a question, but I take your point. What makes you think I did?'

'Just answer the question, please, sir.'

'My client isn't obliged to answer any question which might incriminate him in an offence, Inspector, as you very well know. I advise you not to answer that, Brian,' the lawyer said casually. He was a large, smooth-cheeked man, smelling faintly of aftershave. Girdler kept his eyes fixed on Brian Eden.

'"Hugh Scott was killed because he was a man,"' Brian read aloud. 'Why on earth should I write something like this?'

'If you have any evidence linking my client to this letter, you're obliged to tell us.'

'I know that. And your client hasn't been charged with any offence, though of course whoever wrote this could eventually be charged with wasting police time. We're simply asking the question.'

There was a long pause. Girdler added thoughtfully, 'I'm sure you'll agree, Mr Eden, that for our part we've been extremely co-operative when you've asked for our help.'

Brian flushed and tried to hand the letter back. 'I've never seen it before.'

'Did you notice that it's written in iambic pentameters?' Girdler asked. He kept his hands on the table, and after a moment Eden studied the letter again. He raised his eyebrows and nodded slowly.

'Do you read a lot of poetry in the course of your work, Mr Eden?'

'The more interesting question, Inspector, is do you? Did you spot this? Are you perhaps a part-time Coleridge or a weekend Wordsworth? Do you scribble *terza rima* in the officers' canteen? Or was it someone else who put you on to it? One of my own dear colleagues perhaps?' He stopped, as if struck by a thought. 'It wasn't that silly bitch next door, was it? Only just moved in, and already she's helping the policeman with his enquiries. Let me warn you, Inspector, you're wasting your time there. She promises more than she delivers. One of the followers of Lesbos, if you take my meaning.' His solicitor laid a warning hand on his arm, and he stopped.

For fully twelve seconds Girdler stared him out, not moving a muscle. 'Interesting you should say that,' he said at last. Jane Hughes, sitting quietly behind him, was surprised to hear a tremor of anger in his normally even speech. 'She's also been the victim of some sexual harassment of a particularly nasty kind. Now I wonder who's responsible for that?'

'Not I, Inspector.'

'Then perhaps, given your expertise in that area, you could suggest where we might start looking.'

'That's enough,' the solicitor snapped. 'This is most unprofessional. You're asking my client to repeat hearsay.'

'I'm asking him to repeat nothing,' Girdler said smoothly. 'In fact, I'm trying to make sure that nothing is repeated. Like no repeats of last week's little pranks, if pranks they were. There are a lot of gossips round your neck of the woods, Mr Eden, and you of all people should know how easy it is for gossip to spread.'

Eden was on his feet. 'Anything in my statement is confidential unless relevant to the inquiry,' he hissed. 'I've been assured of that by officers of much higher rank than you, Inspector, and if you attempt to threaten me again, I'll have them down on you.'

'I think we've both made our point.' Girdler stood up, towering over the man on the other side of the table. 'Thank you for coming in, Mr Eden.'

*   *   *

'What do you think?' he asked the DC when Eden and his solicitor had departed.

'It's hard to say, sir. But given his reaction, I think there's a good chance he wrote it. What about the rapist thing, though? Whoever wrote the letter knew about it.'

'He could have got that from anyone. One of the woodentops on the door. Whoever first interviewed him the day after the murder. Or most likely one of those senior officers he keeps going on about.'

'Is he serious about that?'

Girdler stretched. He hadn't realized how tensed he'd been during the interview. 'Oh, sure. You'd be surprised how many top coppers like to be invited to dine at High Table every now and again. I've been left in no doubt that I'm to tread carefully where the University's concerned. Not to mention a couple of cryptic conversations with the funny-handshake boys on the way to the washroom.'

'So you agree Eden wrote the letter himself?'

'We shouldn't leap to any conclusions without evidence. But on balance, and given what Mrs Williams has told us, yes I do think he wrote it, though we'll never get him to admit it. We got the letter before we found out his little secret, remember? He probably had some idea that he'd deflect attention away from his own goings-on.'

'So if Eden wrote the letter, and we're still convinced he had nothing to do with the murder, where does that leave us on the murder investigation?'

'There's still the writing on the wall. Rapist, and

the use of lipstick, do suggest a woman,' Girdler said thoughtfully.

'Hang on. What if Rapist was meant to refer to the killer himself, rather than to Scott? A signature, and not an accusation?' Jane suggested. 'Scott could have been raped before he was killed. The soldering iron would have destroyed all traces of it. Who knows – the killer might even be aware of DNA testing, and deliberately chosen to kill him with the soldering iron to prevent it.'

'Good thinking,' Girdler said. 'OK, you'll need to go back and check all the records of sodomy without consent over the last year. Look for anything that links to Scott. And get Bob to go back to the pathologist and go over the PM results with a fine tooth comb.'

'That still leaves the lipstick. Maybe it belonged to someone at the party?'

'That bloody party. OK, let's have another go at tracing everyone who was present. The students are all back now, so it should be easier than it was six weeks ago. I want posters, an appeal on local TV, a request to the heads of all the colleges for help. And check all of Scott's girlfriends again to see if any of them wore flame red lipstick.'

Miles Lambert sat in his tutorial, not hearing a word that was being said.

For two days he had barely left his room. He found himself reliving the rape over and over again, playing it in his head like an endless loop of film. Each time the loop went round it became a fraction

168

less vivid, a fraction less clear, but it still blotted out everything else. Sometimes he found himself playing alternative scenarios – what would have happened if he'd run, fought, been more friendly, carried a weapon, offered to suck the man off. Sometimes he found himself watching the loop like a porn movie, and getting turned on. That was the worst part – the suspicion that the rapist had been right, that he had enjoyed it as much as the man who had attacked him. It was shameful. But it was also, in some strange and terrible way, the best part too. Sometimes he imagined himself as the rapist, masked and armed, stealing up on someone helpless and violating them savagely. Or he'd look at strangers in the library and imagine them dragging him off and buggering him viciously. Then he'd become aroused and start trembling, putting his head in his hands until the awful arousal was over.

Once, a straight boy he'd seduced and gone to bed with had told him afterwards that he was a filthy queer because he'd do anything for sex. He'd put it out of his mind, but now he remembered and wondered if he really was different to other people. No-one else, surely, would react like this to being assaulted. Women who were raped, he'd read, felt ashamed and disgusted. But that, surely, was different: they were ashamed of what had happened, not of how they had reacted.

He was also worried about AIDS. He needed to get a blood test, and he wasn't sure what would happen if he went to the college doctor and asked for one.

He suddenly realized that his tutor and David, his tutorial partner, were looking at him. 'I'm sorry?' he said.

His tutor sighed. 'I asked you if you had given any thought to Moore's *Principia* yet,' he said acidly. A closet homosexual for thirty years, he couldn't conceal his dislike of these blatant young gays who turned up at Oxford nowadays, with their cropped hair and their earrings. 'But you were clearly thinking about something far more important than the philosophy of ethics.'

'I'm sorry,' Miles muttered. 'I'm listening now.'

Julia Van Glught called on Brian and found him in a foul mood, drinking lapsang souchong and smoking small cigars.

'Oh good. I'll have a cup of that.' When he didn't move she put the kettle on herself. 'What's put you in such a temper?' she asked.

He stabbed with the point of his cigar at the wall. 'The dyke next door has been telling tales on me.'

'Oh dear. No longer quite the apple of your roving eye, I take it? Mind you,' she added archly, '*someone* owes little me a big favour.'

'Why?'

'Because *someone* wrote her a silly note, which *I* tore up and flushed down her khazi.'

He grunted.

'I know you, Brian Eden. You're relishing the challenge, aren't you?' She drained her cup, and said lightly, 'I really came round to see if you fancy a shag. Dorling, or should I say Dickie the

Dragonling, is still refusing to perform his conjugal duties.'

He glanced at her. 'I think that's all over now, don't you?'

Julia smiled bravely. 'If you say so.' She got up and put her cup in the sink. 'Shame I'm not Terry Williams, isn't it?'

Brian smiled. 'Yes, it is rather. A great shame.'

It was the first time Terry had entertained in her new home. A leg of lamb sizzled in the oven, a bottle of wine breathed next to the cooker, and there were flowers on the little kitchen table.

'Sorry I'm late,' Girdler said when he turned up at eight thirty. 'I hope nothing's ruined.'

'No, it's all fine,' she assured him. 'I wasn't planning on eating till later, and I haven't made the salad yet. You can come and talk to me while I cook.' She washed leaves in the sink while he reached across her and poured himself some wine. He kissed her neck, and when her body swung against his he put the glass down and reached round her to cup her breasts.

'Pig,' she said, flicking her wet hands at him. 'I'm in the midst of feminine servitude here, and all you can do is grope me.'

'The last time someone called me a pig,' he said thoughtfully, his fingers stroking her gently, 'I beat them up and framed their confession.'

'Beat me up and I'll beat you back,' she murmured, not caring if she was making any sense or not. He slipped his hand up her dress, hooked a finger into the cleft of her knickers, and tugged. She wriggled sensuously, and obediently lifted first one leg, then the other, to help him. The knickers lay discarded on the floor, a frail figure-of-eight.

'My hands are wet,' she said after a moment, as he undid his trousers and guided her hand. He laughed throatily, his questing fingers having discovered a different kind of wetness. Then, without further preamble, she pulled him inside her, bracing herself against the edge of the sink as he thrust.

'I'm sorry,' he said a couple of minutes later, 'I was too quick.'

'I've been ravished,' she gasped jokingly as he pulled out. Then, more seriously, 'Don't worry. I'll make sure I get my turn later.'

They ate the lamb, their legs wrapped together under the table.

'Brian Eden tried to tell me that you were a lesbian,' he said casually as she made coffee.

'You saw Brian? When?'

'Today. Just warning him off. If he did have anything to do with those attempts to scare you, I don't think he'll do it again.'

'My hero,' she said ironically.

'Why did he think you were gay, though?'

She saw no point in lying. 'I was, briefly. That is, I had an affair with a girlfriend. One of the locals saw her help me move in and put two and two together. Does it bother you?'

'Of course not.'

She smiled at his tone. 'I've never understood why men think two men together is grotesque, and two women is cute and rather innocent.'

'I've never understood why *women* always generalize about the opposite sex.'

'Nice one,' she said approvingly. 'You're pretty sharp, aren't you?'

'And you're pretty patronizing. Goodness me, an intelligent policeman. And in answer to your previous question, it's because what two women do together is simply less threatening. It's much the same as heterosexual foreplay, isn't it, so of course it seems more innocent.'

She looked into his eyes. 'If I thought you could stand it, if I thought it wouldn't threaten your masculinity, I could show you some things my lover taught me that would blow your little copper mind.'

He smiled. 'Try me.'

'Tell me why you went into the police,' she said, changing the subject.

But later that night, when they had finished another bottle of wine and gone to bed, she got one of the toys she'd used with Mo out of the bedside table and showed him a little, a very little, of what she had been talking about. This was her turn. It wasn't the same as with Mo. With Mo the two bodies with their two double-ended shafts, each body both a plug and a socket, each body both soft breasts and hard buttocks, had rocked and ridden and made one endless circle that went on spinning inside her for days afterwards. But it was good enough. It was certainly good enough.

*　　*　　*

When she woke he was already getting dressed. She glanced at the alarm clock. Half past six.

'Doing a runner?'

'Doing a press conference. At nine. I want to be sure I'm prepared.'

She grinned. 'I know what we did last night was a bit out of the ordinary, but does it really warrant a statement to the press?'

He climbed onto the bed and took hold of her wrists. 'Actually the ladies and gentlemen of the press are coming in to hear about the case, not the Inspector's sex life. Thank God.'

'Why? What's happened?'

'It looks like we were right to look for a male killer. There's nothing conclusive, but – well, it's a story of police incompetence really.'

'Tell me,' she said, freeing herself and sitting up.

'A couple of years ago we set up a separate Rape Centre in the St Aldate's nick. You know – comfy sofas instead of desks, a dedicated examination room, a separate entrance, the whole thing staffed entirely by women officers. It was designed to be a less threatening environment, take a bit of a PR initiative.'

'So what happened?'

'Perhaps not surprisingly, it looks as if the unit developed a bit of an anti-male culture. Anyway, I asked someone to look through all the reports of sexual assault on men and they turned up a case from a few weeks ago. A young man came to the Centre saying he'd been raped. They sent him away. Told him that it was for women only and that he should report his attack to the front desk in the normal way.' He shrugged. 'In fact, the Centre *wasn't* set up for women only, so far as I can tell. The women officers concerned were making their own assumptions. There's no record of the assault being logged in the Crime Book, so presumably he decided he couldn't face it and gave up. Hardly surprising after the way he'd been treated. But when my officer talked to the WPC who'd noted it in the files at the Rape Centre, she recalled thinking that the young man was a transvestite or gay because he had lipstick on his face. He wasn't very good at putting it on, she said, because there were smudges of it everywhere, all over his face.'

'Jesus. So you think the lipstick came from the rapist?'

'Well, it's certainly possible.'

'And you're going to tell the papers all this?'

'Good God, no. The one thing the police never do is wash their dirty linen in public. No, the WPCs at the Rape Centre have been reprimanded and told to bring in a male officer next time they get a male victim. The press conference is to ask for help from any men who've been raped or sexually assaulted in Oxford and to try to track down all the students who came to the end-of-term party. We've still not identified most of the fingerprints.'

'Why didn't you tell me this last night?'

Richard looked blank. 'Why should I?'

She laughed out of sheer exasperation. 'Because it was me who gave you the idea. Because I'm involved.'

'What do you mean, your idea? It was detective work by one of my officers. You're out of this now.'

'Out of it? How can I be out of it? I still live here, don't I?'

'Look, Terry. If I thought you were in any way involved in this investigation, I wouldn't be here. I couldn't be, it would be against regulations. Your bit, such as it was, is over. The rest is police business, which I shouldn't even be discussing with you. The Force frowns on pillow talk, you know.'

'Pillow talk,' she said scornfully. 'This is pillow talk, is it?'

'I really don't understand what's bugging you,' he said, getting off the bed and reaching for his tie. 'Most police wives are only too glad if their man doesn't bring the job home with him.'

'Forgive me if I refrain from pointing out the obvious,' she said acidly. She lay back and ignored him while he finished dressing. When he kissed her goodbye she allowed him only a token peck on the cheek before turning her head away.

Eleven

Terry sat sandwiched between one of the cleverest mathematicians in the country and one of the most eminent geologists in the world, wishing she were somewhere else. Even if she had been about fifteen feet to her right, she reflected, it would have been a distinct improvement: then she'd have been in amongst a group of rather jolly professors of music and theology.

Being invited to High Table was one of the occupational hazards for a female academic at Oxford. Doctoral students were meant to be invited in rotation, but so many of the dons were either gay, unmarried or having unsuitable liaisons with their students that even when partners were invited as well, balancing the sexes was nigh on impossible unless the females like Terry were asked more frequently than their male counterparts.

The food, of course, was terrible. There were no banquets of roast swan stuffed with foie gras here,

St Mary's being one of the poorer colleges. And even if there had been, she reflected, the contractors responsible for the college kitchens would have made it taste like lamb chops. Their primary function was to cook for two hundred students at the least possible cost: haute cuisine had not been part of their catering HNDs, or whatever the basic qualification was called these days.

In any case, better cooking would have been wasted on most of those around her. Terry tried to ignore the way the mathematician kept poking his finger in his ear and wriggling it round before taking another swig of his wine. She did, however, glance at his glass, and was faintly repelled by the way the rim was already opaque with the combined greases of the food and his body.

To add to her discomfort, none of the men around her had any conversational graces whatsoever, and were apparently incapable of including her in their conversation, unless sporadic covetous glances at her breasts counted as inclusion. Not that it was particularly worth being included in: the brightest minds in the land seemed interested only in discussing college gossip and bitching about each other. So much, she thought, for Reg and his Beauty, Truth and Goodness.

Inevitably, the murder of Hugh Scott was the hottest topic of debate.

'I hear some of our delightful undergraduates are up in arms about the sale of the murder house,' the geologist said. Terry's ears pricked up.

178

'Why? Did they want it kept?' someone opposite asked.

'No, not that. It's the proceeds they're concerned about. Over a hundred thousand pounds which *they* say should be put back into student housing.'

'That's ridiculous,' the mathematician scoffed. 'It's St Mary's money, not theirs. Anyway, it's a ludicrous time to buy.'

'They have a moral argument though, do they not? A student is killed and our response is to sell a house, thus forcing more undergraduates out into the dubious safety of the bed-and-breakfast market.'

The mathematician pursed his lips. 'By moral I take it you mean emotional, rather than ethical?'

'I think I mean neither. I mean that, while we are not legally obliged to provide housing for them, we *are* obliged to ensure their safety . . . and there's a practical dimension too, of course: if the students take umbrage and start to pressurize the college for more housing, they will ultimately get it by sheer force of numbers. Which in the long run will mean less money for research and fellowships.'

'This place would be so much better', the mathematician said, 'if we didn't have students at all.'

Terry had the feeling that these were tired old arguments: conversational fillers which allowed the participants to indulge in ritual sword-crossing.

'We are all students,' rejoined the geologist. 'And more to the point, those who fill these seats in the future will all have been students too.'

Any moment now, Terry told herself, I'm going to

179

scream at the pointlessness of it all. But she didn't. Instead, she suppressed a yawn.

The pudding plates were being cleared away. She saw Brian Eden get to his feet at the other end of the table and walk towards her, carrying his wine glass. He tapped the person opposite on the shoulder.

Oh no, Terry thought, that caps it all.

'You are boring Miss Williams,' he said solemnly. 'And I therefore invoke rule number thirty-eight in the college statutes, and request that you change places with me.'

'Oh piss off, Brian,' the don said irritably. 'There's no such rule.' But such was the force of Brian's personality that he got up anyway and took the other man's seat. The geologist and the mathematician fell silent, eyeing Brian cautiously.

He ignored them and spoke directly to Terry. 'I haven't seen much of you recently. You really must drop in to see us.'

She tried to smile politely. 'Thank you.'

'We were discussing your poor ex-neighbour, Brian,' the geologist said. 'I was just suggesting that his ghastly, ghastly death—'

Interrupting him, Brian kept his smile fixed on Terry and quoted:

' "He hath awakened from the dream of life—
'Tis we, who lost in stormy visions, keep
With phantoms an unprofitable strife,
And in mad trance, strike with our spirit's knife
Invulnerable nothings." '

'I don't recognize that particular quotation,' the geologist said. 'But I must say it's not a view of death which I imagine the coroner's court would, ah—'

' "The one remains, the many change and pass." '

Terry picked up the quotation,

' "Heaven's light forever shines, Earth's shadows fly;
Life, like a dome of many-coloured glass,
Stains the white radiance of Eternity." '

Putting down his wine glass, Brian put his hands together and applauded her, slowly and ironically. The noise caused one or two heads to turn towards them, listening.

'Bravo. I wasn't aware that you were a fan of Shelley's, Terry. Or do I have my book to thank for that?'

'I wouldn't say I was a fan, exactly,' she said cautiously. 'To be perfectly honest, I find it hard to admire his poetry when I so despise his morals.' Damn, she thought, that hair-splitting mathematician's going to tell me that I don't mean morals, I mean ethics.

But he didn't. Instead, Brian was saying, 'Ah, the tired old feminist argument. Presumably you're referring to his first wife?'

'His first wife, who drowned herself in the Serpentine when he eloped with Mary Godwin. But there were many others as well, weren't there? He had an affair with Mary's own sister Claire, not to mention Jane Williams.'

'Step-sister, actually,' he murmured. 'But he was a poet, Terry. Jane Williams inspired some of his greatest love poetry. Would you have wished all those verses unwritten?'

'If it had meant a little less human misery, then yes I would,' she retorted. 'Poets are no different from the rest of us.'

His eyes widened in mock surprise. 'But that's where you're wrong. "Poets are the hierophants of an unapprehended imagination; the mirrors of the gigantic shadows which futurity casts upon the present; the words which express what they understand not; the trumpets which sing to battle, and feel not what they inspire; the influence which is moved not, but moves . . ."' He cocked an eyebrow at her, challenging her to finish for him.

'". . . Poets are the unacknowledged legislators of the world." A very useful philosophy for someone who himself entirely disregarded all forms of legislation.'

'Ah,' he said, his eyes bright with interest. 'The law. I see where this is heading now. You prefer detective fiction to poetry, don't you? Sexton Blake to William Blake; Conan Doyle to Coleridge; law enforcers to poetic legislators. Isn't that right?'

'I'm doing my doctorate in detective fiction, certainly,' she said, colouring. 'But after all, wasn't Shelley's first work a mystery novel?'

'He scribbled it while he was still a schoolboy at Eton,' he said dismissively. 'He grew out of all that.'

She was on weak ground here, and she knew it. Trying a different tack, she said, 'I have no problem with most of the Romantics, actually. Keats, for example, was neither a chauvinist nor a blinkered idealist, unlike Shelley.'

'Idealism is long-range realism,' he rejoined. He saw her frowning as she tried to place the quotation, and smiled. 'Brian Eden. From the introduction to my book.'

'But not one of Shelley's ideals has happened yet, has it?' she asked innocently. 'Or did you mean even more long-range than the twentieth century?' Now it was his turn to look defensive. Seizing her opportunity, she ticked them off on her fingers. 'He prophesied an end to marriage. That hasn't happened yet, has it? He predicted that England would become a Republic. No, that neither. He thought that the lyric poem would become more widely read than the novel. Wrong on that count too.'

'The philosophy was just a means to an end. It helped him to write great poetry.'

It was like one of those magicians' duels in folk stories, she thought: he turned into a mouse to frighten your elephant, so you turned into a cat to chase his mouse. All conversation had ceased around them now. The other dons were listening agog, those further down the table craning their necks to hear.

'That's a subjective opinion,' she scoffed. 'What was it Spender said about Shelley – too much brother body-soul melting into sister body-soul?

And then there's all that self-pitiful shrieking he goes in for – "Oh lift me from the grass! I die! I faint! I fail!" '

Brian Eden shrugged. 'Doesn't a poet have the right to be judged, not by his life, or even by his worst poetry, but by his best?' His eyes still fixed on hers, he recited softly:

' "The fountains mingle with the river
And the rivers with the Ocean,
The winds of Heaven mix for ever
With a sweet emotion;
Nothing in the world is single;
All things by a law divine
In one spirit meet and mingle.
Why not I with thine?—" '

The words resonated in the big hall, their pure beauty robbing her of any answer she might have had.

'That was written to a mistress, as I'm sure you're aware. If he had never had affairs, it would never have existed,' Brian murmured. 'Romanticism isn't a way of writing: it's a way of life. All or nothing. Most of us only have the courage for nothing.'

There was a long pause. 'Someone told me', the geologist said, 'that Keats used to put pepper on his tongue when he drank claret, in order to increase the sensations.'

'He must have drunk wine as filthy as this, then,' the mathematician suggested. 'When is the Master going to invest in a decent cellar?'

Brian, though he said nothing more, was still holding her eyes triumphantly. Around them a buzz of conversation arose. Terry looked away, cursing herself. What on earth had possessed her to trade quotations with Eden, and on his specialist subject of all things?

But though she had lost, she had to admit to herself that for a few brief minutes that evening she had at least not been bored rigid.

They moved down to the Senior Common Room for coffee. Once again Terry found herself ignored. She did her best to look decorative, since that was clearly all she had been invited for, pretending to look at the pictures of past Masters and eminent Fellows on the walls. Every now and again she caught dons sneaking sideways glances at her, amusement in their eyes. Evidently the story of her impromptu debate was doing the rounds.

Feeling a touch on her elbow, she jumped and almost spilled her coffee. Then, seeing it was Eden, she steadied herself.

'I enjoyed talking to you back there,' he said, his eyes very close to hers. 'I think it was the first sensible conversation I've ever had in this place.'

'There's no need to be condescending. You wiped the floor with me, and everybody knows it.'

'Well, yes. But what only you and I know is how much we both enjoyed it.'

'We were having an academic argument about a dead poet,' she said, pretending not to understand him. 'What's to enjoy?'

'That wasn't an argument,' he said, amused. 'That was foreplay.'

'Don't be ridiculous.'

'"Nothing in the world is single,"' he murmured. 'I've just booked a double room up the road at The Old Parsonage hotel. Room service is bringing some flowers and champagne: if we walk slowly we'll get there at the same time they do.'

She looked at him, and saw that he was entirely serious. 'And what about your wife?' she said icily.

He smiled wolfishly. 'Oh, she can have you too. But not tonight. Tonight I want you to myself.'

'That wasn't what I meant,' she started to say; then, 'Oh, what's the use?' She looked at him directly. 'Go and play your games with someone else.'

'Games?' he mocked, unfazed. 'They're hardly games.' Bending forward so that his mouth was very close to her ear, he breathed,

'For the crown of our life as it closes
Is darkness, the fruit thereof dust;
No thorns go as deep as a rose's,
And love is more cruel than lust.
Time turns the old days to derision,
Our loves into corpses or wives;
And marriage and death and division
Make barren our lives.'

'Bollocks,' she said crisply. 'The fact that it rhymes nicely doesn't mean it's true.'

'And I thought you were going to come back with

186

an equally beautiful and apposite quotation from the philosophy of Hercule Poirot,' he mocked.

'If you'd really wanted to get me into bed,' she said, and paused.

'Yes?'

'You should have let me win.' Then she handed him her coffee cup and walked away. But she wasn't walking so quickly that she didn't hear him call after her, 'No. No, I don't think that's true of you at all.'

Twelve

Terry took a two-handed grip on the sledgehammer
and waggled her shoulders, like a golfer addressing
the ball for a particularly long drive. In fact the
distance to the wall was only a couple of feet, but
then a golf club doesn't weigh twenty pounds. The
wall looked, as walls do when you're about to
knock a hole in them, terrifyingly solid.

She hoisted the hammer up to shoulder height
and swung, feeling the shockwaves vibrate through
her wrists at the moment of impact. The house
mumbled to itself. Again. Back over her shoulder, a
nice big arc, and – whump. She felt mortar loosen-
ing. A plate-sized lump of plaster fell away from the
wall.

Two more blows in rapid succession, and she
reckoned she was getting somewhere. A depression
the size of a manhole cover had appeared in the wall
just in front of her. She paused to shake the dust off
her mask and lifted the hammer again. This time

her blow met less resistance. Bricks fell from the opening like collapsing playing cards, toppling into a pile on the other side of the gap. The dust was phenomenal – not only the white dust of shattering plaster, falling off the bricks like icing falling off a wedding cake, but the pinker lumps of broken brick and the grey of the mortar. For a few minutes she felt the intense, wild exultation of destruction; the thrilling power of reducing everything around her to smithereens. Once the hole had been made extending it was easy, and she was soon standing on a mound of rubble, breathing heavily, surveying one large downstairs room where previously there had been two.

Before she did anything else she got the new lintel in, a long piece of steel temporarily held up by two extending builder's props. She extended the props as far as they would go by banging on the nuts with the edge of the sledgehammer, then she tidied the area round the edges of the opening. There had been some hideous wallpaper on the far side: it hung down around the sides in ragged icicles. She ripped them off methodically, adding them to the debris at her feet.

In the very top corner of what had once been the front room was one last strip of wallpaper. Standing on a wobbling heap of bricks, she could just grasp it with her fingers. She yanked, and it ripped into a dozen pieces, fluttering to the floor. No, it hadn't ripped. The strip of wallpaper was in her hand, having come away whole. So what were the other pieces of paper?

She bent down and picked a few up. They were all the same width, about an inch or so across, though each strip was of a different length. All were on flimsy magazine paper. A colour photograph on one caught her eye. It took her a moment to work out what she was looking at: it had been cut from the magazine without respecting the original border of the photo. A pair of naked female buttocks, pushed towards the viewer. Half the girl's face was missing but you could see that she was grinning inanely over her shoulder and that one hand was between her legs, pulling apart her labia for the camera. Terry picked up another cutting. Again it had been oddly cropped – this time all you could see was three-quarters of a thigh and a shaved crotch, the overall effect not so much erotic as functional, as if whoever had cut them out hadn't been trying to focus on anything in particular. Seen from this angle, the hairless labia looked like nothing so much as a piece of bicycle inner tube.

So. Cuttings from a porn mag, hidden behind the wallpaper. And this, of course, had been the room where the crime had taken place. She supposed she really ought to take them to the police, but they only proved what everyone already knew; that Hugh, though somewhat adolescent, was definitely into girls.

She picked up the third piece of paper. This was the same flimsy paper as the rest, but the picture was totally devoid of pornographic content – in fact, she could have sworn it looked like part of a cigarette advertisement. Turning the fragments over, she realized what hadn't been apparent at first: the reason the photographs were badly cropped was because it was the other sides that had been the point of the cuttings, not the photographs. Each one was covered in text. 'Dear Linzi,' she read at the top of one; a letter. Then, at the end, leaping into sudden focus, the sign-off:

Carla, Oxford.

'Good Lord,' Terry said aloud. Taking off her dustmask, she sat down and began to read.

Dear Linzi,

I'm twenty-eight years old, and my husband and I have been married for seven years. We've always had a wonderful sex life, and have acted out many wild fantasies together. However, there was one particular fantasy that we often discussed but had never had the chance to try, which was wife-swapping. When we made love I used to wonder what it would feel like to have another man's thick cock pounding my pussy, while Brian soon confessed he'd love to see another man ravish me while he watched.

'I bet he did,' Terry murmured. She skipped towards the end.

By this time, needless to say, we girls were horny as hell, and while Brian fixed up some drinks Mary and I did a striptease for her husband. Then it was our turn. We threw ourselves back on the bed and let the men lick us to a wonderful orgasm, Brian bringing Mary off a little before I came – to be honest, I was enjoying the feel of John's silver tongue on my cunt and clitoris so much that I was deliberately holding back until I couldn't bear it any longer. But now it was one all, so to speak, and John announced that it was time for the tie-breaker. Positioning himself behind me, he thrust his enormous cock right into my still unravished pussy, and began to slide it in and out with long, slow strokes that drove me wild.

'Blah blah blah,' Terry muttered. She picked up another.

Dear Linzi,
I am a twenty-eight-year-old woman who has been married now for several years. I have been told I'm still attractive, but for one reason and another sex with my husband doesn't fully satisfy me, and for some time now I've been fantasizing about sleeping with another man. To begin with I didn't think I'd dare to put my fantasies into practice, but then something

The cutting ended there, but something about the cleanness of the cut suggested that it was the bottom of the magazine's page, in which case, Terry reasoned, there might well be another cutting where the column continued. She searched for one that seemed to be from the top of a page. Ah yes, there it was.

happened to make me change my mind.
I've got a little open-top MG, a red one, which

after my husband is one of the things I love best in the world. One very hot morning I was driving in it with the roof down, sunning myself. The shiny red paintwork had been polished, I let my hair out so it caught the wind, and what with one thing and another I found myself going faster and faster.

The fragment stopped, apparently because the letter had been laid out round a photograph. She picked up another one at random.

rammed his huge cock up me from behind and fucked me until I saw stars. He admitted to me later that although he'd always wanted to he'd never have dared approach me if I hadn't made the first move. After that, whenever my husband was out Hugh would pop round for sex – and I never had such good fucking before as I get from my horny young lover.

Since then we've enjoyed several excellent fucks, in every conceivable combination. Hugh says he's getting the best education possible – and as far as I'm concerned, he's a star student!
Carla, Oxford

If the letters were to be believed, her neighbour was either a complete nymphomaniac or had a very fertile imagination indeed. And the reference to Hugh certainly seemed to confirm the gossip that Hugh and Carla had been having an affair. She put the cuttings on one side carefully. She'd keep working while she decided what to do with them.

Now came the laborious process of picking the

bricks up, a stack of four or five at a time, and carrying them out through the kitchen into the back garden. But this too was a kind of pleasure – neatness after mess, the simple sculptural satisfaction of making a tidy and exactly square pile that wouldn't slip or topple. She worked until lunchtime, then popped out to the shop in her overalls to buy a pasty.

Perhaps because her mind was still elsewhere, she was a bit slow on the uptake. She almost bumped into someone as she came out of her own front door, vaguely registered that it was a woman, smartly dressed, talking to some people on the other side of the street, said, 'Excuse me,' and slipped past. It was only when one of the people on the other side of the street shouted, 'Cut,' and the woman glanced sideways at her disapprovingly, that she realized what was happening. She walked on, out of the range of the TV camera, but hearing the man call, 'OK Jem, still running,' she slowed and looked back. The presenter straightened her skirt unselfconsciously and started again.

'Three, two, one. Oxford undergraduate Hugh Scott, brutally murdered in this house in February, may have been the victim of a sexual attack by another man, according to a new theory being put forward by Thames Valley Police. They're asking for male victims of similar attacks to come forward and help them in their investigation. In common with many other university cities, Oxford has a large and thriving homosexual community, and today gay spokesmen reacted with alarm to the news that they may be har-bouring a sadistic sex killer. Local councillor Jerry Fairbanks, however, believes that this was a tragedy waiting to happen, the result of a council policy that has been too liberal towards sexual minorities. He had this to say.' She paused. 'And cut.'

Terry walked slowly back towards her front door. At that point she had no particular intention of say-ing anything, but when the woman looked at her inquiringly she made a snap decision.

'Do you always spout homophobic bollocks?' As an opening it wasn't exactly witty, but it had the desired effect. The reporter's eyes widened and she took a step back nervously.

'This is my house, and my front door, and if you want to do any filming here you should have asked my permission,' Terry said menacingly. She was dimly aware that the camera was pointing at her, and remembered reading an interview with a well-known politician in which he'd said that the only way to prevent footage being used on air was to swear continually. She took a deep breath and went for it. 'All you're fucking well doing by giving air-time to fucking ignorant fascists, which I take it is what you're fucking up to, is turning everyone in this fucking city into rabid queer-bashers. You stupid twat,' she added for good measure. Then she stormed back into the house – well, as near to storm-ing as you can when you've got to find the key to unlock the deadlock – and slammed the door savagely.

She caught sight of herself in a mirror and laughed. God, she thought, I must have been terrifying. A dust-coloured harpy in her ex-husband's painting overalls, several sizes too large.

Not that she could really understand why she'd got so furious. It was something territorial, she supposed: some other bitch had come pissing on her patch, and Terry had seen her off. But it was more than that. Terry had been what Mo had laughingly called a vanilla lesbian – about as straight as it was possible for a dyke to be. Except with Mo's friends, she'd never even come out. But she was damned if she was going to do a St Peter now, and turn her back when gays were being attacked.

The edges of the new opening were still lined with a ragged Lego-like crenellation of bricks, and she set to work knocking them out with the sledge-hammer. This was hard work, the bricks having the strength of the other walls they were attached to, and she was soon sweating again. She was glad when the doorbell went, and she had the chance of a rest.

Much to her surprise, it was Carla. She looked nervous.

'Can I come in?'

'I suppose so,' Terry conceded. 'We'd better go into the kitchen. There's mess everywhere else.' She led the other woman along the hall, past the two doors to the new room.

'Wow,' Carla said. 'I heard banging, but I didn't realize you were doing it yourself.' She shrugged. 'No more Hugh's room.'

'Well, it wasn't very practical, having two small rooms,' Terry said.

'Look, I came to say – I mean, I wanted to apologize. For what I said the other day. It was crass of me.'

'Yes, it was,' agreed Terry, who saw no reason why she should make this any easier for her.

'I suppose – I suppose I was behaving the way I would have', she blushed and swallowed, 'if I was making a pass at a man.'

That made sense, Terry thought. Not many men would have turned down an invitation from the slight, green-eyed redhead in front of her, however crassly made.

'OK, let's just forget it,' she said. 'Though while you're here, you might as well know that I found some copies of your letters behind the wallpaper.'

Carla looked puzzled. 'What do you mean, my letters?'

'Your, er,' Terry tried to think of a euphemism, 'intimate letters. I found them in Hugh's room.'

Carla still didn't seem to understand. 'Look, you probably know by now that I slept with Hugh a couple of times. Everyone else round here seems to know, so it's not exactly a big secret. But why would I have written him letters? He only lived next door to me.'

'Not letters *to* him. Letters about him. And about, um, other people too.'

'What *do* you mean?'

It seemed simpler just to show her one of the clippings. Carla's eyes widened, her hand went to

197

her mouth, and then she started to laugh.

'What's funny?' Terry asked.

'Isn't it obvious? They may have my name on them, but half those letters in sex magazines claim to be by women, don't they? Hugh probably wrote them himself. They're certainly nothing to do with me. I don't think I've written anything longer than a postcard in ten years.' Carla was either a very good actress, or she was telling the truth. She read a little more. 'The mucky little bastard,' she said affectionately.

'It doesn't bother you, then?' Terry asked. 'Knowing that this was the kind of thing he fantasized about?'

Carla shot her an amused glance. 'Oh, come off it. For that matter, I wasn't exactly after him for his mind.'

'But why would he keep them?' Terry wondered aloud.

'Authorial pride maybe? Who knows? Want me to burn them for you?'

'No, I think the police should probably see them. As they're nothing to do with you.' Terry deftly removed the clippings from Carla's hand.

'Suit yourself,' Carla shrugged.

Terry put the clippings into an envelope, thinking hard. Presumably Carla was right, and the letters had been written by Hugh himself, in which case they might throw some useful light on his personality. Equally, if Carla did know about them but was lying, Girdler should also be told that she had something to hide. And there was something else too, something she'd read in the letters them-selves, that she couldn't quite put her finger on.

Carla was looking at the lintel where the wall had been. 'How do you know the house won't collapse?'

'Oh, it wasn't a load-bearing wall. Don't worry, I know what I'm doing.'

'And you just bash these bricks with the hammer till they fall down?'

'Something like that. Want a go?'

Carla looked puzzled – almost, Terry thought, as if she had offered her a turn at putting the rubbish out or cleaning the loo.

'It's very satisfying, believe me,' she said mildly.

'Oh, I couldn't. I haven't got your strength, for one thing.'

'No really, it's all technique. Here.' She arranged Carla behind the hammer, and helped her heft it up onto her shoulder. For a moment – or did she imagine it? – she felt the other woman's body arch minutely, like a cat instinctively stretching to be stroked. 'Now, the biggest swing you possibly can. Aim for that point in front of your knees, so gravity will be helping you.'

Carla swung, rather inelegantly. But it had the desired effect. 'Wow! The whole house moves,' she said breathlessly. She moved aside. 'Come on then. Show me how it's done.'

Terry hit, as hard as she could, one of the remaining outcrops of brick, and had the satisfaction of seeing them tumble away from her.

'What happens to those?'

'I'm sticking them in the garden. I thought I might make a barbecue, later in the summer.' She looked at Carla's dress doubtfully. 'It's going to be rather dusty from now on, I'm afraid.'

Carla took the hint. 'OK, I'll be off.'

Alone again, Terry stuck some Hendrix on the tape deck and got back to work. But even as she sledgehammered the last protruding bricks from the edges of the oblong, her mind was still worrying at the rough edges and protuberances of what Carla had been saying.

Why would she deny writing the letters? True, they weren't the sort of thing you'd want to own up to in polite company, but given that both Carla and her husband had made a pass at her, and both had talked about the open nature of their marriage, it hardly seemed in character for Carla to disown them out of embarrassment – particularly when she could have asked Terry to give them back.

No, Carla must have been telling the truth. In which case, the only possible explanation was that Hugh had written them himself. So why was she still uneasy?

She phoned Girdler at the station, was told that he was out, and left a message for him to call back. She finished tidying up and hoovered thoroughly. Although she'd draped dustsheets over the bookshelves, she was annoyed to discover that the dust had got everywhere, and all her academic texts were covered in a thick film of pink and grey. Oh well, there wasn't much point in cleaning them up until the plastering was completed. With luck, she'd get that done tomorrow.

She watched the teatime news, partly to see whether she was on it. She was, though the shot of the house had been cut to a few seconds. Terry herself, scowling ferociously and grey-haired with mortar dust, was no more than a passer-by in the background, thank God. A picture of a young man wearing a formal university gown appeared, obviously blown up from a matriculation photograph. It coincided with a reference to Hugh Scott, and Terry realized she was looking at the murder victim. She started. It was eerie to put a face to the name after so long.

Hugh had been a beautiful young man, about six foot tall, but with just enough muscle on him not to seem lanky. His blond hair was tight and curly, like a cauliflower, and although the photograph was in black and white she could tell he was blue-eyed. In the photo he was scowling, which only added to his attractiveness. A very English type, she decided.

The report rolled on. The councillor whose interview the reporter had been linking to when Terry had accosted her appeared, ranting about the use of ratepayers' money to subsidize 'gay this, gay that, gay everything'. A female academic from one of the women's colleges pointed out that for every man sexually attacked there were three hundred women raped, battered or sexually molested. But despite this brief sop to common sense the overall tone of the piece was entirely hysterical. A cut to a doctor talking about the spread of Aids into the heterosexual population was left without commentary but made its point anyway: even if this pervert doesn't knife you, he can still kill you. They finished with a shot of Girdler looking worried and appealing for information. Two minutes after the report began they were back with the newsreader in the studio, who started talking about an agricultural show in which a local farmer had won first prize.

In the Thames Valley Police headquarters at Kidlington, Girdler was watching the report too. He sighed and turned it off. He never got used to how oafish he looked on television.

He lit another Hamlet and picked up the pile of messages on his desk. The top one was Terry's. Glumly he decided that he'd better not put it off any longer.

'I'm sorry about yesterday,' he said as soon as she answered the phone.

'Don't worry about it. I've been hammering out the aggression,' he thought she said. 'Listen, I've got something for you.'

She told him about the letters, and Carla's theory that Hugh had written them himself. 'She's probably right,' he agreed. 'Though authorship can't be proved one way or another, I seem to remember you saying.'

'That's true when you've only got one text. There are plenty of computer programs that can compare one text with another, and tell you if they're written by the same person.'

'What do you mean, computer programs?' A

202

subordinate came in with a report and he scanned it quickly, marking the important bits with a highlighter pen.

'They count up the number of, I don't know, adverbial clauses or colonic prepositions or something, and match them to another text with the same grammatical quirks. A bit like fingerprints, I suppose. One of my colleagues is using it to try to prove that a particular Old English poem was written by the same person who wrote another, much more famous poem.'

'Sounds fascinating,' he said, dropping the report into his out-tray.

Her voice, suddenly cold with anger, drew his attention back to the phone. 'It's not meant to be interesting, Inspector. The point is that you asked if authorship could be proved, and I was just telling you that it can.'

'I'm sorry,' he said, wincing. 'You're right. My mind was elsewhere, I'm afraid.' He was starting to realize that a relationship with Terry Williams would rarely be comfortable, nor would he ever be allowed to take her for granted.

'Who's next?' the nurse called. Miles stood up, his legs shaking. He advanced to the hatch and tried to smile.

'Do you have a card?' she asked him.

'What card?' he asked.

'Who was it sent you for a blood test?' she asked.

'No-one,' he said. 'I thought I could just turn up.'

'Wait there a minute,' the nurse said, and withdrew. Miles wondered if he should leg it. Then a young doctor came out, and invited him into one of the cubicles.

'If you need a blood test, you're meant to go to your GP,' he explained. 'The GP fills out a card, and you bring the card to us.'

'I don't want to go through my doctor,' Miles muttered. The other man looked at him sympathetically. There was one overriding reason why young men came for blood tests nowadays.

'Well, we can do a test and send the results to you ourselves,' he offered, pulling out one of the request cards. 'But if it's an HIV test, you'll have to come in for counselling before the results are in. Name?'

'Radcliffe' he lied. It was a bad lie, he realized: they were in the John Radcliffe hospital. He made an appointment for counselling, then made up an address as well.

Thirteen

A glass of Guinness in her hand, Terry edged back against a pillar and looked around her at the mayhem that was Hugh Scott's wake.

It was quite a sight. The Catamites had hired the ballroom of the Randolph Hotel for the night, and if the rumours were to be believed, a number of the bedrooms upstairs as well. The huge room was entirely swagged in black theatre drapes, and illuminated only by the light of the black candles which burned in enormous silver candelabra. In the centre of the room stood a black-draped table on which had been placed two vast silver punchbowls of Black Velvet – champagne mixed with stout – surrounded by bowls of Black Sobranie cigarettes, platters of oysters on crushed black ice, and glistening tubs of caviar. The noise level was deafening. Over two hundred people had been invited, and despite the bouncers standing guard outside rather more than that had clearly managed to talk their way in. In one corner a string quartet struggled gamely against the deafening roar of conversation and the increasing crush of bodies, but when the cellist found herself unable to use her bow for lack of room they gave up and stormed out in disgust.

Terry had come on an impulse. The invitation had been lying around on her kitchen table for days. A thick white card edged with black, it had come in a black-edged envelope embossed on the back with an obscene satanic drawing. The writing on the card itself was embossed in gold. *The Committee and Familiars of The Catamite Society request the pleasure of your company at a wake in honour of the recently deceased Hugh Harford Scott. Dress: Red, black, too fast to live.* Someone, presumably Giles, had written across the top, *I hope I'll see you at this.*

Even though she'd know virtually no-one, and had no intention of staying more than an hour or so, she decided it might be fun to go and see what the rich and arty undergraduates were up to these days. Her only black dress was the Ozbek one she'd worn to Brian Eden's party, but she had a short red one in satiny material that showed off her legs.

She got there around eleven, and was immediately almost knocked over by a very drunk girl who was removing her dress in order to prove to a group of leering young men that she was wearing black underwear. Edging away, she found herself a small amount of room and looked around. Shrieking, shouting, drinking and groping seemed to be the order of the day. She spotted Dorling and Julia Van Glught in the crowd, but gave them a wide berth. Then to her surprise she heard her name being called and saw her tutor, Reg, standing with an enormously fat man.

'What on earth are you doing here?' she shouted over the din.

'They always like to invite a few dons. They think it gives them credibility,' he yelled back. 'Do you know Roddy?'

She shook the fat man's hand. He ran his eyes over her muscular body and shouted, 'Do you row?' She shook her head, puzzled.

Someone fell on her from behind, covering her neck with kisses. She turned and saw that it was Giles. He was very drunk. 'This man saved my life,' he said incoherently, pointing at Roddy. 'I love this man.' A pretty young girl watched them from a distance, smiling timidly.

'You've had enough, Giles,' the fat man bellowed. 'Come on, let's get you outside.' He and the girl each took one of Giles's arms and marched him away.

'Roddy coaches the college boat,' Reg explained. 'Actually, I was just leaving. It's getting to the stage where I shouldn't be here.'

'I thought students today were meant to be boring,' Terry said, leaning back to avoid a bare breast that was squeezing past her.

'They are, generally speaking. But the rich ones aren't affected by the forces that shape the behaviour of the great mass. They go to five- hundred-year-old public schools, they live in five-hundred-year-old houses, they derive income from five-hundred-year-old trust funds, and then they come here. You can't expect them to be affected by anything so transitory as a recession. They just get a little less imaginative, that's all.'

She watched as a passing young buck in black tie took a huge mouthful of Black Velvet, grabbed the girl next to her, and pressed his open mouth to hers. Liquid dribbled down her chin onto her dress.

'Like birds feeding their young,' Reg remarked. 'It's all harmless fun.'

'If you're leaving, I think I'll come with you,' she said. 'I've seen all I want to see.'

Outside they found Roddy propping Giles up against a wall and talking to him quietly but with some force. A stubby finger was stabbing into Giles's chest, emphasizing his point. The girlfriend, apparently unconcerned, was talking to some friends a few yards away. A couple of paparazzi loitered around the entrance, but they were apparently waiting for something specific and ignored them.

'This lad needs to get home,' Roddy said.

'He can come with me,' Terry said. 'I live opposite him.'

Together they manoeuvred Giles into one of the waiting minicabs.

'Osney Island,' she told the driver, climbing in the other side.

'Is your bloke all right?' he asked in an Oxfordshire accent. 'Only if he chucks up, I'll have to charge fifty quid for the cleaning.'

At that moment Giles began to retch. 'Shit,' Terry hissed. She leapt out, raced round and pulled the door open. Crouching down, she tried to yank his shoulders out of the car. Giles swayed like a jack-in-the-box, then his head toppled towards her and a stream of black vomit cascaded into the gutter. Terry recoiled and went sprawling backwards, the dress that had showed off her legs now showing off rather more than that. A couple of flashlights popped, and she heard male laughter.

Grant and Paul were two of the last to leave the Scotch Pony. It had been a quiet evening: some of their friends were in a new play that had just opened, and they'd been to the opening-night party. The theatre had been almost empty, and the cast had been subdued.

'What a dreary evening, dearie,' Grant chanted as they walked back towards their college. 'What a dull, dull day. God, I was so bored tonight I nearly fainted.'

'Oi!' someone called. Grant turned. There was a group of young men behind them.

'Ignore them dear, they're rough boys,' Paul said.

One of them was coming towards them, smiling. ''Scuse me, have you got the time?' Leather jacket, Elvis fringe, Levi's.

'Ooh, look at the meat on that,' Grant said out of the corner of his mouth. Instead of answering him directly he held out his arm. It was a purposefully ambivalent gesture: the other man could either just peer at his wristwatch, if the time was really all he wanted, or he could take hold of his wrist as if to steady it. He felt the fingers close round his wrist and winked sideways at Paul.

His arm was wrenched up behind his back and a boot stabbed into the back of his knees, bringing him down. He was dimly aware of others running towards them – rescuers, he thought, until he heard Paul shout and a boot exploded into the side of his ribs, so hard that his head left the ground and came down again with a crack, making his ears ring. He saw a sudden cinematic close-up of the tarmac in front of his eyes and felt something hot and phlegmy flowing from his nose. Another boot slammed into the small of his back, and with a faint shock of surprise he felt something inside him move, below the skin where you took it for granted everything was solid. 'Fucking pansies,' a voice shouted. There was a howl of feedback, and he passed out.

He drifted in and out of consciousness, dimly aware of being in an ambulance, of Paul wailing beside him. He came round again as a doctor started to examine him. 'I'm all right now, actually,' he said, and passed out again.

The next time he came round he was on a hospital trolley in a cubicle. Paul was sitting beside him. There was a cut down the length of his cheek. 'I hope I look better than you do,' Grant said feebly.

'We were queer-bashed,' Paul said. He looked as if he was on the verge of tears. 'Oh darling, I tried to rescue you but I couldn't.' Grant squeezed his hand reassuringly. A Chinese doctor came and said,

'Feeling better? Let's have a look,' tapping and probing in places Grant couldn't even remember getting hit. Then a policeman came, and asked him what happened. He took some details, but it was obvious that they wouldn't be able to catch them.

Detective Constable Stradling closed his notebook and went to find a phone to make his report. The Inspector had predicted that there would be a spate of incidents like this after the press conference: it was the price you paid for going public.

It was well after midnight by the time Terry managed to deliver the drunken Giles to his own home and pay off the irate taxi driver. Puking had sobered him up a little, but even so she felt she couldn't just dump him on his sofa and leave in case he passed out and vomited again. She went into his kitchen and made them both coffee. By the time she returned with the mugs he was sitting, sprawled but upright, his eyes reasonably focused.

'Alone at last,' he said thickly, taking the mug from her. The coffee slopped dangerously as he raised it to his lips.

Terry sighed. 'Don't start all that.'

'Oh, come on. We both want a shag, don't we?'

'No, Giles. For one thing you're a student, and I don't shag students, and secondly, you're nearly ten years younger than me.'

'Doesn't stop some people,' he muttered.

'You mean Carla?' she said, suddenly interested.

'Carla. Not only Carla.' He put a finger to his lips. 'My lips are sealed.'

'About what?'

He shook his head. 'Oldest friend. Dead now. Poor bloody Hugh.'

'Yes,' she agreed. 'Poor Hugh. And it can't have been easy for you, either.'

'I knew him when he was both – we were both – little boys. Little boys at school,' he said sadly.

'Tell me about Hugh and Carla,' she suggested.

For a moment he looked as if he was about to tell her. Discretion fought drunkenness, and discretion won. 'Not fair on Hugh,' he said eventually.

She sighed. 'Come on, Giles. You should get to bed.'

He leered at her. 'Put me to bed?'

She smiled and stood up. 'Goodnight. Drink some water, won't you? You'll feel bad enough in the morning as it is.'

To her annoyance, she discovered when she finally got into her own bed that she was not in the least sleepy. Sighing, she switched the light back on and went to her desk, looking for some work to do. The porn cuttings were still where she had left them and she picked them up.

It wasn't straightforward to assemble complete letters from the fragments in her hand, but after a few minutes she had three separate letters laid out in three columns on the desk in front of her. Carefully, she began to read.

Dear Linzi,

I am a twenty-eight-year-old woman who has been married now for several years. I have been told I'm

212

still attractive, but for one reason and another sex with my husband doesn't fully satisfy me, and for some time now I've been fantasizing about sleeping with another man. To begin with I didn't think I'd dare to put my fantasies into practice, but then something happened to make me change my mind.

I've got a little open-top MG, a red one, which after my husband is one of the things I love best in the world. One very hot morning I was driving in it with the roof down, sunning myself. The shiny red paintwork had been polished, I let my hair out so it caught the wind, and what with one thing and another I found myself going faster and faster.

Suddenly I see a blue flashing light behind me, and I'm pulled over by these two young traffic cops. They get out of the car very slowly and come towards me. One's dark, almost foreign looking, with a touch of stubble and a very cleft chin. The other's blond and very well built. I tell them that I know I've been speeding, but that I'll do anything to avoid being given a ticket. 'Anything?' the dark one says, shooting a meaningful look at the other one. The way he says it leaves me in no doubt as to what they intend. I'm still sitting in my car, and they're standing. So my eyes are at the level of their crotches, and I'm staring straight at the bulges in their trousers as they start to grow and stiffen. 'OK,' the second one says at last, 'get into our car.'

I clamber over the seats, revealing in the process that I'm not wearing any knickers. As I do so a hand reaches out, casually flips up my miniskirt and squeezes my bottom. I shriek, but I've enjoyed it, and they can tell I won't be objecting too much to whatever they want to do. By this time they're unbuckling their belts and climbing in behind me. The dark one gets his cock in my mouth first, and while I'm made to lick and suck him the other one is rubbing his hands all over my body, undoing my bra and playing with my nipples. Then he takes me from behind while the dark one watches. He's quite rough but I'm loving it.

While we're still screwing a call comes through on the radio. They have to chase a getaway car. They don't want to let me go yet so they bundle me into the back. The blond one drives, impossibly fast, while the dark one continues to ram his cock between my legs. When they eventually catch up with the stolen car and arrest the driver, he sees me in the back seat, and in order to keep him quiet about it they offer me to him as well. He's delighted because he knows he's going to prison where there'll only be homosexuals, so this is his last chance to screw for seven years. They hold me down on the bonnet of the car and take it in turns to have me.

Eventually they take me back to my own car, and the dark one tears up the traffic violation ticket he started to write out for me earlier. Then they drive away, and I do too, feeling bruised and sore from the fucking I've received, sperm dribbling out of me onto the leather seat I'm sitting on.

That's it. I hope you enjoy reading this as much as I enjoyed writing it!

Carla, Oxford

Dear Linzi,
I'm twenty-eight years old, and my husband and I have been married for seven years. We've always

214

had a wonderful sex life, and have acted out many wild fantasies together. However, there was one particular fantasy that we often discussed but had never had the chance to try, which was wife-swapping. When we made love I used to wonder what it would feel like to have another man's thick cock pounding my pussy, while Brian soon confessed he'd love to see another man ravish me while he watched.

About a year ago we got our chance, when I accompanied him to a conference down in Brighton. Although a big dinner had been organized for all the delegates, another couple and ourselves agreed that it was so boring we'd rather slip off somewhere alone. We found a little Italian restaurant, and proceeded to play some very silly drinking games that got all four of us totally drunk. The other couple, Mary and John, were obviously sexually adventurous and quite uninhibited. They were feeding each other spaghetti and making a big show of waggling their tongues. We did the same, and when a bit of sauce fell on my blouse John quickly dipped his napkin in some water and began sponging my breasts with it. His wife was laughing and joking, saying that she could tell who John would be spending the night with. However, it was all banter and although we were all feeling pretty horny by the time we left the restaurant no one had actually taken it any further.

When we got back to the hotel and asked for our keys the receptionist mistakenly paired us with the wrong partners. John immediately grabbed my arm for a joke, saying to Brian, 'So how do you like your new wife, Brian?' My husband immediately said he wasn't sure, as he hadn't had his wedding night yet. 'I promise you won't be disappointed,' Mary said, and I saw her hand reach down to the front of his trousers. The receptionist couldn't see anything because we were all standing close to the desk, but I could tell from the way Brian was smiling that he was enjoying what she was doing to him.

John kept hold of my arm as we went upstairs, still laughing and joking, and led me into his room. Then he said something like, 'Alone at last,' and took me in his arms for a really passionate French kiss. I was so aroused I could have screwed him then and there, but after a few minutes I said I thought we ought to go and see what the others were doing. They hadn't locked the door, and when we walked in I got the shock of my life: there was my husband with his trousers round his ankles, being given an expert blow-job by Mary.

Brian would have stopped when we came in, but Mary had a good hold of him and obviously wasn't about to let go. Two can play at this game, I thought, so I turned to John and said, 'Looks like we've been left behind,' running my finger down the bulge in his trousers as I did so. 'Oh, I expect we can catch up,' he replied with a wicked smile. I sat down on the edge of the bed and unzipped him. His cock was huge, and hard as a rock. Grasping it in one hand, I ran it round and round my lips like a gigantic lipstick – it always drives Brian wild when I do that, and to judge from the groans above me it was having the same effect on John. Then I took all of him into my mouth, and started tonguing him for all I was worth. Pretty soon I felt his knees sag, and my mouth was filled with lovely come. We beat the others to it by just a few seconds, and when I looked over I saw that my husband had come so much, it was dribbling out of Mary's mouth and down her chin.

By this time, needless to say, we girls were horny as hell, and while Brian fixed up some drinks Mary and I did a striptease for her husband. Then it was our turn. We threw ourselves back on the bed and let the men lick us to a wonderful orgasm, Brian bringing Mary off a little before I came – to be honest, I was enjoying the feel of John's silver tongue on my cunt and clitoris so much that I was deliberately holding back until I couldn't bear it any longer. But now it was one all, so to speak, and John announced that it was time for the tie-breaker. Positioning himself behind me, he thrust his enormous cock right into my still unravished pussy, and began to slide it in and out with long, slow strokes that drove me wild. I was dimly aware that Mary had climbed on top of Brian and was riding him noisily. At one point she leaned over to John and kissed him, and I did the same with Brian, and when Mary eventually reached down with her hand and started to squeeze and rub my breasts, I shouted, 'My God! I'm coming,' and I came and came in great waves of pleasure. Mary came too, and then Brian, and finally John, so the 'contest' was an honourable draw.

After a moment I felt John's limp cock sliding out of me. We were all too exhausted to fuck any more, though we exchanged addresses and promised to meet up at the next conference. So far we haven't seen them again yet, but it's certainly done wonders for our sex life. Brian has confessed he got such a thrill out of watching me with John that he'd like to see me screwing a few other men, and though no one suitable has turned up yet, he's still looking!

Carla, Oxford

Dear Linzi,
Recently a very good-looking young student moved in to the house next door to me. My husband soon remarked that Hugh, as the young man was called, seemed rather smitten by me. I hadn't noticed it before, but now that he'd mentioned it I quickly realized that he was right. Hugh was always looking at me with undisguised lust, and once when I was up a ladder cleaning windows and he rode past on his bicycle, he was so distracted by the view he had of my legs disappearing into my rather short skirt that he almost fell off.

I must admit that his attention was rather flattering, and I soon resolved to get him into bed. However, being young he was also rather bashful, and it quickly became clear that he wasn't going to make the first move.

To begin with I simply led him on. Whenever it was warm enough I used to sunbathe topless in the garden, making sure that I chose times when he'd be around. Then, one night when my husband was away and I knew Hugh would be there on his own, I went next door and asked if he could help mend my bed, which had come off one of its legs. Hugh came round with a screwdriver and slid underneath my bed on his back, looking for the problem. 'I've found it,' he said at last. 'It just needs a screw.'

Well, I knew I was never going to get another chance as good as this, so I took a deep breath and said, 'I know just how it feels.' Then I got down on top of him and started stroking his cock through his trousers. Of course, trapped underneath the bed he couldn't move, and pretty soon I had his trousers undone and his lovely cock buried deep in my mouth. When he was completely turned on I tore off my clothes and impaled myself on him, riding him frantically until we both came, breathing in fast thick pants.

He was shattered by the time I finally let him get up, but he was grinning from ear to ear and I could tell from the amount of spunk dribbling out of me that he'd thoroughly enjoyed the experience. But he also wanted his revenge. Grabbing me, he threw me roughly across the bed and spanked me roughly with his hand. Naturally, this turned me on even more and I was soon groaning and writhing in ecstasy. Getting on top of me, he rammed his huge cock up me from behind and fucked me until I saw stars. He admitted to me later that although he'd always wanted to he'd never have dared approach me if I hadn't made the first move. After that, whenever my husband was out Hugh would pop round for sex – and I never had such good fucking before as I get from my horny young lover.

Since then we've enjoyed several excellent fucks, in every conceivable combination. Hugh says he's getting the best education possible – and as far as I'm concerned, he's a star student!

Carla, Oxford

Terry put down the last letter and shifted uncomfortably on her chair. Her watch told her that it was twelve twenty-five. 'Sod it,' she said aloud. She went and got the phone.

When Allison answered her voice sounded surprised, rather than sleepy.

'It's Terry. Did I wake you up?'

'No, I was working. What's the matter?'

Briefly Terry explained about the letters and read her a few of the less alarming extracts. Allison whistled occasionally but otherwise said little until Terry was done.

'The thing is,' Terry said, 'I've had an idea. I need to talk to someone about it, and – well, you're the only person who won't tell me I'm mad.'

'Sure, go ahead.'

Terry marshalled her thoughts. 'Look. The police now accept that Hugh was probably attacked by a man, right? And the circumstances of the attack are, if not kinky, then certainly sexually suggestive.'

'Agreed.'

'And at the moment there's no evidence that Hugh was anything but heterosexual, which suggests some sort of random attacker. A male rapist, in other words.'

'Sure. The police were on the news today, saying something like that.'

Terry cut across her impatiently. 'On first reading, these letters seem to confirm that. Assuming that Hugh wrote them, of course, though that seems a reasonable assumption given that they were in his room. But look at it this way. What sort of man writes his fantasies from the point of view of a woman?'

'You're saying he might have been gay after all?'

'Well – it's a thought, isn't it? Imaginatively, he's putting himself in the shoes of the woman. Not that she's wearing shoes, or anything else, in most of these.'

There was a pause while Allison took in what she was saying. 'I'm no expert, but don't thousands of men write letters like these? Come to that, no-one suggests that a novelist is gay just because he writes from the point of view of a female character.'

'Sure, but now look at the content of the letters. If you think of the writer as a closet homosexual, it all falls into place. The one about the car, for example.' Terry picked it up as she spoke. 'Don't think of it as a piece of pornography for a moment, just think of it as a text. What's it about? Crime and punishment. The narrator is a criminal: he's caught by the police and what happens next is a sort of retribution. What's his crime? "For some time now I've been fantasizing about being screwed by another man." That can be read two ways, can't it? Said by a woman, it means someone who isn't her partner, but said by a man, it means he's been fantasizing about homosexuality.'

'Hmm,' Allison said thoughtfully.

'But he can't help it, he's just doing what comes naturally – when we first see him he's enjoying the sun, becoming free, unshackling the restrictive bonds of society. "I let my hair out so it caught the wind, and what with one thing and another I found myself going faster and faster." But society catches up with him: the speeding car – for which read the fantasy – is brought to a sudden halt on the hard shoulder.'

'Go on. I'm not saying I agree, but it's interesting.'

'He's pretending to be a woman, because that makes the letter acceptable for publication, but also because it's about his feminine side. A beautiful woman in a sports car: the female hidden inside the ultra-masculine machine. A metaphor for the feminine side of him, hidden inside his everyday, masculine persona.'

'But isn't that a bit obvious? You'll be saying the car's a phallic symbol next.'

'Well, why not? Just because it's a cliché doesn't mean it isn't true. Look, he's driving along. He's got the top down: for which read, he's opening up. Going faster and faster – the speed a kind of symbol for the ecstasy he's feeling. But of course, he's breaking the rules. So society sends the real men to stop him.

'But this is a fantasy, right? In this special wonderland, he does a deal with them. Suddenly everyone's happy – they take off their belts, the place where a policeman keeps his gun, and they divest themselves of their uniforms, the mark of their authority. They start to speed again, chasing the bad guy – the bad guy is someone else now, not the narrator. Sex has made him innocent again. Of course, he knows it isn't really true: the car is going "impossibly fast"; it's all a dream. But he doesn't care. He's in some special place where men don't compete any more. They take turns. They even share him with the robber – good and bad coming together in a moment of synthesis. "He's delighted because he knows he's going to prison where there'll only be homosexuals." That's the logic of the subconscious mind: bad men go to prison, prison is full of homosexuals, therefore homosexuals are bad men.'

'Hmm. And the car gets in on the act too: the last screw is on the bonnet.'

'Exactly. There might even be an unconscious pun there – a bonnet is a piece of feminine clothing, isn't it? Anyway, the fantasy has to come to an end. His speeding ticket – his ticket to wonderland – is torn up. Sperm dribbles onto the leather seats – living cells becoming dead cells. And a movement of withdrawal, of disengagement after engagement.'

There was a long silence. 'So what do you think?' she demanded. 'Am I mad?'

'Not mad. It's clever, but is it a bit far-fetched? And what about all the other letters? How do they fit in?'

Terry picked up the next letter. It was the one about the foursome having sex in the hotel.

'Group sex. Well, that's potentially pretty bisexual, isn't it? And don't forget, it's a story about *pretending*. The receptionist thinks they're married when they're not: perhaps on the subconscious level she's not really even a she.'

'That's interesting. There's a psychologist here who wrote something about pretence in sexual fantasy recently. It was quite well received.'

'Here in Oxford? Maybe we could talk to him.'

'It's a woman, actually. Professor Byres. She's at the Faculty, although our paths don't cross much. This is certainly more her field than mine.' She laughed. 'Rats haven't got round to sex crime yet.'

'Could you ask her?'

'Certainly. But haven't you forgotten something? According to the letters, and other people you've spoken to, Hugh was having an affair with this Carla woman. Why's he doing that if he's really gay?'

Terry thought for a moment. 'I don't know,' she admitted. She looked at the last letter again. *Hugh came round with a screwdriver and slid underneath my bed on his back, looking for the problem. 'I've found it,' he said at last. 'It just needs a screw.' Well, I knew I was never going to get another chance as good as this, so I took a deep breath and said, 'I know just how it feels.' Then I got down on top of him and started stroking his cock through his trousers. Of course, trapped underneath the bed he couldn't move, and pretty soon I had his trousers undone and his lovely cock buried deep in my mouth.*

Into the long silence Allison suddenly chuckled and said, 'Boy, this is some weird conversation we're having, isn't it?'

'This one doesn't fit,' Terry conceded. She read the passage out loud, and added, 'It's almost, I don't know, tongue in cheek. Like a bawdy postcard or something.'

'From what you say, her tongue's got somewhere a bit more adventurous than her cheek.'

224

'I need to show them to your professor,' Terry decided. 'Can you fix it up tomorrow?'

'What about the police?'

'I'm having a slight personal disagreement with the man in charge. I don't want to go to him till I'm certain.'

'OK. I'll phone Ann Byres in the morning. If you're sure that's what you want.'

'Oh yes. I'm involved now, whether I like it or not. And Ali? Thanks for listening to this. I'm sorry I phoned so late.'

'Any time,' the other woman said, yawning. She hung up. Terry sat on for a while, the phone still pressed to her ear, listening to the distant clicks and bumps of late-night static, the fax-songs and the sparrow thumps, the chatter of distant satellites and the faint ghostly echoes of other people's conversations. Then she too put down the phone and went to bed.

Fourteen

The next morning Terry went to the Osney shop and photocopied the letters under the watchful eye of Mrs Evans, the owner. Putting the clippings face down on the copier meant leaving the photos on the reverse side buttocks up, but although the other woman was making furtive attempts to see what she was doing, Terry managed to distract her by ordering a particularly complicated combination of provisions she didn't really need. Presumably her own reputation as a rampant lesbian had spread round Osney like wildfire: the last thing she needed was to be labelled a rampant lesbian with a penchant for pornography.

'And you'd better take down the notice,' Terry said, pointing to the card she'd put up in the window about the cat and kittens.

'Found the owner, did you?'

Terry nodded – it was the truth, sort of, and now wasn't the time to go into details. Mrs Evans folded her arms and said seriously, 'I used to get ever so much pleasure from my old pussy, but ever since Don and I started trying for a family, I'm not allowed so much as to stroke her.' Perhaps it was the unexpected juxtaposition with the material Terry was copying – she wasn't usually susceptible to cheap *double entendres* – that made her snort with laughter.

'Why's that?' she asked, to cover her embarrassment.

'Because of – what's it called? Toxic something or other. It can make you miscarry.'

A word drifted up from the depths of Terry's memory. 'Toxoplasmosis?'

'That's the one. Ever so dangerous it is if you've got my blood group. The doctor said a lot of people don't realize.'

'Oh shit,' Terry said with considerable feeling.

'Ooh, I'm sorry. You're not . . . ?'

'No, I'm not. But I know someone who is, and she wanted one of the kittens. I'd better check. And I suppose you'd better leave the card up for another week, just in case.'

'That'll be another pound, then, please dear.'

As she got home Terry phoned the woman who'd wanted the kitten. Sure enough, she'd never had a cat before and had never heard of toxoplasmosis. 'I think it depends on your blood group,' Terry explained.

'I'm A Negative. Do you think that could be a problem?'

'I'm not sure. But I suppose you'd better ask your

midwife. And if there's any sort of problem, I could always keep the kitten for you until after the birth.'

'Can Polly still come and visit her?'

'Er – of course.' The little girl had called in a couple of times with friends to show them her cat. They'd been no trouble, but Terry wasn't used to having children round the place and she was always relieved when they went. She felt a bit guilty about it, and wondered if she was turning into a crusty old spinster.

The two surviving kittens had developed little teeth as sharp as hypodermics now and, having destroyed their box, were gradually venturing further and further from their lair under the stairs. A variety of objects had become theirs, by virtue of being partially destroyed by them: the cotton reels from her sewing box, her rolling pin, one half of a pair of Russell and Bromley court shoes. She'd turned an old box file into a temporary cat litter for their mother, but the kittens chewed that as well and Fuller's Earth was starting to slop onto the floor whenever the cat used it. Terry knew that she had to accept that this makeshift state of affairs was effectively permanent. She was stuck with the mother and the unsold kitten now.

She was aware that her reluctance to keep them was more psychological than anything else. For five years now she'd been rootless, moving house as easily as she moved bank accounts, changing her life whenever she'd needed to. She'd tried marriage, and when it hadn't worked out she'd tried a different sexuality altogether. She'd extricated herself from her affair with Mo in a way that could, she supposed, be construed as ruthless. She'd only done what had to be done, of course, but she hadn't exactly pussyfooted around. To coin a phrase. She smiled wryly to herself.

She went and pulled the mother out of its box and put it in her lap, stroking its black and white fur thoughtfully.

'Pussy Galore,' she said aloud, 'I'm going to give you a new name. From now on, you will be known as Guinness. Because you've got white ears and Guinness is what you look like.'

'And you,' she said to the second kitten, 'can be Half-pint.'

As her favourite poet had said, the naming of cats is a serious matter.

The phone rang. It was Allison.

'I've talked to Ann Byres,' she said. 'She'd be happy to have a look at the letters.'

'You will come too, won't you?'

'Of course, if you want me to. I'll come and pick you up in the car.'

'Should we be handling these?' Allison asked when Terry handed her the sheaf of papers.

'They're copies. I've kept the originals safe, just in case we spill coffee on these. But there certainly won't be anything physical like fingerprints. I'd covered them with rubble before I realized they might be important.'

Allison drove her to north Oxford, pulling up outside a lovely Edwardian town house next to the playground of a junior school. A lanky and startlingly beautiful girl of about fifteen opened the door to them, said, 'This is for Mum, right?' and showed them into a study.

A large oil painting of a nude hung above the glowing computer on the desk. The walls were lined with books, and the sound of children's play drifted through the open window. It was, Terry decided, exactly what she wanted her own workroom to be like.

Ann Byres was a glamorous professor, to say the least, a tiny woman in her forties with jet-black hair that was liberally streaked with grey.

'Pleased to meet you,' she said, coming in and shaking Terry's hand. 'Sit down, please. If you want coffee, we might be able to bribe Jessica into making us some.'

'Make it yourself, I'm watching *Neighbours*,' the girl's voice shouted from upstairs.

Ann smiled. 'Believe me, sexual deviants are a doddle compared with teenagers,' she said cheerfully. 'Can I get you something?'

Terry volunteered to make the coffee while Ann read the letters, and was directed down to the basement. This was the garden level, and the kitchen ran the whole length of the house, dominated by an enormous refectory table. Academic papers and journals of psychology were strewn all down one side, mixed up with *Smash Hits* and *Sky Magazine*. A life-size pull-out poster of some floppy-haired pop idol, his chest bare, hung on the back of the door.

By the time she came back Ann was finishing the last letter, her lips pursed in concentration. She put it down, her eyes still thoughtful. 'A very interesting little collection,' she said. 'Now, what do you want to ask me?'

Terry took a deep breath. 'Mainly, I suppose we want to know what you can tell us about the person who wrote them. For example, can you tell which bits might be real and which bits are fantasy? And if they were written by a man or a woman? I had an idea these sorts of letters are usually written by men, even if they've got a woman's name to them.'

'Mmm. You're not a psychologist?'

'No. I'm doing a doctorate in detective fiction at St Mary's.'

'OK. Well, I'll try and keep this non-technical. The answer is, as it always is, that I can't tell you anything for certain. All I can do is give you some probabilities, yes?'

Allison nodded, evidently expecting this.

'What you have to understand first of all is that this is a bit different from what I normally do. I've published some studies about sexual fantasies, but those were sexual fantasies that I came across in patient therapy.

'The reason that's important is that the same fantasy, written by two different people, could mean two completely different things. For example, it's been shown that rapists and serial killers typically fantasize about domination and power. But fantasies like that don't *necessarily* signal that the fantasizer is a sex killer. In fact, they can signal the reverse: quite meek, mild-mannered people also fantasize about power, because that's a psychological need that isn't being met in their everyday lives. The difference between the two is what psychologists call integration. In the case of the serial killer, the fantasies are never fully integrated into their personalities, so they're unsatisfied until they move on to the real thing. Do you follow what I'm saying?'

Terry nodded. 'I think so . . . is there any way you can tell from the fantasy itself whether the writer has an integrated personality?'

Professor Byres looked doubtful. 'Sometimes. If the fantasy is obviously left unresolved in some way, or if it seems obsessive, it might point to a non-integrated personality. But I don't think you could ever say for certain.

'The issue of who wrote the letters is a bit more complicated. I'm sure that a lot of the letters from so-called women in those magazines are written by men, but that's not because nice girls don't have sexual fantasies. It's got more to do with the readership profile of the individual magazine. If it *is* the work of a man, it might mean that the subject of the fantasy is something that matters deeply to him – it's so important, or so forbidden, that he has to approach it indirectly through the medium of a surrogate. It's as if the imaginative leap required to see the fantasy through someone else's eyes makes the whole thing more possible.'

'In literature it's called the suspension of disbelief,' Terry said.

Ann nodded and went on, 'As for the question about what's real and what's made up, it's not a distinction that has much meaning for a psychologist. A fantasy can be based on a real event, if it touches something important in an individual's sexual needs: equally, a made-up fantasy can be much more important than a person's real experiences. You've got to understand that fantasies aren't lies. They're private myths, if you like; a psychodrama that the subconscious writes for itself. Where the material for the fantasy comes from is irrelevant.'

'But we fantasize about what we subconsciously want,' Terry suggested.

'Not necessarily – if you'll forgive me saying so, that's a classic layman's assumption. A lot of fantasy is to do with permission, you see. Fantasies are often about breaking taboos, and we have to give ourselves permission to do that. Take the old chestnut about the woman who fantasizes about being raped. It doesn't mean that she *wants* to be raped. In real life, she'd be totally traumatized by the experience. What it might mean is that she wants sex, but she doesn't want to admit she wants it. She invents a rapist who makes her have sex, and the conflict is resolved. So the fact that so many of these letters are about coercion—'

'Hang on,' Terry interrupted. 'I'm not with you there. What coercion? There's no rape here.'

'No, but look how often *events* conspire to force the author into sex. Being caught speeding and needing to avoid a ticket. Being paired with the wrong partner by the hotel receptionist. Being trapped under a bed. These are all permission strategies – it wasn't me, I had no choice.'

'OK. Sorry, go on.'

'I was just going to say that, statistically speaking, these sorts of fantasies suggest a woman writer. In general, men don't have such a problem admitting what they want.'

Terry absorbed the implications. 'You're saying Carla – the woman – wrote them after all?'

Ann Byres smiled. 'No, I'm saying it's statistically likely. As I said before, it's also possible that they're written by a man who is atypical – who has unusual difficulty in admitting to himself what his real desires are.'

'Terry had an interesting idea about these letters,' Allison said, nodding at her friend.

'Oh yes? What was that?'

Terry marshalled her thoughts and explained, as briefly as possible, her theory that Hugh Scott might have been secretly homosexual.

'Mmm. Well, that's very *ingenious*. I have to say it doesn't seem likely to me. But then, working from text is more your field than mine.'

'This stuff about sharing a woman between two men seemed as if it could be a sign of latent homosexuality to me,' Terry said.

The professor shook her head impatiently. 'That's another layman's way of looking at it, I'm afraid. The word "latent" doesn't really have any meaning to a psychologist. We'd see it more in terms of competition. In our culture, men compete with their father for their mother's love, and they compete with their closest friends for the most sexually desirable women. By sharing a woman with another man, they're opting out of the competition. In the same way that a game of football integrates competitive urges that might otherwise become dangerous, sharing your woman is a way of letting the stronger male take her temporarily, with no real harm done. And this being fantasy, you can have your cake and eat it too.' She picked up the pile of letters and shuffled through it. 'Take the four-in-a-bed scene in the hotel. The whole thing is described as a competition, which the prime male ultimately wins. However, even though he's won, there's this rather touching scene where they all kiss their own partners as they fuck someone else.' The Anglo-Saxon word seemed to hang in the air: it was with a slight shock that Terry remembered they were discussing soft porn, rather than analysing some nineteenth-century novel.

'This letter's absolutely classic of its type, by the way,' Professor Byres said, tapping it with an elegant finger. 'First of all, look how *many* permission elements there are. There's all this reassurance about how wonderful their sex life is: the implication is clearly that sex with another couple won't threaten their marriage, it'll actually help it. And then it's initiated by this other couple, who are described as sexually adventurous: it's their suggestion, so it's their responsibility, not the writer's.

'Then there's the whole thing about the mistaken identities I mentioned. The hotel receptionist gets the couples mixed up; I suppose you could say that

235

since he runs the hotel, the mini-society in which they find themselves, he also represents society as a whole, saying that it's OK. But notice how the narrator figure, despite having started the letter by saying she used to fantasize about this sort of situation the whole time, is actually the last one of the group to go along with the idea of shared sex. She's been cast as a nice girl, you see, and nice girls don't do this sort of thing.

'However, once she's given in, and *her* permission is fully established, look how the emphasis suddenly switches from her to her husband. 'Brian would have stopped . . . but Mary had a good hold of him." "I ran it round and round my lips like a gigantic lipstick – it always drives Brian wild when I do that . . . when I looked over I saw that my husband . . ." et cetera et cetera. The competition game has started by now, but see what's happened to the permission motif. This nice girl who was holding back is now the one who's doing all the initiating: "Two can play at this game . . . we beat the others to it by just a few seconds . . . Mary and I did a striptease for her husband. . . We threw ourselves back on the bed . . ." And what's Brian doing now? He's wandering around fixing drinks, like a nervous host. Even when they all start screwing, Brian's underneath, passive, being ridden by Mary.'

'What conclusion do you draw from that?' Terry asked.

'Well, up to this point the letter could have been written by either a man or a woman. But this second bit is certainly more consistent with the

236

writer being male. First of all he has to persuade himself that his wife really would take part in a scenario like the one he's describing. Then he has to persuade himself that the competition game is being initiated by her, not by him, because the taboo is too dangerous for him to handle directly. She's now the one giving *him* the permission.'

'When you say "his wife",' Terry said slowly, 'does that mean you think Brian wrote this letter? I thought it must have been Hugh – someone else, that is.'

Ann looked thoughtful. 'It's hard to say. I think it was *probably* written by "Brian", yes. Though I suppose that might not be the real-life Brian, but someone who simply identified with Brian for the purposes of this fantasy.'

'And the competition, as you call it, is a draw,' Terry said. 'Does that mean this is what you'd call an unresolved fantasy?'

'Ah. It's declared a draw – what was the phrase? An 'honourable draw', that's right – but as I said, in every other sense the Brian character wins. It's the other bloke's manhood which we see shrivelling in the final close-up, as it were. As far as Brian's subconscious is concerned, he's come out best. He gets to go home with his wife, and he's back in full masculine control – at the end of the letter he's busy making arrangements for future encounters.'

Terry thought for a moment. 'I'm confused,' she admitted. 'I found these letters in a room that previously belonged to a student. I think he may have had a fling with the woman who lives next door, who is really called Carla and really does have a husband called Brian, so I assumed that he wrote these himself as a way of bragging about his conquest. Could that be possible?'

'Possible, yes. He may have felt so in awe of the prime male whose wife he'd stolen that he needed to write a fantasy about the wife being shared voluntarily. But I have to say I don't think it's likely.'

Terry leant forward. 'Assuming that these letters were written by the same person, and that it is a man, what could you deduce about him?'

Ann turned her head out of the window and thought for a long time. The sound of the television drifted down from upstairs, and a door closed.

'He's in a long-term relationship,' she said at last. 'Hence the consistent theme of sharing his partner. But by the same token, it's not a relationship which satisfies him sexually. He's overtly masculine, and insecure about his masculinity – he's probably either a womanizer or at the very least a serial flirt. He has a strong need for attention. He is ruthlessly competitive. He's probably manipulative, a player of mind games. He is a control freak who has the urge, and probably the ability, to make others do what he wants. He has a strong exhibitionist streak; well, we know that from the fact that he published the letters in the first place, but it's also there in the way he fantasizes about public places and group situations. He idealizes women – hence the strong sense that he needs his partner's permission to indulge in these fantasies. He may well be quite attractive to women but he will still behave child-ishly around them to get their attention. And deep down, probably very well hidden beneath his enthusiasm and his idealism, he is full of sexual anxiety.'

'Could he be bisexual? Could that be the source of his anxiety?'

'I'm not sure – I'd have to think about that.'

'And if it wasn't a man, but a woman? If they were written by Carla?'

Ann shook her head. 'No. I just can't see it myself. Not unless there's something I can't figure out.'

It's Brian, Terry thought. Not Hugh, not Carla, but Brian. Brian wrote the letters, and somehow Hugh had got hold of them. She wondered if she would find any iambic pentameters when she looked through the letters again.

A thought suddenly struck her. 'Can I see the one about the foursome for a moment?' she asked. Ann handed her the photocopy, and she scanned it quickly.

'Of course,' she breathed.

'What is it?'

'When I first read this, there was something that bothered me, but I couldn't work out what. I've just realized what it was. "He thrust his enormous cock right into my still unravished pussy." That's a quote from Keats – well, not the enormous cock bit, obviously. But the opening line of Keats's "Ode on a Grecian Urn" is "Thou still unravished bride of quietness".'

239

'I'm sorry, I'm not with you,' Professor Byres said.

'Me neither,' Allison agreed.

'Don't worry, it's a long story. But it's all starting to make some kind of sense. Please, go on. What about the last letter?'

'Oh yes. The one where she seduces the young next-door neighbour. This strikes me as being very different to the others.'

'Why's that?'

'There's no permission element. I'd say that's curious, wouldn't you? "His attention was rather flattering, and I soon resolved to get him into bed." After all that protesting our narrator does in all the other letters, here she just comes straight out and decides to have sex. The only person who's got any degree of permission is the young man himself, since he's trapped under the bed.'

'What can you say about that?' Allison asked.

'I'm not sure, to be honest. It's oddly . . . I don't know, impersonal. The other letters are quite well constructed as pieces of narrative – well, again, that's more your area than mine. Whereas this one seems more functional.'

'That's certainly true,' Terry agreed. 'This is the only one without any real characterization, if that's not too upmarket a word for what we're discussing.'

'Could it be two different writers?' Allison suggested.

'Or the same writer, but at a later date?' Terry added.

240

'That's possible,' Ann conceded. 'But it's something else too . . . I know: it's hostility. That's what I'm getting here. Whoever wrote this is working off some fairly serious anger.'

Terry felt the hairs on her forearms rise. 'The young man described in that letter was murdered. The police aren't sure, but the motive was probably sexual – he'd had a soldering iron forced into his arse.'

'Oh, I *see*. The Osney murder.'

'Could the man who wrote this . . .' She stopped, aware of the enormity of what she was saying. 'Could the husband – the man who you say wrote these – be hostile enough to rape and even kill another man? Given all the insecurities in the other letters? Could he be the person the police are looking for?'

'I really shouldn't speculate—'

'*Please*,' Terry begged. 'This individual lives next door to me.'

Professor Byres sighed. 'It's possible. Of course it's possible.'

'And don't forget, the letters were written for publication,' Terry said. She had got to her feet and was pacing up and down nervously. 'You said yourself, it's the context that matters. He knew they'd never print the things he really fantasizes about.'

'Again, we can speculate all we like,' Ann Byres said nervously. 'I'm not sure that the police would—'

'You said earlier', Terry interrupted, 'that it was all to do with integration. How much a person's fantasies are integrated into their personalities. How integrated are these fantasies?'

Ann Byres spread her hands. 'I simply can't tell from so little material.' She paused. 'There is a kind of fantasy I haven't talked about, that you get with some kinds of personality disorders, particularly very well-disguised ones.'

'Yes?'

'At this very deepest level, fantasies aren't just about sex. They can be about the invisible made visible. Do you see what I mean? A fantasy that isn't just a record of a sexual event, real or imagined; but the event itself, so that the fantasy becomes a kind of ritual, a ceremony of the subconscious.'

'I'm afraid you've lost *me*,' Allison confessed.

'Then let me put it another way ... most fantasies exist to excite the fantasizer. That's their sole purpose: anything we learn about their creator we learn simply because it's impossible to do anything without revealing something of yourself. But fantasy can fulfil another purpose too. It can be like an insomniac pacing up and down or a schizophrenic obsessively stroking the same piece of cloth: something compulsive and uncontrollable, the psychological equivalent of scratching an itch. If it becomes attached to a particular object we might call it a fetish.'

'In Japanese drama,' Terry said, 'someone who dies in the midst of a great passion, like a love affair, is condemned to come back and relive their last hours over and over again, until all the passion is gone.'

Ann nodded. 'Or think of Lady Macbeth, obsessively reliving the murder of Duncan. That's the kind of fantasy I'm talking about. But it doesn't have to be about anything as grisly as a murder. It could be something that is outwardly completely normal.' She glanced down at the papers by her feet. 'Or something that could be published in a top shelf magazine.'

'You're saying that these letters could be proof of a disturbed mind?'

'No. No, they're proof of nothing.' She hesitated. 'I'm just saying that they *could* have been written by someone with a mind like that. A possibility, not a probability.'

'Why? What's making you think this?'

'They're all about different things. But if you look at them as a whole, they're all about the same thing. The thrill of the group orgy, driving at speed and being stopped by the police, trapping the boy next door – they're all about *transgression*, and the sex that follows is both a punishment for wrongdoing and a reward for being so brave.'

Terry pushed her hair back impatiently. 'What does that mean?'

'I don't know. This is uncharted territory, I'm afraid. Or rather, uncharted by psychology. You people have been thinking about it for centuries.' She nodded at Terry. 'Why does an artist return to a particular theme time and time again? Why does a poet write about the same love affair for a lifetime? The disordered personality and the creative mind are two points on the same spectrum.'

In the adjoining room *Neighbours* was coming to an end. Terry heard the incessant, catchy jingle of its theme tune, before the television was abruptly switched off. She thought of the man in the house next to her own, the man who might or might not be a rapist and a killer, and she shuddered.

Fifteen

Clive Trevelyan and Helen Sayers got off the late bus and kissed in the shadow of the bus shelter. It was Helen who pulled away first. 'Get off, you,' she said fondly. 'We're late enough as it is.'

'Plenty of time for a goodnight kiss, though,' Clive protested.

She put her arm round his waist and squeezed as they started the short walk up Headington Road to the roundabout. 'Course there is. When we get home. That's why I'm in a hurry. I promised them I'd be back by eleven.'

'Your dad still be up, then?'

'You know what he's like. He likes to make sure I'm back in one piece. Don't worry, Mum'll keep him inside.'

'Hey – not quite in one piece anymore, eh? Not after last weekend.'

'Shut up about that!'

'Why? It's the truth, isn't it?'

Helen turned her nose up. 'I suppose you've been telling all your mates.'

'I have not!' He laughed. 'They thought we were doing it months ago.'

'Why did they think that then, Clive Trevelyan?'

'Search me,' he said innocently. She tutted indignantly and he laughed again as he took her hand to guide her over the ring road. A lorry came up from the Banbury direction and took the roundabout too fast, so they had to run for it.

'I'm so sick of that Derek, though,' she said as they linked up again on the other side.

'Pizzaface? What's he been saying now?'

'He gave me another bollocking tonight, just because you were hanging around.'

'I'm allowed to wait for my girlfriend, aren't I?'

'He reckons it looks bad to the customers.'

'Well, sod him,' Clive said hotly. 'If he gives you any more trouble, I'll have him.'

They were walking through the Bayswater estate now: Helen's house was just up the road. 'Say goodnight here if you like,' she suggested, 'then you definitely won't run into Dad.'

'I'm walking you home,' he insisted. 'You can't be too careful.'

'It's only just there.' But she allowed him to go on. When they got to her house and he drew her into the shadow of the garage she sighed happily and turned her face up to his.

Fifteen minutes later she finally pulled away from him, carefully straightening her blouse. She rang the bell. 'You ought to get a key,' he said, 'you're eighteen aren't you?'

'Dad likes to be woken up,' she whispered as the door was opened.

'Evening, Mr Sayers. Goodnight Helen,' Clive said formally, kissing her on the cheek.

'Goodnight, Clive.' Tom watched as the young lad walked down the path. 'Bit late, aren't you?' he said to his daughter, loud enough for Clive to hear. It didn't do any harm to remind him that you were keeping an eye on the time. In Tom's book, eleven o'clock meant eleven and no later.

Clive walked slowly down the hill in the direction of his own house. At this point the ring road ran adjacent to the residential streets, and traffic occasionally roared past him. Used to it, he paid it no attention. His mind was on Helen. She'd got him so aroused, though of course they hadn't been able to finish it outside her parents' house. Next weekend, he decided, he'd take her out for a walk. Just the two of them, into the countryside. And he'd get himself some more rubbers from the machine in the pub.

It was only when he reached the relative quiet of the recreation ground that he realized there were footsteps a little way behind him. He didn't look round: there was always a chance it might be someone looking for trouble. You got all sorts after the pubs closed.

He was walking across grass now: both his own footsteps and the other's were silent. Not knowing where the other person was unnerved him a little, and he quickened his pace, glancing quickly to left and right.

He almost ran into him, and sucked in his breath with an audible gasp.

The man standing in front of him, blocking his way, was dressed in dark clothes. Three points caught the light: the two eyepieces of a pair of swimming goggles protruding through the black balaclava and the silver sheen of the Stanley knife in his hand.

'Where are you off to, bitch?' the figure said conversationally.

He thinks I'm a bird, Clive thought with a strange sense of relief. 'I'm going home,' he said.

The man laughed. 'No, you're not. You're out looking for it, aren't you?' He paused, and raised the knife. 'You fucking little tart.'

Clive turned and ran. He was young and fit, and his body was full of adrenaline. But as he ran he heard the other right beside him, still saying things, filthy things. And then a hand grabbed his neck and he crashed to the ground, his fists flailing.

Richard Girdler read the letters slowly, occasionally stopping to refer back to something on a previous page. 'Does it upset you, finding this?' he asked.

'I've read de Sade in the original. This is hardly in the same league, is it?' Seeing his look of surprise, Terry sighed. 'Just because I'm a woman doesn't mean I've never been exposed to pornography, Inspector.'

He thought for a moment. 'But even if this isn't particularly violent pornography, isn't the current thinking that all pornography incites violence towards women? That pornography is violence, in fact, because it reinforces sexual contempt? I seem to remember reading something by Andrea Dworkin to that effect.'

Her surprise obviously showed, because he added mildly, 'Just because I'm a policeman doesn't mean I've never been exposed to feminist thinking, Doctor.'

'Touché,' she admitted. 'Though I'm not actually a doctor until I've finished my thesis. Anyway, I'm not sure about that theory. I know lesbians who read *Playboy*. And some critics think that de Sade was the most radical philosopher of his time.'

'Not much philosophy here.' He indicated the sheaf of papers. 'Where's this quote from Keats you were telling me about?'

She showed him.

He looked doubtful. 'It's not a great deal to go on.'

'It's also riddled with iambic pentameters. Listen.' She picked up the first letter and read out a few lines in a sing-song voice, emphasizing the rhythm.

'The shiny red paintwork had been polished,
I let my hair out so it caught the wind.

Or how about this:

While Brian soon confessed he'd love to see
another man ravish me while he watched.

Those are just two examples, but there are plenty more.'

'I've read better pornography in the *News of the World*,' he commented.

'And I've read better poetry in undergraduate magazines. The point is, they were written by someone who is quite possibly disturbed, who unconsciously uses blank verse, who also wrote that letter to you after Hugh's death, and who in the opinion of one of Oxford's most eminent psychologists is probably Brian Eden.'

'Fair enough. But I have to tell you that I still know for sure that he couldn't have murdered Hugh Scott.'

'Your famous alibi.'

'Partly.' He didn't elaborate. 'By the way, you're famous now too.' He opened the copy of the *Oxford Chronicle* he'd brought with him and showed her the article. 'Rich students wreck hotel' was the headline. It was illustrated with several photographs, of which one showed Terry sprawling on the ground, her legs akimbo, while Giles threw up in front of her. There was a small caption underneath: *For one couple it was all too much*.

'Oh, bollocks,' Terry said. 'I was just getting out of the way.' She threw the paper in the bin.

They went to bed, but Richard didn't seem to want to make love. Terry wondered if it was the effect of reading the letters or simple tiredness. She was just going to sleep when she realized with a start that this, and not their previous sexual encounters, was the emotional milestone, the act of commitment. When you were comfortable going to bed with someone and not making love, you were turning into lovers. She examined the thought uneasily until she fell asleep.

It was almost 6 a.m. when his pager went off.

Sixteen

'He was found in this playground, about five hundred yards from his own front door,' Girdler explained, tapping the wall map with a broken snooker cue which doubled as his office swagger stick, wall pointer and also came in useful for banging on subordinates' desks. 'Multiple stab wounds with a sharp knife. The autopsy can't be fitted in until later today, but it looks like a razor blade or a Stanley.'

'Who found him, sir?' one of the constables asked.

'Milkman,' Girdler said economically. 'It was quite a warm night and there's post-mortem hypostasis, but it looks as if there was some tearing of his clothes. One lipstick mark, the same colour as was used on Hugh Scott, on his face. Obviously, we'll be looking to the autopsy to tell us whether or not he was raped. Everyone with me so far?'

The bleary-eyed DCs nodded.

'Adams, could you remind us what hypostasis is?'

The constable looked surprised. 'Er, no, sir.'

'Blood draining under the influence of gravity to the lowest point of the body. If you don't know something in future, ask.' Girdler looked at his team in exasperation. Two murder investigations under way, and he was lumbered with two detective constables just out of the woodentops. Jeffries and Adams were barely older than the boy who'd died: not stupid necessarily, but terminally gormless. Had he himself ever been this fresh faced and wet behind the ears? In the canteen, he'd heard, the two of them had been dubbed Tweedledum and Tweedledumber.

'The body's been identified already, by his mum. Name is Clive Trevelyan: IC1 male, eighteen years old. Mum expected him home from a date with his girlfriend around midnight, but she didn't panic when he didn't show because she thought he'd be with his mates. She phoned the local station an hour ago when a neighbour told her the milkman had found a body. A WPC's bringing her here. I'll be taking her statement and the statement of the girlfriend, Helen Sayer. DS Warner will divvy the others up between you, then it's straight on to house-to-house. We'll be doing that together with Uniform: if they find anything at all, take a statement and let me know. Uniform will also be helping us make a fingertip search of the playground. That's being organized as we speak. Jeffries and Adams, you attend the post-mortem, write me an interim report. I want to know the pathologist's best estimate of time and cause, whether or not he was sexually abused, what's in his stomach. All right?' There was a general nodding. 'Get going then. Bill, you spare me a moment.'

As the room emptied his sergeant, Bill Warner, came over.

'They've not put the A-team on this one, Bill.'

'Thanks very much, sir,' Warner said evenly. In appearance he was not unlike Girdler himself, big and solid. They'd worked together off and on for four years, though these days resources were so tight that a DS generally handled an investigation on his own. Warner's main headache at the moment was car crime; the youth of Oxford had recently discovered the joys of hotting, or doing stunts in stolen high-performance cars.

'I don't include you, obviously. But keep a bloody good eye on those two kids for me, will you? If we can give them a crash course in coppering, they might just be some use to us.'

'Ah. I was wondering why it took two of them to cover the autopsy.'

'Precisely. There's nothing like the sight of someone else's breakfast to sort the men out from the boys. Particularly when it's still in someone else's stomach.'

Jane Hughes stuck her head round the door. 'Mr and Mrs Trevelyan are here, sir. Interview room five.'

'Let battle commence,' Girdler said, picking up his papers.

*　　*　　*

Five hours later, Jeffries was feeling distinctly queasy.

He, Adams and a forensic photographer were in a basement room in the John Radcliffe hospital, watching Professor El-Shamir dismember the body of Clive Trevelyan.

'Your first post-mortem?' he had said as he tied a thin polythene apron over his shirt and tie. Jeffries wondered how he'd known to ask, and decided Warner must have phoned to let him know.

'Watch and learn, gentlemen. Ask questions if you wish but not while I'm talking: I'll be using a Dictaphone and we don't want to confuse the typist.'

'Ready for the patient, sir?' a porter had enquired, sticking his head round the door.

'Certainly. Wheel him in. They get so used to thinking of them as patients', he explained to the two policemen, 'that it doesn't occur to them to use the word "corpse".'

Now, watching the professor at work, Jeffries was trying hard not to think of the figure on the table as anything other than a lifeless and impersonal piece of meat. Occasionally he would find himself remembering that only twelve hours ago this body had been on a date with its girlfriend, walking around just like Jeffries himself, but he managed to stop himself thinking those thoughts too often.

His first sight of the corpse hadn't been too bad. It was wheeled in on a trolley, still covered in white linen, then slid longways onto a grooved stainless steel platform not unlike the draining board on Jeffries' sink at home. An assistant placed a small wooden pillow under the neck, its scrubbed oak strangely medieval-looking in contrast to the gleaming steel. Then he wheeled over a second trolley, this one dominated by a huge pair of hanging scales like a fishmonger's. Jeffries tried not to imagine what this was going to be for.

The assistant removed the linen and began to cut away the clothes. Jeffries was surprised by how unlike a living person, a sleeper for example, the cadaver was. Quite apart from the preposterousness of the wounds in the neck and chest, the skin had a pale candle-coloured quality to it, like a very bad waxwork. The fingernails, he noticed, were dead white. On the top of the body only the penis was dark, though the calves and feet were blotchy and almost black in places. That would be the draining effect Girdler had been talking about, he guessed. A single gold earring stud glinted in the boy's left ear. The face had been slashed with flame red lipstick.

El-Shamir was reciting some information into the Dictaphone, bending down and squinting at one of the ankles. Jeffries realized that something had been written on the skin there, a message scrawled in biro. Adams had seen it too: the two policemen moved towards it simultaneously.

El-Shamir waved them away. 'Relax gentlemen, it isn't a clue. It's a substitute toe tag. When the government decides that we're not to have any more money for labels the technicians have to write the details on the body. Now, if I might continue . . . ?'

Chastened, they stood back.

The professor measured the neck wound, speaking the details into the recorder. 'Take a look at these other wounds,' he called over his shoulder. 'See?' There were a number of smaller cuts and grazes just above the main wound, under the left ear. 'He was holding him from behind, I'd say, like this.' He demonstrated on Adams, locking his arm round his neck. 'Hand me that scalpel,' he instructed. Jeffries put it into his hand. The blade rested just behind Adams' jaw. 'He got those when he was struggling,' the professor announced with satisfaction. He released the constable, and turning back to the body made a small incision in the throat.

'Notice how easily it cuts? There's not much rigor mortis,' he said, glancing in their direction. 'That helps us determine the time of death. Rigor generally sets in after about four hours: less after a very violent struggle such as we're probably seeing here, because exertion depletes the body of oxygen. We'll get a more accurate picture, though, when the forensic lab takes a look at his eyes.'

'Why's that, sir?' Jeffries asked.

'Flies,' the professor said. 'They're attracted by the death scent within hours, if the body's in the open. The lab will be able to look at the eggs laid on the cornea and work backwards from there.' He leant over and peered into one of the eyes. 'Your man's wearing contact lenses, but they should be able to do something.' That was when Jeffries had begun to feel nauseous. Glancing across at Adams, he saw that he had gone almost as pale as the corpse.

El-Shamir examined the outside of the body, muttering occasionally into his Dictaphone. He carefully cleaned under the fingernails, swabbed each wound, and finally took a swab from the penis before summoning the assistant to help turn the corpse over. Clive's head lolled and hit the wooden pillow with an audible thunk that made Jeffries wince. A small stream of creamy vomit bubbled through the white lips onto the floor. El-Shamir ignored it, and began searching meticulously through the hair of the scalp for minor wounds, like a chimp checking for nits. After a while he moved down the body and began to examine the anus. Jeffries looked away, embarrassed.

'There's nothing to suggest that he was raped, anyway. But I'll send the swabs to the lab for them to check.'

Jeffries hadn't been prepared for the sheer physicality of what happened next. Together, the pathologist and his assistant turned Clive back over and cut all the way down to the navel. It was hard work, as if they were battling with the body and it was resisting them. Despite the wooden pillow, the head waggled from side to side, and at one point one of the legs slipped sideways off the table. Both men were breathing heavily by the time they were done. Then they made two smaller cuts, branching off their main opening like the two branches of the peace symbol, down towards each of the hips.

Like a man pulling yards of stockings out of a tightly packed drawer, El-Shamir plunged his hands into the opening and impatiently hauled yard after yard of intestine out of the stomach cavity. The assistant opened up a section of it and carefully bagged a sample of the contents. Despite the air-conditioning, the stench was now almost unbearable. Then – it was a conjuring trick, Jeffries thought dazedly, it wasn't real – El-Shamir reached right into the chest with both arms, hugging something to him, and with a shock Jeffries saw Clive's lips move, forming a word helplessly. He must have twitched himself, because the pathologist grunted and said, 'Air in the oesophagus,' pulled, and the whole lung assembly came away in his hands, complete with the tube leading up to the Adam's apple.

He suddenly remembered the report they were meant to be writing. 'Can you tell us what he ate last?' he asked.

'Looked like pizza,' the professor said. 'Mind you, a lot of things look like pizza after a few hours. Want to see for yourself?'

Jeffries glanced at Adams, who shook his head emphatically.

Blood was dripping continually from every orifice now, the sound of it drumming into the stainless sink below the table filling the room. Everything was a blur of impressions – the extraordinary colours of the body's insides, colour-coded and packed together, as neat and as complex as the engine of a Japanese car; the assistant weighing livers, kidneys and heart, taking a thin slice of each for the lab to analyse, finally weighing the slices themselves, waiting for the scales to settle with pursed lips like a butcher trying to judge whether he'd given too little or too much; and then the work on the head and face.

A wedge-shaped incision was made across the top of the head so that for a moment Clive appeared to be wearing a hairband, then the skin was pulled forward to expose the bone, effectively scalping him. The assistant fastened a clamp to the top of the skull, tightened it, and produced a small, square-ended saw. After a few moments, he removed the brain from its eggcup and weighed it.

When the internal work was over, and the assistant was sewing Clive up again with rough, huge stitches like the webbing of a tent, El-Shamir suddenly seemed to notice their silence. 'Well, gentlemen, are you finding this useful?' he enquired.

Jeffries tried to remember the instructions Girdler had given them. 'Can you say how he died yet, sir?'

'Well, that's straightforward enough. Asphyxiation as the result of having his windpipe severed. There's some pleural fluid I'm having checked that'll confirm it, but I don't think it'll throw up any major surprises. Most of this', he waved at the lumps of organ behind him, 'is just because we have to check everything, or you lot get clobbered when it comes to court. A defence lawyer could claim he'd had a heart attack, for example.' He sighed. 'As it happens, he's the healthiest young man I've cut up in years.'

The assistant was replacing the top of the skull and fastening it in place by wrapping a bandage round it. The earring stud still glinted in Clive's left lobe. He removed it with a pair of tweezers, sealing it in an evidence bag. Then something seemed to catch his attention. 'Excuse me, sir,' he said. 'Could you have a look?'

'What is it?'

'There's a hair wrapped round this,' he said. Jeffries realized that until this point the assistant hadn't spoken. He had a soft Oxfordshire accent.

'Probably one of his own.' El-Shamir bent down to have a look, and whistled. Holding the bag up to the light, he said, 'That's not a hair. I'd say it's a clothing fibre. Dark coloured wool, at a guess.'

'If they were standing the way you showed me,' Jeffries suggested eagerly, 'their ears would have been almost touching. If the attacker was wearing something over his head, the earring might have got tangled in it.'

'It's possible, yes. But don't get carried away. He might simply have caught it in his own pullover when he put it on. Anyway, the labs will be able to tell us more.'

Neither of the constables spoke much in the car on the way back to the station. They found the incident room empty. Girdler had left instructions that Adams was to write up the report, while Jeffries was to join him in the interview with Helen Sayers.

He got there just as the DI was taking the girl through the events of the previous evening. Jane

Hughes was sitting at the back of the room, and he slipped into the chair beside her. After what he had just witnessed, it was a shock to hear this pretty young woman talking about Clive as a living person, to imagine the lips that he had seen bubbling with gore pressed against hers, the lungs that he had seen pulled out of their cavity grunting words of passion. He realized he was sweating. Although Girdler was taking notes himself, he got out his notebook and tried to concentrate on what she was saying.

'We met up at work,' she was explaining patiently. No doubt she'd been through it all a dozen times already. She looked tired, he thought, and suddenly realized that he was exhausted himself. 'That's the American Pizza Company in Gloucester Green. Mr Bennet – that's the manager – got a bit upset because Clive came to wait for me. He didn't like him moping around, he said. I told Clive later not to do it again.' Suddenly, without warning, she started to cry. Jeffries looked away. Girdler said nothing, simply waited while she sobbed, nodding to himself as if agreeing with something she was saying. Eventually she composed herself. 'Is it true he was interfered with?' she asked.

To Jeffries' surprise Girdler turned to him. 'Is it?' he said quietly.

For a moment he was unsure whether or not he was supposed to lie. 'It looks unlikely,' he said. 'We won't know for sure until we get the lab results back.'

'I spoke to his brothers,' she said bitterly. 'They said the fact that he was dead proved that he'd fought them off, whoever did it. They said he must have been killed because he resisted.'

Remembering the pathologist's reconstruction, Jeffries nodded. 'We think he did.'

'Well I wish he bloody hadn't,' she said hotly. 'I wish he'd done bloody anything to stay alive.'

Girdler put his hand on her arm. 'I have to ask you this, Helen.'

'What?'

'Was Clive homosexual at all? Had he ever mentioned any homosexual experiences?'

'No. Course he wasn't queer. He fancied me, didn't he?' Her eyes filled with tears again. Jeffries had a sudden flashback to El-Shamir standing over the corpse, peering at its eyes and wondering aloud about flies' eggs. He had worn contact lenses and an earring, and there had been rough skin on the heels of his feet, where his trainers had rubbed him.

'How long had you been going out together?'

''Bout two months.'

'Did you have sex?' Jeffries was embarrassed by the insensitivity of Girdler's questioning. But he recognized that they were questions that had to be asked.

Helen seemed to recognize it too. Setting her face, she said, 'Once. Just the once,' and folded her hands in her lap.

'It was . . . normal?'

'I wouldn't know any different,' she said. 'Since

263

you must know, he was the first. But yes, it was normal.'

'Did you have sex last night?'

'No.'

'Would Clive have become aroused at all last night?' When she didn't answer immediately he explained, 'We'll need to know for the forensic tests.'

'I guess so,' she said at last.

'Had he ever mentioned anyone making unwanted sexual advances? A man or a woman?'

Helen shook her head. Girdler raised his hands, a gesture of frustration. 'Is there anything at all you can think of that might help us?' he asked. 'Anyone who bore him a grudge, anyone you might have seen on the bus who was behaving oddly, anything out of the usual?'

Helen shrugged. 'Nothing. It was just an ordinary night.'

'How about at work? Did you serve anyone out of the ordinary? Did anyone approach Clive while he was waiting for you?'

'I can't remember,' she wailed, her shoulders heaving.

'OK. Let's go back over your journey home. Can you remember any of the other passengers on the bus?'

'Not really. We were kissing.'

'Was the bus full?'

'I don't think so.' She thought for a moment. 'Maybe half-full. I remember there was an Asian guy, an old bloke, who was looking at us.'

264

'All right. After we've finished here the WPC will take you to try and get an identikit likeness. You know what that is?' She nodded. 'What about when you got off? Did anyone else get off with you?'

'A few people. They were behind us, though. I didn't get a look at any of them.'

'Anyone waiting at the bus stop?'

'I'm not sure. No, maybe there was someone. I remember because Clive and me stopped for a kiss by the bus shelter, and the bus didn't move off straight away. I just felt a bit embarrassed, because they'd all be looking at us through the windows, you know? And it was like the driver was waiting to see whether whoever it was was going to get on, or if he was waiting for a different bus. Loads of buses use that stop, see, it's on the coach route to London.' She sighed. 'I remember hearing the hissing noise as the doors closed, and thinking maybe now we'll get some peace and quiet.'

'You're sure you didn't see anyone yourself?'

Helen shook her head.

'You couldn't say if it was definitely a man, for example?'

'I told you,' she said, 'I didn't see anything.'

'How about the lorry you had to run across the ring road to avoid? Can you remember anything about that?'

'It was just a lorry.' She screwed up her face, trying to remember. 'Maybe a Sainsbury's lorry.'

'Sainsbury's? Can you be sure of that?'

'Pretty sure. It was definitely a supermarket. Yeah

– I remember now, Clive said he'd nearly had us for the meat section.'

Girdler patiently took Helen through every step of her journey home, then pushed his chair back. 'You've been remarkably helpful and brave, Helen. If anything else occurs to you, will you let us know?'

She nodded. 'Then thank you for coming in,' he said. 'If you go with Jane here to try and do some work on the Asian man you saw, I'll bring you your statement to sign in a few minutes.' He stood up. 'I really am most sorry.' Jeffries wondered if he should tell him about the hair on the earring before she left, but thought better of it. He stood up too. As Helen left, ushered out by Jane Hughes, she stopped by Jeffries and wrinkled her nose.

'Christ,' she said, 'you smell terrible. What have you been doing?' With a sudden flash of panic Jeffries realized he must still smell of formaldehyde and offal, wondered whether she could possibly know that she was smelling her lover's guts on him. 'Eating chips,' he blurted out. Luckily she wasn't really interested. He managed a nod as she left the room, then sat down hastily.

'Well done,' Girdler said when he told him about the post-mortem. 'That was about as much as we could have hoped for. Now get yourself over to Cowley. I've fixed up for you to see the personnel officer at the Rover works. Woman by the name of Lindsay Sayers, no relation. Get whatever you can out of her, and then wander down onto the shop floor, see if you can have a chat with some of Clive's workmates.'

He was being kept busy, Jeffries realized. The way he felt at the moment, that was fine by him. He took one of the unmarked cars from the pool, a blue Escort, and reversed it out of its parking bay. There was a banging on the roof: he looked round to see Girdler standing by his passenger window. He leaned across and wound it down.

'Better take one of the Metros,' his boss said, indicating the row of marked police cars behind him. 'Sounds daft, but they're touchy about people who drive the opposition.'

Cursing himself for being a fool, Jeffries swapped cars. If only he'd been more alert, the same thought would have occurred to him. It was just the sort of detail, he knew, which made the difference between an average CID copper and a good one.

The Rover car works straddled the ring road by the Cowley roundabout, its crumbling clock tower and ugly squares of Fifties buildings almost like a grotesque parody of one of Oxford's ancient colleges. Indeed, while the university tended to get all the attention, this sprawling complex of workshops, paintshops, bodyshops and assembly lines actually had more employees than the university had undergraduates. If the colleges were Oxford's brain, this was its brawn; in economic terms, it was a moot point as to which was the more important. It was ironic, Jeffries thought to himself as he showed his police ID to the security guard at the main gate, that while the university produced graduates entitled to call themselves Master of Arts, one of the cars produced up here had been called, with unconscious competitiveness, the Maestro.

Lindsay Sayers was unable to tell him much. Clearly she had never met Trevelyan, and though she made sympathetic noises about his death it wasn't going to spoil her day. A bustling blonde in her early thirties in a sharply tailored female version of the executive suit, Jeffries found himself wondering how anyone so clearly uninterested in people ever became interested in Personnel. He learnt how much Clive earned, and how often he had been absent, but little else.

After she had shown him out he asked a secretary to direct him to the part of the assembly line where Clive had worked. She took him there herself, evidently glad of the break. This was a different world again. All around him the unpainted carcasses of cars were slowly being stuffed with their constituent parts: an engine dropping in here, a seat assembly being added there. It was, he thought, a bit like the post-mortem room in reverse, assembly after disassembly.

He watched for a while, fascinated, until a foreman came over to see what he wanted. The foreman, a Sikh, took him over to meet the man who had worked alongside Clive, putting in windscreens; rather than stop the line, the foreman took over while the two of them went outside, looking for a quiet place to talk. The man introduced himself as Eddie Bowman.

'Have you heard the news about Clive?' Jeffries asked.

'I've heard he was killed. Bloody terrible, isn't it? They're saying he was killed by a queer, if that's right. I don't know, he didn't seem the type to me.'

'He wasn't,' Jeffries said. 'It looks – well, it's too early to be sure, but it looks as if it was a random attack.'

'They say queers can tell, though, don't they? Takes one to know one.' Eddie shook his head. 'Someone must have thought he was, any road. He used to wear a ring in his ear, you know. I told him it looked daft, like a bloody pirate. Or a bloody queer.'

'How long had you worked with him?'

'Not long. Maybe a year. Seemed a good enough lad. I know his brothers too, of course. There's a bunch of that family in the works.'

'Do you know where I'd find any of them?'

'Well, I doubt they'll be here. They'll be at home, won't they? With their mother. I'll tell you what, though. You better catch him before they do. They stick together, Trevelyans, and they won't like this.'

At the end of the day Girdler called a case conference to pull together what they'd learned. It was depressingly little. The house-to-house had thrown up a man who claimed to have seen a gang of marauding transvestites armed with knives. Another report seemed to suggest that it was simply three girls returning from a Saturday night out at the Apollo. The driver of the bus Clive and Helen had taken from the city centre couldn't remember them, let alone anyone else who might have got off with them. Nor could he remember waiting at the bus stop to see whether anyone else was getting on.

'The truth is, we've got nothing,' Girdler told the assembled policemen.

'Any links to the Scott case, sir?' Bill Warner enquired.

'Only the lipstick. And it's hard to see what other links there might be. Trevelyan and Scott were a different class, lived in very different parts of Oxford, had different friends – it doesn't seem likely their paths would ever have crossed.'

A uniformed PC brought in a fax and handed it to Girdler, who scanned it in silence. 'This is interesting,' he said at last. 'They've traced the lorry driver who nearly ran Clive and Helen over. He's in Wolverhampton now, but the local boys have faxed a statement through. According to him, he reckons there were three people in the group that ran across the road: two who went for it, and one who hung back till he'd gone past. He can't give us a description – he only saw them for a moment and his attention was on the two he was trying not to hit. But he thinks the third person might have been wearing a tracksuit.' He picked up his snooker cue and thwacked it into his hand rhythmically while he thought for a moment. 'We're going to have to do it all again tomorrow,' he said finally. 'All the house-to-house, all the same people, all the same questions. Adams and Jeffries, you get up to Wolverhampton tonight. See if you can get anything else out of this driver.'

*   *   *

After a day spent working at her desk, Terry's head was aching. She decided to take her latest reading matter, a nineteenth-century detective story by Wilkie Collins called *The Law and the Lady*, down to the riverside pub and read in the fresh air with a drink beside her.

Ordering her pint of lager at the bar, however, she heard a familiar voice behind her.

'Ah, Terry. Out on the town? I'm afraid you won't find much action in here. The singles bars are all in the city centre.'

She turned. Brian Eden, his sidekick Dorling Van Glught and a third man she didn't know were standing at one end of the bar, watching her.

'Please, come and join us,' Brian Eden continued.

'No, thank you,' she said curtly, picking up her drink and moving away. She hadn't seen him since the night of the High Table, but after what Ann Byres had said about the authorship of the letters, she was in no mood to talk to him.

She found herself a table in the tiny beer garden and sat down, but to her annoyance she realized that Brian had followed her outside and was pulling up a chair.

'You're very standoffish,' he murmured.

She stared at him. He seemed so ordinary, she thought, so harmless in every way except for his obvious and heavyhanded flirtatiousness. Could he really be the monster she imagined him to be? 'I have work to do,' she said, indicating the book.

He plucked it out of her hands and examined it thoughtfully. 'Hmm. Written in 1875. That's just a little after my own period, but still fascinating, I'm sure. Still, all work and no play. At least let's have a drink together.'

She got up, intending to go.

'Oh, come on,' he said impatiently. 'You can't still be cross about that little flirtation the other night? I'll tell you what. I will entirely refrain from flirting for the duration of our conversation.' He reached up with his hand to pull her down and she stiffened involuntarily, terrified, as his hand made contact. 'Why . . . ?' he began; then, seeing her distress, 'You're frightened of me, aren't you?'

She didn't reply.

He glanced at the book again and nodded thoughtfully. 'Oh, I see. This isn't about the other night at all, is it? This is something else. You think I might have had something to do with Hugh Scott's death. You've been reading too much of this stuff, Terry. Do I really look like a homosexual psychopath to you? And if I was, would I behave towards *you* the way I do?'

She pulled away, breaking his grip. For once, she was at a loss for words. Abandoning the full pint, but snatching up the book, she beat a hasty retreat back to number fifty-seven.

Seventeen

'E. M. Forster once said that a good book contains a beginning, a muddle and an end. He was referring particularly to comic fiction like his own, of course, in which the muddle is usually a matter of miscommunication in human relationships. In detective fiction, it might be fairer to say that there's a beginning, a *riddle* and an end: there is always a point at which the hero, having set out on his quest, is forced to confront a conundrum or mystery that seems to defy logical analysis. Perhaps the murder has taken place inside a locked room: perhaps the prime suspect has turned up in the library with his own throat cut. There *is* always a logical explanation for these events, but it may not be an explanation that can be reached through logic alone.'

Terry paused and drank some more water. There were even fewer students than last week, some of her listeners having evidently decided that detective fiction wasn't the easy option it had promised to be. She could hardly blame them. She'd distributed a reading list at the end of the previous week's session: even though she'd kept it as short as possible, the subject demanded that any serious student read at least twenty novels in the space of a few weeks. Suddenly, she knew, lyric poetry would seem a remarkably attractive option.

'Earlier this term I drew an analogy between detectives and the knights of the medieval quest,' she continued. 'But both detective fiction and Romance quests also have something in common with another oral tradition, the fairy story. When the detective is confronted by his locked-room mystery, or the knight is enslaved by a magic girdle, they are in much the same position as the fairy-tale prince who has to answer the witches' riddle before he can rescue his princess.

'Let's take a look at a classic detective story in detail. Last week you should all have read *A Scandal in Bohemia*, the first story in *The Adventures of Sherlock Holmes*.' Terry picked up her own copy and read the opening lines out loud: ' "To Sherlock Holmes she is always *the* woman. I have seldom heard him mention her under any other name. In his eyes she eclipses and predominates the whole of her sex. It was not that he felt any emotion akin to love for Irene Adler. All emotions, and that one particularly, were abhorrent to his cold, precise, but admirably balanced mind. He was, I take it, the most perfect reasoning and observing machine that the world has seen: but, as a lover, he would have placed himself in a false position." Comments, anyone?'

There was a long, agonizing silence. Terry searched desperately for someone she could pick on, and found Emily Harris, the girl who'd come round with flowers for Hugh. 'Emily?' she said.

Turning bright red, Emily said, 'Doesn't sound very admirably balanced to me.'

It got the ball rolling, Emily being easier to argue with than Terry.

'Or perhaps Watson is showing us his ambivalence towards Holmes,' suggested a spotty-faced boy in a rugger shirt. 'That phrase "a false position" makes him sound like a bank clerk. And why does Watson say "I take it"? It's almost as if he's saying "according to himself".'

'Hold on,' Terry said. 'Be careful not to project our own values on to Conan Doyle. We don't approve of people who deny their emotions today, but in 1900 it was still considered, if not normal, then at least heroic. The point is, does setting Holmes and Irene Adler up as polar opposites like this simply get the plot off to a good start, or is there an element of the myth being re-enacted here? I'm just wondering if you can compare Holmes's attitude to women – and Irene is certainly being set up to represent her sex, she's *the* woman, after all – to the attitude of the medieval knights, Gawain for example.'

More blank looks. One or two of them shrugged, and turned their attention back to their notes.

'OK,' Terry said grimly. 'Let's go through it together, shall we?'

*   *   *

At the end of her hour, as most of the students were wearily packing up their backpacks and carrier bags and Terry was putting away her notes, a boy approached the lectern. It was Edward, the boy who had taken up Hugh's place on the course. She smiled at him encouragingly.

'That was really brilliant,' he said.

'Thank you,' Terry said, somewhat surprised. He hadn't been particularly forthcoming during the lecture itself: perhaps, she thought, he was nervous about speaking in front of the others since he was technically a year behind them.

'I'm thinking of making detective fiction one of my special subjects, and I was wondering . . . Do you think I could have some extra tutorials?' he asked.

'Sure, I'd be happy to,' she said. It was more work for her, but the extra money would come in useful: the university rate for a one-to-one tutorial was a lot higher than for lecturing. 'When d'you want to start?'

'It'll have to be later in the term,' Edward said. 'I'm doing the Romantics with Brian Eden at the moment, so I'm pretty busy.'

Terry sighed. 'Well, when you've finished with Dr Eden, why don't you drop me a note,' she said acidly. He looked slightly taken aback – reasonably enough: it wasn't his fault that he was being taught by the foremost Romanticist in the university, after all.

'I'll do that,' he said, backing away.

276

*　　*　　*

That afternoon, working at home, Terry heard a knock and found an Interflora van at the door, delivering a huge bunch of red roses.

'Oh, they're beautiful,' she said, taking them into her arms.

'There's a note inside,' the driver said. 'No name, though. We just wrote the message down for him.'

She knew instinctively, even before she got them inside and took the wrapping off, that they were from Brian Eden and not from Richard. When she saw the note she knew she'd been right.

'O Rose, thou art sick,' was all it said.

She called Richard at the police station.

'Hello,' he said cautiously when he heard her voice.

'What about dinner tonight?' she suggested.

'That sounds great. I've been up to my eyes in a murder, but I'll be free about nine.'

'And Richard?'

'Yes?'

'You didn't send me any flowers today, did you?'

'No,' he said, puzzled. 'Should I have done?'

She laughed. 'Do you want to know what I like about you?'

'Um. Yes, please.'

'It's the fact that you're not the least little bit romantic.'

'Sorry?'

'Don't worry, I'll explain when we meet.'

'Baxendale wants to see you,' Jane Hughes said,

sticking her head round Girdler's door. 'He said it was urgent.'

Girdler groaned. A summons from the Chief Superintendent rarely meant a pat on the back. 'Tell him I'll be five minutes. No, on second thoughts I'd better get it over with.'

He walked through the Incident Room, still busy although it was nearly eight o'clock. Most of the legwork now revolved around tracing and painstakingly eliminating from both murders those who were around but unlikely to have done it: the partygoers in the case of Hugh Scott, the other people on the bus in the case of Clive Trevelyan.

He trudged up the stairs to the Chief Super's palatial offices, knocked on the closed door, and waited for an answer. Despite recent attempts to modernize the police by bringing in management consultants to talk about such new concepts as 'open-door management' and 'teamworking', his boss was one of the old school. He wore his uniform whenever possible: all but the most senior of his officers were expected to knock and then, on entering, to salute him before speaking.

'You wanted to see me, sir.'

'Ah, Richard. I wanted an update on the two murders. Any news from the labs?'

'Some. We found a wool fibre on Trevelyan that probably came from a military-style balaclava – there are a couple of army surplus shops in the city centre that sell them, mostly to students and sportsmen. However, we have asked the military police up at Headington Camp if there are any squaddies we should be talking to. There was also some flesh under his fingernails that's being DNA tested – we'll have the results of that in a couple of days, though we'll need to check that it isn't the girlfriend's.'

'Is the link between the two murders definite yet?'

'Only because of the lipstick. Same composition, same colour: Forensic are ninety-nine per cent certain it's the same one.'

'And you're confident the motive was sexual?'

'As confident as we can be about anything, sir,' Girdler said, unsure where this was leading.

'But you're nowhere near to a result?'

'No, sir.'

'Right.' The Chief Super nodded. 'I've been asked what we're doing about this, and this is what I've said. CID and Uniformed are going to do a trawl of all the gay hidey-holes, pubs, clubs, cottages, houses of known offenders, the lot. See if we can flush this pervert out.'

'With respect, sir, I'm not sure that's the best option,' Girdler said cautiously. 'Our best hope of finding a link between the murders is finding someone who's been raped by this character and survived. If we come down hard on the homosexual community, they're extremely unlikely to want to help us.'

'They haven't helped much so far, have they?' Baxendale nodded again. 'They've had their chance. We can't afford to let this one drag on any longer.' He gave a short bark of laughter. 'No pun intended.'

*   *   *

The next day, lunchtime drinkers at the Scotch Pony would be startled to see a posse of half-a-dozen uniformed policemen charging in amongst the regulars, most of whom were just having a quiet pint and a bite to eat. The toilets would be inspected for cottagers, and then the whole lot would be bussed back to the police station, their names and addresses checked against records of previous offences. The same thing would happen that night at the Coven, much to the amusement of its mainly straight student clientele. All over Oxford those with previous arrests for any kind of homosexual activity would be brought in for questioning, though the backlog was soon so great that interviews were having to be arranged for two or even three days ahead.

Arrests were made, though only for under-age drinking.

They went to a Lebanese restaurant in Jericho and drank red wine with spicy food.

'How do you know the flowers are from Eden?' he asked curiously. He hadn't meant to get her on to the subject of her neighbour, but he was too tired to tread diplomatically. 'Anyone could have chosen that quotation.'

'It's from a famous poem by Blake. Another of the Romantic poets,' Terry added, seeing his look of incomprehension.

' "O Rose, thou art sick!
The invisible worm
That flies in the night,
In the howling storm

Has found out thy bed
Of crimson joy:
And his dark secret love
Does thy life destroy," '

she quoted.

'What does it mean, then?'

She thought for a moment before replying. 'There are two interpretations most people go for,' she said at last. 'The first, traditional one is that it's about losing your sexual innocence.'

'It is?' he said, astonished.

'The rose was a traditional symbol of purity and maidenhood,' she explained. 'The worm – well, that's the penis, flying in the night because it comes in a sort of moral darkness. So the bed of crimson joy is the virgin's bed in which the maidenhood is lost, stained crimson with her blood.'

'Blimey.' He shook his head. 'I'd love to see what you lot could do with a Taking Without Owner's Consent statement.'

She ignored him, and went on, 'On the other hand, a very famous critic quite recently suggested that it means exactly the opposite, and that's the view most people take nowadays. This guy's followers – his rather wonderful name is Wolf Mankowitz, by the way – see it as a poem about how sex is joyful until it's corrupted by social guilt.

281

So the rose represents the female sexual organ, and the invisible worm is the guilt and secrecy that the world sends to feed on it; hence the "dark secret love".'

'Double blimey. It's like two lawyers arguing over two different versions of the facts, isn't it?'

'I suppose it is, yes.'

'But why does it have to mean either of those? Why can't it just be a poem about a worm eating a rose? It still makes perfect sense that way. The worm can be invisible because it's very small, not because it's a metaphysical symbol. The bed of crimson joy could just be a flower bed. Worms eat roses – they love them, hence dark secret love, and the rose dies, so no more crimson joy.'

'Case closed,' she teased. 'The baffling murder of the rose solved at last: the worm dunnit.'

'Well, why not?' he demanded. 'Why does everything have to be a, a sort of parable that means something else?'

'Actually, you're dead right,' Terry agreed. 'I think people like Blake just write about the conflicts they see around them. It's us academics who need it to mean something.'

'This Blake character. Is he the one who said something like, It's better to commit murder than to bottle it up inside you?'

'That's right. "Sooner murder an infant in its cradle, than nurse unacted desires." However did you come across that?'

He shrugged. 'Some student I nicked once vandalizing a fountain quoted it at me. I think I asked him where this Blake lived. Said I was going to go and nick him too, for incitement.'

'Mmm. Blake may not have meant murder literally, anyway. You can read it two ways again. Either, it is better to go out and kill someone than to bottle up the unacted desire to murder, which is the obvious meaning, *or*, don't nurse unacted desires – murder them in their infancy, before they become really dangerous.'

'Meanings again,' he sighed.

'Oh, this is nothing,' she assured him. 'You should see what the structuralists can make of a line like that.'

'So why did Eden send the roses to you? What does *he* mean by it?'

She thought for a moment. 'There's a meaning, and there's a message,' she said at last. 'In this context – the context of our relationship – the meaning of the poem becomes, don't let this stupid idea that I'm a murderer eat away at you like the invisible worm ate the rose. The worm is suspicion, I'm the rose, you see.'

'And the message?'

'Oh, that's easy. He's saying he wants to go to bed with me.'

Putting his credit card on the bill, Richard waved at the waiter. 'In that case,' he said, 'O rose, thou art sick.'

But bed that night was not a great joy, crimson or otherwise. Richard was willing but tired, and altogether too eager to please after their argument.

After a while his endlessly circling fingers on her clitoris felt more like someone trying to rub cream into a spot than any transports of delight. Aware that he was only holding back until she came, she debated whether or not to fake an orgasm. But she hated doing that – even if her head told her it was just the simplest solution, it always felt like subjugation. So she struggled on, groaning and grinding, until he finally gave up and came to a rather weedy orgasm.

He was asleep within moments, still inside her. After a while she eased off him, unplugging a flow of now-cold come onto her thighs and bush.

Getting up to wash, she became aware of moaning sounds coming from the garden. It was a warm night, and the window was open. Her first thought was that someone had heard them, and was deliberately mimicking the noises she'd made herself. Angrily, she strode to the gap in the curtains and looked through it.

The night was dark but there was enough moonlight for her to be able to see the two figures in the Edens' garden, their naked bodies gleaming like phosphorescence against the dark grass. The woman's red hair and very white skin identified her immediately as Carla. She was sitting astride the man, obscuring him with her body, so that it was a moment before Terry could identify him as Brian. As she watched, Carla arched her back with a soft cry and pushed herself against him: a moment later he came, his hips lifting and locking as he shuddered and jerked inside her. Terry turned away quickly, wondering if they had seen her. Then, fury getting the better of embarrassment, she went back, slammed the window down noisily and locked it.

Eighteen

Terry spent the morning working through her reading list. But she found it impossible to concentrate. Her thoughts kept straying back to Brian Eden.

Having struggled through a particularly turgid passage in *Myth and Metaphor: Conan Doyle and the New Atheism*, she came to a decision. Shutting the book with a snap, she picked up Eden's book on Shelley.

On the inside back cover was a smirking photograph of the author and a brief publisher's blurb. 'Dr Eden is a renowned critic and commentator on the Romantic period. A Fellow of St Mary's, Oxford, he is the author of two volumes of poetry: *Bulldozers* (1978) and *The Big Hymn* (1981), as well as numerous works of criticism and television documentaries . . .'

That was interesting. She hadn't been aware that he was a poet himself. A failed one, presumably, given the long gap since he'd last published.

Precocious, of course, to have published so young, but that was hardly surprising. She wondered what had happened to make him dry up.

Flicking idly through the book, looking for anything that might relate to the authorship of the letters, she came upon a passage describing Shelley's death. Her brow furrowed, and then she read it again with mounting interest.

Brian quoted at length a description by Edward Trelawny, one of Shelley's friends. Shelley had drowned when his boat was hit by a storm off the coast of Italy. Trelawny and Byron had supervised the disposal of the body:

Three white wands had been stuck in the sand to mark the Poet's grave, but as they were at some distance from each other, we had to cut a trench thirty yards in length, in the line of the sticks, to ascertain the exact spot, and it was nearly an hour before we came upon the grave.

We were startled and drawn together by a dull hollow sound that followed the blow of a mattock; the iron had struck a skull, and the body was soon uncovered. Lime had been strewn on it; this, or decomposition, had the effect of staining it a dark and ghastly indigo colour. Byron asked me to preserve the skull for him; but remembering that he had formerly used one as a drinking cup, I was determined Shelley's should not be so profaned . . . The corpse was removed entire into the furnace. I had taken the precaution of having more and larger pieces of timber, in consequence of my experience of the day before of the difficulty of consuming a corpse in the open air with our apparatus. After the fire was well kindled we repeated the ceremony of the previous day; and more wine was poured over Shelley's dead body than he had consumed during his life. This with the oil and salt made the yellow flames glisten and quiver. The heat from the sun and fire was so intense that the atmosphere was tremulous and wavy. The corpse fell open and the heart was laid bare. The frontal bone of the skull, where it had been struck with the mattock, fell off; and as the back of the head rested on the red-hot bottom bars of the furnace, the brains literally seethed, bubbled, and boiled as in a cauldron, for a very long time.

Byron could not face this scene, he withdrew to the beach and swam off to the Bolivar. Leigh Hunt remained in the carriage ... the only portions that were not consumed were some fragments of bones, the jaw, and the skull, but what surprised us all, was that the heart remained entire. In snatching this relic from the fiery furnace, my hand was severely burnt; and had anyone seen me do the act I should have been put into quarantine.

Terry shivered as the implications of what she had just read slowly sank in. According to this eyewitness account there was no way anyone could have made a death mask from Shelley's corpse.

But if the mask in Eden's hall wasn't Shelley's, then whose was it? Some other young man in his twenties, with a beautiful girlish face ... God in heaven, could it have come from Hugh Scott? No – too many people would have recognized it. Then it could only be one of Eden's previous victims.

'You don't know there were any previous victims,' she heard Richard's calm, logical voice say inside her head. 'And even if it did turn out to be the death mask of a student, it isn't proof that Eden was responsible for his death.'

'Bullshit,' she said aloud.

'I told you not to worry about Brian Eden being the murderer. He's been thoroughly checked out,' the voice inside her head reminded her.

But you've been wrong so many times, she thought.

Coming to a decision, she kicked *Myth and Metaphor* under the bed. She was going to sort this out once and for all.

Getting out the telephone directory, she found the number of the Birmingham Hyatt, the hotel Girdler said Brian had been staying at on the night of the murder. She asked to be put through to their conference organizer, and after a few minutes of music-box Vivaldi a breezy voice came on the line.

'Birmingham Hyatt, Gillian speaking, how may I help you?' Both name and question were said with an efficient, practised fluency which robbed them of any trace of personality whatsoever.

'It's Theresa Williams here, from Oxford University,' Terry explained, matching her tone to the other woman's. 'I'm writing the report on a conference you held in February, and I just wanted to check some delegates' names with you.'

'Certainly, no problem,' the disembodied voice said helpfully. 'Which conference would that be?'

289

That was more tricky. It would have been something to do with the Romantics, but if she didn't get the title right she'd blow her cover story. Hang on, though: the murder had been on the last day of the academic term, so the date would be in her University Diary. Leafing through it quickly, she said, 'The one on the twenty-third of February.'

'Just let me have a look.' She heard fingers tapping on a keyboard. 'Yes, here it is. Which names were you after?'

'Well – one in particular, really. Brian Eden. I've got one bit of paper here which lists him as Dr Eden, and one as Professor, and I was wondering which title was correct at the time of the conference.'

'Eden. Let's see. No, there's no Eden here.'

Terry felt her skin crawl. 'Are you sure?'

'Oh, sorry. My mistake. Here we are, Eden. Doctor, it says here.'

Terry relaxed. 'Oh, thanks. Um, you've been a great help.'

'I almost missed him then,' the voice explained, 'because I was looking at the list for the day you gave me, the twenty-third, that's all.'

'What do you mean?' Terry asked carefully.

'Well, he obviously wasn't there for the last morning. Quite a few do that, skip the final night and leave after the dinner, if they've got planes to catch or whatever. But he was definitely here for the rest of the conference.'

'What time did the dinner finish that day?'

'One moment, please.' More tapping. 'It was scheduled to finish at eleven thirty.'

'Thanks,' Terry said.

'No problem. Pleased to have helped you.' The voice disconnected.

So Brian wasn't at the conference after eleven thirty. That gave him ample time to catch a train back to Oxford and kill Hugh Scott in the small hours of the morning. He'd have been back even sooner if he'd slipped out of the dinner early.

And if I can destroy Dr Eden's alibi with a simple phone call, Terry thought, what on earth are the police up to?

She sat motionless by the phone, thinking about the obscene letters. If there was an answer to this mystery, she was convinced that it would be reflected somehow in the text, however obscurely hidden or deeply buried.

Clearly, the letters told a story of sorts, though what the story was she couldn't for the moment begin to imagine. It was, she reflected, not unlike trying to puzzle out Shakespeare's sexual relationships from the evidence of the Sonnets, without knowing what order they came in and with the added complication that the author was quite possibly deranged or making the whole thing up.

She had an advantage over Shakespeare's editors, though: her subject was no shadowy Mr W. H., but someone who had lived in this very house.

What I need to do, she decided, is find out more about my main character. But how to go about it?

Coming out of her trance with a start, she suddenly realized that one possible avenue was quite literally staring her in the face. She still hadn't got round to painting the wall on which the phone was mounted: the messages, phone numbers and doodles Hugh and his housemates had scribbled around the instrument were still there, bleached but still legible. She started to work her way through them. 'H call Jamie.' 'Rollo – John called, confirmed tomorrow.' 'Pizza – deliveries – 351982.' 'Mum's B'day Jan 18th.' The notes were dotted with drawings: a love heart with an H and 'Angie – wow!' inside it; cartoon faces; a headless naked woman drawn by someone rather talented; a comic spider sitting in a web of doodles.

Something else caught Terry's eye, a scribble amongst all the other scribbles: 'Everyone – please note my home number for the vac. T. 01472 876549.' T. would have been Trish, the girl Julia Van Glught had told her about. That sounded promising.

She dialled the number, and waited until a horsy-sounding woman answered with a crisp 'Hello?'

'Hello, I'm a friend of your daughter's from Oxford,' Terry said. 'The most recent phone number I've got is for that house in Osney, and I was wondering if you could tell me how I could get hold of her now.'

'Trish has rooms in college at the moment,' her mother said. 'There's a payphone in the hallway. You have to let it ring quite a while, but someone usually comes and answers it in the end. Have you got a pen? I'll give you the number.'

Terry thanked her, dialled the number she'd been given, and waited while it rang and rang. Eventually a boy answered, and promised to look for Trish.

At last she came to the phone, her voice a softer version of her mother's plummy tones. 'Hello? Who is it?'

'You don't know me,' Terry began, 'but I bought the house you used to live in, the house in Osney.'

'Oh yuh?' Trish sounded wary.

'And – I don't really know how to explain this – but I need to talk to someone about Hugh. It's a bit complicated, but I found some stuff that might be his. Could I come round and talk to you, just for half an hour or so?'

'You're not a journalist?'

'No, I'm a post-grad at St Mary's.'

The other girl thought for a moment. 'OK, why not? But don't come here, it's a tip. I'll come to you in about an hour.'

In the meantime, Terry wondered, who else could she talk to? It occurred to her that the local gossips, Sheila Gibson and Julia Van Glught, might be worth a try. Of the two, Julia seemed closer to Brian and Carla, as well as the more indiscreet. She went across and knocked on the Van Glughts' door, hoping to be invited in for coffee.

It was Dorling, not Julia, who answered it. He was wearing a pair of khaki overalls liberally spattered with paint.

'I was looking for your wife,' she said. 'But it's

nothing urgent. I'll come back later.'

'She's asleep,' he said. Terry raised her eyebrows – it was well after noon – but he offered no further explanation. 'Come in anyway. I wanted to talk to you, as it happens.'

'You're sure I'm not disturbing you?' she said, following him inside.

'I'd just put the kettle on. Taking a break from wristing.'

'Wristing?' Terry said cautiously. After all the other activities she'd read about in the letters, it sounded distinctly obscene.

Dorling caught the expression on her face and laughed. 'Colouring an illustration. Boring mechanical work that involves the wrist but not the brain, hence wristing.'

'Oh. I see.'

'My publishers are making me revise my latest book, for the tenth time,' he explained. 'It's only a simple story, but they're never bloody satisfied. They keep wanging on about making the characters darker. I thought they meant darker in colour, but after I'd redrawn them all it turned out they were talking about their sodding motivation. I told them dragons don't have motivation, but they won't bloody listen.' She had followed him through to the kitchen by this time. The large pine table was strewn with drawings. Terry picked one up. It was still only a line drawing, uncoloured pencil on paper. A tiny, bespectacled dragon was cuddling up to a little girl. The drawings were charming, a cross between the crude simplicity of a Walt Disney

294

cartoon and something more detailed. They reminded Terry of the old Guinness advertisements she'd seen hanging in pubs.

'So this is Dickie,' she commented. There were doodles round the edge of the paper, and she twisted her head to examine them.

'My bank manager's best friend,' he agreed drily. He took the drawing from her and shuffled it, along with the others, into a pile. 'I'm paranoid about coffee getting spilt on them,' he apologized.

'I'm not suprised. They're very good.'

'Oh, well,' Dorling shrugged off the compliment. 'It's the stories I really enjoy. Children are very gratifying to write for – they're not in the least bit interested in literature, which makes them much more straightforward as an audience.'

'You don't have any children yourself, though?'

His mouth twisted wryly at the corners. 'Can you really imagine Julia as a mother?'

When she didn't reply, he added, 'Sorry. That was unfair of me. Most of our friends seem to be taking sides, and after a while one forgets there's any such thing as a neutral party.'

Terry felt herself being sidetracked. 'You're going through some . . . problems, I take it?'

He looked surprised. 'You mean you hadn't heard? Most people seem to know every last detail.'

'I try not get involved in local gossip,' she said lamely. 'Being the victim of it myself, to some extent.'

He laughed drily. 'Oh yes. I heard about *that*. Homophobia and other forms of communal hysteria. Lesbianism is next to witchcraft in this place. It's a good thing you weren't living here at the time of the murder, otherwise you'd have been a prime suspect yourself. They were trying to pin it on a woman for a while, you know.'

Of all the reactions to her sexuality she'd encountered amongst her neighbours, this wry detachment was the friendliest. She found herself warming to Dorling.

'Don't tell anyone,' she said, 'but I'm not even a card-carrying lesbian. I had a brief excursion in that direction, a couple of people here found out, and it seems to have got out of hand.'

'Well, I'd certainly better not tell Brian,' he murmured. 'He's fixated on you enough as it is.'

'Hmm,' she said, neither wanting to appear boastful nor to change the subject.

'That's what I wanted to talk to you about, actually,' Dorling said. 'The other day at the pub . . .'

'Yes?'

'What was all that about?'

She trod cautiously. 'He's a good friend of yours, isn't he?'

He snorted. 'Hardly. We were friends once, but after he and Julia had their little fling our friendship cooled somewhat.'

'Ah,' she said.

He shot her an amused glance. 'You didn't even know that? You really haven't been keeping up with the gossip, have you?'

'Apparently not.' She sighed. 'I found some . . .

things Brian had written. I showed them to the police. There's probably nothing in it, but I can't be sure.'

'Let me tell you about Brian,' Dorling said carefully. 'The man is a monster. It took me many years to realize it, but he is the only person I have ever met with an obsessive need to control anybody and everybody who comes into his orbit. He's like a black hole that sucks in light and never lets it out again. If you ever get involved with him in any way at all he will certainly destroy you.' He was still talking with the same light, casual tone, but the intensity in his eyes was unmistakable.

'Do you think he's capable of murder?' Terry asked.

'Yes.' She looked at him and he shrugged. 'Capable of it, I mean. But that's a different question from asking whether he killed Hugh Scott, isn't it? The police interviewed all of us at the time, and pretty gruelling it was too. They didn't pull any punches. One presumes they would have found out if he'd done it.'

'I see,' Terry said. There was a thumping above them; presumably Julia waking from her sleep. 'I'd better go.'

'But you'll keep away from him?' he persisted.

'Of course. The warning was unnecessary, believe me.' And with that he seemed to be satisfied.

Nineteen

Half an hour later Trish came to her house, a pretty
girl with richly conditioned blond hair as soft as her
cashmere sweater, and a string of pearls round her
neck as white as her expensive teeth. She could have
been the product of any one of half-a-dozen expensive girls' boarding schools: the way she pushed
her hair back from her forehead reminded Terry of
Giles Chawker. She wheeled an old black bicycle
into the hallway and leaned it against the wall with
a practised, familiar movement, looked around her
and smiled.

'Gosh. I hardly recognize the place. It looks
almost habitable now.'

'Thank you,' Terry said, liking her at once despite
herself. You could see instantly what sort of life she
had had, and what sort of life she was going to go
on having – a few years in Fulham, working in an
office and escaping to the country at weekends,
then marriage to a banker, a move out to the

country to have kids and Labradors, the boys put down for their father's old school at birth, the girls sent to somewhere that reminded her of her own school – but for all that there was a straightforwardness about her that was instantly attractive. 'Do you want to have a look round?'

'Love to.'

Terry gave her the guided tour. 'This was our room,' Trish explained when she came to Terry's bedroom. Then she saw Guinness and the kittens, curled up on the bed, and gave a shriek of delight. 'Oh, Pussy Galore, you're here. And a mum, too.' Guinness recognized her and lay back to be loved. 'I'm so glad she's safe. I spent ages looking for her when – when it all happened, but she'd just disappeared.'

That made sense, Terry thought: if Guinness had been burnt with a soldering iron on the night of the murder, she'd probably have made herself scarce. By the time she'd plucked up courage to return, the house would have been empty.

'Why you, particularly?' Terry said curiously. 'She was Hugh's cat, wasn't she?'

Trish sat on the bed and lifted Guinness onto her lap to stroke her. 'Sort of. Hugh's cat, but I bought the food, the cat litter, the flea collars, the bowls, I fed her and let her in and out. Hugh liked the idea of having a mascot, but he certainly wasn't going to do any of the work.'

'Just like a man, eh?' Terry said sympathetically. Trish looked at her curiously. That was the wrong approach, Terry realized: no latent feminism here. 'He was a bit lazy?' she suggested.

'Lazy, selfish, irresponsible, anti-social. Hugh was all of those.' She sighed. 'Living together in the first place was another of Hugh's great ideas. Roland, my boyfriend, was a friend of his. It was going to be like a commune without all the hippy bits, you know? We were going to give dinner parties together.'

It was, Terry reflected, an interesting ideology for a commune. 'But it didn't turn out like that?' she guessed.

'It turned out the others couldn't cook. I wouldn't have minded that, but they wouldn't even do the washing up. And it always seemed to be me who went out in the middle of the night because we'd run out of loo roll. Rollo's all right, of course, but the others treated me like a scrubber.'

'Did you have rows?'

'Not really. Hugh got quite frightening if you tried to complain about something. That's why I came today when you phoned. Everyone's always telling me what a great bloke he was, how he could drink this and play that and how everybody liked him. Well, I didn't. I thought he was ghastly, once I got to know him. It's a relief to be able to talk to someone about it, actually. Roland still won't hear a word against him. He thinks it's speaking ill of the dead or something.'

'Was there anything in particular he did that you minded?' Terry asked.

Trish rolled her eyes. 'Where do I start? He got

worse once he realized I wasn't one of his adoring fans, that's for sure. Like, when he came back drunk once and I had a go at him because he'd left the sink full of dirty plates. So he got his, his thing out and pissed on them. That sex maniac friend of his, Giles, was with him, egging him on. They thought it was hilarious.'

'Did he have many girlfriends?'

'Girlfriends?' She snorted. 'Not girlfriends. Scrubbers and one-night stands, mostly. Not that he wasn't good-looking, but he never went out with anyone for more than a few weeks. God, you should have seen some of the tarts who came out of his room at breakfast time.' She gave an embarrassed laugh. 'He had a real scrubber once. Someone who actually worked in the college kitchens. And there was this on-off thing with a don's wife.'

'Carla Eden.'

'Oh, God.' Trish laughed again. 'You know about that.'

'Do you remember a girl called Emily? A first year at St Mary's?'

Trish frowned. 'I don't think so.' She thought for a moment, and added, 'He didn't like the fact that Rollo and I had a steady relationship, that's for sure. Rollo couldn't tell – he thought it was just more horsing around. But he used to do things like barge into our room without knocking, as if I wasn't there. And there was this running joke about how he was going to take me to bed one day.' She rolled her eyes. 'As if I would. You just had to ignore it.' She looked at Terry inquisitively. 'Why do you want to know all this?'

'It's complicated . . . partly, I'm just curious, but it's also because I've been finding things, and I don't like to bother the police with them unless they're actually relevant. I told them about the cat, obviously, but this other stuff is a bit different.'

'What sort of things?'

'Pornography.'

Trish laughed. 'Porn mags? They all used to read porn mags, even Rollo. Hugh had a little stash of them in his bedroom.'

'Didn't you mind?'

She shrugged. 'I've got three older brothers, I know what public schoolboys are like. No point in trying to change them.'

'Could any of them have written pornography themselves? You know, for the letters pages?'

'God, I don't think so. I mean, that's a really,' she struggled to find the word, 'really *naff* thing to do. I don't think any of them took it that seriously.'

'Tell me about the murder,' Terry said, switching tack. 'Were you here when it happened?'

'Oh, yuh. We all were.' The girl looked down at the cat in her lap. 'We had an end-of-term party. It was pretty impromptu – we were just finishing up the booze in the house before we moved out. Anyway, word got around, there weren't any other parties going on that night, and it ended up being quite a crowd.'

'Did any of the neighbours complain about the noise?'

'The old bag next door came round at one point, I think. We turned the stereo down for a few minutes, and then Emma, Giles's girlfriend, turned it back up.'

'The old bag – that was Carla?'

'No, the woman on the other side. Sheila. She was always complaining, and since it was the end of our lease, none of us really cared if she called the police or not.'

'Was that why you were moving out? Because the lease was up?'

Trish nodded. 'We'd all been given places in college. Third years get priority. If it had been Brian or Carla who were complaining, that would have been different, because they could have made things difficult with our tutors. But Brian was away, and Carla came round anyway.'

'Carla was at the party? I hadn't realized.'

'Oh God,' Trish said, 'I'm not sure I was meant to say that. I'd gone to bed by that time.'

'Why's it a secret?' Terry asked, curious.

The other girl looked embarrassed. 'Well, you know about it anyway. It's just . . . Carla and Hugh . . . I think there was a sort of feeling that we shouldn't go around telling journalists about it, that sort of thing.'

'And it wasn't mentioned at the inquest. The college asked the police not to talk about it, so it was all nicely hushed up.' Terry sighed. 'What time did you go to bed?'

'About one, I think. We had to throw some people out of this room, and then we were so

303

pissed we went to sleep straight away.'

'Do you know what happened later?'

'After Hugh . . . after he was found, we all talked about the party, obviously. But I don't think anything happened that had anything to do with the murder.'

That line again, Terry thought: something happened but don't worry, it wasn't relevant. She wondered what the girl wasn't telling her.

'What time did the party finish?'

'About two, I think. You'd have to ask one of the others for an exact time.'

'You mentioned a Giles just now. Was that Giles Chawker who lives across the road?'

Trish nodded.

'So if I wanted to know what happened after you'd gone to bed, I could ask him?'

'Well, you could. But I'm not sure he'd talk to you. Hugh was his oldest friend, you know. They were at school together.' She giggled as the cat took a swipe at her pearls. 'Ow! Sharp claws! Do you like cats?'

'Giles asked me if I'd look after her now,' Terry said, accepting that she wasn't going to get any more out of her, 'but I suppose she's yours really, and the kittens too, if you want her.'

'Oh, I couldn't. This is her home, and you obviously love her.'

When Trish had cycled off, Terry crossed the street and rang Giles Chawker's bell. She wasn't sure exactly what she hoped to learn from him, though it would be interesting to see whether his version of the party differed from Trish's.

No-one came to the door, although she could hear music playing inside. She pushed it open. The hall was full of boxes and carrier bags: someone was either in the process of moving in or moving out. As she stood there a girl of about seventeen came down the stairs carrying another box stuffed with clothes. She didn't look particularly surprised to see her. Terry guessed she'd heard the bell and deliberately ignored it.

'Hello? Is Giles around?' she asked.

The girl dumped the box with the others and turned to go back up the stairs. 'He'll be back later,' she said tersely.

'You're Emma, aren't you? Giles's girlfriend? I saw you at the Catamites' party.'

'Well, you're half right,' the girl said viciously.

'Sorry?'

'Yes, Emma; no, girlfriend. Ex-girlfriend.' Suddenly the brittle exterior cracked and her eyes filled with tears. 'Excuse me,' she sobbed, and fled up the stairs.

Terry followed her, and found her in a bedroom strewn with clothes. 'Did you have a row?' she asked.

'No,' said the girl, wiping her eyes on her sleeve, 'that's the worst thing. He just bloody announced he was bored with me. Said I was an impediment to picking up other women.'

Terry thought it best not to mention that she was one of the women Giles had tried to pick up. 'Have you got somewhere to go?' she asked practically.

'I share a room at the secretarial college. I'll have

to go back there. Bastard. He didn't even give me any warning.'

'Perhaps he's still upset about Hugh Scott's death.'

'Perhaps he just wants to me out of the way so he can screw the stuck-up bitch himself.'

'You mean Carla?' Emma said nothing. 'She doesn't seem to have many fans around here.'

She gave a hollow laugh. 'Rather depends on whether you're talking to a man or not, doesn't it?'

'Look,' Terry said, 'I don't know if you know who I am.'

The girl nodded. 'I've seen you around. You're living in number fifty-seven, aren't you?'

'That's right. I've met Giles a few times. And – it's all a bit complicated – but I'm curious about the way Hugh died. I sort of got adopted by his cat, and then I started hearing all sorts of conflicting things about him, and then I found some stuff, and that made me want to find out what happened.' She was aware how feeble it sounded, but she was fed up with lying. 'So basically, I came round to ask Giles what happened, the night of the party.'

'Giles wouldn't tell you anything, you can be sure of that.'

'Because he wouldn't speak ill of the dead?'

'Because he's bloody embarrassed. And Giles does hate to be embarrassed.' Emma sat down on the bed, staring at her through red-rimmed eyes. 'There's no reason why you shouldn't know, though. Enough other people do, so why not you?'

'You were there?'

'Not for all of it. I walked out, actually. But I got the rest out of Giles afterwards . . . This was all before the murder, of course.'

'What was?'

Emma found a packet of Silk Cut and offered her one. When Terry shook her head, she said, 'I was giving up, but I haven't a hope now,' and lit one for herself.

'First of all, you've got to understand how pissed we all were,' she began. 'It was the last night of term – well, not for me because the secretarial college terms are longer, but for all the others. There was a whole load of booze which I think had been left over from a Catamites bash that had been cancelled – it was all pretty spontaneous. There were loads of people there we didn't even know. But the general rule at these parties is, anyone's welcome so long as they bring a bottle, yuh?'

Terry nodded.

'Also, we'd had to keep the noise down for a few weeks because of the neighbours, but now we were all moving out no-one really gave a shit anymore. So there was lots of silly shouting, and the music was pretty loud.

'Hugh was on top form, actually. I mean, he was showing off but no-one minded that, it was just the way Hugh was. He used to make me laugh, any-way. Then – it must have been around midnight – some of us were in the garden and someone said something about the neighbours, I can't remember what exactly, and Hugh said it wasn't a problem because his bird was next door. That was the word he used, bird, like it was all a big joke, and he started yelling up at Carla's bedroom window for her to come down. She stuck her head out and they shouted at each other for a bit.' Emma took a drag of her cigarette and made a sour face. 'You know, flirting like mad, and eventually he went round and got her. He carried her through the front door, the whole caveman routine. She looked like she was loving it, she was stroking his chest and kissing him in front of everyone. Loads of people knew she was Brian Eden's wife, but she didn't seem to care.' She shrugged. 'I was with some girlfriends, and then we were all dancing, and then at some point Hugh and Carla came up to Giles and they – well, Hugh – were all talking about a foursome. You know, Giles and me and Hugh and Carla.'

'How did you feel about that?' Terry asked quietly.

'Oh, bloody ecstatic.' She stubbed out her cigarette. 'Giles says I'm a prude, well, maybe I am. But I certainly didn't want to get into anything like that.'

'You said no?'

'Not for a bit. I just kind of acted like it was all a big joke – well, I thought it was, till I realized none of them were going to back out. Then I told Giles he could stuff it and I came back here.'

'Do you know what happened?'

'They made it pretty clear before I left that they were going to go ahead without me.' She shuddered.

'Did you go back to the party?'

'No. Giles came home about an hour later. I pretended to be asleep, but I wasn't. I was so miserable. I mean, I knew he hadn't been faithful but he'd never flaunted it in front of me before.'

'And what about Brian? Did anyone see him?'

Emma shook her head. 'He was away that night. They wouldn't have been stupid enough to risk it otherwise, would they?'

'When did you next see him?'

'He came back the next day, I think. He'd been at a conference or something.'

'And did anyone tell the police about all this?'

Emma shrugged. 'Someone must have done. The police already knew about it when they spoke to Giles.'

Did this explain the murder? Terry wondered. She'd established that Brian Eden had the opportunity. He could easily have come home unexpectedly, found Carla drunk and post-coital, and discovered what had happened. But what about the motive? Could he have gone round to murder Hugh in a jealous rage, and then tried to make it look like a random sexual attack?

Leaving Emma, she walked back to her own house, deep in thought. No, it was full of holes. First of all, if jealousy was the motive, why kill Hugh and not Giles? Secondly, Brian and Carla had an open marriage. Jealousy seemed unlikely, given such a set-up. And thirdly, if she was right in thinking that Brian wrote the letters, he already knew that Carla and Hugh were having an affair and was using it to fuel his own fantasies.

But hang on a moment. Ann Byres had said that what we want in fantasy may be what we can't handle in reality. If Brian hadn't actually known about Hugh and Carla – if he had conceived the letters as pure fantasy – then what effect might it have on him to discover that the line between reality and his fantasies was becoming blurred? That what he had pictured in his imagination – and even more than he had pictured – was actually taking place, without him, when he wasn't there? In a man with a compulsive need to control everything, even his own homoerotic sexuality, might it not cause him to spin out of control?

That was more like it. What the letters suggested was an intense inner struggle between heterosexuality and homosexuality, a struggle so repressed that Brian might not even have been aware of it himself. When he found out about the two students bedding Carla, he suddenly recognized his homosexual tendencies for what they were. Unable to accept his feelings, he would have gone round to Hugh's room later that night and savagely murdered him – allowing himself, through the manner of the death, to experience a sort of substitute sexual penetration. He couldn't do the same to Giles because Hugh, unlike Giles, slept alone: in any case, it was Hugh, not Giles, who was the instigator.

She went to the phone and got through to Girdler at the police station. As concisely and clearly as she could, she told him everything she'd learnt.

'So what do you think?' she demanded when she'd finished.

'I think you've fitted a theory to most of the facts, as you know them,' he said cautiously. 'But there are some things that still don't quite hang together. How did the letters come into Hugh's possession, for example?'

'Maybe he found them himself, in the magazine,' she said.

'Why did he keep them hidden?'

'They had his neighbour's name on. He might have thought she really had written them herself, and if he was attracted to her, he would have taken it as proof that she was ripe for an affair.'

'How does it explain what you told me yesterday, about one of the letters being more hostile than the others?'

'I don't know. That's a detail, for God's sake. Maybe Brian was already becoming suspicious.'

'The problem is, Brian has an alibi.'

'No. No he doesn't,' she said urgently. 'I phoned up the hotel and checked. He missed the final night. He could have come back here, killed Hugh, and then made himself scarce.'

There was a long silence. 'I think you'd better come into the station,' Girdler said at last. 'There's something I want to show you. Not now, I'm tied up. Can you come at three?'

'I'll be there,' she promised.

Twenty

Girdler was late. He kept her waiting in the front office of St Aldates police station for three quarters of an hour: when he did see her, he looked tired and harassed. 'I haven't got much time,' he apologized as soon as he saw her. 'We've got every man available on the latest murder. There were traces of flesh under the victim's fingernails. He must have scratched the killer. Once we get the DNA, it's just a matter of legwork.'

'What murder?' she asked, puzzled.

'A young man up in Barton. The poor bastard had been walking his girlfriend home, ironically enough.'

'Why haven't you arrested Brian Eden?' she said. Even to herself her voice sounded shrill and accusatory.

Girdler sighed. 'Look, love, Brian Eden didn't do it.'

She was getting angry now. 'Don't call me love.

You may not want to accept my interpretation of the letters, but you can at least believe me when I tell you that Brian wasn't at his conference on the night Hugh was murdered.'

'Have you interviewed him? Have you taken a statement?'

She flushed. 'Don't patronize me. That's your job and you know it.'

'I'm not patronizing you, Terry, believe me.' He stared at her inscrutably for a few moments; she got the impression his thoughts were somewhere else. 'Dr Eden has an alibi. We checked him out. As you say, that's our job. Our job, rather than yours.'

'An alibi that doesn't stand up,' she said, slapping the table in frustration.

'When you said you were going to have a think about the letters,' he said mildly, 'I imagined you sitting in a library somewhere, not charging round the city like Agatha Christie.'

She flushed. 'I was checking the facts. Any researcher would do the same. And talking of research, what about the death mask? It isn't Shelley's.'

'Death mask?' he said, puzzled.

'He's got this death mask on the wall inside his front door. He claims it's Shelley, the poet.'

'Oh, that thing. He told me it was a mould of his own face, done when he was younger. What's this about Shelley?'

Furiously she tried to remember what had happened when she'd identified the mask as Shelley's. Eden must have been winding her up.

'The reason I wanted you to come in was to see

these,' Girdler said, taking some papers from a thick green file. 'Brian Eden's alibi. A sworn statement by him, affidavits from witnesses, all checked and double-checked. You're not supposed to see them.'

'Why not?' She reached for the papers, but for a moment he didn't release them.

'We promised the college we'd keep them confidential.'

'Half of Oxford already knows about Hugh's relationship with Carla,' she said dismissively.

'True. But they don't know about *this*. Go on, read them. But I'm relying on you not to mention them outside this room.'

Puzzled, she picked up the first page and began to read.

STATEMENT BY CURTIS FISCHER, OF 8 PARK DRIVE MANCHESTER, IN THE PRESENCE OF HIS SOLICITOR, MR HOWARD GILL, AND SIGNED BY MR FISCHER.

For about four years my wife and I have been members of a loosely knit group of adults who get together for the purposes of recreational sex. We were introduced to this group by a fellow academic, Dr Mary Simpson of Cambridge University. Before this we had met couples with similar interests via advertisements in the contact columns of adult magazines.

I first came across Dr and Mrs Eden at an academic conference in July 1987. Dr Eden and I specialize in the same field. We were introduced by Dr Simpson, who together with her husband had had recreational sex with the Edens on many previous occasions. We had sex on that first meeting. After this we got together on frequent but irregular intervals.

On the night of 22 February Dr Simpson, her husband John Simpson, my wife and myself were all attending a conference in Birmingham. After the final paper had been given we went to my hotel room, by prior arrangement, to have recreational sex. Mrs Eden was not present on that occasion. Although it is generally understood that single men are not welcome at group gatherings my wife and I decided to make an exception in Dr Eden's case as we both knew and liked him. Brian Eden was present at all times until the party broke up at about 5 a.m.

On the advice of my solicitor I would like to point out that whenever the members of the group meet no money changes hands, no payment is solicited or given, and that we consider that what we do in private as consenting adults is entirely our own affair.

I have read this statement in the presence of a police officer and agree that it is a fair and accurate record of my words.

(Signed) CURTIS FISCHER

STATEMENT OF DR MARY SIMPSON OF CLARE COLLEGE CAMBRIDGE AND SIGNED BY HER.

I have known Dr Brian Eden since 1977, and have regularly been involved in group sexual activities with him, his wife, my husband and several others. On approximately 1 February Curtis Fischer, a mutual friend, contacted me to say that there was a conference in Birmingham from the 19th to the 23rd which he and his wife would be attending. We made plans to meet then, and I phoned Brian Eden to let him know of the arrangement and to ask if he would be there. He agreed to come. We decided to meet for a session on the last day of the conference, partly because we did not want to miss any of the speakers and partly because I had formed the impression that other academics were starting to gossip. On the last night of a conference some people always leave early and we were therefore unlikely to be missed.

We met at seven o'clock in Curtis Fischer's room and drank wine and chatted for about half an hour. I had sex with Dr Eden. My husband and Diane Fischer then started to have sex, at which point Curtis joined Dr Eden and I. We rested for twenty minutes or so, and then resumed sexual intercourse. This time Dr Eden did not participate, but remained present throughout. Soon after Curtis and my husband had finished, Brian Eden had intercourse with Diane. We then ordered some room service and briefly got dressed while we waited for it to arrive. Then we got undressed again to eat, before resuming sexual intercourse. By this time it was two in the morning: I am quite certain about the time because I wanted to order some more drinks and realized when I looked at my watch that room service would now have finished. We took it in turns to use the shower. This involved some further sexual activity and it was at least five a.m. by the time my husband and I left the room. At that time Dr Eden was dozing on the bed.

I have read this statement in the presence of a police officer and agree that it is a fair and accurate record of my words.

(Signed) MARY SIMPSON

STATEMENT BY ROBERT LEIGH, WAITER, AND SIGNED BY HIM.

For three years I have been employed as a service waiter at the Regency Hyatt Hotel, Birmingham. My normal shift runs from six o'clock in the evening to half past midnight, in the course of which I both wait on tables in the restaurant and deliver room service. In common with the other waiters I prefer to deliver room service, as the tips come quicker. We therefore work a roster system. On the night of 22 February I delivered an order of white wine, scampi, champagne and oysters to room 507. I was asked to provide five glasses. The time on the order was ten past one. I can confirm this because it was my last delivery of the shift. There were five people in the room. When I went in all were dressed, though one lady was only wearing a bath robe and none of the men were wearing ties or socks. I took this to be because the rooms are quite warm. I did not look at any of them closely enough to be able to identify them now. I was given a tip of five pounds which although

317

generous is not unusual for that time of night.

I have read this statement in the presence of a police officer and agree that it is a fair and accurate record of my words.

(Signed) BOB LEIGH

Terry put down the third statement and stared coldly at Girdler. For a moment she was too angry even to speak.

Finally she managed to say, 'And you've known this all the time? You knew it before I even came to Oxford?'

'Yes. As I said, I agreed to keep it confidential. I'm sorry if that's caused you to worry unnecessarily.'

'If someone wasted your time the way you've wasted mine,' she said bitterly, 'you'd be able to lock them up.'

'I tried to tell you,' he protested. 'Over and over again I tried to tell you that I knew he didn't do it.'

'But you didn't tell me why or how you knew. You never gave me proof. In effect, you lied to me.'

'I didn't lie to you. I kept a confidence. There is a distinction.'

'You let me believe something that you knew wasn't true. That's lying in my book. And coincidentally, you were able to come on to me as the big male protector. You lied your way into my bed, you fucked me, and then you lied to me some more.

And all because I was frightened of Brian Eden.' She laughed scornfully. 'I should have been frightened of *you*.'

'Now wait a minute,' he said, reddening.

They stared at each other, both knowing she was overreacting, both knowing the words couldn't now be unsaid.

'Personally, I feel a bit inadequate now I've read this lot,' Terry said sarcastically. 'Dr Simpson really gave you all the gory details, didn't she? Who was doing what to whom, how long it took. I bet you and your detectives were having the time of your lives. When you question me, remind me to have a solicitor present. Mr Fischer got off much more lightly.'

'I'm sorry you were misled,' he said formally.

'What the hell. You're a policeman. I'll know better next time.'

There was a brief silence. When Girdler spoke his voice was neutral, any emotion hidden behind the professional detachment. 'Going back to the letters,' he suggested, 'do you still think your latest interpretation stands up?'

'It doesn't matter now, does it?' she snapped.

'You see, it seems to me that the explanation is very straightforward,' he said, ignoring her. 'He gets a kick out of seeing his wife being screwed by other men, and he gets a kick out of fantasizing about the same thing. He writes down the fantasies and sends them to his favourite magazine. It's a bit sick, I grant you, but it's nothing like the guy we're chasing.'

'I wonder why Carla dropped out that night.'

'By that time she had Hugh. Perhaps a group of middle-aged swingers didn't appeal. Hugh was a lot nearer her own age.'

Terry suddenly remembered how, the morning after Brian's party, she'd seen two half-naked women coming out of his house. Presumably there had been some sort of swinging scene happening that night as well. 'You must think I'm a mug,' she said bitterly.

'Not at all,' he murmured.

'Have you left anything at my house?' she asked icily, getting up to go.

'Terry,' he said quietly, 'I know you feel stupid, and I know that you are so incredibly intellectually arrogant that being made to feel stupid is the one thing you find it hard to forgive. But I really don't see why this has to change our relationship.'

She searched for something expressive and memorable to say. In the event, all she came up with before she walked out was, 'Go fuck Carla Eden.'

Twenty-one

'"For me, as for many others, the reading of detective stories is an addiction like tobacco or alcohol. The symptoms of this are: firstly, the intensity of the craving – if I have any work to do, I must be careful not to get hold of a detective story for, once I begin one, I cannot work or sleep till I have finished it. Secondly, its specificity – the story must conform to certain formulas. (I find it very difficult, for example, to read one that is not set in rural England.)" Question: from which famous poet is this a quotation?'

A boy in the middle of the vast auditorium, now even emptier than on the occasion of Terry's last lecture, raised his hand. It's always the boys, Terry thought. He won't know the answer, but he'll have a go anyway. The girls never put their hands up because they don't want to risk getting it wrong.

'T.S. Eliot?' he ventured.

'Good try, given what I've told you previously

about Eliot, but incorrect. No, it was W. H. Auden, in his essay 'The Guilty Vicarage', written when he was Professor of Poetry here at Oxford. This essay can claim to be one of the first serious critical studies of detective fiction; it's an attempt by Auden to analyse what he calls the "magical function" of the genre.

'For Auden, as I've just indicated, the single most important aspect of the detective novel is that it takes place in a certain type of society. Partly, this is because it's a structural requirement. There has to be a closed circle of suspects, so that one of them and not an outsider is the murderer. But Auden believes it's also something more than this. For him, the world in which the murder takes place, whether it's a remote country house, a village, or a professional group, represents what he calls The Great Good Place. This is an innocent society, a society where there is no need of the law, until the murder reveals that one member is no longer in a state of grace. Then the law becomes a reality, and everyone must live in its shadow until the fallen one is identified. With his arrest, innocence is restored and the law retires again. Am I going too fast?'

Her listeners were flagging now. One girl was massaging her wrist, having got cramp from trying to write it all down exactly as Terry was saying it.

'You really don't have to get every quotation,' Terry said despairingly. 'I'm just trying to give you a sense of the different ideas that other people have come up with.'

They looked at her with blank, unseeing eyes. Oh well, she thought, on with the show.

'From this observation Auden creates his theory. He touches on the popular notion that detective fiction allows us to share vicariously in the violence of murder and dismisses it, pointing out that we rarely see the murder or any violence in these books, certainly by contrast with the pulp thrillers of the time. Instead he suggests that what we, the readers, actually share is the resumption of innocence. In the classical detective story it is a prerequisite that the guilty are ultimately expelled – as Auden says, 'In real life I disapprove of capital punishment, but in a detective story the murderer must have no future.' So for him the detective novel is ultimately a fantasy, a fantasy of being restored to a state of moral innocence.

'He sees the detective genre as an essentially Protestant one, and notes that it flourishes most in Protestant countries, where there is no tradition of confession to a priest. One might think that Chesterton's Father Brown gives the lie to this, but it's interesting to remember that Chesterton began the Brown stories while still a Protestant: the conversion to Catholicism came later.

'Now let's think about the relationship between the detective and the murderer. It's a fundamental requirement of the detective story that the detective "must solve the case by logical deduction from facts fairly put before the reader", as H.R.F. Keating puts it. Think about that a moment. The murderer is an agent of passion: the detective is an agent of logic.

The solving of the crime is therefore a contest between passion and reason, just as its commission was. Or to look at it another way, for logic read order, stability, society: for passion read chaos, anarchy and the individual. With this reading we are very close indeed to Nietzsche's famous analysis of the origins of Greek tragedy, which he sees as being born out of the conflict of Apollo, god of reason, and Dionysus, god of chaos. So one can also say that the magical function of detective fiction is the ritual re-enactment of this archetypal conflict in the human psyche.'

She was losing them now, she could see. Neitzsche, they'd be wondering – he wasn't even English, was he? Let alone a detective writer. So why should we have to read him as well as all this other stuff?

'Thirdly, let's think about the crime itself. It's usually a murder, though Wilkie Collins's *The Moonstone*, which Eliot called 'The first and best English Detective story', was based on nothing more than the theft of a jewel. So why a murder, anyone?'

No one raised their hand.

'Come on,' she encouraged them. 'Someone must have some ideas.'

Uneasily they glanced at each other, waiting to see who was going to put themselves forward.

'OK,' Terry said at last, 'let's look at some of the possibilities.'

Two hours later she was on a coach to Cambridge, drowsy in the afternoon sunlight.

There was only one way to check the statements that cleared Brian of Hugh Scott's death, and that was to go and see one of the people he was with that night. She'd chosen Mary Simpson because she reckoned that she'd been given the hardest time by the police. In addition, Dr Simpson's statement had indicated that she'd known Brian for longer than any of them. Terry wanted to talk to her about his past.

As the coach struggled through endless traffic jams on the M40, Terry tried to struggle through the two slim volumes of Brian Eden's poetry she'd got out of the library. She wasn't sure what she was looking for, though she suspected that anyone who had been a published poet and then given up writing poetry, only to find fame as a biographer of other poets, must have some kind of story to tell.

The two books were markedly different in tone. The first, published when he was still an undergraduate and entitled *Bulldozers*, was much what you'd have expected from a first collection: precocious, fluent, but full of echoes of other writers, overlaid with the ironic posturing and self-important puns of a young man eager to impress. The second, *The Big Hymn*, was more obscure but also more personal, the self-conscious cleverness of the earlier work metamorphosised into a denser linguistic playfulness. For her money it was the better of the two books by far, being less glib and cocksure, but as she worked through it she thought she could detect an increasing hesitancy towards the end of the volume, as if even then he was struggling to fit his vision into the limitations of the form. The poems got steadily shorter: it was almost as if he was running out of things to say before her very eyes. Although it was the slimmer of the two collections, she saw from the date stamps on the front that this second volume had only been borrowed once, about four years previously, whereas the more accessible first volume had been taken out half a dozen times.

Most of the poems in this second book were too difficult to grasp at a first reading, and she wasn't sure she could be bothered to spend time puzzling them out. She had always preferred prose to poetry herself, distrusting the kind of single-minded idealism that allowed a poet to reduce every loving emotion to a lyric and every individual woman to a symbol of her sex.

At the very end of the book she came across a poem entitled 'Song of the Circle':

There were ten in the bed
and the little one said: Roll over.
So we all rolled over

and suddenly we were naked.

All clothes, all conversation,
all politeness gone.
Savaging each other like animals
tearing at a corpse,
and in our turn, each of us
savaged by the pack.

A blur of fragments:
a belly button like the knotted
mouth of a balloon, the bracelet
impressed by a sock on the soft
skin of an ankle, a cock wriggling
through the neck of its vest.

And afterwards, all passion spent,
the slither of skin on skin,
a spaghetti tangle of legs,
a circulating cigarette.
No body spoke.

And I, becoming I again,
saw with a soar of exultation
how everything was changed,

how many kinds of knowledge and belief
had come and touched our foreheads,
lightly, with their dust.

Terry felt the small hairs along her forearm prickle with goosebumps, and rubbed them irritably. In general she had no patience with this kind of pseudomystical rubbish, but even she had to admit that these last poems had a kind of music to them that spoke directly to the body. She suddenly felt sticky and hot, the rough texture of the coach seat pricking the backs of her knees. Putting the books on the empty seat beside her, she rested her head against the window and slept.

*   *   *

When she reached Cambridge she felt groggy. She made her way from the bus station towards Clare College, her spirits gradually revived by the cool breeze that was coming off the Backs. At the porter's lodge she asked for Dr Simpson. Taking a slight liberty with the status of her own PhD, she said that Dr Williams wanted a quick word. Luck was with her: Dr Simpson was both in, and free to see her. Terry followed the porter's directions through the maze of medieval quads, and eventually found the right staircase.

She wasn't sure what she'd expected – some vampish femme fatale, perhaps, provocatively dressed and covered in make-up. But the woman who greeted her was in her late thirties or early forties, small and neat with short hair and lively eyes. Terry was suddenly at a total loss.

'I'm sorry to disturb your work,' she began. 'I just wanted to ask you a couple of questions.'

'Please, have a seat. I'm always happy to help a fellow academic.' Dr Simpson's voice matched her eyes: cool and full of intelligence. Terry took a deep breath as she sat down.

'It's not strictly an academic matter. I've come over from Oxford to ask you about Brian Eden.'

The cool eyes widened slightly, but the well-plucked eyebrows above them betrayed no emotion as they lifted enquiringly.

'I've read your statement to the police,' Terry said.

'Why,' Dr Simpson began. Then she did a double take. 'What do you mean, you've read my statement?'

'I was shown it in confidence. It's a long story.'

'What can I do for you, then? You seem to be in a position to ask whatever you like,' she said caustically.

'I'm not going to threaten you with exposure, if that's what you mean,' Terry said, flushing angrily. 'If you don't want to talk to me I'll go.' She stood up, but the other woman waved her down again.

'Forget I said that. All right, ask me what you want to know.'

'I want to know how your thing with Brian started.'

'*Thing*? I take it you genuinely are an academic of some description. Can't you bring yourself to be a little more precise?'

'The sex, then,' Terry said bluntly.

Dr Simpson nodded, opened a drawer and took out a packet of Stuyvesants before replying. After a moment's pause she offered one to Terry, who lit up too.

'You say sex,' she said matter-of-factly. 'But it wasn't about sex to begin with, or at least not exclusively. This is going back, what, eighteen years?' She shot Terry a glance. 'You would have been still at primary school, wouldn't you? Anyway, we met at Oxford, in a study group in our second year – we were all interested in the Romantics, but quite by chance the group contained a high proportion of seriously intelligent people, people one could see straight away were going to go on and become academics or artists or whatever. You can't imagine what a relief that was,

329

when three-quarters of the undergraduates one came across were just public school idiots. Well, perhaps you can. I don't know you. Anyway, we were inseparable, and in the way of inseparable undergraduates, we decided to form a society.' She took a drag of her cigarette and stared into space for a moment, remembering.

'What did you call yourselves?' Terry asked curiously.

'The Parnassians. As in those who live on Parnassus, the mountain of the muses.'

'Go on.'

'Brian was the driving force. I mean, one could see even then that he was something special. It wasn't that he was necessarily cleverer than the rest of us. But he had a special quality: even his scholarship was always more imaginative, more *committed*.'

Terry said nothing. After a moment Dr Simpson went on, 'The idea was that we were going to bring back the principles of the Romantics. To live lives of pure sensation, as Keats put it.'

'But everyone was doing that around that time, weren't they? Sex and drugs and rock and roll?'

'People were playing at all that, yes. But this was slightly different. For one thing, we were intellectuals: we had the words of the poets ringing in our ears. As Brian used to remind us, it was less than a hundred years since a mob of undergraduates in Oxford rioted over the banning of a poem by Swinburne.

'In any case, this was the Seventies, not the

330

Sixties. The hippy stuff had passed us by – we'd all been in fairly strait-laced middle-class schools – and by the time we got to Oxford, all that was left was a kind of nostalgic feeling, a sense that we'd missed the party. Sure, there was a lot of experimentation. Even in our little group, we'd all changed partners a couple of times every term, until it got to the stage where everyone had slept with virtually everyone else anyway. And everyone did drugs, of course. But the difference between us and the public schoolboys was that while they were dropping acid and smoking pot, we were getting intoxicated on poetry and pints of claret.'

'And sex.'

'And sex. I think there was a feeling that until we'd done that, we were only playing at it.' Dr Simpson smiled slightly. 'You've really no idea what it was like. To shed your inhibitions, hold nothing back. You kids these days are all so uptight.'

Terry fished Brian Eden's book out of her bag, turned to the last page, and read aloud:

'And I, becoming I again,
saw with a soar of exultation
how everything was changed,

how many kinds of knowledge and belief
had come and touched our foreheads,
lightly, with their dust.'

'Actually, he's caught the feeling rather well,' Dr Simpson said. She held out her hand for the book and Terry gave it to her. For a few moments she leafed through it, nodding thoughtfully.

'And what you do now – the meetings in hotels, at conferences and so on. Are those transcendental experiences as well?' Terry asked. The words came out rather more sarcastically than she had meant them to, but she was getting a little riled by the other woman's smug superiority.

Dr Simpson shrugged. 'Perhaps not. But we do what we can to keep the magic alive.' She shot Terry a look. 'You must know what I'm talking about.'

'Me?' Terry said, astonished.

'Yes, you. You're an academic. Why do any of us do what we do, if not to try and recapture some of the excitement we felt when we first read a particular author and felt that shock of recognition, that knowledge that someone in another age has felt what we felt?'

'Who else was in your society?' Terry said, refusing to be sidetracked. 'Not Carla, of course, she's a lot younger than you. I suppose Brian introduced her later. What about Dorling Van Glught and his wife?'

She nodded. 'Julia and Dorling were part of it, yes. Some of the other original members dropped out, of course. They met new partners who didn't get what we were about, or moved too far away to take part. But others, like myself, introduced our new partners to the group, so the numbers have stayed pretty much the same.'

'Brian doesn't only write poetry. He also writes

pornography about his wife being screwed by other men,' Terry said evenly.

'Does he? So what? I've always thought that poetry and pornography are pretty similar when you get down to it. They're both extreme, stylized literary forms. I must ask him if I can read some of his stuff one day. It's probably rather good.'

'This wonderful sex – was it heterosexual, or a bit of both?' Terry asked casually, and had the satisfaction of seeing the other woman look, for the first time, a little shocked.

'We're none of us gay. It wouldn't work if we were.'

'How do you know you're all heterosexual if you never tried anything else? Not very broadminded of you, if you don't mind my saying.' Terry reached uninvited for another one of the cigarettes. 'It must have been quite comic, really. I have this sort of picture of all these middle-aged men with flapping erections, terrified that they might accidentally touch each other.'

'It isn't like that,' Dr Simpson said curtly.

'And Brian Eden – all the time he's screwing you, or one of the other women, he's having a good look at what the other men are doing. Particularly to Carla. She's the wildest one, isn't she? I bet she can take on several of them at once. And I bet she looks fantastic while she does it. That lithe young body.' The other woman smiled thinly without replying, and Terry knew she'd hit a nerve. Oh well, she'd better ease off a bit. 'When did Brian get Carla involved?' she asked.

'About four years ago. She was one of his students originally, you know. We celebrated their wedding night together, as a matter of fact, half a dozen of us in a room at the Randolph Hotel.' She smiled slightly at the memory.

'But Carla doesn't come to the group sessions anymore. I wonder why she went off your little orgies? Perhaps they got a bit boring for her.'

Dr Simpson gave her a triumphant look. 'What gave you that impression? She always comes with Brian. They're inseparable.'

'But not on the night of the murder,' Terry said quietly.

There was a long pause while the other woman realized her mistake. 'That was a rare exception,' she said at last.

'Oh no. It wouldn't be, would it? Brian gets his kicks from watching other men screw Carla. He's not going to come along without her. The reason he *says* he came alone that particular night is because there are witnesses who can confirm that Carla was in Oxford.'

The other woman didn't reply.

'That alibi you all gave him – it could easily be a lie, couldn't it? You wouldn't have any qualms about doing that. What was it Forster said? "If I had to choose between betraying my friend and betraying my country, I hope I would have the courage to betray my country." That's how you'd feel about the police investigation: the group comes first. Or was it more basic than that? After all, if he'd been arrested, the activities of your little group would

334

have been all over the papers. Much better to tell one little lie and rely on Brian's contacts with the police to keep the whole thing hushed up. And since you'd have thought your precious Brian couldn't really have done the murder, you'd have thought no harm was done.'

'I think you should go,' Dr Simpson said angrily.

Terry decided she had nothing to lose now. 'I wonder how long Brian will go on wanting the Parnassians,' she mused. 'After all, the attractions of older flesh, even in abundant quantities, must pale eventually. Look what happened to the mistresses of the original Romantics. Ditched without a qualm as soon as the muse touched someone younger.'

Dr Simpson picked up the internal telephone. 'Security, please,' she said curtly. 'John, I've found an intruder in my rooms. Can you come at once?'

Terry searched around for one last parting shot. 'By the way,' she said, 'we lesbians prefer the word queer to gay. Gay sounds a bit old-fashioned these days.'

She slipped out of the room and went down to the quad, careful not to run and not to meet the eyes of the two porters who hurried past her up the stairs.

Her heart was still pounding when she reached the coach station. She realized she'd left the book of poetry in Dr Simpson's room: oh well, the library would have to do without it. She went into John Menzies and found herself a detective book instead. She still couldn't work out why she'd been so foul to Dr Mary Simpson. 'Baby, it's because you're a bitch,' she murmured to herself out loud, and saw the elderly woman next to her start to edge away. Well, that was certainly true – she *was* a bitch, particularly with certain women, and once she'd started attacking she never knew when to stop. But it wasn't the whole truth. She was just settling herself back in the coach when she realized something else: she had been just the tiniest bit jealous. She pushed the thought away, trying to concentrate on what she'd learned.

The alibi Girdler had shown her might be a tissue of lies, or it might not. There was simply no way of knowing. What had she said to her students, way back at the beginning of term? The truth isn't about knowledge, it's about insight. Conviction. But how could she convince anyone else of what she believed? It seemed a hopeless proposition. In academic terms, what she was offering was an interpretation rather than scholarship: something which got a doctoral thesis failed instantly.

She sighed, opening the paperback and folding back the first page with deliberate determination. But the words in her head were the words Brian Eden had written before his own muse deserted him, the delicate iambic rhythm as catchy in its way as the chorus of a pop song . . . *how many kinds of knowledge and belief / had come and touched our foreheads, / lightly, with their dust.*

The coach station in Oxford was in Gloucester Green, just round the corner from St Mary's, so she

336

decided to call in on her way home. At the porter's lodge she paused to check her long-neglected pigeon hole, which was crammed with mail. Most of it was circulars, flyers for student dramas and forthcoming concerts, the university equivalent of junk mail. Scanning them quickly, she binned them. That left only two envelopes. One contained a brief note from Reg, informing her that a representative of the Pensung Corporation was in town to talk to colleges about the new Chair and asking Terry to come to a drinks party at which the representative would be present. Terry groaned: she'd have to think of some way of getting out of it.

The second envelope was thicker, sealed and with her name typed on the front. She opened it, her mind still on Reg and his corporate politicking.

The letter inside wasn't addressed to her. She had already scanned the first few lines when she realized what she was reading.

Dear Linzi, as before.

But this time – her eye flicked over the familiar litany of obscenities to the end – not written in Carla's name. This time the sign-off was different.

Terry, Oxford.

'Bad news, Miss?'

It was the porter, pushing a new batch of messages into the pigeon holes beside her.

'Sorry?'

He indicated the letter. 'Bad news, is it?'

She managed a smile. 'Nothing important. Did you see who left it here?'

'Sorry. It's been that busy. Is it not signed, then?'

He started to peer over her shoulder and she folded it up quickly and stuffed it back in the envelope.

She mumbled something dismissive and took the letter up to the relative privacy of the library. Across the table from her a young student, still in his sports kit, chewed his pen and wrestled with a translation from what looked like Russian.

Dear Linzi,

I am a twenty-seven-year-old woman who split up from my husband about six months ago and moved to a new house here in Oxford. My new neighbours, Brian and Carla, are both very pleasant, good-looking people and made a real effort to make me feel welcome.

On the night of my birthday we went out to a local restaurant and got very drunk before heading back to their place to start on the whisky. By midnight, when the conversation turned to sex, Brian and I were sprawled across the sofa, while Carla sat on the floor, leaning against us. She was rhapsodizing about how wonderful it was to give a man a blow job, going in to a lot of detail. Through the corner of my eye I could see that Brian was getting a considerable erection, though I pretended not to notice.

I suppose it was partly mischievousness that made me say something to the effect that if she was such an expert, she had better give me a demonstration sometime. She looked me in the eye and asked if I was daring her, and I replied that I was. In a trice she had her husband's zip open and was freeing his enormous hard-on. It was just as impressive as Carla had always said it was, a good

338

eight inches of throbbing meat, which she proceeded to lick and stroke. Brian lay back on the settee, groaning in ecstasy.

Noticing that his eyes were closed, Carla quickly motioned for me to take her place, taking my hand and placing it where hers had been. In this way we managed to switch places without her husband even noticing. Whilst I ran my tongue and fingers up and down the pulsing shaft just as she had done, Carla had stood up and was taking off her clothes. She had a superb figure, slim but with very well-developed breasts. Then she leant over Brian and kissed him on the lips. Thinking it was me, his eyes opened, and you can imagine his surprise when he realized what had happened.

By this time I had his lovely cock buried deep in my throat, and Carla turned round so that her cunt was in his face for him to lick and suck. In this position she could also reach his cock, and the two of us took it in turns to feast on his manhood, occasionally breaking off to French kiss each other. I was by now dripping with desire, and pretty soon I couldn't stop from fingering myself through my panties.

Seeing this, they got up and turned their attention to me, stripping me and kissing me all over until I was lying on the carpet squirming and moaning with lust. Carla worked her way up my thighs with her tongue, teasing me, circling my clit until I thought it would burst. Then at last she found the spot and started to lick me as only a woman can and I came with a great shriek.

After that we all got onto the sofa. Brian took me gently from behind whilst Carla and I did a sixty-nine, then she rode him while I sat on his face and kissed her beautiful breasts. Then we all curled up and slept, waking a couple of hours later to have another joyous fuck.

Since then we have had several more wonderful nights together. They confessed that they had been looking for an opportunity to share their sex life with me for some time – and am I ever glad they found one!

Terry, Oxford.

She read the letter twice, then folded it up and put it back in the envelope. The student opposite glanced at her, and she realized that she had just sighed heavily. Catching her eye, he smiled at her. She looked away coldly.

Dr Simpson must have phoned Brian Eden as soon as she'd gone. This letter was his way of saying that whatever was between them was out in the open.

Twenty-two

The Psychology Faculty was just round the corner. Hurrying there, she asked at the Common Room if Ann Byres was in. She was in luck. Professor Byres was there, and not teaching.

Terry followed the directions she'd been given up to the top floor, where she eventually located room G9. She knocked, and Ann opened the door.

'Terry, how nice to see you again. Come in, come in. Can I get you some coffee? It's only some revolting machine, I'm afraid, but it's better than nothing.'

Terry said she was fine and made a space on which to sit amongst the papers stacked on every available surface.

'I've just got this,' she said without preamble, giving Ann the letter.

Ann read it, then glanced at Terry. 'And how do you feel about it?'

'Furious.'

Ann laughed. 'Well, that's quite a healthy re-action. Anything else?'

'A little bit frightened,' Terry admitted. 'I mean, if he is the murderer, I suppose I may be in some physical danger from him.'

'By he, I take it you mean Brian Eden?'

'It must be him.' She explained about her trip to Cambridge that morning.

'Hmm. Well, for what it's worth, I've studied many fantasies, and I wouldn't have said he's plan-ning anything hostile to you at the moment.' She handed the letter back. 'Quite the reverse, in fact.'

'What do you mean?' Terry said curiously.

'From the evidence of this letter, I'd say he's try-ing to charm you.'

'What!'

'I'm serious. Those last letters were all about Carla – you remember how we found the per-mission theme? Well, here it's you he's trying to give the permission to. I think that on one level he's genuinely trying to entice you into his fantasy world. May I see the letter again?' She re-read it. 'It's all about innocence, in a way, isn't it? When he – or rather you, in his words – talks about having 'a joyous fuck', that seems to be the keynote. Notice the way it's all supposed to take place on your birthday? Subconsciously, he's thinking of it as a gift to you, a birthday treat. And, of course, birth-days are all about childhood, the age of innocence: being the centre of the grown-ups' attention.'

Terry snorted. 'That's ironic. His innocence or guilt is precisely the issue I'm trying to settle.'

'If nothing else,' Ann said thoughtfully, 'it proves that he isn't homosexual, as you thought last time.'

'Bisexual, homosexual, what's the difference?'

'But from the evidence of this, I'd say he wasn't bisexual either. There isn't even another man to share the action.'

'But the other letters,' Terry began.

'You remember you asked me about this the last time we met, and I said I'd need more time to think about it? Well, I did spend a bit of time looking up a couple of studies in this area. And they confirmed what I suspected. Whilst it may be true that a man could get involved in group sex for covertly homo-erotic reasons, it would be very rare indeed – in fact, unheard of – for him to fantasize about group situations and not use the fantasy to indulge his real desires.'

'I'm not sure I buy that,' Terry said, shaking her head.

'Why not?'

When she didn't answer, Ann Byres said gently, 'Terry, may I ask you a personal question?'

'Sure.'

'Is it possible you're projecting your own anxieties on to these letters?'

Terry shot her a puzzled look.

'You're intent on reading this fairly straightforward pornography as an expression of an inner struggle between homosexuality and heterosexuality,' Ann said gently. 'Sometimes a theory tells us as much about the one doing the theorizing as it does about the subject. I'm sorry, I don't mean to be nosy.'

Terry gaped at her. It was so obvious, so blindingly, self-evidently obvious. 'Jesus. Why didn't I think of that?' She slammed her fist into her palm. 'Damn!'

'Do you want to tell me about it?' Ann prompted after a moment.

Terry sighed. 'No. Yes. After my divorce – I had an affair with a girlfriend. My best friend. She's gay. I suppose, with hindsight, that was partly why she became my best friend, wasn't it? I must have been subconsciously interested, even then.'

Ann tutted. 'Don't denigrate yourself. The sub-conscious isn't a rogue we have to constantly watch to make sure it doesn't misbehave, you know. You may just have liked her.'

'Possibly. Anyway, one of the reasons – the main reason – I moved to Oxford was to get away from all that.'

'Hmm. Were you trying to get away from her, or to get away from yourself?'

Terry laughed ironically. 'Both, I guess.'

'Perhaps you imagined lesbian Terry would be left behind in London, and heterosexual Terry would come down here and start afresh. Let me guess: as soon as you got here, you found yourself a man and jumped into bed with him, to prove to yourself how heterosexual you really are.'

'Yes,' Terry said, surprised again. 'Yes, that's exactly what I did.' She thought of the way she'd thrown herself at Girdler. 'Damn!'

'Why damn?'

She shrugged. 'I hate to think it was that predictable, that's all.'

'Like I said, don't run yourself down. There's nothing wrong with doing the predictable. The question is, how do you feel about it now?'

'That he was the wrong man,' Terry admitted. 'If I'm honest, I've been looking for reasons to fight him, right from the start.' She thought for a bit. 'He's a policeman. Do you think I wanted to sleep with him because he's an authority figure?'

'I've no idea,' Ann said. 'What do you think?'

'That was what I said about that letter, wasn't it? The one with the two policemen and the speeding car? I said the policemen were there because having sex with a policeman – being accepted by him – was a way of saying you weren't really a bad person.' She laughed out loud, a bark of exasperation. 'It's so obvious, isn't it? It wasn't what Brian thought, it was what I thought myself.'

'Don't be angry with yourself,' Ann warned her again.

'Oh, it's not that which bothers me. It's just such bad scholarship, that's all.' She grimaced. 'If I was wrong about the letters, if Brian simply isn't in the least bit homosexual, then what could his motive have been for killing Hugh Scott or raping the other kid? There isn't one.'

'Hmm. Men who rape other men aren't necessarily homosexual, you know. Just like the rape of a woman, it's as much to do with power and the need to inflict fear as it is about sex. But if Brian didn't do it, how does that make you feel?'

'Stupid.'

'I meant, how does it make you feel about him?'

Terry shrugged.

'You see – you really must forgive me, you're not my patient and I wouldn't dream of suggesting that you need my services – you see, when you told me just now about going to Cambridge to check on his alibi, I couldn't help wondering whether it was his guilt you were trying to establish,' Ann paused delicately, 'or, perhaps, his innocence.'

'Ah.' Revelations were crowding in on each other so fast Terry had no time even to be surprised. 'You think I want him to be innocent, because I fancy him.'

Ann smiled gently. 'My professional training is in what's called non-directive therapy. I don't tell patients what to think, I just try to allow them to think for themselves.'

Terry thought for a moment. 'I've become a little obsessed with him, haven't I? Chasing his involvement in the murder like this. So I must have some sort of relationship with him. If I'm absolutely honest,' she said, 'I always found him attractive. Well, not attractive, exactly, not *nice*, but I find his arrogance – his certainty – provocative. One of the reasons this letter' – she picked it up and read it through, frowning – 'makes me so angry is because as well as finding it childish, manipulative, presumptuous and sexist, I also find the scenario it describes . . . rather . . .' She clenched her fists. 'Damn! Damn! Damn!'

Ann waited, saying nothing.

'I mean, I don't *like* him. I don't like either of them. He's an egomaniac, she's a flirt. I think they're unprincipled – sleeping with students is just unforgiveable. And they're so bloody smug about themselves.'

'We're just as likely to fancy our enemies as our friends,' Ann pointed out. 'We can't control our instincts. Perhaps it's arrogant of us to even try.'

Terry sighed. 'You're not the first person to accuse me of being arrogant.' She waved away the other woman's protestations. 'My policeman friend, quite rightly, pointed out the same thing. Perhaps that's why, deep down, I find Brian Eden so interesting. We're both of us arrogant bastards.' She mused for a moment. 'But we needn't be at the mercy of our instincts, need we? Even if we can't choose who we fancy, we choose who we sleep with.'

Ann nodded agreement. 'Absolutely. I'm not suggesting you go and sleep with this man.'

Terry was silent.

'Of course, I'm not suggesting you shouldn't, either,' Ann said. Terry smiled ruefully.

'Can I suggest something?' Ann asked. 'I think you need to get his possible involvement in this murder out of your system somehow. Until you do that, I don't think you'll ever see him clearly.'

'How do I do that?'

'Non-directive, remember? Only you can decide what you do now. I think you'll discover the right way, if you look for it.'

Terry nodded thoughtfully. 'There's one other person I need to talk to,' she said. 'Depending on what he tells me, I'll know what to do.' She stood

347

up, feeling lighter than she had done for weeks. 'Ann, I can't thank you enough.'

The other woman stood up too, a diminutive figure amongst all the papers and books in the little room. 'Come and talk to me any time. That's what sisters are for.'

Terry stepped forward and embraced her. She had to be careful not to squeeze all the air out of the woman's tiny frame, so exhilarated did she feel.

It was late evening by the time she got back to Osney. She went in and dropped off her things, then crossed the street and knocked on Giles Chawker's door.

'I want to talk to you,' she said when he opened the door.

Clowning as ever, he put a hand to his forehead in mock surprise. 'An invitation! Don't tell me I've melted that stony heart at last.'

'If you must be facetious, try at least not to mix your metaphors,' she said sternly. 'Stones don't melt.'

'If you must be pedantic, at least smile at me while you're doing it. It makes it all worthwhile.' He opened the door and bowed low. 'O princess, enter.'

'I think we'll go to my place,' she said firmly. 'Student houses tend to be a little grimy for my royal tastes.'

'Do you have any booze?'

'I could probably find some whisky.'

'In that case, lead on.'

As they went across to number fifty-seven, she

glanced at his tracksuit. 'Been training?'

He put a hand to his lower back and winced. 'I pulled a muscle in my back on the erg this morning, so I'm sitting at home catching up on my work. I'll be OK tomorrow.'

'Should you be drinking, then?'

'No,' he said, making a bee-line for the half-full bottle of Lagavulin in her kitchen and pouring them two large measures.

'I'll have water with mine,' Terry said. 'And I suggest you take it easy, too. The last time we met you threw up all over me, remember?'

'Ah. Yes. I never thanked you for getting me home that night, did I?'

'And I never thanked you for providing such a charming photo-opportunity.'

He added water from the tap for both of them. 'Bloody snappers. I suppose I had been overdoing the fun and games a bit.'

'But you haven't only been drinking for pleasure, have you?' He didn't reply, and she went on, 'You've been carrying around a lot of guilt and you can't handle it.'

'Oh dear. The psychoanalyst is in,' he murmured, pushing his hair back out of his eyes.

'A psychoanalyst would probably say that pushing your hair back like that is a way of blocking out the world.'

He blinked, half-raised his hand to his face again, then realized what he was doing and stopped. 'Can you tell my star sign as well? I'd love to know if we're compatible.'

'And as for this ludicrous flirting, I don't believe that's much more than a nervous tic either. You'd run a mile if you thought it would lead to anything. Emma was sweet, but an eighteen-year-old secretarial student and a twenty-nine-year-old academic are very different propositions.'

Giles put his drink down with an expression of exasperation. 'Terry, there's nothing I normally find more fascinating than talking about me, but if all you wanted to do is tell me that I'm a loathsome gibbering wreck I think I'll be on my way. I've got an essay to write before tomorrow.'

'I want to talk about Hugh,' she said, refilling their glasses. 'I know most of it already, but I want to fill in the gaps.'

There was a long pause.

'And don't give me any of that crap about how he was your oldest friend and you don't want to talk about it. It'll probably do you a lot of good to get it all out.'

He looked at her, and she suddenly saw how terribly young he was.

'You mean about Carla?' he said at last.

She nodded. 'I want to know what happened the night of the murder. I've heard Emma's version, but I'd like to hear it from you.'

'It's not something I'm proud of,' he said quietly. 'I was rat-arsed, for Christ's sake.' He stared at his glass. 'Hugh and I – we used to talk about Carla and Emma. You know, what it would be like if we could get them together. Carla was quite keen on the idea, apparently, but I wasn't sure how Em would take it. Anyway, the night of the party, Hugh and Carla were both here, and so were we, and Hugh told me that it was now or never. Brian was away, and Hugh's lot were moving out the next day.'

'So you asked Emma, and she told you to forget it.'

He sighed. 'Yeah. Can't blame her really, can you? But by that time we were all pretty excited about it, so we went ahead anyway.'

'I want to know exactly what happened.' He raised his eyebrows at her, and she said, 'This isn't prurient interest, for God's sake. I want to know if it could have any bearing on the murder.'

'We went through it with the police,' he pointed out.

'Tell me anyway. I don't need to know who did what to whom, just where it all took place.'

'Upstairs, in the Edens' bedroom. Why?'

She leaned forward. 'Was there any sign of Brian? Any sign at all?'

He shook his head again. 'If there had been, I'd hardly have gone ahead and shagged his wife, would I?'

'What about the bedroom? Was the door left open? Any funny business with mirrors?'

He shook his head. 'I was drunk, but I'd have noticed something like that.'

'So it was just the three of you?'

He glanced at her sideways. 'Not quite. Julia was there. Carla's friend from across the road.'

'Yes, I know who she is. What was she doing there?'

'When Emma backed out, Hugh said we were going to be a bit light on women. So Carla got her pal over.' He grimaced. 'Not my type, really, but I wasn't in a position to say no, was I?'

'How did she contact her?'

He shrugged. 'She gave her a ring. Said something like, come on over, we're having a private party.'

'Well, that makes sense. She'd been part of their little swinger group for years.'

'So . . . Now you know all the sordid details, do you really think Brian might have killed Hugh?'

She took another swig of whisky. 'I did think so for a while. But now I'm not sure. It all hinges on whether Brian knew about the foursome and was planning to come back and join in, or whether Carla set it up on her own account, while he was away.'

'But why would he have killed Hugh?'

'I don't know.' She sighed. 'You see, it's perfectly possible that Hugh was simply the first victim of someone who had no connection with Brian or Carla at all. A random attacker, in other words.'

'Which is what the police have been saying all along.'

'Bugger it,' she said succinctly. She seemed to be running faster and faster to stand still, just like Alice in that other famous Oxford story. She had thought the letters would lead her to the truth, only to find that they were a very small part of the truth. She had thought Brian's alibi was the key, only to get sidetracked into his activities with an undergraduate society nearly twenty years before. And she had been convinced that when she understood the events of the night of the murder, she'd know whether Brian did it, only to realize that she was no closer to solving the mystery than she had been at the beginning.

Except that somehow, the letters were still the key. If Hugh was a willing partner in Brian and Carla's activities, why had he felt it necessary to conceal the letters in his room?

The one thing she now could be sure of was that Eden *was* a danger to undergraduates, and that the university authorities, when they found out about his activities, had hushed it up rather than discipline him, at a time when bad PR would have caused them considerable embarrassment.

Terry had once had a discussion with a moral philosopher on the difference between wrong and bad. There were two sorts of people, the philosopher maintained: those who saw moral issues as being about right or wrong, and those who saw exactly the same issues as being about good or bad. For the former, morality was a shifting, pragmatic affair, a matter of adhering to social laws; for the latter, a series of individually felt absolutes. Terry hadn't been sure at the time which category she fell into, but she felt strongly now that what the Edens did with Hugh Scott, and had done to God knew how many other young men, was fundamentally and immutably bad. Not because the sexual activities themselves were unacceptable – like most liberals she believed that what anyone did in the privacy of their own home was entirely their own affair – but because those over whom you have power should never be exploited.

Ann Byres had told her that she would know what to do when the time came. And she was indeed beginning to see clearly what path she must go down now, though where it would lead her she was still uncertain.

She suddenly realized that they had both been silent for a long time. 'What happened with you and Emma?' she asked gently.

He shrugged, avoiding her eyes. 'I couldn't, er, face . . .'

'You became impotent,' she guessed. 'Partly because she knew about you and Hughie sharing Carla, but also because you've been worrying about whether it had anything to do with the murder. And because you're an idiot, you didn't tell her the truth. You decided to maintain this charade that you're some kind of undergraduate Casanova. And when you couldn't avoid bonking her any longer, you kicked her out.'

'I bet you do know my star sign,' he muttered. 'Bloody hell! Anything else the doctor wants to tell me?'

'A doctor would say, stop drinking.' She deftly removed the whisky from his grasp.

'Oi!' He tried to grab it, wincing at a sudden pain in his back.

'A fit person like you shouldn't be pulling muscles, either. You're obviously far too tense.' She looked at him thoughtfully for a moment, then got up and rummaged in one of the cupboards until she found a small phial of yellow liquid. She stood it in a saucepan with some water from the kettle.

'What are you doing?'

'I'm warming some massage oil,' she said matter-of-factly. 'Or would you rather run away?'

'Um . . .'

'Take your shirt off, then. Don't worry, I won't eat you.'

'Shame,' he murmured, 'I bet you're rather good at that.'

'I'm good at this. I was taught by an ex-lover. You'll probably become aroused,' she told him, 'but don't take that as an invitation to make a pass. I don't sleep with students, OK? However good-looking they are.'

'OK,' he agreed meekly, pulling off his top and lying down.

'How's the training going, anyway?' she asked conversationally as she poured a little of the oil into the small of his back. 'Isn't it Eights week pretty soon?'

'I lost my place in the boat,' he said quietly. 'Roddy said I'd fallen apart.' Under her fingers she felt the muscles of his neck suddenly become as hard as pieces of bone.

Twenty-three

The street alongside the Oxford Union was lined bumper to bumper with generator trucks, lighting vans and Outside Broadcast units. Inside one of the latter the programme producer, Freddy Brandreth, watched a small monitor and yawned. The debate, on the subject of Law and Order, was long and tedious, the speakers eminently reasonable and fair-minded. Only when it had been edited down to a three-minute current affairs slot would it look as if either side had disagreed with what the other had said minutes before.

Having finished a speech full of the usual plati-tudes, and ending with a plea for a balanced and fair crime policy, the Chief Constable, Sir Andrew Haig, sat down and an undergraduate in the regulation white tie and tails stood up. Freddy consulted his clipboard. Dominic Ashbury. The absence of any notes next to his name suggested that this was not a person of any importance. Freddy reached out and turned the sound down.

Many years ago Dominic Ashbury had decided that he would one day become prime minister, and had sat down to work out how he would do it. Whilst still at public school he had decided that he needed a mentor, and had written to a politician on the right wing of the Conservative Party, an elderly bachelor, asking to meet him. In return for work as the politician's unpaid assistant in Westminster and the constituency during the holidays, all he had to do was feed the old man's ego and be taken out to dinner. He soon discovered that the other man liked to talk about the canings he had received in his youth at his own public school. In fact Dominic's school had abolished corporal punishment well before Dominic's time there, but in order to keep the old boy happy he invented a series of stories about sadistic slipper-wielding prefects and whip-happy masters. One day he would use his mentor's influence to become a parliamentary researcher. He would then be expected to fight one election for a seat he had no possibility of winning, just to show keenness, before his connections would ease him into the sort of safe Tory seat reserved for those with future Cabinet potential. Then he would be able to ditch the old man, move himself towards the centre of the party, and concentrate on currying favour with the electorate.

So far, Dominic's life plan, written on a scrap of paper when he was seventeen, had gone exactly as it should have done. Next to the first four boxes on his diagram were four small ticks.

But while he had achieved one of his ambitions for the current year – becoming President of the Oxford Union – he had not yet achieved the other, which was listed on the piece of paper simply as 'Get Noticed'.

His problem was that the political world was full of former Presidents of the Union. What he needed was to be tipped as a face to watch, preferably by a few eminent journalists. Later on, when he got into Parliament, the newspaper editors would look through their cuttings files in search of an angle on him, discover that he had already impressed their predecessors, and give him a glowing write-up as a precociously brilliant wunderkind.

In order to get noticed by the national media, he was going to have to do or say something controversial. But his politician's instincts made him shy away from controversy. Anyone he offended now would have it in for him later. The alternative was to find some subject which was inherently newsworthy, and stir it up without offending any of the pressure groups involved.

The debate on Law and Order seemed the perfect opportunity. He'd managed to get a Chief Constable along, so the television cameras would be there in the hope that the mad old fool would make yet another stupid gaffe.

Dominic took a deep breath.

'I want to talk about Law and Order, not in the abstract as the Chief Constable has done, but with reference to one particular example here in this very city,' he began. 'I want to talk about a rapist and

358

murderer known as the Beast of Oxford.' He paused for a moment. He knew the media would love that tag, which he had made up the night before. 'All rape is foul, but this rapist is especially degenerate. He is a homosexual, and his prey are the healthy young men who come to this city, often leaving the safety of their family homes for the first time, to pursue their education.'

In the van, Freddy's interest suddenly flickered. He leaned forward and adjusted the volume back up to its normal level.

'Are we still rolling on three?' he asked the technician. 'This might be interesting.'

'Who created this monster?' Dominic pointed theatrically at the Chief Constable. 'He created him. He gave this man, and other perverts like him, his own pubs, his own television programmes, his own sordid nightclubs. He gave him the impression that he was willing to condone and even encourage his sexual deviancy. Instead of clamping down on homosexuals, he has let them believe that they are immune from prosecution. Small wonder that even after the Beast has murdered at least two young men, and raped who knows how many more, the Chief Constable is unable or unwilling to put him behind bars.

'I suggest that the police force no longer enjoys the confidence of the citizens of Oxford. How long can it be before those citizens decide to do for themselves what the police are so clearly failing to do, and organize themselves into groups of householders, ready and able to defend themselves, thus creating a constant deterrent on every street and in every neighbourhood?'

'He's calling for armed vigilantes,' the sound editor said, incredulous.

'He didn't actually call for them,' Freddy said admiringly. 'And he didn't actually say armed. But that's what everyone will hear.'

'Oh well, he's only a kid,' the mixer said dismissively. 'No one's going to give a shag.'

When Dominic sat down, Freddy got up. 'Just going for a wazz,' he said to the others. When he was safely outside he pulled a mobile phone from his pocket. He looked at his watch. Eight o'clock. The news desk on the tabloid paper he was calling would still be open.

'Phil?' he said when he got through. 'I might just have something for you.'

Richard Girdler was about to leave to catch some sleep when a constable came running to say that the Chief Constable was on the phone for him. He went back to his desk and listened to the torrent of anger in silence, only saying 'yes, sir' when it was expected of him. When it was over and the other man had rung off he allowed himself a slight wince.

Sighing, he looked at the phone for a moment, then dialled Terry's number. It rang half a dozen times before he heard her cool, measured voice saying hello.

'Terry. It's Richard.'

There was a slight pause before she said, 'Oh yes?'

'Look, I've just learnt that some spotty schoolboy has made an inflammatory speech about the killer at a televised debate tonight. It's a safe bet that the national press will get hold of it soon. You may find a few photographers hanging round your house over the next few days.'

'Thanks for letting me know.'

'It's going to be pretty hectic here for a while.'

'That's fine. I'll see you when I see you.'

'Bye, then,' he said.

'I went to Cambridge today,' she said suddenly. 'I saw Mary Simpson. I think she lied to you.'

'Terry,' he said sadly. 'Not this again.'

'Are you going to give Brian a DNA test?'

'We can't make him take one, no,' he said patiently. 'Not without reasonable evidence. The only reason for Eden to take a DNA test now is if he himself volunteers for one.'

She put the phone down slowly, then turned to Giles, who was perched on the edge of the kitchen table. 'I'm sorry, Giles. You're going to have to go. I don't think I'm in the mood any more.'

'Why? What's wrong?'

'That was a former boyfriend. He still has the ability to make me absolutely bloody furious, that's all.'

'In that case, why not come to bed with me? It'll make me feel much better.'

'Don't be silly, Giles.'

'I was only asking,' he said meekly, pulling on his top.

When he had gone Terry sat for a long time on

her own, watching the light drain out of the room and wondering what she was going to do next. Then she went to the phone book, and found the number of the local TV station.

From the depths of her memory she dredged up the name of the reporter who'd filmed outside her house, and whom she'd been so rude to. Jemma.

She asked for Jemma in the news room, trusting that there wouldn't be two female reporters with that name. She was put through to a recorded message, but it included the reporters' mobile numbers. She had to dial two or three times before she got through.

'Jem Parker speaking.'

To judge from the background noises, she was in a pub.

'My name's Terry Williams. I think I may have a story for you. It's connected to the murder in fifty-seven West Street.'

When the other woman replied her voice was cautious. 'Have you been to the police with your information?'

'Oh yes.' Terry laughed. 'That's what the story's about. You see, there's a don, a man called Brian Eden, who's been getting sexually involved with his students. The police found out about him, but kept it quiet because the university asked them to.'

The background noises were quieter now. Terry guessed Jem had taken the phone outside. When she spoke again her voice was slightly muffled, as if she were lighting a cigarette.

'I'm sorry, we can't use this. Without proof, it's almost certainly slanderous.'

'I can give you the names of the other people involved. You'll be able to check the story with them.'

Another pause. 'Even so, we'd be accused of victimizing him. I'm sorry: it's one thing to report allegations someone's gone public with, but it's quite another to make them ourselves. Thanks, but—'

'Wait,' Terry said quickly. 'What if I were to be the one to go public? Could you use the story then?'

The other woman thought about it. 'I think we'd better meet,' she said at last. 'Where are you?'

Twenty-four

In the event there was much they couldn't use, but what they could use was enough. After Terry had recorded a piece to camera for Jemma the other woman had nodded curtly and trotted off with her prize without so much as a handshake. Jemma clearly thought her a harpy, but so long as she was going to use the story Terry wasn't that bothered either way.

The police, of course, had been obliged to confirm that the Edens had been investigated and that the investigation had included their other sexual partners. Since, Jemma had explained, such a police statement counted as corroboration, the story was now in the public domain.

Terry tried not to think what all this would do to Girdler's career.

Once the piece was on air the phone calls started. Terry refused to comment further, not even answering the door to the journalists from the national papers who camped outside, shouting questions through the letterbox. But she allowed herself to be photographed as she came and went, and within twenty-four hours the story had made the tabloids, already hungry for a new angle on the story initiated by Dominic Ashbury's speech at the Union.

It was Brian who got the full treatment, pursued by reporters every time he entered or left his home. She never saw him talk to any of them, but she guessed the university would use its influence to protect their star. She was sickened but not surprised when Mo called from London to say that one of the more upmarket papers had sent someone round to ask about her relationship with Terry. Mo had sent him away with a flea in his ear, but Terry knew it was now only a matter of time before her sexuality was used against her. She checked in the University Register: the editor of the paper had been an Oxford man.

She had stopped reading the papers by that stage, knowing that some of them would portray her whistle-blowing as the stridency of a feminist, the nosiness of an embittered neighbour, or – worst of all – the delusions of an academic unable to distinguish between the detective fiction she studied and real life. But she was aware of changes in the city – in her pigeon hole at the college she found a university circular advising male students to go out in pairs late at night, and to avoid wearing provocative clothing, whatever that was. She crumpled it wearily and dropped it on the floor. There was also a note from the Master, asking her to come and see him urgently. This she didn't drop on the floor, but otherwise she paid it no more attention than the circular.

In the event it was her tutor, Reg, who came to personally escort her to the Master. Seeing that a refusal now would only make the situation worse, she went. Wisely Reg avoided asking her any questions in the car, so they were both largely silent until they got to St Mary's.

'Jesus,' she said as she walked through the porter's lodge, 'what's going on?' The entire college seemed to be milling around on the grass of the main quad, most of the men in black tie, the women in cocktail dresses. In the centre of the grass a long rowing boat had been laid upside down on a plinth of wooden blocks.

'Mighty St Mary's, as we are now unofficially known, became Head Of The River today. Roddy's boys have done us proud yet again.'

'Oh, of course. Eights week.' For a moment, in her paranoia, she had thought all this must be something to do with her.

'Whatever happens, you should stick around to watch the ceremony. It's quite a sight.'

'Stick around? You make it sound as if I'll be leaving, Reg.' When he didn't answer, she said angrily, 'I thought I could count on your support, at least.'

'You haven't asked for it.'

'I'm too bloody proud to ask for it.' That, at

least, made him smile. He touched her arm. 'Come on. The Master will be wanting to go and join the festivities. The longer we keep him waiting, the less time we'll have to put your case.'

Whatever she was expecting, the atmosphere in the Master's chambers was eminently civilized. His wife showed them into the drawing room with a brief, professional smile. A decanter of sherry and a cluster of elegant glasses stood on the side table. The Master rose to greet them, a tall, elegant man also wearing black tie.

'My dear Reg. And you must be Theresa. I'm rather sorry we didn't have the opportunity to meet before this. Is dry sherry all right? The students appear to have drunk me out of sweet.'

'Wonderful,' said Terry, who wouldn't have known the difference. She accepted a glass of sticky brown stuff and moistened her lips with it obediently.

'Now then,' the Master said, hitching the creases of his trousers a little before settling into an armchair opposite her, 'what are we going to do about all this?'

Terry thought it prudent not to reply.

'These are mixed days for the college,' the Master mused. 'Triumph on the water, disaster on land. What do you think, Mrs Williams?'

'I'm sure the Eight deserved their win,' she said politely.

'Ah. I meant, what do you think about the disaster on land. And believe me, it is a disaster. We have just heard that Magdalen are to get the new

Pensung Chair of Detective Fiction. One feels that possibly this is not unrelated to the wild and unsubstantiated allegations made by a St Mary's postgraduate against one of her own colleagues.'

He paused. 'No-one is more broadminded than we. It is a requirement of our profession, after all. But the thing one cannot tolerate is disloyalty to the college.'

It was time for her to speak. 'Brian Eden has been abusing his position in the college for years. He is a sexual pervert—'

He interrupted her with the crisp assurance of the barrister he had once been. 'Don't be naïve. For that matter, so are you.'

Shaken, she tried to continue. 'He is a pervert who has certainly been involving St Mary's students in group sex practices. I believe he lied to the police about his whereabouts on the night Hugh Scott was killed. If this institution is about anything, it is about truth. I merely told the truth.'

He regarded her for a while. 'Where do you think the money for your employment here came from, Mrs Williams?'

'I don't know,' she said, confused by this sudden change of subject.

'It came from the sale of one of our properties. Ironically, the property I believe you now live in yourself.' He nodded towards Reg. 'I was asked if I could find some extra funds to subsidize an attempt to get the new Chair. It was a sound investment – the new Chair would have paid for itself many times over. Do you follow what I'm saying?'

She did. 'You're saying that with the Chair assigned to Magdalen, you'll have no reason to keep me on.'

He spread his hands in a gesture of resignation. 'No reason, and no funding. Cause, and effect. As it happens, you are both the cause and the effect. How felicitous. The fact that you have attempted to disgrace one of the most respected members of the college has,' he paused, 'has, you might say, nothing to do with it.'

So what Reg hadn't told her when he took her on was that she would have been out on her ear anyway, if the Chair hadn't come to St Mary's. For some reason this was almost as unbearable as the loss of the job itself.

There was no point in arguing. 'May I see the term out?' she asked. 'I've already prepared my last seminars.'

'Hmm. Reg?'

'I should like Terry to stay as long as you think possible, Master.'

So much for Reg's support, she thought.

'Given that there are only two weeks of term left, I think that's reasonable. Assuming that you stick to your subject this time. And assuming that you put your name to a public retraction and apology.'

'Retraction! You must be out of your tiny mind.'

He ignored her sneering tone. 'It will not in any case make much difference. Now that Dr Eden has cleared himself of all involvement in the murders, the rest will be taken for malicious speculation.'

'Cleared himself?' she said suspiciously. 'What do you mean?'

'Dr Eden went to the police and took a voluntary DNA test a few days ago. The results came through today. There is now less than one chance in one billion that he could be the man the police are looking for.'

'He's faked the tests somehow,' she said. 'He's an academic, he'll have found some way round it.' She stopped, aware that she sounded like a hysterical maniac.

The Master stood up. 'Are you sure you do want to stay for the rest of the term?' he enquired solicitously. 'I think you might benefit from a rest. But it is your decision. A public retraction, and you may stay for the next eleven days. And now you must excuse me. We are celebrating tonight.'

It was late afternoon as she left the Master's chambers. An expectant hush had fallen on the people hanging round the quad, and she stayed to watch.

From the dining hall there came a low rumble, which grew in volume to a roar as the doors were thrown open and the members of the college boat club poured onto the steps. They stood five abreast, their jackets discarded and their bow ties undone, arms linked around each others' shoulders for support. Many were plastered with sweat. They were mightily drunk, and they swayed as they received the adulation of those below.

The boat on the grass had evidently been doused

in petrol. A groundsman put a lighter to it and it went up in moments, a line of flame twenty feet long leaping three or four feet into the air. Immediately the first of the victors was off, sprinting down the steps and across the grass as a great shout went up from those watching. He jumped clear through the flames and raised both arms, but the shout which greeted this achievement was already turning into another roar for the person behind him.

They jumped the flames individually, and when they had all done that they linked arms and jumped in pairs, in threes and even in fives. As they jumped they sang, or rather chanted, songs that Terry couldn't hear over the hubbub but which she knew would be obscene.

Josie Graves and Neil Mather had taken a picnic out to the meadow. After they had eaten, and drunk the bottle of wine they had with them, they lay down in the long grass and kissed. They had chosen a spot well away from the path, and they were not disturbed as they lay in one another's arms. After a while Neil's hands slipped inside Josie's dress and began to stroke her through her panties. She murmured something and closed her eyes. Although they were living together, sharing Neil's room in Jericho, it was sweet to be out in the open air like this, warmed by the evening sun, gently arousing each other.

Neil rolled on top of her, pushing his hardness against her thigh, working his fingers further into her. She didn't want him to stop, but she was nervous about someone coming and finding them. She opened her eyes lazily to check that no-one was there, and looked straight into the eyes of the man who was watching them.

He was wearing a woollen balaclava and swimming goggles, but he was so close, kneeling over them, that she could see the eyes behind the goggles, as cold and steely as the Stanley knife in his hand.

Alerted by her sudden stiffness, Neil looked over his shoulder. Then he too froze as the knife came to rest on his neck.

'Hello, bitches,' the stranger murmured softly.

Neil jerked once, and in terrible close-up she saw the point of the knife dip into the unresisting skin. A tiny ball-bearing of blood, Neil's blood, welled out of the puncture. She drew breath to scream but the man's hand was over her mouth and nose. For an instant she actually tasted the salt of his palm before her mouth closed again and he took his hand away.

'Don't move a muscle, bitches,' he said calmly.

For the rest of the afternoon and most of the evening Terry walked. The city was achingly beautiful at this time of year, the brilliant sunshine revealing a myriad of warm hues in the local stone, the quads and corridors of the great colleges oases of coolness after the heat and din of the streets. Escaping the tourists, Terry found herself heading out through Christ Church meadow towards the river. She walked along the towpath, watching

372

the huge globes of gnats as they wobbled across the surface of the water. Once she saw a trout, fat as a flexing bicep, balancing itself against the current with lazy motions of its tail. By dusk she was in an unfamiliar part of the city, a colourful jumble of student bedsits and immigrant housing. Her feet were sore, but she had no real wish to return home yet. Darkness gave her anonymity. She sat outside a pub on her own, drinking Guinness and smoking. When the pub called time she got to her feet and walked some more. The Guinness had gone to her head: she felt detached and numb, insulated from the world.

She needed a pee, and walked across to some public toilets she could see on the other side of the street. When she got there, though, she found the Ladies closed and padlocked. A small handwritten sign apologized, with unconscious irony, for any inconvenience. The men's side, however, was open and lit up.

She looked around. The street was completely deserted. She waited a few moments to make sure she wouldn't meet someone coming out, then slipped into the Gents.

She had been in men's toilets before, for one reason or another, but never one as uninviting as this. She was in a grubby concrete bunker lined with high slit windows. Someone had run amok with a blue spray can – here and there she could just make out 'United FC', but for the most part the author had been content to draw meaningless knots and squiggles of paint, incomprehensible hieroglyphs of male aggression. In front of her a row of urinals protruded from the wall, each bleached white jawbone sucking a mint of disinfectant. Quickly she found a cubicle with a lock – the only one, in fact – and wiped the seat carefully before allowing herself the luxury of emptying her bursting bladder.

The graffiti was universally obscene. 'I like big cocks.' 'I'll suck your big one.' 'Come here at midnight and I'll fill your mouth.' She searched for anything witty or amusing, anything that could have been in one of those anthologies of toilet-wall wisdom some of her friends kept beside the loo, but found none. And now that she came to think of it, which was odder: this sad outpouring of human misery and frustration, or what normal people did, keeping a collection of toilet-wall scribbles in their toilet, but in a nicely printed book instead of spraying them over the Laura Ashley wallpaper?

As her eye travelled over the graffiti she suddenly noticed that there was a hole in the wall, a couple of inches in diameter, roughly hacked with a penknife. Someone had pasted a piece of paper over it for privacy, which explained why she hadn't spotted it before. She was just realizing what it must be for when she heard footsteps on the concrete floor.

She kept very still, hoping that he would just relieve himself and be gone. But after a moment the footsteps came into the cubicle next to her own. She felt a surge of adrenaline that made her shiver. She waited for him to lock his door, to start; then she would make a calm but hurried exit.

He knocked on the partition, and she jumped.

'Hallo?' he said quietly. His voice reverberated on the concrete walls.

There was a long silence.

'If you're not here for the same reason I'm here,' he whispered, 'just say.'

Running through her mind were all the options: a firm, acerbic 'Go away' – though what might that precipitate? And if the worst did happen, wouldn't a judge say she had been guilty of provocation, simply by being there? – answering in a whisper that might disguise her gender; making a run for it; doing nothing. But somehow she was paralysed, unable to decide on any of them.

So she did nothing.

'I thought so,' the voice was saying. 'I had a look under a moment ago. That's a pair of women's knickers, isn't it? You dirty bastard.'

She heard him chuckle, and then a belt chinked. Cloth rustled on cloth. The circle of paper over the hole in the wall darkened and split as he poked a finger through it. The toes of two training shoes appeared under the partition. Then – she held her hand to her mouth, a reflex action – his penis pushed into her space, half erect.

The urge to scream died in her throat. It was so ridiculous – not because it was small, or flaccid: on the contrary, it was becoming harder every second, twitching upwards with the beat of his blood. It just looked so incongruous, poking out of a squiggle of graffiti, ringed with hairs. It was almost as if the wall itself had sprouted feet and a sexual organ.

Afterwards, she would never know what it was that had made her reach out to touch it; whether it was the Guinness, or wilful curiosity, or simple weariness with the whole sexual nonsense, the clamour and urgency of bodies that all ultimately came down to this: flesh touching flesh. It shuddered at the contact. As if in slow motion, she saw her hand moving on him. 'Now your mouth,' he hissed, but she heard nothing. After a minute he groaned and came, a torrent of hot candlewax that fizzled and leapt and ran down the opposite wall to the floor. Instantly he withdrew, and she heard the sound of tissue paper being torn off, the belt being refastened. Then he was gone.

She sat there for a while, staring into space. She was dimly aware that there were noises outside, shouting, some kind of struggle, and that some of the noise was directed inside, at her. Then she heard the concrete chamber outside her cubicle fill with running footsteps, and the doors to the cubicles were kicked open one by one. Before they reached her, she undid the bolt and walked out. The place was full of men now, police constables and others not wearing any uniform whom she also took to be policemen. For a moment she had the absurd thought that they had all come to use the facilities.

Seeing her, they fell silent. She ignored them and went to wash her hands. At last one stepped forward and said formally, 'You'd better come with us.'

At the police station she emptied her pockets and was put into a bright cell. Here there was no graffiti, but otherwise it was no more hospitable or pleasant than the toilet had been, a disinfected cubicle of concrete with a tiny hole through which she could be observed. Periodically eyes came and looked at her briefly: she guessed that she was the subject of much curiosity now.

She lay on the bench and stared at the pulse of the fluorescent bulb above her head. In the car she had spoken Girdler's name and eventually, after what might have been one hour or many hours, he came.

'Are you all right?' he asked, his bulk filling the door.

'I'd like to go home.'

'In a minute,' he said, and led her to another functional room. Here there was a tape recorder, empty of tapes, a table and a few metal chairs. He sat down opposite her. A WPC she remembered from the first time she had come here, to tell them about the cat, brought her a plastic cup of something hot.

'Will I be charged?' she asked through teeth that were suddenly chattering.

'Of course not,' Girdler said. She had thought he would be contemptuous, though his voice radiated only concern.

'If I was a man what would I be charged with?' she asked.

He rubbed his eyes. 'Does it really matter? Look, I'll take you home.'

'I'd rather get a taxi.'

'It's no trouble.'

'I don't want to be with you,' she said. Meeting his eyes, she said. 'I'm sorry, Richard. It isn't going to work.'

He looked away before she did. 'No,' he said quietly. 'I can see that. Anyway, Jane here can take you home.'

'I'm sorry,' she said again. 'I expect I got you into trouble by talking to that reporter about Eden, didn't I?'

He shrugged. 'There's been another attack, by the way. This evening, out by the river. The victim's with the medic now. I haven't interviewed him yet, but I think we may be getting closer.'

'Eden?'

He shook his head. 'Was in College, at a Rowing Club celebration. Come on, Terry. What did you expect?'

Twenty-five

In the examination room the policeman broke the seal on a box and handed it to the doctor, who told Neil to take his clothes off and lie down on the examination table. Miserable, naked and shivering uncontrollably with shock, he climbed onto the table and saw the other men eyeing his body with dispassionate concentration. He was asked if he'd showered or had a bath since the attack: he hadn't. A paper towel was placed under his buttocks. The doctor started to comb his pubic hair with a comb he took from the box, while the policeman began to examine and bag up the clothes he had been wearing. After a while Neil knew he was going to cry. He bit his lip to stop himself. If you cry, he told himself, they'll think you're queer, they'll think you asked for it. The doctor was keeping up a running commentary in a low, sympathetic voice, explaining everything he was doing. 'Now I'm going to take some swabs.' The doctor took hold of his penis now and pulled back the foreskin with his gloved hands so that he could wipe it with a swab: Neil could feel the warmth of the man's fingers, the calluses on his palms, through the thin plastic of the gloves. He shut his eyes. 'I'm going to cut some of your pubic hairs,' the doctor explained. He felt the snipping round the base of his penis, then he heard the doctor, absurdly, counting up to ten. 'Two more,' the policeman said. 'I thought it was ten,' said the doctor. 'No, twelve,' the policeman insisted. There was a pause while they consulted some notes; as if, Neil thought, they were reading an instruction manual for a particularly complicated and un-familiar piece of DIY furniture. 'Twelve,' the doctor conceded, cutting two more. 'Neil, I'm going to cut your fingernails.' For a few surreal minutes he lay there, still shivering, while the doctor gave him a manicure and scraped under his nails, picking the clippings up off the examination table carefully with tweezers and putting them in yet another envelope.

He suddenly remembered about the thing the rapist had dropped. 'Look in the pocket of my trousers,' he said to the policeman who was bag-ging his clothes. 'He dropped it.' The policeman found the lipstick and looked impressed. He took it out of Neil's trousers carefully, putting his hand inside a plastic bag and then flipping it inside out so that his fingers didn't come into contact with it. 'Flame red,' he said, squinting at the label. 'We'll talk in a minute. Let's get this part over with first.'

If he had been on his own when he was raped Neil would probably never have called the police. But Josie had insisted. It was something she and her friends had thought through more than he or any of his male friends, of course: she pointed out that if he reported it, there was at least a chance that the rapist would be caught. If he didn't report it, others would be raped. She hadn't even let him have a bath or change his clothes, making the phone call for him while he sat vacantly on the bed in his room, holding a blood-encrusted tissue to the cut in his neck.

'OK,' the doctor said at last, 'I'll need some help with this next bit. You have to stand up and bend forward over the table.' He had known this was coming, known they would have to do it, but he found himself hyperventilating with fear and shock as he did as he was asked. The policeman was writing on the envelopes, deliberately not catching Neil's eye. The first swab was gentle, like a mother wiping a baby. 'You may feel some discomfort now, I'm afraid,' the doctor said. He did, he felt more than discomfort, and couldn't help himself from crying out as the fingers probed inside him. Looking round, he caught a glimpse of the swab the doctor was holding, a bright smear of blood. 'No bodily fluids,' the doctor muttered to the policeman. 'Oh well,' the policeman said, sounding disappointed. 'Right, Neil, you can get dressed now.' Neil moved towards his clothes but the doctor had produced a jumpsuit made of white paper-like material. 'We'll need to keep your clothes,

I'm afraid,' the policeman said. He climbed into the suit. It was incredibly thin and did nothing to stop him shivering. 'I'd like a cup of coffee,' he pleaded. 'In a minute,' the doctor said. 'I've just got to take a swab from your mouth, and a sputum sample.' He was made to spit onto a piece of tissue, which was carefully folded up and placed in yet another envelope. Finally, there was just the blood sample. As the needle pressed against his forearm and disappeared into the solid flesh Neil had a sudden flashback to the rape, the point of the Stanley knife resting against his neck, the sudden agony as the man had penetrated him. He closed his eyes. 'Right, we're done,' he heard the doctor say cheerfully. Neil opened his eyes and counted nine envelopes on the desk. 'How do you take it?' the policeman asked. Neil gaped at him. 'Your coffee?' he prompted gently.

The police car dropped Terry outside her front door. Too late she realized that this was not the most inconspicuous way of returning to Osney. Luckily, the street was empty apart from Dorling Van Glught who was posting a letter, though even he looked somewhat alarmed at the sight of the car.

'Don't worry,' she muttered as she got out. 'I've only killed twenty of them and I'm out on bail.' She looked across at Sheila's house, where the net curtains fortunately remained drawn.

She slept for a few hours, then got up and ran a bath, lying in the hot water stroking Guinness, who for unfathomable reasons of her own liked to come and balance precariously on the edge of the bath

382

when Terry was using it, lapping the soapy water delicately with her neat little tongue. Then she wrapped herself in an old dressing gown and went to her desk. She groaned out loud and rested her head in her hands.

Wrong, wrong, wrong. Everything she had said or done since she had returned to Oxford had either been mistaken or misguided. She had made a complete balls-up of everything, and now she was out on her ear. Doubtless news of her inadvertent cottaging would spread round the university like wildfire, ensuring that her reputation would plummet even lower.

The envelope in which she had placed the original letters lay in front of her, the most recent letter on top of it. Pulling them towards her, she skimmed through them once more, her eye registering a blur of body parts and positions.

Taking a clean sheet of paper, she wrote out the text of the very first letter again, the one that the police had been sent on Women's Centre notepaper and which Girdler had showed her in the police station, so many ages ago. *Hugh Scott was killed because he was a man. Save fuel, burn men. All men are rapists. The sisters of unmercy will prevail.* On a second piece she wrote out the text of the letter that Julia had flushed down her toilet. How had it gone? Ironically, the iambic rhythm made it easier to remember the words. *You will be glad to know that someone was watching the two of you at it last night. Please keep it up (and keep the curtains open). Believe me when I say your little shows are much appreciated.*

And, of course, there was also the word written above Hugh Scott's mutilated body. *Rapist.* She wrote that on a third piece of paper, then placed them next to the porn letters.

She tried to think of them as a sequence, written by one person. In which case, the porn letters she'd found in Hugh's room came first, followed by *Rapist*, followed by the letter to the police. Then came the note to her and the final porn letter, the one written in her name.

Why had Hugh hidden those first letters in his room? Could it have been because he had known, not that Brian had written them, *but that he hadn't*?

Had some detail of the letters made him aware that they could not have been written by either of the two people whose bed he was sharing? Perhaps the events they described just didn't tally with Hugh's experience. Perhaps he even mentioned them to Carla and Brian and got a blank look.

As she rearranged them, a phrase from the most recent letter leapt out at her. *She started to lick me as only a woman can.* Would Eden, with his monumental male arrogance, have written those words? Surely not.

Looking back over the sequence, she noticed something else. *When Mary eventually reached down with her hand and started to squeeze and rub my breasts, I shouted, 'My God! I'm coming,' and I came and came in great waves of pleasure.* Eden wouldn't have written that, either. To him, lesbians were simply women who hadn't found the right man. In his fantasies, women wouldn't come just because they were touched by other women.

It wasn't even credible as a scene – what had Mary Simpson said? 'We were none of us in the least bit gay. It wouldn't have worked otherwise.' Terry had been asking about homosexuality among the men, which was why she hadn't noticed the discrepancy at the time. But Mary's 'we' clearly referred to both sexes. And Carla's inept pass at Terry suggested that she'd never had the chance to experiment with lesbianism in the swingers' group.

Two things she was certain of. First, if Brian had been writing about the Parnassians, he'd have been accurate. He was a scholar, after all.

Secondly, the person who wrote the letters felt inadequate sexually. Women didn't need him. Other men were more sexually successful than he was. That was why he wrote from the point of view of a woman: he felt himself a failure as a man.

It wasn't Brian. Who, then? It clearly had to be one of the Parnassians – the iambic rhythms confirmed that.

Dr Simpson had said there were half a dozen of them originally. And that – Terry's memory strained to recall the exact words – some of them had moved away.

Like a flashbulb going off and flooding the papers in front of her with light, she suddenly saw what had been staring her in the face all along.

Dorling Van Glught.

Like Brian, the Van Glughts were Parnassians who had stayed. 'The clever ones got jobs and the thick ones like me stayed on however they could,' Dorling had told her at the party. 'A friend of Brian's got me a commission for a children's book.'

Dickie the Dragon. Julia had laughed at it. A little dragon which wasn't fierce or fiery enough to be a proper dragon.

Fire. Dragon flames. A soldering iron. *Burn men*. Was there a connection? Deep down in the twisted mind of a psychopathic rapist, were fire and sexual assault one and the same thing?

From the depths of her own brain a line floated up. *He wasn't very fierce and he wasn't very tall, Dickie the Dragon was very very small.* The doggerel in which Dorling wrote his children's books. The iambic doggerel.

All this time she had been looking at the wrong writer. She had imagined that the iambs of the letters were the result of a career spent writing books about Shelley and Keats. It had never occurred to her that anyone was still using those same rhythms today. But of course, they were. There was still a ready market for crap like Dickie the Dragon.

In one sense, she had been right all along. Her mistake had been to fasten her suspicions on the wrong person.

Ann Byres had described the first letter she'd looked at as a competition, which the prime male ultimately wins. Terry had assumed that meant Brian was the author, because he was also the winner. But if the letter was written because the author hated Brian, hated his success – both academic and sexual – and hated his fame, it might make sense that he was acting out the reasons for his hatred in fantasy.

Just as a transvestite dresses up in women's clothes and expresses his feelings about women through camp, Dorling was escaping the harsh reality of his failed masculinity. Except that while a transvestite simply puts on the clothes of a woman, here Dorling was dressing up in women's minds.

Dorling Van Glught hated men, for much the same reason that some extreme feminists did. He hated them for all the things they had which he didn't: power, confidence, authority, success.

His alarm when he'd seen her in the police car earlier made sense now. It hadn't been her he was alarmed about, but the car itself. If he'd attacked someone else that very day, he was probably terrified of being arrested.

She debated whether or not to call Girdler, but decided against it. This time she was going to get proof before she made a fool of herself.

She glanced at her watch. At any moment, the mail would be collected from the postbox.

She ran outside. Sure enough, the red mail van was at that very second drawing up next to the postbox on the street corner. She raced towards it, waving and shouting. As the postman unlocked the postbox door, letting the letters inside tumble into his sack, he saw her.

'I wonder,' she said, 'if I could possibly retrieve a letter I put in here a few minutes ago? It's a bill, you see, and I've just realized I've forgotten to put the cheque in with it.'

The postman looked doubtful. 'Strictly speaking,' he began. Terry flashed him her most winning smile, widening her eyes and all but fluttering her eyelashes. 'Please,' she begged, 'I'll get into the most terrible trouble if I send it without a cheque.'

'Oh, all right then,' the postman said, weakening. He held open the sack. 'Help yourself.'

'It'll be on top, because I've only just posted it,' Terry said, to cover the fact that she didn't know exactly what she was looking for. She bent lower into the sack and arched her back, hoping that he'd be too distracted by her bum to notice that she was rifling through the letters one by one. Would it be typed or handwritten? Typed, she guessed. He was a professional writer, after all.

Then she saw it. *Linzi's Letters*, read the first line of the address.

'Thanks,' she said, backing out and clutching her prize.

'Anytime at all,' said the postman, meaning it.

She took it back to her house thoughtfully. She mustn't open it, she realized, or she'd be accused of tampering with the evidence. She placed it on the desk with the others and went to the phone.

Girdler wasn't there, but she got his voicemail.

'It's me, Terry. Look, I know you won't want to believe me, but I've finally worked out who really did it. And this time I've got proof.' She paused. It wasn't the right time or the right medium, but she wanted to say it anyway. 'Richard, I've been a fool, and I don't mean about the case. Come round as soon as you can, will you?'

He was there ten minutes later, ringing the doorbell impatiently and banging on the door for her to come down and let him in. With a light heart she ran to the door, seeing his silhouette framed against the frosted glass. She started to pull it open, falling back with a gasp as it was suddenly forced all the way, sprawling on the floor in the narrow passageway while above her Dorling Van Glught carefully closed the door, having first checked the street to see that no-one had observed him, before wrapping a fist in her hair and hauling her roughly before him up the stairs.

In her bedroom he picked the envelope up off the desk and stowed it in his pocket without a word.

'How did you know I had that?' Terry said, trying to keep her voice calm. Her scalp ached where he had lifted her bodily up the stairs by her hair, and her cheek felt bruised where it had banged on the steps, but she knew that she had to keep the situation as normal-seeming as possible. Dogs only bite you when you run away.

'I saw you running after the post,' he said. 'So I waited to see what you were up to. Then I saw you coming away with my envelope. I couldn't risk you opening it. It's a little incriminating, you see.'

'You write them on Women's Centre notepaper,' she guessed. 'You write them in Carla's name – or my name, for that matter – and you put them on Women's Centre paper to make them seem more authentic.'

'Smart bitch,' he whispered.

She suddenly ran to the phone on the other side of the bed and punched 999. It was answered almost immediately.

'Emergency, which service do you require?'

'Police.' But it was all too slow. Casually, Dorling had moved behind her and disconnected the call with a finger.

She did then what she had always promised herself she would do in such a situation. She scraped her foot down the inside of his shin and then stamped hard on his toes. If she had been wearing shoes, she would probably have disabled him. But she wasn't, and she felt her naked heel bounce ineffectually off his foot.

So she hit him with the phone handset instead, crashing it against the side of his head. He bellowed with pain, and put his hand to the spot.

For a moment they stood there, regarding each other cautiously. She wondered whether she should hit him again. But it was hard, this deliberately hurting someone, and when he reached out his hand and took the phone from her she offered no resistance.

Then he punched her, full in the stomach, punched her as a man might punch another man. Winded, she collapsed, and she felt his fingers reaching for a nipple through the thin material of her T-shirt, twisting it cruelly. The pain was like

390

something visual, something brightly coloured that fizzed and bubbled behind her eyes. She screamed, and he put his hands to her neck and ripped. The T-shirt came away. Underneath it she was bra-less.

She lay there, panting. Again, she was astonished how normal it seemed, to be lying here half-naked while a madman decided how he was going to hurt her next.

'Take your clothes off,' he said calmly.

She did as she was told. When she was standing naked in front of him she said, 'If you would like to have sex with me, it will be better if you don't hit me.' But he shook his head with an expression of distaste and pointed to the bed. 'Lie there, bitch. I need to think.'

She obeyed. She needed to think too. She thought: why does this man rape other men? What had Ann said? It's about the need to inflict fear. Perhaps if she showed him how frightened she was, he would let her go.

On the other hand, perhaps the first sign of fear would trigger his bloodlust. So she kept quiet.

'You have paint, don't you?' he said suddenly. The question was so bizarre she didn't answer him at first, and he prodded her viciously in the ribs with the heel of his shoe. 'Answer me, bitch.'

'Yes,' she said meekly.

'Get it.'

The paint was stored in the spare room next to hers, four or five large three-litre drums of White with a hint of Lavender. She lugged it in, two at a time, and set it at Dorling's feet.

'Turps?' he asked. 'White spirit? Anything like that?'

He's mad, she thought. Any moment now we're going to start discussing colour schemes. But then she saw that he was reading one of the labels on the paint tins, and realized what he was up to.

Satisfied, he set the can down. 'Open them,' he said, nodding at the cans.

She prized the cans open with an old bike tyre lever she kept for the purpose.

'Good. Now back over there. I tried to burn this house down once before,' he said conversationally, 'but the bastard I set fire to didn't burn very well.'

'Why did you kill him?' she asked.

'Kill who?'

'Hugh Scott. Why did you break in here and kill him, that night? It must have been more risky than attacking a stranger.'

Dorling nodded. 'He was the first,' he said at last. 'I found him on the towpath one night. He was out running. I was out . . . hunting. So I had him.'

Dear God, she thought: so Hugh Scott had been raped himself, and never told a soul.

'Stupid of me. To strike so close to home, I mean. And afterwards . . . I saw him looking at me sometimes. As if he was wondering. As if he suspected. So I decided to kill him.'

'He'd found the letters, by then,' she said. 'He used to read the magazine you sent them to. I thought Brian wrote them, but Hugh realized he couldn't have done.'

'Of course Brian didn't write them. Brian couldn't write a fucking shopping list.'

She was trying to keep him talking, it having occurred to her that Girdler might have heard her voice-mail message by now. Would he come? Would he think she was a neurotic cow who'd wrecked his career, or would he still want to see her?

'He got you your book commission, though, didn't he?'

'Oh, yes,' he sneered. 'I've got so much to thank *Brian* for, haven't I? Everyone loves *Brian*. Brian's a fucking *visionary*. Brian's so fucking *magnanimous*.'

'I never liked him either,' she said. Offering him common ground. Trying to make him feel that she was on his side.

'You tried to give him the credit for my work.'

'I didn't realize,' she said. 'I'm really very sorry.'

He nodded. 'You and I have both tried to destroy him,' he said solemnly. 'The difference is, I shall succeed.' He picked up the bottle of white spirit and looked at it thoughtfully. 'I wonder what this stuff's like to drink?' he wondered. Then he held it out to her. 'After you.'

'No, really, I—'

'Fucking well drink,' he roared, and she obediently moistened her lips with the foul-tasting liquid.

'It's fine,' she said, handing it back to him. An idea struck her. 'More of a man's drink, though.'

Glaring at her, Dorling put it to his lips and threw his head back. She wondered whether to rush him, but he kept his eyes fixed on her all the time.

'Call him,' he said, putting down the bottle.

'Who?'

'Brian, of course. It's time to get superstud round to join our little party.'

'He won't come.'

Dorling leered at her. 'He will if you say what I tell you to say.'

Twenty-six

Girdler sat at his desk, with Jane Hughes and Mike Jeffries taking the seats opposite him. 'Let's get some coffees,' he suggested.

Jane got up. There was no reason why she should get them just because she was a woman, but she didn't want to make a point of it. 'I'll go,' she offered.

'Thanks,' Girdler smiled.

'So,' Mike started to say, but Girdler shushed him. 'Let's wait for Jane,' he suggested. He doodled thoughtfully on the pad in front of him while they waited. Flame red. Flames. When he had finished drawing the flames he started to draw a beast behind them, a mythical dragon belching smoke, then he put cartoon lips on the dragon as if it was wearing lipstick. It looked so comic he added false eyelashes and a handbag, then quickly scribbled over it to rub it out.

Jane Hughes came in with two coffees. 'Sorry, I

could only carry two at a time,' she said cheerfully. 'Won't be a tick.'

Girdler sighed and reached for the phone. 'I'll just phone Forensic while we're waiting. Oh, I've got a message,' he said, noticing the change of tone. He keyed in the numbers that replayed his voice-mail.

'You have two messages,' the mechanical voice said. 'The first is . . .' Girdler listened to a long tirade from the Chief, most of it concerning the newspaper reports, which he had evidently just read, about Brian Eden.

Jane Hughes came back and sat down. His two juniors sat waiting for him expectantly. Girdler started to talk over the jabbering in his ear.

'What's so important about this last attack', he said, blowing noisily on his coffee to cool it, 'isn't just the lipstick, or the fact that we've got someone who might recognize the killer if we get him into a line-up. It's the fact that we've got someone who's prepared to go on television and announce that he's been raped. It might help persuade someone else to come forward – hang on—'

In his ear he heard Terry saying, '. . . finally worked out who really did it. And this time I've got proof.'

'But it'll also alert the killer,' Jane began. Girdler held up his hand. '. . . been a fool,' Terry was saying. 'Come round as soon as you can . . .'

He put the phone down thoughtfully. A WPC from the Ops room was waiting at the door. 'Sir? I thought you'd want to know. This came through on

999. I was going to log it, but then I noticed the address and I thought you'd want to see it.'

He took the slip of paper from her. *57 West Street. Duration 12 seconds. Female caller. Caller abort.*

He called Terry's number, but the line was busy.

'OK, I'll go and check on this myself,' he said, putting the paper in his pocket.

'D'you want it logged, sir?'

'No.'

Hughes and Jeffries exchanged glances. The boss's obsession with the highly strung academic in Osney was becoming the talk of the canteen.

'While you're out, sir,' Jane suggested acidly, 'we could do with some more milk.'

Terry put down the phone. The things Dorling had made her say to Brian might have been corny – as crass as anything Dorling had written in his letters, in fact – but they'd also been effective. He would be round in a couple of minutes.

She glanced at Dorling. He had drunk his way through about half the white spirit by now. It didn't seem to have affected him particularly, though even the small amount she'd had was making her own head feel light and disorientated.

'When did you start writing pornography?' she asked.

'Less talk, more action. On the bed with your legs spread. Face down. Like that.' He took a piece of her T-shirt and tied it into a makeshift gag. 'When he comes in, you're not to say anything, you hear?'

She nodded. She doubted if she could make a sound through the gag in any case.

For a moment he stood looking down at her. She felt, as much from the sudden stillness of his attention as anything else, that he was for the first time sexually interested in her, now that she was exposed like this, laid out powerless like an image in a girlie magazine. She guessed that for him some wires must have long ago got crossed in his brain, making him respond only to situations where he could feel powerful, dominant; his sexual urges totally at the service of his massive insecurity.

He ran his hand down her flank once, a lingering caress that made her blood run cold, then stood back, sighing. 'Don't waste any sympathy on Brian,' he said. 'He's an idiot. It always pissed me off, you know, that someone like him was considered so attractive, while the ordinary decent quiet people get ignored.'

You're hardly an ordinary decent person, she thought, but even if she had not been gagged she would have kept the thought to herself for fear of provoking him. Bizarrely, she found herself thinking about Holmes and Watson, or for that matter Shelley and Trelawney. So often a charismatic, Promethean figure seemed to call into being their opposite, someone who was attracted by the very qualities they lacked. Only in this case it hadn't been admiration and love which bound Dorling to Brian Eden, but envy and hatred.

The door creaked open, and a footstep entered the room. But then she heard a faint *miaow*, and realized to her horror that Half-pint the kitten was there, back from her afternoon's hunting. Which probably meant that Guinness was somewhere in the house too.

Dorling laughed. 'A cat disturbed me once before,' he said chattily. 'Don't move, bitch, or I'll slice your cunt open and ram your ovaries down your throat.'

There was a kissing noise as he scooped the kitten into his arms, then he was gone. She listened. He was in the bathroom. She heard a sudden, piercing howl from the animal, then the toilet flushed.

Suddenly she was terrified, really terrified, shaking uncontrollably with fear and panic. She realized that whatever happened, she wasn't going to get out of this alive. Her bladder convulsed, and she felt a trickle of urine seep onto the bed. She moaned softly, fighting the urge to let go, fighting the shame of it. Vomit surged into her mouth, her throat locking in sudden spasms around the cloth between her teeth. There was nowhere for it to go, and she forced herself to swallow it before she choked.

Dorling returned from the bathroom and stood over her, wiping his hands on his trousers. At that moment the front door opened downstairs, and her heart leapt – Richard? – only to hear, a moment later, Brian Eden's voice floating up the stairwell.

From the corner of her vision she saw Dorling take a thin dark woollen roll from one of his pockets. He shook it out: inside were a Stanley knife and a pair of goggles.

'Time for me to get dressed,' he whispered. 'Remember, not a sound.'

Richard put the carton of milk into the glove compartment of his car and paused a moment before starting the engine. Osney was just round the corner, but he felt a curious ambivalence, a reluctance almost, about seeing Terry again. On the one hand she had affected him powerfully, but on the other hand her ludicrous antics had almost certainly cost him a promotion, if not his whole career. He could see in his mind's eye what might happen when he got to her house – the crazy theories, the anger if he refused to take her seriously, the intellectual arrogance she'd display towards him. He had never in his life felt as patronized as he sometimes did with Terry.

But he could also see the possibility of reconciliation, bed, a new beginning. He had always felt that her theories, though impetuously gathered and dogmatically defended, stemmed from a deep and passionate desire to make sense of the world. It was this, as much as anything physical, that he liked about Terry: her refusal to take anything for granted, her ability – rare, he felt, in a woman – to disregard what most people thought of as the normal rules of civilized behaviour. A similar feeling in himself was one of the reasons he had joined the police.

Removing the keys from the ignition, he went back into the shop to see if they sold flowers.

* * *

Brian Eden walked into Terry's bedroom and saw her naked on the bed. She had her face turned away from the door, and Dorling had arranged a pillow so that the gag was barely visible. To all intents and purposes it must have looked as if she were laid out for him, waiting. She heard him take a step forward. Then he smelt the urine and fear, saw the cloth in her mouth and started to hesitate. But by that time Dorling had swung the door shut behind him. She heard Brian draw breath to shout, but the sound died in his throat.

She turned her head then and spat out the evil-tasting gag, reckoning that Dorling's attention would no longer be focused on her, and that even if it was, there were better ways to die than choking on her own vomit.

Dorling had pulled the balaclava over the goggles, so that his eyes glinted green in the midst of the black wool like some strange bug – an ant, she thought, or a wasp. In his hand was the knife.

'Hello, darling,' he said conversationally.

'Jesus Christ!' Brian stepped back towards the bed. It caught the back of his knees and he sprawled backwards beside Terry.

'Something like that,' agreed Dorling calmly. 'You're lying in her piss, Brian. The mare has pissed the bed. Isn't that sweet?' Leaning close over them, the knife rock steady in his hand, he whispered, 'You're going to piss yourself too, you know. Or if you don't, I'll cut your bladder open and spill your stinking piss over the bed that way.'

'Dorling. You're,' Brian swallowed, 'you're upset.

Put the knife down and let's talk about it.'

Dorling laughed. 'Upset? *Upset?*' He reached out and, almost casually, stroked the blade across Brian's cheek. 'Wrong answer, Brian.'

In horrible close-up Terry saw the skin of Brian's cheek ladder like a stocking. An inch-long globule of blood, as wide as a man's tongue, swelled from the opening.

'Besides, why talk when I've brought you this present?' He indicated the naked Terry with the knife. 'Any man would want to fuck that. You do want to fuck her, don't you Brian? And remember, no more wrong answers.'

Brian said nothing.

'Take your clothes off.' Dorling's voice was hard now, devoid of any inflection. Brian did as he was told. When he was too slow the knife darted again, nicking and slashing at the exposed flesh.

Naked, he stood before them.

'Now fuck her,' Dorling ordered.

There was a pause. 'I can't,' Eden said.

'Why not?'

Eden spread his arms a little. 'I can't get a hard on like this,' he said quietly. 'That's what you wanted me to say, isn't it? That I'm impotent.'

'Two flaccid bitches, then. I'll just have to show you who the real man is around here. Get down next to her.'

He gestured with the knife towards the bed. At that moment Brian grabbed the hand with the knife, pulling it over his shoulder so that Dorling was forced off balance. But Dorling instantly headbutted him, knocking his own wool-covered head into Brian's nose, twisting on top of him so that he could get his knee into Brian's groin.

Terry slid sideways off the bed, giving them space. She suddenly saw that there was a screwdriver on the floor under the bed, a Phillips screwdriver she had used to refasten the floorboards in here. It must have rolled under the bed and been forgotten about.

Every instinct in her body told her to run, or to cower in the corner until they were done. But her brain told her to act.

She acted.

Coming up behind Dorling, she selected a spot under his chin and with one long, hard thrust drove the screwdriver up through his throat and into his brain, holding on for dear life as he tried to buck and shake her free, until the bucking and the shaking had stopped and she could close her eyes gratefully and think about nothing, nothing at all, just blackness and calm and pure, perfect silence.

When Girdler rushed in through the open front door, only moments later, that was how he found the three of them: toppled together on the bed, while Guinness the cat prowled round them, jealously trying to work her way between the warmth of their bodies.

'Today, as we reach the end of this series of lectures, I want to talk about endings in detective fiction and what they signify.'

Terry stopped, and glanced at her notes.

She was in the largest of all the lecture theatres this time, having been warned by the faculty administrator that her final session of the term was likely to have rather more attendees than previously. Even that had turned out to be an understatement. She was famous now. The rows of seats rising in front of the podium were crammed with students, and more were sitting cross-legged in the aisles, their files open on their knees.

'My theme this week is certainty and its opposite, ambiguity. The ending of the detective novel is, classically, a victory for certainty. Social order has been threatened by human passion: passion which has spilled over into bloody murder. On one level, then, the detective is an emissary of the forces of order, restoring proper balance to a disrupted society. Wrongdoers must be brought to justice; mysteries must be laid bare; Apollo, god of order, must triumph over Dionysus, god of misrule. It is perhaps no accident that when we speak of the law, we habitually call it "law and order", so intertwined are these two concepts in our public imagination. The neat, ordered resolution of the classical detective story is in a sense returning us to this public world, the world outside the novel, with a renewed sense of the rightness and immutability we will find there.

'Why should this be so? Well, if you look at those periods when the detective myth in its various guises has been most popular, they are periods of the greatest spiritual and social upheaval. Would Miss Marple have existed without Keir Hardie? Her little village is a microcosm of an unchanging

England, England as it would have been before the First World War changed that way of life for ever. As many observers have pointed out, if you want to find the villain in a Christie novel, look no further than the person who is trying to change his or her social class. Would Sherlock Holmes have existed without Charles Darwin? Sherlock, it is suggested on several occasions, is an atheist and a rationalist: his household gods are the opium pipe and the violin, his personal devil a terror of boredom – boredom which for him takes on a spiritual dimension, so that we might even be tempted to use a different contemporary term, and call it ennui, that precursor of existential angst. And similarly, the quest narratives I have been comparing detective fiction with over the past weeks were at their most popular in the eleventh and twelfth centuries – a time of spiritual and social darkness in which European civilization came close to breaking down altogether.

'In other words, the detective's desire for order once reflected, and perhaps even helped to satisfy, a similar hunger in society at large. Today, we might like to believe that we are more sophisticated than that. For us, certainty equals naïvety. This belief has been reflected in all the arts, of course, but it has had a particularly dramatic effect on the detective novel. Gradually, as the century has unfolded, the nature of the detective novel has changed. The great detectives of the first part of the century were, quite simply, never wrong. Certainty came easily to them: their authors simply could not

405

conceive of a case they could not solve. A Sherlock Holmes or an Auguste Dupin looks down on events from a god-like height. Contemptuous of the police, impatient with indecision; these are figures of myth rather than of humanity.

'In the post-war period that changed, and in the work of Raymond Chandler and other writers we see heroes, or rather anti-heroes, who are themselves fugitives from justice. Evil is not always vanquished: good is not always triumphant. In short, we moved from what might be termed closed endings to those that are more open.'

She watched as the girl directly in front of her in the first row wrote down *Closed*, and next to it *Open*, underlining the two words neatly. The girl's hair brushed the paper as she leant over it.

'Following this path to its logical conclusion, however, we can see that the detective novel is caught in a cleft stick, a paradox of its own making. Having abandoned the comforting fantasy of certainty, all that is left is the chaos of ambiguity. What sort of detective story would it be in which the detective was, quite literally, incapable of solving the crime? What would happen if real life, with all its mess and confusion, was allowed to destroy the illusion of order, so painstakingly created? Is the quest only valid if the Knight does indeed lay his hands upon the Grail?'

She paused. A hundred pairs of eyes watched her, expectantly, waiting for her to answer her own questions so that they could write it down in their files. To them, she thought suddenly, I'm the Great

Detective. I read the texts and hey presto, out of my lips spills forth the truth. She suddenly felt unutterably weary. Putting down her notes, she said:

'When I began this series of talks I said that the real goal of the detective quest is not justice, but understanding. I believe I quoted Eliot:

' "And the end of all our exploring
Will be to arrive where we started
And know the place for the first time."

'Yet Eliot, we should remember, was a Christian, someone who had embraced the certainties of a dying faith. He believed in one knowledge, one truth, one moment of revelation: more, he believed in the possibility of such a revelation.

'For most of us today that possibility does not exist. For most of us, as a modern philosopher has said, truth is a pathless land – a land, in other words, where there are a multiplicity of truths; all equally valid, all equally false; a land where – as a lesser poet than Eliot has put it, but in a lesser age – many kinds of knowledge and belief have come and touched our foreheads, lightly, with their dust.'

She paused for a long time, so long that those who were taking notes stilled their pens and looked at her, perplexed.

'Today, we see the world as flies do: as a million unrelated fragments. We look, not for patterns, but only for movement. The detective novel has become the crime thriller, pandering to the public's taste for the grotesque. The quest for truth has become mere police procedural: the Mystery has become the formula whodunit. And a living literary form has died, become something to be dissected in lectures and seminars.'

She gestured towards her listeners, a gesture which took in not only the rows of undergraduates, their ring-binders open like the gaping beaks of so many ravenous fledglings waiting to be fed, but also the auditorium, the overhead projector, the podium, herself. 'Who killed the detective novel? We did.'

In the ensuing silence she picked up her notes and looked at them thoughtfully. In her hand were half a dozen more pages, a litany of quotations and textural references which were ultimately completely irrelevant and completely meaningless. She had said everything she wanted to say. Without another word she turned on her heel and left the room.

Epilogue

By mid-November all the leaves had fallen from the trees along the towpath, and the students walked from lecture to lecture wrapped in ever-increasing layers of baggy sweaters. The two men who walked shivering along the pavement of West Street were more sombrely dressed than students, in identical dark suits and overcoats. But a keen observer might have noticed that the suits were of a cut no longer quite fashionable, while their coats smelled faintly of the mothballs in which they had been stored for the summer.

The cars parked on either side of the road were frosted over, their windscreens opaque as ground glass. One car, however, was clear, parked with the engine running. As the two men approached, its doors opened and a man and woman got out, followed by two small children.

'Mr and Mrs Prescott?' Nick enquired, hurrying forward to hold the car door open.

'That's us. You must be from the estate agents. Shall we get inside?'

Nick unlocked the front door. It was just as cold inside the house as it was out: the heating had been off for some time.

'It's a charming property, as you can see. Beautifully restored, as well, and ready for immediate occupation.'

'It's not part of a selling chain, then?' the husband asked.

'Absolutely not. Mrs Williams, the owner – or rather, Ms Carran, I should say: she's reverted to her maiden name – has gone to work at the University of London. Our instructions are simply to sell as soon as possible. She's very pragmatic about these things – I think you'll find she'll accept any reasonable offer.'

'This is a lovely big room, John,' the woman said, standing in the main living room and looking around her.

'Used to be two rooms, actually. Ms Carran knocked them through herself.'

The little girl ran back towards them. 'Mummy! Mummy! There's a garden!'

'You've just got the two children, have you?' Nick asked.

Mrs Prescott patted her stomach. 'And another in the oven, I'm afraid,' she said cheerfully.

'Really? My wife's expecting our third as well.' He smiled at her encouragingly. 'It'll be a lovely house for the right family. Plenty of space for the money.'

The little boy came back from the garden more slowly than his sister. 'Mummy,' he said, 'there's a man next door who's giving some little cats a bath.'

'In this weather?' his mother said. 'I don't think that's very likely, Jonno.' She smiled at the estate agent. 'Shall we look upstairs?'

In the garden next door, Brian Eden had heard the noise of the children, but paid it no attention. He had laid out neatly on the white grass everything he would need: a washing-up bowl full of warm water, some rags, a towel, and a stick that Terry had used for stirring tins of paint.

Going inside, he went to the space under the stairs and gently lifted Guinness out of the cardboard box in which, the previous day, she'd given birth for the second time. The cat let herself be taken without protest upstairs and locked in a bedroom.

Carrying the cardboard box out to the garden, Brian lifted the first newborn kitten out and held it in his hands, feeling the tinyness of the bones inside the sack of skin. Then he pushed it underwater and held it there with the stick. Pinned on its back to the bottom of the bowl, it doggy-paddled feebly for a few moments, its mouth open in a yawn. A tiny amount of air bubbled up, so tiny that it seemed impossible that it was enough to keep such a complex mechanism going in the first place. The paddling slowed and finally stopped. He counted to ten. Somewhere inside the house he could hear their mother starting to mew. He fished the dead animal

411

out with the stick and reached into the box for another. Soon there were four dead kittens laid beside the bowl.

He emptied the steaming water onto the grass, put the corpses into the bowl, and went back into the house.

THE END

FAREWELL TO THE FLESH
by Gemma O'Connor

'Gemma O'Connor, a real writer in the great tradition of Irish storytellers' *BBC Kaleidoscope*

Stebton Place in Oxfordshire and the convent of Holy Retreat overlooking Dublin Bay: two great houses whose histories are curiously entwined by shameful, forgotten secrets. Forgotten, that is, until Jeddie Stebton-Hillyard knocks on the convent door...

Anxious to salvage what remains of their decaying convent, the nuns of Holy Retreat seek the help of Terence Murphy-Dunne, a suave, manipulative Dublin solicitor who persuades them to move their graveyard and sell off the site to raise funds. But just as the last coffin is exhumed, an extra, unmarked lead casket is unearthed. Who is in it, how long has it been there, and what has the eccentric Jeddie Hillyard to do with it?

When lawyer Tess Callaway is drafted in, she too begins to raise awkward questions – questions which set in motion a disturbing chain of events. And all too soon Tess finds herself caught in a spiral of intrigue that places herself and her baby daughter in mortal danger.

A Bantam Paperback
0 553 50586 6

THE JUROR
by George Dawes Green

You are a juror in a murder trial. They tell you your child will be safe. Your career will flourish. Your friends will remain alive. All you have to say are two words: *Not Guilty*.

Prospective Juror number 224 is a perfect jury candidate. Annie Laird is honest and old-fashioned enough to think a syndicate hit is still murder. She is also a perfect candidate for the Teacher. He needs a single juror to return a not guilty verdict. This one is smart and she has just one person to love and protect – her twelve-year-old son, Oliver.

But it is a mistake to underestimate a woman protecting her only child. This butterfly's wings may have tips of steel.

'A heart-pounding, blood-chilling, page-turning *tour de force*'
Scott Turow, author of *Presumed Innocent*

A Bantam Paperback
0 553 50386 3

SEXTET
by Sally Beauman

'This is a peach of a novel . . . *Sextet* is a hugely entertaining read, seriously romantic and with a terrific sense of atmosphere' Kate Saunders, *Daily Express*

Journalist Lindsay Drummond is about to re-make her life: she plans to move out of London, change her job, and above all cure herself of her hopeless love for her unfairly handsome colleague, Rowland McGuire – but then a chance encounter teaches her that the best-laid plans can go delightfully awry . . .

In New York, actress Natasha Lawrence is also trying to rebuild her life. Pursued by a stalker for the past five years, still bound to her ex-husband, the celebrated film director Tomas Court, she retreats with her son to the precincts of the exclusive – and haunted – Conrad apartment building. But will it provide her with the security she so desperately seeks, and will she and her husband be able to lay to rest the ghosts of their past?

Lindsay's and Natasha's lives become inextricably entangled; when the cast of characters gathers for Thanksgiving at the sinister Conrad building, anything can happen, for romance and retribution, marriage and murder are in the air.

'A complex cracker of a plot with vivid characters and atmospheric locations'

Daily Mail

A Bantam Paperback
0 553 50326 X

A SELECTION OF NOVELS
AVAILABLE FROM BANTAM BOOKS

THE PRICES SHOWN BELOW WERE CORRECT AT THE TIME OF GOING TO
PRESS. HOWEVER TRANSWORLD PUBLISHERS RESERVE THE RIGHT TO
SHOW NEW RETAIL PRICES ON COVERS WHICH MAY DIFFER FROM
THOSE PREVIOUSLY ADVERTISED IN THE TEXT OR ELSEWHERE.

40791 0	DEATH OF A GOSSIP	*M C Beaton*	£3.99
40792 9	DEATH OF A CAD	*M C Beaton*	£3.99
50329 4	DANGER ZONES	*Sally Beauman*	£5.99
50630 7	DARK ANGEL	*Sally Beauman*	£6.99
50631 5	DESTINY	*Sally Beauman*	£6.99
40727 9	LOVERS AND LIARS	*Sally Beauman*	£5.99
50326 X	SEXTET	*Sally Beauman*	£5.99
50540 8	KILLING FLOOR	*Lee Child*	£5.99
40922 0	THE JUROR	*George Dawes Green*	£5.99
50611 0	THE SHIFT	*George Foy*	£5.99
50475 4	THE MONKEY HOUSE	*John Fullerton*	£5.99
40846 1	IN THE PRESENCE OF THE ENEMY	*Elizabeth George*	£5.99
40238 2	MISSING JOSEPH	*Elizabeth George*	£5.99
17511 4	PAYMENT IN BLOOD	*Elizabeth George*	£5.99
40845 3	PLAYING FOR THE ASHES	*Elizabeth George*	£5.99
40167 X	WELL-SCHOOLED IN MURDER	*Elizabeth George*	£5.99
50385 5	A DRINK BEFORE THE WAR	*Dennis Lehane*	£5.99
50584 X	DARKNESS, TAKE MY HAND	*Dennis Lehane*	£5.99
40884 4	FAST FORWARD	*Judy Mercer*	£5.99
50619 6	DARK SKIES	*Stan Nicholls*	£4.99
50586 6	FAREWELL TO THE FLESH	*Gemma O'Connor*	£5.99
50438 X	MOUNT DRAGON	*Lincoln Preston*	£5.99
50496 7	THE RELIC	*Lincoln Preston*	£5.99

All Transworld titles are available by post from:
Book Service By Post, PO Box 29, Douglas, Isle of Man, IM99 1BQ
Credit cards accepted. Please telephone 01624 675137,
fax 01624 670923, Internet http://www.bookpost.co.uk.
or e-mail:bookshop@enterprise.net for details.
Free postage and packing in the UK. Overseas customers: allow
£1 per book (paperbacks) and £3 per book (hardbacks).